Walks
In
Stardust

Lynn Sholes

Praise for Lynn Armistead McKee's previous novels

KEEPER OF DREAMS
"Poignant …effectively entwine[s] the emotional whirlwind of
a modern-day romance with the
primitive instincts of the Native Americans."
—*Ft. Lauderdale Sun-Sentinel* (FL)

"Lynn Armistead McKee is a master storyteller as she weaves a
powerful story of an early civilization …Tremendous!"
—*Rendezvous*
"This wonderfully written novel is a real page-turner."
—*Romantic Times*

TOUCHES THE STARS
"Engrossing!"
—*Rave Reviews*
"[A] compelling and enthralling tale of the dawning of time in
the ancient Everglades …Superb!"
—*Rendezvous*
"Fans of Clan of the Cave Bear will relish this."
—*Heartland Critiques*

WOMAN OF THE MISTS
"A fascinating read."
—*School Library Journal*
"An engrossing story …will satisfy fans."
—*Rave Reviews*

WALKS IN STARDUST

Published by Stone Creek Books
Oakland Park, Florida

Originally published by Diamond Books

Cover art by Joe Moore

ISBN-13: 978-0692535455
ISBN-10: 0692535454

DEDICATION

For the ones who fill up my memories

ACKNOWLEDGMENTS

Very special thanks to the Broward County
Archaeological Society and the Graves Museum of
Archaeology and Natural History.
As always, I owe so much to the Thursday night group
that stripped the "taffy" out.
Also, gratitude to Nancy O'Leary, my friend.

"Strength and courage can sometimes be lonely friends—
but those who reach, walk in Stardust."
—Flavia Weedn

Prologue

THE CINDERS OF THE FIRE darted about, flickering red lights, like fireflies suddenly brought to life by the stirring of a stick.

"Move back, little one," Tamar, the big man, said, slowly shifting his stiff leg out from under him. Hidden beneath his thinning skin still resided the muscles he had developed in his youth. But deep within, his old bones protested that he sat in the same position too long, especially on such a cold evening. He winced with discomfort as he moved the leg, helping it with his hands.

The small girl looked at him with respect and adoration, drawing her stick out of the fire.

"Come and sit with me," Sola said, patting the ground between her and Tamar.

The child dropped her stick, and a puff of dust spewed up as it hit the earth.

Restrained in a net of wrinkles, Sola's black eyes reflected the flames of the fire, and it was clear she held the lessons of age. "Never mind them," she said to the child, flashing her wise eyes at a gossipy woman across the way. "Pay no mind to their babbling. It is just prattle."

The girl crawled up to sit between the old man and woman, feeling the rampart of their bodies shield her from malicious chatter. Still, some eyes in the dark glared at her, made her pull up tighter against Tamar and Sola, shrink into the comfort of their shadows.

Her small fingers played with the feathers and shells that dangled from Tamar's arm band. The shells tinkled as she fingered the different strands, making them clink together to a song she hummed.

"One day you will teach me the words to your song," Sola said, stroking the back of the child's head.

The girl's face lit up with a smile. The old woman slid her arm around the child and cradled her against her shoulder, gently rocking. Wisps of clouds drifted across the icy moon, and a quick breeze made the people bundle up in their skin robes and fur blankets.

"Look!" a young man screeched. The villagers squinted over their fires, looking into the sky.

"Ayee!" they cried, seeing the streak of golden light.

Tamar stood and lifted the girl, pointing to the sky. "There, little one. Do you see?"

All of the villagers had gotten to their feet, mouths agape, in wonder of the brilliant light that lit the heavens. But in a moment, one by one, they began to fall to their knees in prayer.

"It is coming."

"Save us!"

Tamar remained standing, whispering into the child's ear. "It is a hearthstone from the fires in the sky. The spirits' fire. It comes this way."

The girl's eyes widened. She could feel Tamar's arms tense with pride as he held her, and his chest swelled. He was not afraid like the others, and so neither would she be.

"They send it to us," he whispered to her, as if she were the only one who could understand.

Rapidly the fireball came upon them, streamers of colored light trailing behind it. There was a loud noise, an explosion, and the people covered their ears, crying for the spirits to spare them, to save them.

Tamar lowered the girl to the ground as the people looked up again to see a shower of golden lights sprinkle down from the sky.

"Wait!" Sola called as the child ran toward it. Tamar held out his arm, blocking the woman from going after her.

"Let her go into the stardust."

Everyone watched, and a hush fell over the village as the child vanished into the shadows of the night.

Finally, emerging from the stillness of the deep night, the child reappeared and walked back to the fire. In her hands she carried a slender oblong object. The people stared, edging closer to get a better look.

"From the heavens," the child said, holding out the still-warm, sharp sliver of the hearthstone that had come from the sky.

Tamar took it from her and examined it. He uttered sounds of deep contemplation. He had never seen anything like this before. The stone was not a rock, as he knew rock.

But of course it would not be ordinary. It was from the fire of the spirits.

"The child has brought us a piece of the stars," Tamar said.

"Yes," a woman from the back of the crowd agreed, bowing her head in reverence.

"From out of the golden light," another said.

Tamar backed the girl against his leg, facing her toward the crowd, his hand resting on her shoulder. "The spirits smile on her, and she is one of us." His heart was full. The spirits had answered his prayers, and in such a grand way. There was no doubt now that she was as much his child as if she had come from his seed.

The child looked up at the big man, putting her hand on top of his as it so firmly sat upon her shoulder. "It is good?" she asked.

Tamar lowered to one knee. "It is very good," he said, her innocence bringing the faintest smile to his lips.

The girl's arms went around him, and her little eyes filled with tears.

Again Tamar stood to face the crowd, lifting the child so that all could look upon her face and the object she had given to them. "Behold, a gift from the spirits!"

He let the child down to the ground and took her by the hand. "Come," he said, leading her into the crowd. "They wish to touch you."

As she passed, nervous, anxious fingers stroked her arm, touched her face, traced lines down her legs. They walked through the crowd, filling the need of the People. The vision of them, moving in the shadows and the firelight, captivated the villagers, causing some to hold their breath while others began to cry.

Sola stood in the distance, her arms around her middle, overwhelmed with happiness. She watched them until they faded into the darkness of the trees.

High in a cypress the feathers of a white bird captured the silver light of the moon. Tamar and the child stopped beneath the tree, and he mumbled a prayer. The child watched as another white bird came out of the night and perched beside the first. Tamar's prayers became louder, a song she had never heard him sing before.

Sola came and stood at the edge of the woods searching for their silhouettes. Strange, she thought, they had just been there, beneath the tall tree, and now she saw nothing but the black of night. Suddenly she heard the fluttering of wings. The sound made her look to the sky. Rising out of the shadow of the cypress to soar in the moonlight, two graceful white birds glided above the treetops and over the village.

CHAPTER 1

SHE WAS RUNNING, heaving for air, her lungs on fire, her muscles cramping with exhaustion. The shallow water splashed in her face as she stumbled and went down, the peat gushing beneath her knees and oozing between her fingers. Quickly she drew herself up and froze, the hammer of her heart battering her temples. She looked in every direction as a jolt of fear swept through her. Horrified and engulfed by the shock, she suddenly was aware that she did not know who she was, why or where she was running, from or to what. She remembered the last few steps, the fall into the water, but the time before that was a blank. Her mind was empty, as if the spirits had dropped her here in the midst of the saw-grass prairie, grabbed her in the middle of a nightmare, and abandoned her with no warning and no explanation. A chill ran down her spine.

The woman felt terror course through her as again she turned, looked deep into the distance, and whimpered. A storm was brewing, the dark belly of the clouds protruding, bloating with rain. Her breath exploded from her, and her heart beat heavily in her chest. She had been running hard, fiercely. Why? She held still, listening, watching for some clue.

As far as she could see in all directions stretched the shallow water and the tall saw grass that whipped in the wind as the storm approached. Thunder rumbled, and the first raindrops fell on her face.

The woman spotted a small hammock close by and

trudged through the water, keeping low, hiding in the toothed sedge, feeling it tear at her moss skirt and slit fine shallow, stinging cuts on her body. Finally she collapsed on the island. The rain fell harder, driven in sheets by the wind. She clawed at the mud, scrambling on her hands and knees, and crawled farther under the canopy of trees. She peered out, scouring the rim of the island, watching for someone or something. She still made noises when she breathed, wheezing from exertion and fright. She wrapped her arms around herself and shivered.

Who was out there? What was coming after her? Why?

She wiped away the raindrops from her face, realizing for the first time that she clutched something in her hand. Again she brushed the water from her eyes, and then focused on the object she held. It was a knife, its handle fire-polished and intricately carved from bone. She knew the designs had been made with the tip of a shark's tooth, but who had made them? She didn't even know if it belonged to her. And the blade—what peculiar substance was it made from?

The woman tried to catch her breath, shielding her eyes from the rain that made its way through the lush foliage. She rubbed her thumb up and down the sharp blade, then the handle, feeling the tiny ridges and grooves as she looked closer. The edge of the blade was so sharp and thin she thought it would break away if she pinched it. After a quick attempt, she was astounded by the strength of the material.

The knife handle was long with carved turtle-effigy wedges securing the blade through the ferrule and into the handle. At the tip of the handle was another turtle. Along the length of the carved bone were hatch marks and lines as well as a series of dots and swirls. Beautiful and elaborate.

Her attention suddenly turned to her chest. A stream of pink rainwater streamed down the crevice between her breasts. She put the knife under her arm, scooted to an opening in the trees, cupped her hands, and held them out to catch the rain. From the pool that formed in her hands, she saw that the rain was clear. She looked down. Several small pink rivulets flowed down her chest. Pink water streaked her arms and trickled from her chin. The rain dripped from her hair into her eyes. Her fingers raked the side of her head in an attempt to sweep back her long black hair. She found her hair hard, stiff, and matted. She withdrew her hand and held it in front of her. Her palm and fingers were red. Blood! Her hair was soaked in blood! The knife fell to the ground.

She ran her fingers over her head, feeling for the wound. But there was no soreness anywhere, no lump, no gash. Lightning lit the sky, and the thunder cracked. Again she felt her head; there had to be a wound somewhere.

She found nothing—no cuts, no gashes, not even any scrapes, no reason for the blood.

She stood and inspected her body, touching, probing, looking. She made noises, sounds of panic as she examined herself, small gasps, noisy exhalations, hysterical whimpers. Her fingers searched her body— nothing but the small cuts from the teeth of the saw grass.

The blood had to have come from someone else. The knife. She lifted it and examined it, but it had been washed clean. She had fallen with it in the water, and there was the rain. If the knife had been covered with blood, it was all rinsed away.

The woman peeked out across the stormy saw-grass prairie, looking for some hint, some indication that would tell her what had happened. She heard the lashing of the saw-grass blades and the rumble of the thunder, but there was nothing to see—nothing but the fury of a summer thunderstorm.

Was it morning or late in the day?

A loud crack behind her made her turn. The wind had ripped a limb from a bay tree. It dangled and swung, twisted, then was wrenched from the tree, falling free. Afraid of the weather and what might be pursuing her, she moved deeper into the cover of trees, into a thicket of tall weeds and thin saplings. She curled over her knees as she huddled close to the muck and waited out the storm, quaking from the wet chill and the terror.

Finally the lightning became infrequent, the thunder distant, and the rain a drizzle. She wanted to creep out of the heavy brush. The mosquitoes were worse here, and the weeds scratched her. But she was too afraid to move out of the cover. Who was after her? What still might be coming for her?

She hunkered low, feeling jumpy, her eyes wide. The squawking and tweeting of the birds slowly returned. The hammock quickly soaked up the moisture, and the steaming, musty scent of the layers of rotting leaves, the heavy odor of the muck, wafted in the air. Mud streaked her face and body, and a few brown leaves and small brittle twigs were caught in the tangle of her hair.

A sudden flurry of birds taking flight from the trees made her start and leap to her feet. When she realized what had frightened her, she expelled a cry and held her forehead in her hand, unsure if she was really laughing or crying.

Why couldn't she remember?

She squeezed her eyes shut, then opened them, shook her head, and pressed her hands to her temples. The blade of the knife lay flat against her cheek.

Whose blood was in her hair?

CHAPTER 2

THE WOMAN ANXIOUSLY AWAITED sunrise. She had slept on and off through the night. Each time she awoke, the trauma of realizing she was actually living a nightmare jolted her into heedful, rousing wakefulness. After the last time, she had not been able to go back to sleep. Sunrise could not be too far away.

Before nightfall, she had managed to cut and pile some soft ferns to use as a bed. Exhausted, she had at first found the bed suitable, but as the night wore on, she didn't like the feeling of being so exposed and unprotected. The moonless night had come upon her quickly, and even the shadows were lost in the blackness.

She felt relief with the return of the sun. The woman sat up and scratched the welts that covered her body. The mosquitoes had found her an easy target. The mud with which she had coated her body had not been much help.

The sunlight that sprinkled through the trees made her eyes burn. She rubbed them and vowed never again to spend another night as she had the last night. Never again would she leave herself so vulnerable. The time for crying like a child was over. Now she had to survive—had to fend for herself.

She wondered where all this determination came from. Was that what she was like ... determined? Did others see the same thing in her? Did they see her as determined, or did they think she was uncompromising?

The thought brought on a chain of questions. She remembered the blood in her hair, and her stomach coiled. Had she lost her temper with someone? Who was she?

"My name," she said aloud. "My name." Desperately she attempted to sift through her mind, trying to hook on to some clue.

Concentrate!

She tried again, but the effort went unrewarded. She slammed her fists down, making a low thud as they struck the ground through the shield fern cushion. She rummaged through the ferns searching for the knife until her fingertips finally felt the blade, then the handle.

She lifted the knife and held it against her chest. It was her only link to her past. Gently she let her fingers caress the handle. She felt the ridges of the finely crafted carvings. The knife grew warm in her hand, a pleasant, comforting warmth. She dared not lose this. This was no ordinary knife.

With the yellow morning light coming like splinters through the trees, she made her way to the edge of the mound, picking berries and eating them along the way. The caked mud cracked on her body as she moved. The woman wrinkled her nose and stretched her mouth open, feeling the mud fissure. At the water's edge, she washed her face, and then splashed handfuls of water down her arms, trunk, and legs.

She pulled some nut grass and chewed it, the sweet grass making her mouth feel refreshed.

How selective her memory loss was, she thought. How did she know to coat herself with mud if she had no fish oil, and what about the nut grass? How did she even know how to wash? How did she know that the berries she ate were not poison? Why had not everything except knowing how to breathe been snatched away at the same time as the rest of her memory? The heat of anger flushed her face and burned in her stomach.

What other things could she remember? The small white flowers growing in patches beside her were good for abrasions. She picked one, pulverized it, and then rubbed the pulp on her skinned shin.

She looked across the watery land. The sun begins its journey in the east and ends it in the west. Another fragment of information that her mind had held on to. It seemed she could remember everything—everything except her life.

Her hands trembled as she held them over her face and bowed her head into them. "I do not understand." she shrieked.

She sniffled and wiped her nose with the back of her free hand. Her jaw tightened as she looked behind her into the small hammock that was her new home.

Well, she thought, if she was to keep the promise to herself that she would never spend another night as she had last night, there were things she needed to do.

She turned back to the water and scooped some up in her cupped hands. Just as she lifted it to her face, she let it spill out, recoiling at what she saw.

In the distance were canoes. Many of them. Moving silently.

The woman crouched, picked up her knife, and backed into the trees. She waited and watched as the canoes came closer; she studied them and the men in them.

Had they come to save her?

When they were near enough for her to see detail, she knew she would be in danger if she stayed where she was.

Were these her people coming for her, or were they

her enemy?

Behind her, farther into the forest of the hammock, was a large strangler fig. Quickly she ran to it and climbed up, hoping to get a better look.

She thought the canoes were going to pass the hammock, but then a voice rang out, and suddenly the canoes took a deliberate turn toward the end of the tree island.

Her heart raced, and her hands grew cold and sweaty.

Who were they?

As they came closer and closer, she watched the men, scrutinizing their clothing, tattoos, and ornaments as they approached. The tribe these men belonged to should have been apparent. Even the style of their canoes should have told her who they were. But she didn't recognize them. There was nothing familiar about them; even their stature was curious to her. Was this part of her memory loss, or did she really have no knowledge of this tribe?

The men poled two of the canoes up to the island at the southern tip, banked them, and came ashore while the others waited quietly in their dugouts. She shifted on the branch to see better, craning her neck as if it could make up the distance.

She dropped the knife, and the shock of her mistake sent a sensation like fire channeling down her arms. The knife had tumbled from her hands, plummeting to the ground and impaling itself straight up like a stake to mark her presence. The noise she made when she gasped was so loud she was sure they heard. She looked at the advancing men and then back at the knife, wondering if she had time to climb down, retrieve it, and again scale the tree. No, she decided. Better that she remain still and hope the knife would be overlooked.

The woman realized she had bitten into her lip when

she tasted the salty blood. Afraid to breathe, she watched the men move into the cover of the hammock.

They appeared to be looking for something, and they were being careful not to make any noise. They moved like seasoned, masterful hunters, executing every step with adeptness, knowing the earth and how to blend with it. Yet the woman was certain they were not on the hunt. They spread out, skulking in a near dead hush. The fan of warriors edged closer, the sleek brown bodies slinking through the brush, never alarming so much as a bird.

In the tree, huddled against the trunk, the woman was so alert, her senses so sharpened by fear, that she could smell them.

One man noiselessly stole closer to her. She cringed at the sight of him, a fish bone through a perforation in his nose. He was near enough that she could see his heart beat heavily in his chest and beads of sweat roll down his forehead. She looked at the knife below, its ornate handle protruding like a death marker. Surely he would see it.

There was a low rumble of fear in her ears, like thunder far in the distance. For an instant she was dizzy. She wrapped her arms around the trunk of the tree and pressed her cheek against it. Her mouth was dry, and she was unable to swallow. An icy chill flooded her hands and feet until she was sure they were numb. Her teeth scored her sliced lip as the man stopped and looked around after stepping on and snapping a twig.

In response to his mistake, the warrior dropped to a squat and hunkered low. With fluid expertise he nocked an arrow and drew back the sinew string, clearing the bark protector around his arm before his thumb rested under his jaw. His eyes smoothly searched the area, the tension of the bowstring straining the practiced muscles of his arm.

The woman watched in dread, certain that she would give away her position with the pounding of her heart or the sound of her breathing.

Finally he stood again, keeping his arrow ready for flight until he was certain there was no threat. He lowered the bow, but kept the arrow nocked, waited a moment longer, then turned around and trod back toward the canoes.

She clung to the tree, watching all the men return to the dugouts as stealthily as they had come. They pushed off, met the other canoes, and continued on their journey.

The woman leaned her head back and closed her eyes in relief. If the twig had not cracked under his foot, surely he would have discovered the knife and then her. She silently watched them move away. She climbed to a higher branch to see the canoes finally fade into the distance.

A sudden twisted thought changed the expression on her face. What if she had hidden herself from rescue? Were those men her people, come to save her? There was no way of knowing, and she realized that this questioning would not lead her anywhere except to more tears. There were already too many questions that she couldn't answer.

She climbed higher until she could see across the whole island. She needed to know this hammock, its length and breadth, its position in the trail of islands that blotched the otherwise bleak saw grass. The top of the tree was less sturdy and swayed with her weight, persuading her to climb down.

She pulled the knife out of the ground and decided that she needed a sheath for it so she could strap it around her waist. For that she needed to hunt, to kill an animal that would give her its skin and sinew. But she had no weapons.

Except the knife.

She pulled off the leaves that had been skewered onto the knife blade when it stuck into the ground. The tip was so sharp. What if she could learn to use this knife the way the men used a lance? Perhaps it could serve as the point of the lance. She would think more about the possibilities.

And what about a shelter? Something to conceal her from the nocturnal animals and the weather, a place to return to each night, a place to fashion baskets and tools. The sun would not provide enough daylight in one day for all the things she needed to do.

By afternoon she had built herself a lean-to deep within the hammock. She knew that a place in the sunlight would have been drier and more pleasant than this spot beneath the heavy canopy of trees, but exposure on the edge of the island was too great a risk. The warriors might return, or others might travel past. Even if they intended to pass the island, they would be attracted by the shelter. She decided she was wiser to settle for perpetual dampness.

The lodging was simple, something she could break apart and scatter if someone came. She hoisted a long ridgepole onto the top of a stump and then braced branches against that, forming a framework. She covered that with thicker, smaller boughs, then deposited rubble in front of the entrance so she could seal herself in at night. There was room inside for her to sleep comfortably, and a little room for dry storage. The sides were dense enough to prevent rain from easily passing through, and, she thought with trepidation, if she was still here when winter came, the shelter would help insulate her from the cold air and wind. Spending the winter here was something she had to consider, since she could not tell how much of the warm season was left. Winter might be only one sleep away.

Building the shelter took all morning—searching for a stump in an acceptable place, gathering the branches. Her hands were cut and sticky with sap, and every muscle ached. But she kept on. Then, after a brief rest and a meal of berries, other fruit, and stalks, she made a fire drill. She sacrificed the thin strip of sinew that was the waistband of her skirt to make the bow. She collected the down from thistles and cattails for tinder that would quickly spark into flame.

As she sat ready to start her fire, she felt herself stiffen and heard the rustle of birds' wings. A sudden image flashed in front of her. She saw the large hand of a man wrapped around the end of a bow drill like the one she had made. The hand was moving the bow back and forth, and smoke was streaming from the notch in the fire board. Her eyes were wide and watching, as if the event were taking place now, but then the vision disappeared as suddenly as it had come, leaving her staring at the barren, gently sloping fire pit she had sculpted out of the earth.

Desperately she tried to hang on to the thread of memory. She threw down the cattails and thistles in frustration and reached for her temples. Buried inside her head were the memories, the things that made her the woman she was. She took a deep breath and realized that the image was gone and she could not recover it.

In a moment she returned to her tasks. Twilight would be upon her soon. She piled small dry kindling twigs and the larger wood, wrist-sized in diameter, that would maintain the fire.

As the first evening star glittered in the sky, she blew on the small coal she had created. She nested it in some cattail and thistle fluff, gently blowing on it until it flamed, nurturing the small ember, adding to it very slowly so she wouldn't smother it.

When the fire was complete, she sat back on her heels in admiration. Using the right wood, finding the correct tension of the cord so that it did not ride up or down on the spindle of the fire drill, bracing her arm so that she held the spindle straight—all those things she had learned during the afternoon, repeating or altering her efforts over and over until at last she was rewarded with a fire.

Either fire making had been stricken from her memory, or she had never built one before. Obviously she knew the technique, but the experience had been sorely missing.

She felt great satisfaction as she watched the flames dance in the dark. By its light she ate from the pile of plant food she had gathered. Then she fumbled with the knife and a long stick.

The woman held the stick beneath her eye and looked down the shaft. This was the straightest one she had found. She rested the middle of the stick in the palm of her hand, checking for balance.

The end of the stick was blunt where she had cut it off. She made a slit in the end of the stick to slide the knife handle inside. After inserting the handle she attempted to bind it. The grapevines did not hold tightly enough, and the knife wobbled. Tomorrow she would remove the sinew from the bow drill and securely bind the knife to the stick.

The flames of the fire danced, holding her spellbound, and her mind slipped back. Suddenly the blaze appeared larger and more frightening, and the sound of screaming made her scramble to her feet. She blinked as if awakening from a dream. There was nothing but her small fire in front of her—the haunting call of an owl and the singing of the crickets. Another small flash of a memory had come to her. A sliver of her past had managed to pierce the black cloud that held everything else back.

The time had come to stop working for the day. She must sleep, she thought, succumbing to exhaustion.

The woman added hardwood to the fire, knowing it would slowly burn down to coals during the night. Satisfied that the fire was fed well enough, she sat still, humming the tune of a song. She wished she could recall the words or remember where she had learned them.

When the melody ended, she prepared for sleep. Earlier she had brought water in her mouth back to her camp and spit it out onto a pile of leaves. She had done this several times so that the leaves were damp even now. She spread a light covering of them over the fire, creating instant smoke that drove away the mosquitoes. The fresh mud covering on her body, the smoke, and the shelter would help protect her during the night.

The sky glittered with the stars. So many of them, she thought. How many spirits and ancestors sat by their fires in the sky just as she sat by hers?

The woman crawled into her lodging and filled in the entrance with the debris. The fern bed was cool and soft against her naked body. Instantly her eyes closed, but the noises of the night made her anxious. The footfalls of waddling raccoons and opossums, the croaking of the frogs, the bellow of an alligator, echoed in the night. She recognized them all, but still they troubled her and kept her from sleep. Surely she had heard these same sounds every night of her life; they frightened her now only because she was alone, confused.

And did not know who she was.

CHAPTER 3

IT WAS NOT THE SEASON she had hoped it would be. As many days passed, they grew shorter. The nights grew cooler, not nearly as stifling and humid as they had been. The booming of afternoon thunderstorms ceased.

The woman pulled a skin blanket about her shoulders as she sat next to the fire in the chilly evening. She had not bothered to fashion a new skirt. She thanked the spirits they had shown her how to use the knife to hunt, to provide for herself. The skill had not been easy to master, but endless practice made her successful.

Every night before sleeping she cut a small gash in the stick she kept to record the passing of each day. Tonight she took the knife from the sheath at her side and notched her stick with a long slash to mark the full moon, then stared at the cuts in the wood. Too many long slashes, too many cycles of the moon, she thought. She feared that she would spend the rest of her life on this hammock, alone, without ever remembering anything about herself.

Tonight, like every night, she strained to see the few points of stars that peeked in and out of the rustling treetops of the woodland. She called to the spirits in prayer, thanking them for providing yet another day for her. But tonight she felt so empty, so abandoned. Did the spirits not see her here?

Near the shelter she had dug a hole and lined it with a

grass-woven mat. Inside the hole she stored her belongings: a few clay pots she had made, skins from animals stuffed in baskets, pouches, sinew, fire-making tools, and antler. She covered the hole with broad Sabal palm branches and other leaves so that it could not be seen. She had learned to sleep on the ground without a mat, lying only on a few ferns. If the enemy came, she would scatter the components of her simple lodge, extinguish the small fire, cover it, and hope that it might go unnoticed.

Next to the fire was an otter stomach of water to douse the fire in an emergency. She had the procedure planned so that it would take only a moment, and then she would hide in the forest. The only thing she would carry with her was the knife.

Tonight she pulled the deerskin wrap snugly about her shoulders, guarding against the cold. Myths told that long ago the People believed the cold air was the breath of a giant beast that lived to the north. She wondered what it might be like farther north, in the land from which her ancestors had followed the legendary creatures with curling tusks. They had followed those giants here to the land of the water. And how her imagination spun when she thought of the stories of those beasts that lived alongside her ancestors, beasts that stood three or four times higher than a man, beasts whose steps made the earth tremble, animals whose flesh could feed a whole clan for days and days.

How peculiar, she thought. She could remember tales of her ancestors and descriptions of animals she had never seen, but she could not recall her name. She let out a sigh. Perhaps it didn't matter if she took all these precautions—secret holes, water to put the fire out. No one was coming for her—not the enemy, not her people.

She didn't matter to anyone, so why should she matter to herself? She was no one.

At first light she began her daily routine. She stirred the coals of the fire and fed it, then took care of her personal needs.

The hammock's shrubs and vines no longer provided fruit. There remained nuts, stalks and tubers, leaves and stems. She had dried some fruit, but because storage space was limited, so was her supply. Another reason she had stored so little was that she had started gathering provisions late in the season, so certain was she that she would regain her memory any day, or that someone would come for her. When she realized she might be here a long time, the fruiting season had nearly ended. She also stored dried meat, which she continued to save for emergencies.

The days passed, one so much like the last that she often found herself ready for a short sleep in the afternoon. At first she had been busy with the tasks of learning to live here and take care of herself. She had learned to hunt with the knife. Becoming skillful with it had kept her occupied for a long time. Finally she could bring down a moving target with ease—rabbit, raccoon, even deer. Now there was nothing new, only the day-to-day chore of subsistence.

Tiny flashes of memory continued to come to her, but nothing that she could make sense of or hang on to. Such visions only teased and tormented her, reminded her of how much she had lost. Her treks to the water to bathe became less frequent, and her appetite dwindled. She picked at her food, hunting less, eating less, spending more time lying inside the shelter. Her life was as empty as her memory.

This night she crawled into her lean-to and did not bother to put away the bowl she had eaten from. She left the secret storage hole uncovered. If someone came in the night, let him find her and take her life, she thought as she curled up to sleep.

She had a dream, one that she had had before. When she waked from it, all she could remember was the stirring of the wind and how it blew gently on her face, and then looking up to see a beautiful white bird so close the feathers touched her. She turned over and opened her eyes, staring in the darkness. She liked the dream. In the dream she felt safe and content. Finally she closed her eyes again and slipped into a dreamless sleep.

No one did come in the night. No one came to rescue her. No one came to kill her and end her misery.

As the morning light twinkled through the leaves, the woman turned on her earthen bed. Unlike all other mornings since she had been here, she did not crawl out of the shelter. Instead she turned to her side, pulled the skin blanket more tightly around her, and closed her eyes. There was no reason to get up. There was no reason to go on. She lay there and hoped the spirits would do just one kind thing for her—let her starve to death without much pain.

She wanted to sleep, had no intention of getting up. After a while she found that she dozed on and off but still felt more and more tired. All she wanted was to sleep until the spirits took her.

Twice the sun traveled from the east to the west without the woman emerging from her shelter. Finally she became so thirsty and uncomfortable that she came out for water. She was surprised there was no hunger. Perhaps the spirits had heard her prayers.

Her sunken hearth was cold, and she kicked the

charcoal, creating a cloud of ash. She took with her the pot she had left out days ago and trudged to the water. At the hammock's edge, she sat on her heels and scooped water into her dry mouth. She filled the black pot and went back to her lean-to.

From the hole she took out a basket in which she had stored small pelts. From her waist she unstrapped the sheath that held the knife and put it inside the basket. If her people ever came for her, they would want this knife. This way they would be sure to find it. They would go through a woman's basket because it contained her most treasured and valuable belongings. She wished she knew more about this incredible knife.

How long was this going to take? she wondered. When would the spirits relieve her from this anguish? How long before they ended it?

A thought came to her; she was certain it came from the spirits. She knew a plant that helped people sleep and took away pain, but too much of it would …The vine bloomed sweetly at night. She knew where it grew.

Without further deliberation, she found the plant, harvested sprigs of it, started a fire, then steeped the plant in a bowl of water. She knew the unripe green berries were the most effective part of the plant, but there was no fruit. She hoped the parts she had would do what she wanted.

When the tea had cooled enough to drink, the woman took a large swallow and waited for the effect. Nothing happened. She raised the cup to her mouth again, allowing the sweet scent to swirl up to her nose. A sleeping death had to be just as sweet. As she again held the bowl to her lips, she felt a wave of dizziness. She dropped the bowl, and it smashed on the ground.

No matter, she thought. The tea was already working

on her. She set the basket with the knife just inside the opening of the lean-to. Off-balance, she crawled into the shelter, bundled up in the deerskin, closed her eyes, and waited for the sleeping death.

Her first sensation was one of floating. Her body felt so heavy, yet she was floating. Yes, this was much better than the life she had been living. There was nothing to be afraid of. Clouds whirled around her, wafting through the shelter, touching her with long soothing fingers, caressing her tired body, and lulling her mind.

Soon she became confused and wasn't sure if she was awake, asleep, or in some strange dimension on the way to the Other Side. Were her eyes open or closed? The sounds in the woodland became enhanced, and she could even hear the voices of the spirits that were coming for her.

"There has been a fire nearby. I smell the smoke."

She heard the voice and smiled. At last the end was approaching. "Come and take me," she said softly.

"There. Do you see the small lodge?" the spirit voice said.

They had found her. "Here," she whispered to the spirits, calling them to her. All about her, though her-eyes were closed, she saw lights—small, glittering, brilliant lights in the darkness. But then those lights were engulfed by blackness, and so was she.

"Is she alive?" Talasee asked as he watched Cherok crawl inside the shelter.

Cherok placed his fingertips on the side of her neck. Her face was chalky pale, and she was cold. He didn't feel any pulse and lowered his head in front of her face, turning his cheek toward her, waiting to feel her breath.

"Yes," he answered, "but barely. Help me with her."

Cherok turned her onto her back and lifted her shoulders. "Take her feet. Let us get her out of here so I can see what is wrong."

The two men maneuvered the woman out of the shelter and laid her on the ground. The deerskin fell away, her nakedness catching them by surprise. Cherok quickly replaced the blanket.

"She is bony," Talasee commented.

Cherok cradled her head and shoulders against his body, giving her his warmth. "Woman," he called softly. He lifted one of her eyelids. "Give me some water," he told his friend.

Talasee handed him his water pouch.

"No, in my hands."

Talasee poured some in Cherok's palms. Cherok splashed the water on her face. "Woman," he called again, gently tapping her cheeks.

The woman groaned and turned her head. The air was cold on her wet face.

"Good," he said, elevating her head even more as he rested it against his chest. "Wake up." He looked at his friend who knelt next to them. "Put more water," he said.

Talasee obeyed, rubbing the cold water on the woman's face.

The woman protested, shaking her head, her eyelids fluttering.

"Help me get her up," Cherok said. "Keep her wrapped in the deerskin. We must take her with us."

When he moved her, her eyes opened for a moment and looked hazily at him.

Talasee hesitated. "Wait, Cherok. You act too quickly. Is she Tegesta? She is not one of our clan."

Cherok's face showed his displeasure. "What does it matter? She could die if we leave her here."

"But what if she is from another tribe? What if she is not Tegesta?"

"And what if she is?"

Talasee wrapped the blanket around her, and Cherok hoisted her over his shoulder, his arm under her buttocks, her head and arms dangling down his back. "Go through those things in the pit," Cherok said. "Bring whatever we can use." The woman's black hair tumbled past his waist and brushed against his legs. "And do not forget her basket," Cherok added. "It looks as though that is all she has."

Talasee sorted through the supplies in the storage pit. He picked up a few of the pots, ate a handful of berries, and then retrieved the basket. His arms were full when he joined Cherok at the canoe.

"Do you think anyone else is on this hammock?" Talasee asked, looking down at the woman Cherok had laid in the bottom of the canoe.

"Perhaps you should scan it quickly. I will stay with the woman."

Talasee put the things he had salvaged into the canoe and went back into the forest.

The woman groaned again as Cherok sprinkled more water on her face. "Wake up, woman, and drink," he said, holding the pouch to her mouth. He poured a little across her cracked lips, then a little more. She sputtered and coughed. "You will have to wake up if you do not want to choke," he said.

Slowly the woman strained to focus. The sky was a blinding blue and hurt her eyes. She heard a voice beside her and turned to see who it was. She saw a fuzzy image of someone. Perhaps a man and not a spirit.

"What has happened to you?" he asked.

It was a man. The voice was deep.

"Are you ill?"

She shook her head.

"Then what is wrong? Tell me so I can help you."

The woman closed her eyes and turned away.

"No," he said, splashing water on her face. "I cannot help you unless you tell me what is wrong. There are no wounds, no bleeding. We saw your pit. You were not starving."

The woman did not answer him. She tried desperately to slip back into that dark, serene sleep where the spirits would come for her.

Cherok jostled her again. "Why do you not want to let me help? At least tell me your name."

The woman shivered. Then she realized she understood his language. Maybe she was one of his people. "Cimmera," she whispered, making up a Tegesta name for herself.

"Cimmera?" he repeated.

The woman nodded. Maybe she was Tegesta. He was rescuing her. Then she remembered the poison she had drunk. She was going to die.

"Speak, woman."

She had a hard time thinking of the word, but at last she recalled it. Had she also forgotten how to speak her language? Was it coming back to her slowly?

"Poison," she whispered.

"What poison?" he asked, shaking her to make sure she was awake. He watched her lips sluggishly form the name of the plant. Her answer brought a smile to his eyes. "There are no berries now," he said, rocking his head back in relief. "You concocted yourself a very ineffective poison. I do not think you could drink enough of it to kill you. But you are sleepy, are you not?" he said in a sympathetic tone, stroking her cheek with the backs of his fingers to comfort her.

Cherok lifted her into his lap and then higher. She was not going to like this. He bent her over the side of the canoe and forced his finger down her throat, making her gag. She protested, but was too weak to resist. Again he probed her throat until finally she brought up the meager contents of her stomach. He repeated his efforts. She heaved, but nothing else came forth.

"Drink this," he said, lifting her head and giving her water.

She was thirsty and took a big gulp.

Aggressively he again positioned her over the side of the canoe and thrust his finger down her throat once more, making her bring up the water she had drunk.

"Just to be sure everything is out," he said.

The woman wiped her nose and mouth with the back of her hand.

"Here," he said, cutting away a piece of her blanket with his knife. He dipped it into the water and handed it to her.

The woman swabbed her face.

He offered her some more water, but she refused.

"I will not do that again. Drink if you are thirsty."

She sipped the water, expecting at any moment that he would twist her over the side of the dugout again. He smiled at her caution.

"I do what I say," he told her. "I will not lie to you. Feel safe to drink."

Eagerly she gulped some more.

Talasee approached. "The hammock appears clear. Only this woman," he said as he climbed in the canoe.

"Her name is Cimmera," Cherok said. "A good Tegesta name. And let me tell you what we are called," he said to her. "This is Talasee, and I am called Cherok."

She saw Talasee move the basket aside, and suddenly she remembered the knife. What if she was not Tegesta? The knife would give her away.

"Look at this," Talasee said, reaching into the basket.

CHAPTER 4

TALASEE HELD A RARE all-white pelt in his hand.

Cimmera forced herself upright, her head spinning. She grabbed the basket and clutched it close to her.

Talasee looked curiously at Cherok.

"Let it be," Cherok said. "It belongs to the woman. As I said, these things are probably all she has."

"But the fur?" Talasee said, knowing this pelt was very special.

"Put it back into the basket."

Talasee nodded. Cherok was right, he knew that, but the white fur was truly something to covet.

Cimmera let him place the fur on top of her other things. The knife was still hidden. He hadn't seen it.

She lay in the bottom of the canoe with her eyes closed, listening to them talk, understanding everything they said. But there was something very strange. She found that when she thought of speaking, she had trouble thinking of the correct words. Though she understood the two men, speaking their language was more difficult. Even when she had said her made-up name, the sound of it came out a bit garbled, as if her tongue found it unfamiliar. Maybe the cause was the poison she had drunk, and that would wear off, she thought. But as she continued to listen to the two men, she began to believe that her trouble with the language was more than that. The words in her head were hidden deep. Perhaps all her memory was sequestered in the same dark place.

The cool air seeped through her blanket as the canoe moved through the water, and she pulled the fur higher about her neck. If she could remember the language, find the words, then she also might find her memory. Hearing the words spoken had brought back much of the language, so maybe when she saw something, her past, too, would come tumbling back. Eventually all the pieces would come together.

Again she drifted into sleep, the poison still potent enough to make her dull and drowsy.

Cherok stared down at her. She looked so vulnerable and fragile. "I wonder what made her want to drink a poison," he said to Talasee.

"Ask her," Talasee said.

Cherok shook his head at the man's response. It would not be mannerly to question this woman like that. Talasee always saw things so simply. He was a good man, but—

"You stare long at her," Talasee said.

He was observant, also, Cherok thought. Her small frame was thin, yet the deerskin coverlet fell in at her waist and rose at the swell of her hips. He let his eyes linger a moment at the soft fullness of her breasts as they gently distended the deerskin. Her thick black lashes fanned delicately against her smooth, flawless skin. Though her face was pale, he imagined what she might look like with a blush in her cheeks and lips.

"Too bony," Talasee remarked, shaking his head at the man who could not seem to stop looking at the woman in the bottom of their canoe.

"For you," Cherok said, finally looking away and smiling at his friend. "There is ample flesh in all the right places."

"I have never seen you take such an interest in a

woman," Talasee said.

"Curiosity."

"Not curiosity," Talasee disagreed. "Arousal."

Cherok laughed but knew Talasee was probably correct. She did engage him in the most basic way.

Dusk fell over them. Cimmera felt stiff. For an instant her eyes wandered. She had forgotten where she was.

"Cimmera," Cherok said softly, noticing her open eyes.

She looked up at him. He stood above her, his legs long and lean, his torso firm and defined with muscle. His black hair spilled down to his shoulders, and a white feather hung beside his face, contrasting with the deep, rich hue of his skin.

He called her name again, aware of her disorientation.

"Yes," she answered, finally realizing where she was and remembering in pieces how she had come to be in the bottom of this canoe that now was still.

"Talasee will return shortly. He is exploring this hammock. It appears to be uninhabited, but then we thought the same of your hammock before we found you. We plan to stay here for the night."

Cimmera put her hand on her basket, which rested next to her. She felt the furs still on top.

"We have not taken anything."

She looked back at him as he stooped next to her.

"Let me help you sit up," he said, sliding one arm under her shoulders.

She felt dizzy and reached for him to steady herself.

"Better?" he asked as she loosened her grasp on his arm.

"Yes."

"When the sun comes again, you should be well.

Tonight you will eat and drink plenty of water. That should speed your recovery."

Cimmera shook her head.

"I have not gone to all this trouble to have you undo my endeavor."

"No," she said. "I am not hungry. My stomach is …"

What was the word?

"You will do as I say," he said, pulling up the blanket, which had lazily slid down her arm.

Cimmera's eyes darted at him. "I will do as I choose," she snapped, grateful the words had come easily.

"And you will choose to eat and drink," he said firmly, standing up as Talasee approached.

"The hammock is clear," Talasee called.

Cherok held out his hand to Cimmera.

"I can stand alone," she said.

Cherok smiled and drew back his hand, watching her.

Cimmera put one hand on the side of the dugout and attempted to step out. The canoe rocked, and the motion made dizziness sweep over her again. She wobbled, her knees buckling.

Cherok caught her and held her up. Her face was flush against his chest, and her one hand had lost its grip on the blanket, which had fallen to her waist.

The cold air chilled her, and the warmth of him felt good.

"Stubborn woman," he said, pulling up the deerskin. "Why do you resist me so?"

Because I do not know who you are, she thought. Maybe you are the enemy.

He turned her to the side, and one of his arms curved under her knees and the other behind her shoulders. He lifted her and stepped out of the canoe.

Suddenly she felt his arms release her, and she

splashed down into the cold shallow water.

"A bath would be good for you," he said and grinned.

Talasee was gathering their things from the canoe and turned at the splash. He, too, smiled.

Cimmera's face grew red with surprise and anger.

"That is more your natural color," Cherok said, liking the flush in her cheeks. "We will take our time setting up camp. Call to me when you are finished, and I will bring you a blanket."

Cimmera struggled inside the heavy wet hide. She wiped away the water that dripped in her face. "I will never call for you," she said, still kicking and twisting to free herself of the blanket.

"Yes, you will," he said, walking away with Talasee.

Cimmera shivered with the cold. Who was this man? What made him believe he could give her orders? She was not his woman. He did not even know who she was.

For a moment she took satisfaction in knowing that the name she had given him was made up. He knew nothing about her. But then, neither did she.

Finally free of the blanket, she washed herself, having decided that she might as well do so, since she was in the water. The old cracked mud slid away. She lay back and wet her hair, combing it with her fingers, freeing the twigs and leaves that were entrapped in snarls. As she cleaned herself, she thought of what she should do. There was not the slightest chance she would stay with this man. Perhaps this one night would be all that she would have to bear. In the morning they would leave, and she would refuse to go with them.

But as the sky darkened and the stars emerged, she knew her decision was not a good one. Staying alone again would be the same as death. She would think of something.

Before long, it was too dark to see around her. In the moonlight the water was a glittering black. Why did he not come back to check on her?

The wind rustled the leaves in the trees, and the sound of the bullfrogs made her anxious.

Where was he?

"I am finished," she called out. She waited for Cherok to come and lay a deerskin blanket on the bank.

After a few more moments she called again.

The noises of the night grew louder, and she was certain that an alligator would find her soon. She waded out of the water and stood shivering in the trees, smelling the smoke of their fire. She would die of the cold before she would walk into their camp naked and at his command.

The soft fur of rabbits slid around her shoulders. Cimmera started and turned around. Cherok pulled the fur blanket closed in front of her.

In the moonlight her eyes caught his for a moment, and then he smiled and set her free, walking away into the depths of the shadows. When the darkness swallowed him, she trotted to catch up.

"Sit by the fire," Cherok said. "I am sure you are chilled, but you smell better."

She could see the smug smile that wrapped itself around his mouth. Cimmera did not respond to his comment. She sat near the flames, welcoming the heat. She leaned her head to the side, ruffling her hair before the fire to help it dry.

Cherok offered her a skewer of meat. "It is fresh. Thank Talasee."

She nodded at Cherok's companion.

Cherok found himself inspecting her. He liked what he saw even better now that all the dirt was cleaned away.

Her eyes were bright in the firelight. The sheen of her damp hair made him want to touch it.

Cimmera held the skewer but did not take it to her mouth, though the cold water had stirred an appetite in her.

"Eat," Cherok said.

She actually felt her mouth water but refused to give in.

"Please," Cherok said, surprising her.

She looked up at him and found his expression was sincere. Cimmera nibbled at the meat, and it landed warmly in her stomach.

"Was your village destroyed by the storm?" Cherok asked.

Cimmera's mind whirled. "Destroyed by the storm?" she repeated.

"Talasee and I seek survivors of our clan. We were gone on a Big Water journey when the storm struck. We returned to find our village destroyed. Is that what happened to your village? Is that why you were alone?"

Cimmera swallowed the piece of succulent meat. "Yes, that is what happened."

"You have been wandering all this time?"

The woman hesitated, spinning a story in her head as fast as she could. "Yes ...well, almost."

Talasee bit a piece of meat off the stick and leaned to one side to see around the smoke. "Where was your village?"

Cimmera felt the tension inside her, her stomach balled up into a knot, and a cold sweat formed on the palms of her hands. "I do not know from here. I am not sure where I am."

Cherok could tell that the conversation made her uncomfortable. "Of course you are confused. Look," he said, moving close to her and pointing to a bright star. "We found you there, to the north. We have traveled south."

"Oh," Cimmera said, knowing that Cherok had picked up on her nervousness.

"You were out of Tegesta territory. The area where we found you is A-po-la-chee. We took a risk searching there, but we wanted to be sure none of our people had fled that far and needed to be rescued. Why did you go so far north instead of deeper into Tegesta territory?"

Cimmera shook her head. "I was …" She could not recall the word. She looked at Cherok, lines of fright carved around her eyes and the corners of her mouth.

"It is not important," he said. "I just thought perhaps there was a reason that might help us locate any of our clan."

"Frantic. I was frantic. The storm."

"It is all right, Cimmera. I understand how it must have been for you." He touched her hand, which had found its way to her lips as if she were attempting to hide her words with her fingertips. Gently he took her hand in his and guided it down to her lap.

She didn't know what to say in response. Her nervousness was from the lies, not from recalling the fright she had suffered during a storm. She did not remember any storm. And what had he said? She was in the land of the A-po-la-chee. What if she was A-po-la-chee? Perhaps that was why the Tegesta words were so difficult for her to think of and say. Tegesta might not be her language. She must have learned it from prisoners and slaves. She turned away from him, looked at the coals of the fire, and cringed when she thought of the knife again.

"Where is my basket?" she asked, whipping her head back to face him.

"Still in the dugout," Talasee said before Cherok had a chance to answer.

"I want it," she said, immediately realizing how abrupt and demanding she sounded. But it was too late; she had already blurted out the sharp words.

"Then go get it," Cherok said, the softer lines of his face surrendering to the coarser. "If you were expecting a favor, you did not encourage one with your tongue."

Cimmera looked away. She couldn't explain her bad manners.

"Did you have a husband?" Cherok asked.

"No," she answered, wondering how she had known that. This piece of information was not a lie; it had come from her memory. She knew her face reflected the excitement she felt at the prospect of remembering her past, even if it was such a small morsel.

Cherok misunderstood the curl of her lips. "I did not ask for personal reasons. I was curious what man would have a woman who speaks so impertinently."

Cherok's statement cut straight through her. Those questions she had been asking about herself—who she was and what she was like—rose again in a flood, and she wished the poison she had swallowed had worked.

She felt her eyes sting and promptly put a stop to it. This man who had dropped her into the water, who said that she would do exactly as he asked, and who then had the arrogance to call her impertinent—this man would not make her cry. If she decided to cry, it would be her doing.

"Tell me the name of someone from your village. A warrior. I am familiar with many men from most of the Tegesta villages," Cherok said.

Cimmera changed her mind about crying, finding an advantage in it now. She allowed her eyes to fill with tears.

"I did not mean to be insensitive. It must be painful for you to think about those you have lost."

She wiped away the tear that slowly rolled down her cheek. "I do not want to talk about it. Ever."

Talasee tossed his stick into the fire. "There could still be someone alive. You are." He sounded annoyed.

"You are heartless." She fired the insult at him.

Talasee's spine straightened, and he lifted one eyebrow. "If you would think of others a moment before yourself, you would see that I mean no harm. If we knew where your village was, we could search more of that area."

Cimmera looked back at Cherok, putting together the sentence in her head before she spoke. "Your friend lacks kindness."

"I believe my friend is right," Cherok said. "Though thinking of those you love is painful, it might help. If you survived the storm, others from your village also may be alive. Give me some names. I will know the village."

"Leave me alone," she cried.

"Just some names. Then you will not have to think about it anymore."

Cimmera stood up, pulling the fur wrap around her and ran out of the firelight, disappearing into shadows.

Talasee started to go after her, but Cherok held his arm out. "Let her go. She needs to sort through things. If she took poison, her suffering must be great. Perhaps I pushed her too far."

"I suppose you are right." Talasee sat down again. "Do you think she will take the canoe?"

"There is nowhere for her to go."

"She might be angry enough, or want to be alone enough, to take it just to get away from us."

"She might be angry enough, but she will realize she has nowhere to run." Cherok hesitated a moment as he chewed on a long stem of grass. "I will follow her anyway and stay out of sight."

Talasee nodded, and Cherok left the camp.

Near the bank he ducked behind the trees and brush. He could see her silhouette as she climbed into the canoe and grabbed a paddle. She wrestled with the fur blanket and the oar. He could hear her fret and then her quiet sobbing.

Finally she sat in the canoe and threw the paddle into the bottom of the dugout, yanked the furs around her, and buried her face in the soft wrap as she lifted it from underneath.

He heard her scream, muffled as it was. So much had to be hurting this woman. As he watched her, he decided not to press her again about her village. Broaching the subject again would be up to her. He would advise Talasee.

When her crying quieted, he approached the canoe. Cimmera saw him as he touched the bow.

"Please," she mumbled. "Leave me alone."

"I will ask you no more questions," he said, stepping inside the canoe, and then sitting next to her. "Your heart is afflicted with too much anguish." He put his arm around her and encouraged her to rest her head on his shoulder.

They sat in silence, her head leaning heavily against him.

Cimmera's eyes filled with tears again. She had spun herself a chrysalis of lies and had hidden inside it. She was not a real person. She was made up, a fantasy, created in her head as she went along. Even the reasons that this man was trying to comfort her were all lies. Everything he knew about her was a lie. Almost everything she knew about herself was a lie.

CHAPTER 5

"YOU KNOW THE STORY of how the People came to be?" Cherok said, liking the feel of her head against his shoulder, the feel of her silken hair against his chest, the feel of his strength soothing her.

Cimmera did not answer.

"The elders say that in the beginning we were born from the earth. We crawled out of the ground through a hole, like ants. In those days the People lived far away, in a land where there were great rises and ridges in the earth, rises so high that the clouds shrouded the peaks. There was a name for those rises, but our people have forgotten. Those ridges were believed to be the backbone of the earth. And then the Great Spirit caused a vast mist to descend, and the People could not see. They wandered fearful in the dark and calling to each other in the fog. They drifted apart in small groups. These small groups stayed close to one another, frightened that they would become all alone. Finally, after many days, beginning in the east as the sun rose, the Great Spirit blew and blew until he had blown away the mist. The People were grateful, and the members of each group turned to one another and promised to stay together as a family, as close as brother and sister, mother and child."

Cimmera looked up at Cherok's face as he stared out into the darkness and continued.

"Just as the clans were created, it is important that they

stay together. No man, no war, no storm, should ever drive them apart. It should be as the Great Spirit decided. That is why I pressed you about your village. Not only my clan, but all the clans of the People must be together. That is the will of the Great Spirit."

Cimmera hid her face against his shoulder again.

"I will not inflict any more despair upon you. There is no cause for you to flee. The People who are left must cling to each other."

Cimmera felt Cherok's hand smooth her hair, moving from the crown of her head down past her shoulder, and she wished she could take back the lies and tell him what she did and did not know about herself. But she could not trust a stranger.

"Come," he said, "let us go back to camp."

The woman looked at her basket as she took his hand to help her out of the canoe. She noticed he had no blanket and she felt guilty that he had suffered the cold for her. She touched the arm she hadn't been resting against.

"You are cold," she said.

"I had not noticed," he answered as they walked up to the camp.

Cimmera curled up in the fur blanket near the fire, watching the flames flicker in the darkness. In a moment she was asleep.

Wonderful warm yellow fingers of the sun beat on their backs and glinted on the small wake the canoe left behind. The air was chilly, the clarity of the sky and the heat of the sun soporific. A hawk climbed and swooped above them, the undersides of its wings catching a warm current rising from the earth. Cimmera watched as the bird, its wings outstretched, effortlessly glided on the rising river of air.

"Look there," Talasee called, pointing to something in the distance.

Cherok stood up and put the paddle in the bottom of the canoe. "Hand me the pole," he told Cimmera.

Talasee rested his paddle across his thighs and put his hand on the worn leather knife sheath at his side.

Cherok moved the dugout toward the tiny floating peat island. Cimmera leaned out to see better. On top of the island was the outline of a body, but she could not tell if it was a man or a woman, alive or dead. She placed her basket in her lap, worming her hand beneath the pelts until she felt the knife.

"A man," Talasee said. "Cannot tell if he is Tegesta. Looks dead, ill, or pretending to be."

Cherok pushed with the pole, straining to see.

Cimmera wrapped her fingers around the handle of the knife, her muscles tense.

"He moves," Talasee said, seeing the man's head turn to the side.

Cimmera's eyes widened. She had hoped he was dead; she was afraid of who he might be.

Cherok stopped the dugout and waited for the man to give some signal of identity.

The man on the island feebly raised a hand, a gesture that could have meant peace or surrender. Cherok poled closer.

"Wait here," Cherok directed Talasee as he disembarked and waded through the shallow water. The man called out and Cherok drew his knife.

"He wants help," Cimmera said.

Cherok and Talasee both turned to her in surprise. Cimmera's face blanched. The man spoke A-po-la-chee.

"How do you know what he said?" Talasee asked

sharply, twisting around to confront her more squarely.

Her mouth went dry, and she struggled for the Tegesta words. "He seems hurt. He must want our help."

Cherok moved through the water until he was next to the man atop the small floating peat island. "A-po-la-chee," he said, staring coldly.

The man looked past Cherok, at her, as she sat in the canoe. He spoke out, raising a feeble fist to the sky. Cimmera's mouth dropped open. He was thanking the spirits that she was alive. How did he know her? Suddenly she was out of the canoe, wading through the water, holding the blanket above her knees, stopping next to Cherok.

"He needs our help," she said. She pulled a strand of hair from her eyes. There was dried blood on the side of the man's face and neck. "He is wounded."

"Move back, Cimmera. Get back in the dugout," Cherok commanded.

The man spoke again, asking her to help him.

"You cannot leave him to die. That is not the way of a courageous man," she said.

"I will not aid the enemy," Cherok answered.

"Then I will. Take him with us. I will help him. When he can care for himself, we will leave him on his own."

"Why should I let you heal this man? I will only face him in battle someday."

"And if he holds his knife to your throat and sees your face, he will remember your brave and kind deed. He will give you honor and respect ...and your life."

"And when I—"

"Are you a man of valor? There is no ..." Again the words failed her. She knew the word "combat" in A-po-la-chee but not in Tegesta. "You have no fight with this man. There is no glory in leaving a wounded man to die."

She paused a moment and softened her voice. "You did not leave me."

Cherok roughly turned the man's head so that he could see his injury better. The wound had gone bad. "Do what you can for him. I will give you two sleeps, and then we must get rid of him."

"Two sleeps," she said, watching Cherok haul the man over his shoulder.

They waded back to the canoe, and Cherok dumped his burden into the dugout. Talasee shook his head in disapproval.

Cimmera sat with the man's head in her lap. The wound on the side of his head oozed a thick blood-streaked fluid. It was not a fresh wound. It was dirty and had become gravely infected—bad spirits inside. Red streaks beneath the skin snaked down his neck. The man probably would not live. She cleaned the wound with water and bandaged it.

The man beckoned her to lean closer. She lowered her head, and he whispered to her. "You are safe."

Cimmera closed her eyes. This man knew her, and there was something familiar about him. She tried to make the memory come forward from the dark hole inside her head, but she failed, disappointed. She desperately wanted to ask him how he knew her, who she was, what had happened. If she could keep him alive and lucid, she might find some private moment to ask.

Then her thoughts turned to the more obvious. She knew this man's language, and it came to her effortlessly. He knew her. There was only one clear explanation: She was A-po-la-chee, and that meant she was in the company of the enemy. She looked up to see if Cherok or Talasee had observed the man speaking to her and was alarmed to see Cherok staring.

"What did he say?" Cherok asked.

Cimmera shook her head and straightened up. "I do not know. I do not understand the A-po-la-chee language. He mumbles. He is out of his mind."

"He does not look delirious to me," Talasee commented, turning back to them.

"Nor to me," Cherok said.

"He mutters," Cimmera said. "Could be words, but I do not know his tongue. I pretend I understand to comfort him."

Talasee turned away, and Cherok looked to the western horizon.

"I fell," the A-po-la-chee whispered to her, touching his hand to the wound.

Cimmera shook her head and pressed a finger to her lips to signal him to be quiet. She was grateful the sound of the wind had drowned out his whispering. Again she discreetly shook her head and looked at him, eyebrows dipped and lines of worry and fear etched about her mouth and eyes. "Shh," she whispered.

But the man could not clearly see her expression. "Bad spirits inside," he said on faint breath.

Cimmera covered his mouth with her hand. Very bad spirits, she thought.

As the day wore on, the A-po-la-chee man slept frequently. His body was hot even in the cold air.

"We need to stop," Cimmera told the other men.

"It is late in the day. We will stop soon enough. We are on our way back to our village," Cherok said. "We do not need to waste time."

"We must stop," she argued. "This man is dangerously ill." Her words came guardedly. "If you do not allow me to gather the things I need to treat him, I fear he will die."

Talasee turned to face her. "Then he will die."

Cimmera looked down at the man. Even as he slept, he shivered as if he were very cold, yet his body was hot to touch. Bad signs.

Talasee shifted. His face grew red, though Cimmera could tell he fought to control the signs of his anger. First he lifted his head to the sky and sighed, then looked back at her. "He will only live to war with us another day. You do not understand, woman. You have never had to face a warrior who was ready to cut out your heart. You would feel differently if you had seen someone you loved ripped open by an A-po-la-chee's lance. You must never have seen the blood of a loved one being spilled on the ground while you were helpless—or felt the fires burning your face as your village went up in flames. You could not have."

Cimmera's expression changed to a blank stare. Talasee's words had set off images in her mind, as clear as if the event were happening in front of her right then.

Fire. Blazing orange, blue, yellow, white flames. Thatch going up faster than people could get away from it. Heat blistering their hands and feet as they climbed from their platforms. Children running and screaming across a village smothering in black smoke. She saw herself in the crowd, a terrified child. She heard herself coughing from the smoke as she ran, felt the icy-hot chill of fear run down her spine, the stream of tears rolling down her face. She heard the shriek of her voice as she cried. The pounding of her feet echoed in her ears, and the strong vibrations shot up her legs and through her body.

Cimmera broke out in a sweat, perspiration trickling down her body, collecting between her breasts, and clinging to her temples. Suddenly the vision disappeared.

"We told her two sleeps. Only two moons. I do not go back on my word," Cherok was saying. "There." He pointed to a hammock in the distance.

Cimmera was shaken and still quaked. One hand clutched the blanket, and the other dug deep nail marks in her palm.

"Is that satisfactory?" Cherok asked her.

Cimmera had still not recovered and did not hear him.

"Do you hear? You will quickly get whatever you need to treat this man."

Cimmera turned to look at Cherok, her face blank, her skin drenched in sweat.

"Do you understand?" he asked, confused by the bewildered look on her face.

Cimmera hesitated, and then finally answered with a subtle nod.

Talasee helped navigate the canoe in the right direction, craning his neck and scouring the distance. "I would argue again if we had not already surveyed that island a few days before and found that it was safe. Too much time would be wasted."

Cherok looked down at the injured man and touched him with his foot to wake him to hear. "Unlike the A-po-la-chee, the Tegesta are men of their word." He turned to Cimmera. "I told you I would let you attempt to heal him."

When they banked the canoe, Cimmera stepped out.

"And gather some of that," Cherok said, pointing to the air plants that dripped from the trees in curling clumps of small gray-green tendrils. "You need a skirt."

Cherok tossed her a narrow strip of rawhide. "But do not take long."

The thick, lush cover of the hammock quickly cloaked her. She glanced back toward the men, but already the foliage hid them. There seemed to be two worlds: the open, vast, dull saw-grass prairie, and the rich misty green interior of the hardwood hammocks.

The light grew dim beneath the giant oaks, strangler figs, and Sabal palms. She heard a small rustling of leaves and a call from a tree frog. Cimmera suddenly felt anxious and alone, as she had been such a short time ago.

Quickly she spotted the plants with downy leaves that had healing properties. She uprooted them and held them in her hand. There were other plants she could collect, but she didn't see them nearby.

Deeper in the hammock the sunlight faded to a filmy gray, and she felt reluctant to continue her search. She stopped and completed her last task, pulling down pieces of air plants and roughly working them about the rawhide strip to make her skirt. If she had fine sinew and a bone needle, she could attach the plants more securely, she thought, and more time would allow her to plait them.

As she worked, her anxiety grew. The isolation flooded her with that same sense of hopelessness and desperation she had felt before taking the poison. And what had Cherok said? In two moons they would get rid of the A-po-la-chee man. What if they found out that she was A-po-la-chee? What if while she was out here gathering plants and making her skirt Talasee had rummaged through her basket and found the knife? Cimmera's heart sped up. Already they could have abandoned her, left her stranded here. Alone.

Quickly she tied on the skirt, wrapped herself in the furs, picked up the leaves she had gathered, and hurried back to the canoe.

When she finally spotted the dugout and the men through the brush and trees, Cimmera let out a whimper of relief. Even if they were the enemy, she could hide her identity from them. Anything was better than being alone again—even if they killed her, that would be better than being alone.

The robe of furs flopped open as she stepped inside the canoe. "We have no women's tools for you to make your skirt," Cherok said.

"It will hold awhile," she answered.

"What medicine did you gather?" Cherok asked as Talasee pushed off.

Cimmera's expression changed. Perhaps what she had gathered was not a customary medicine for the Tegesta.

"Just a common plant. It will help, but I fear it is not potent enough." The words came easier now as if loosed from a forgotten dark corner.

"Where is it?" Talasee asked.

"I have crushed it in my hand."

"Let me see," Cherok said.

Cimmera's voice quavered when she spoke. "Why do you always interrogate me? I am tired of the questions."

Cherok smiled, curious about her reaction. "Only conversation. I am interested in healing medicines. My father was a shaman, and I learned many skills from him."

Cimmera turned away and looked out across the sedge.

"Where did you learn about medicines?" Talasee asked.

She did not turn to look at him.

"Why are you so secretive?" Cherok asked. "Show me what is in your hand."

Cimmera continued to ignore them, the leaves in her hand soaked in nervous perspiration.

"Turn about, woman, when I speak to you. Open your fist." Cherok's hand was hard and demanding on her shoulder.

Cimmera kept her eyes on her hand as she slowly uncurled her fingers.

Cherok lifted her palm closer. With his first finger he poked the leaves and moved them around. He lifted a leaf and smelled it, then put it back with the others. He stared at Cimmera for a moment as if seeking some answers, and then he looked at his older friend. "Do you know this plant, Talasee?"

CHAPTER 6

CHEROK SMILED AT TALASEE, then at Cimmera. "My father taught me about this plant. Your knowledge of medicine is wise."

Cimmera relaxed with a guarded sigh.

"Is that all you collected?" Cherok asked.

"You told me to hurry."

"There are other plants, other remedies you should make if you want to help this man."

"I know that," Cimmera answered. "But there were none in the small area that I searched. You told me to do this quickly."

"Did you look for the pilosa?" Cherok asked.

"Of course. But the ground was too damp there for it to grow. If you had allowed me more time, I might have found some pilosa and some ..." Her voice trailed off.

"Pokeberry?" He filled the gap in her recall of words.

"Yes, pokeberry."

"The root of the pokeberry?" he asked.

"I have no intention of poisoning the man."

Cherok smiled at her. He was aware the root was poisonous. "How do you know so much about medicines?"

Cimmera swallowed. He had been testing her, probing to see what she knew. "I do not know that much," she finally answered. "There were some medicines that everyone in my village used. I have not given away great secrets. And," she said, "you are questioning me again. I find that an irritating habit of yours."

Cherok shook his head at her defensiveness. "It just seems I have elicited more from you by discussing medicinal plants than anything else."

"Perhaps if you were more considerate I would find other things to talk to you about."

Talasee chuckled. "The woman will forever hold a grudge against you for dipping her in the water.

Cherok's expression changed so that his eyes flashed with mischief. He remembered her face as she looked up at him from the cold water he had dropped her in.

Talasee spoke again. "Women are like that. She will never forget how you dumped her in the water, and if you know her at the end of your lifetime, she will remind you then!"

Cimmera adjusted the blanket around her and ignored both men.

"So what are you going to do with those few puny plants you have?" Talasee asked.

She knew the men would not stop and allow her to brew the medicine properly and make a good poultice. "I will chew them and then put them on his wound." Talasee's attitude toward her effort to save the man annoyed her. "I am sure you will find delight in watching me chew the bitter leaves."

"I suppose," Talasee said, his lips curling into a satisfied smile.

Cimmera took a few leaves, pushed them into her mouth, and chewed.

Talasee did not turn around to watch as she thought he would. Cherok, however, caught a glimpse every chance he could when he thought she wouldn't notice. He found himself grimacing with her as she squinted her eyes, wrinkled her nose, and shuddered at the taste. She was a stubborn, proud, and determined woman, and to his way of thinking, a bit foolish. She could have waited until they camped, and then she could have brewed the medicine. The sun would set in a short time.

The woman pressed the chewed leaves onto the man's wound. Cherok was right. This medicine was weak. The A-po-la-chee warrior had been so long without care, and the wound was so angry, that she doubted he would recover no matter what she treated him with. But she needed him. He had to live at least until she had the opportunity to ask him about herself.

Her last thought troubled her, and she chastised herself for not feeling more concern for the well-being of the warrior she tended. Was she a woman with no conscience?

The warrior groaned as she pressed the medicine against his wound again.

"Do not speak," Cimmera whispered to him, leaning close, pretending to inspect the wound.

Talasee fed the fire until it came ablaze. Cimmera sat next to the A-po-la-chee warrior, helping him drink water.

"Tamar's spirit can rest," the man said, looking up at her.

"Please," she whispered, "stay quiet." She stood up and moved away.

"The sun will go down very soon, and it will be too dark to find more medicinal plants," Cherok said.

Cimmera looked back at the suffering warrior. "I go now."

He saw the disconsolate look on her face. "I will help. Two pairs of eyes can find the plants more quickly."

She thanked him with a nod and started into the forested interior of the hammock. "But your help will not make me forget how you dropped me in the water," she said as she stepped past him.

He caught a glimpse of a faint smile. "You are... I do not know if there is a proper word to describe you," he said, moving beside her. "You sulk about your unwanted plunge in the water and slip a tiny grin across your lips when you talk about it."

With a shake of her head, Cimmera tossed back the hair from her eyes. "Pokeberry," she said, stripping some leaves and stems from the tall plant in front of her.

"I do not think you will find the pilosa here," he said. "The soil is too damp."

"I will do what I can."

"Helping this man is important to you." Cherok paused to look at her before he continued. "He is the enemy."

"We have discussed this before."

"I would have left him where he lay," Cherok said.

"And I could not," she responded.

"I think that is a favorable quality in a woman."

Cimmera tweaked a leaf from its stem and held on to it as she spoke. "Helping others is a good quality in either a man or a woman." She felt the sincerity of the words, and with that came the relief of knowing that she did indeed have a conscience. Besides wanting the A-po-la-chee to live because of the information he could provide her, she worried that he suffered, and she wished to relieve his pain. She felt heavyhearted because she expected that he would die, and she wished she could prevent that.

"That is not the way a clever warrior must think."

"When he is at war," she said. "But there is no war, no battle, between you and this man. He is just a man, and every man's life has value."

Cherok studied her face. There was conviction in her eyes and truth on her tongue. Perhaps her easy talk of her opinions, her passion for things she believed, discouraged a man from taking her as his woman, as his wife. But Cherok found something attractive in her way, something exciting. He was sure she would not be one just to lie beneath a man during joining. No, this woman—

"What do you stare at?" she asked.

"I am not sure," he answered.

They walked back, through the shadows that seeped into every crevice of the hammock.

Talasee stood by the fire taking a bullfrog from his two-pronged spear. "They are abundant," he said, dropping the frog onto a pile of others.

"They will fill our bellies," Cherok said.

Cimmera heated the plant parts in a pouch of water suspended over the fire. She dropped hot stones into the pouch until the liquid inside was hot. She immersed a swatch of deerskin in the liquid, fished it out with a stick, and carried it over to the A-po-la-chee. As Cherok and Talasee cooked the frogs, Cimmera sat with the man, tending to his wound.

"Tell me your name?" she said softly, hoping that his name would stir her memory.

"Kupah," he said, his voice low and raspy.

"Kupah," she repeated. "Kupah." The name meant nothing to her.

He mumbled something again. Cimmera looked toward the fire where Talasee and Cherok were talking and laughing as they cooked the meal. They had not heard her or the A-po-la-chee.

"Star," Kupah said. His voice broke into gurgles and rasps as he spoke.

"What star? What do you mean?"

Kupah started to speak but choked. He coughed and struggled to clear his throat. "Star knife."

Cimmera tensed. He had to mean the knife she had hidden in her basket. "I have it," she told him.

"They come," the man said, squeezing her hand.

"Who?" she asked. "Who is coming?" Suddenly she realized that her voice had gotten too loud. Cherok and Talasee turned to look at her.

"The medicine will help you," she said loudly in Tegesta. "Ask the spirits for their help."

Talasee and Cherok returned to their conversation.

Cimmera whispered again. "Who am I, Kupah? What is my name?"

The man moaned and closed his eyes.

"Kupah," she said, gently shaking one of his shoulders. "Tell me who I am. I do not remember. Do you understand? Can you hear me?"

The man slowly opened his eyes to slits. "You do not know?"

"I have lost my memory. I do not remember anything."

"You have the knife?" he asked.

"Yes," she said. "I told you that I have it."

The A-po-la-chee trembled, his brows twitched, and his eyelids fluttered. "They come." The man's voice rose, and he tried to lift up.

Cimmera gently encouraged him to lie back down. "No one is coming." Her whisper sounded confident, but she searched the dark shadows. "Do not speak loudly. We are among the Tegesta. They think I am one of them."

The man feebly raised his head a little so that he could see the men who sat at the fire. Then his head dropped back to the ground.

"Kupah, tell me who I am."

"Your name?"

"Yes," she said anxiously. "My name."

"Cimmera," Cherok called. "Come, the meat is cooked."

"Yes," she answered. "I am coming."

She did not want to leave. The man was going to say her name.

Kupah closed his eyes again, and his breathing was quick and shallow.

Cherok rose and walked over to her, carrying a skewer of meat. "You must eat, woman," he said as he held it out to her.

Cimmera reached for the wooden stick, but just as she almost grasped the skewer, Cherok pulled it away.

"He sleeps. Come and sit at the fire. You have done what you can."

"I will stay with him a little longer," she said.

"For what? Have you treated him with the medicine?"

"Yes," she answered.

"And does he sleep?"

Cimmera looked at Kupah.

"There is no reason to sit here. Come to the fire and eat."

Cimmera reluctantly got to her feet.

In the middle of the night Cimmera heard Kupah moaning. She crawled over to him. In the dim light of the moon and the dying fire, she saw his face. He was suffering, his lips taut and thin, his eyes shut tight, and all the lines of his face squirming.

She called his name and wiped his forehead.

He groaned and took a gasp of air. "Kill me," he said.

Cimmera shrank back. "No, Kupah. Shh." She

removed the bandage. The wound was no better, and the whole side of his head was swollen, his left eye barely able to open, the corner of his mouth disfigured by the swelling.

"Give me a weapon," he said. "Tell the Tegesta I ..." A sweeping pain cut him off. With his eyes closed he saw the pain as yellow jagged lines that flashed, like lightning bolts slashing through him.

"You are going to recover, Kupah. You will be all right."

"I am dying," he mumbled. "Send a Tegesta to battle with me."

"You cannot fight," Cimmera said, wiping the perspiration from his face.

Kupah grasped her wrist and spoke through clenched teeth. "I am a warrior. I wish to die as one." The man coughed. "A warrior," he muttered again before letting her go.

"I am going to help you," Cimmera said to him, daubing his forehead with a swatch of moss she tore from her skirt. "Stop talking. Rest."

Cherok turned to his side and looked in Cimmera's direction. The A-po-la-chee's legs writhed. Cherok sat up for a better look. "Cimmera," he called.

The woman spun around to look at Cherok, who had gotten to his feet and was walking over to her.

"I am afraid that he is dying," she said.

Cherok squatted next to them. Suddenly the A-po-la-chee reached up and grabbed Cherok's knife sheath. Cherok took the man's wrist and pulled his hand away.

Cherok slowly removed his knife from the sheath. Kupah clutched Cherok's hand with an unsteady grip and guided the knife to his own throat. Cherok focused on the man's eyes and the desperation he saw there.

The A-po-la-chee nodded, pressed the Tegesta's knife more firmly against his throat, and closed his eyes.

"Go away, Cimmera," Cherok said.

"What are you going to do?" she asked.

"Go back by the fire."

Cimmera sat in stunned silence.

"Do as I say." Cherok's voice was demanding, and Talasee now stood next to her, prodding her with a gentle tug on her shoulder.

"Help me with him, Talasee," Cherok said.

Cimmera got up and backed her way to the fire.

"We will take him where she cannot see," Cherok directed Talasee.

Kupah stared hard at his enemy, looking for a sign that the Tegesta man understood. Cherok nodded at him, and Kupah sighed.

After carrying the A-po-la-chee a short distance, they propped him up on his feet, helped him balance against the trunk of a hackberry, the peace tree.

Kupah struggled to stay upright. His vision was blurry, his head pounded, and his heart thumped frantically and uncomfortably in his chest.

"Give him your knife, Talasee," Cherok ordered.

Talasee obeyed, planting his knife firmly in Kupah's palm.

Kupah and Cherok stared at each other for a long time before Cherok bent his knees and assumed a fighting stance.

The A-po-la-chee pulled himself away from the bracing tree, took a deep breath, and gathered all his strength. Then he lurched at Cherok, yelping a war cry, a strong cry, the proud cry of a warrior on the attack.

Cimmera huddled by the fire. She was glad that Cherok had taken Kupah into the darkness where she could not be a witness. She heard Kupah's whoop and then silence.

Talasee trod back into camp first, his knife returned to its sheath.

"Where is Cherok?" Cimmera asked, now feeling her body quake.

"He washes his knife," Talasee told her.

Cimmera put the furs around her, unsure if it was the cold that made her shake or if it was the realization of what had just happened.

Cherok appeared by the fire that Talasee had fueled so that it blazed again. "The A-po-la-chee died with honor."

Cimmera curled her body and lay on her side, her back to the men, wrapped snugly in the fur blanket. "Did you say prayers over him?" she asked, her voice so low that the two men barely heard her.

"He is A-po-la-chee," Cherok answered.

Tears rolled out of the corners of her eyes, one sliding over the bridge of her nose. She could not ask Cherok and Talasee to give Kupah, an A-po-la-chee, the enemy, a proper burial. It was enough that they had given him a chance to die with the dignity of a warrior.

She heard the Tegesta men finally bed down for the night. But she could not sleep. Kupah was dead—the only one who knew her—the only link to her past. He was someone she had known, and she was angry that she could not remember him and grieve as a friend should. His body now lay somewhere in the woods, to be torn apart and eaten by the animals, to rot, to decay without a prayer or a shaman's guidance to the Other Side.

Cimmera shifted as if changing position might help her sleep. She stared at the coals of the fire. If she was a good and decent person, she had to do something, whatever she could, for Kupah. She watched Cherok and

Talasee sleep for a little while. Finally she sat up quietly, waited to see if her movement disturbed the men. Then, confident that they slept soundly, she stood and walked into the trees.

The moonlight did not provide much illumination. She ducked beneath the low branches, moving slowly through the forest. She felt the tackiness of a spiderweb stick to her face, and she wondered if the creature was crawling in her hair. She shook her head, brushed her hands through her hair, and then wiped the web away.

They could have taken Kupah anywhere on the hammock, she thought, and this could be a futile search. But just as she was afraid she would not find him, she saw Kupah's body.

She crouched next to him, cleared a spot that was not soaked with his blood, and sat down. Kupah's eyes were open and stared at the black sky. The last thing he saw, she realized, was the fires of his ancestors that burned above him. She found some peace in that thought.

Cimmera looked up at the stars and talked to the spirits, hoping they would hear her. The words came with surprising ease, flowing from deep inside her, naturally, powerfully. "Please come this way for Kupah, a brave warrior of the A-po-la-chee," she said. "See him as he lies here, as he waits for you to take him to the Other Side. Come for him," she said. And then from her mouth slipped a soft chant, words that were not A-po-la-chee and not Tegesta—an ancient tongue. She felt drained when she finished the short song. Where had such a song come from? Where inside her had it been hidden? Who was she?

She looked back at Kupah's face and felt her body grow weak. His face. There was something she recognized.

Suddenly voices were roaring in her head, and she was barraged by images.

Disjointed pieces and blotches of memory flicked through her mind. The one image that kept returning was Kupah telling her to hurry, the background filled with fire, and smoke, shrieks, and cries.

"Cimmera, what are you doing?"

Cherok's voice ripped her back into the dark hammock and next to Kupah's body.

"What are you doing?" Cherok asked again.

CHAPTER 7

CIMMERA LOOKED UP to face Cherok, her mouth empty of words.

"He is gone, Cimmera. There is nothing you can do for him." He crouched beside her and put his thumb and forefinger on Kupah's eyelids to shut them. "Why do you brood so over this A-po-la-chee?"

"I thought I could help him," she said. "I was wrong."

"Come," Cherok said, standing and extending his hand to help her up. "Walk back to camp with me."

Cimmera rested her small hand in his large palm.

Cherok's fingers curled over hers. She rose slowly, then found herself facing the Tegesta man, standing so close to him that she could feel the heat of his body radiate and cut through the cold air. He held her hand a moment longer than was necessary, and Cimmera finally pulled it away and dusted off her knees.

She could feel his eyes watching her, gliding down her back, drifting to her legs. "There," she said as she brushed her hands together.

A lock of hair fell across her face, and she reached up to move it away. But Cherok stopped her, placing his hand over hers, rolling her hand into a fist inside his. He took the strand of hair and unhurriedly moved it. Fine silver splinters of moonlight sprinkled through the trees and dappled her face.

"I am trying to decide if you are lovelier in the sun or

in moon shadow," he said.

Cimmera forced herself to look away.

"Do I make you uncomfortable?" he asked, seeing how she had become flustered.

You are my enemy, she screamed in her head. "You say things you should not," she finally answered.

"Why should I not speak what I think?"

Cimmera found the strength to pull her hand free of his. "You do not know me," she said, taking a step back toward camp.

Cherok grasped her shoulder and made her turn around. He ran his hand up under her hair behind her ear, exposing the soft and tender side of her neck.

"What is this?" he asked, noticing a small patch of darker skin just behind and beneath her ear. "It is shaped like a butterfly," he said. "Like you—delicate, exquisite."

Cimmera put her hand over his to move it, then felt his palm glide slowly down her neck and over her shoulder. She couldn't move as she felt him lean into her and touch his mouth to hers, taking her breath away. She was dazed, unable to move or think, suspended there, feeling herself grow warm even as the cold air breezed past her. But this man was Tegesta, and she was A-po-la-chee. She turned her head. She wanted to tell him never to do that again, but she could not bring herself to say it, and she knew that if she did speak, her voice would catch in her throat.

Cherok cocked one corner of his mouth into an irreverent smile as he watched her walk back into camp.

Cimmera wrapped herself tightly in the furs and lay down on the deerskin blanket, closing her eyes.

Cherok hunkered near the fire and fed it some wood, his gaze fixed on the woman who pretended to rest peacefully.

"The woman occupies your head," Talasee said.

The voice came unexpectedly. Cherok was so engrossed in his thoughts that he did not note Talasee's approach. "So she does," Cherok said.

Talasee folded his legs under him and sat next to Cherok. "I remember what that feels like."

"Tashi?"

Talasee seemed to let his mind drift back in time. "I remember the first time I saw her. All curves and glossy hair down her back swaying gently to the rock of her hips as she walked."

"We will find her, my friend."

Talasee's expression was despairing. "There seem to be so few who survived. The women and children had no one but old men to help them during the storm. You know what the village looked like when we returned. Nothing left."

"We have found others. Those we have returned to our hammock are rebuilding even as we speak. You must not give up. We will make other journeys in search of our people."

"Perhaps if we had not been gone on the Big Water journey when the storm came, we could have done something. Maybe I could have saved her."

"Talasee, you cannot wonder such things. You will never know the answer. And she may be fine, anxious to return home. If the spirits willed your wife to live, then she is alive. If they willed her dead, then there was nothing you could have done. Make yourself think of her as living."

"I do best if I do not think about her at all. I have finally begun to accept that she is dead. My son gives me reason to go on. I must think of him and how fortunate we were to find him with Gaga-na and other women who survived the storm."

Cherok touched his friend's shoulder.

"Events such as the storm make a man want to live his life differently," Talasee said.

"What do you mean?"

"Do not put anything off. You must live each day as if the next will never come. There are things I should have said to Tashi—things I had not said to her since we were first together." Talasee looked up. "Do you follow?"

Cherok gazed at the form of the woman curled up inside the furs. "I understand," he said. "There should never be time or opportunity wasted. The chance may never come again."

"Exactly," Talasee said, lying back, elbows out, the palms of his hands cradling his head.

Cherok probed the fire with a stick. Perhaps that was why he had acted so hastily, touching this woman's mouth with his, skirting the traditional conventions and formalities of a courtship.

"If this woman really pleases you, let her know it," Talasee said.

Cherok thought about the brief encounter he had just had with her.

"I still think she needs more flesh on her bones," Talasee said and laughed, bringing a smile to Cherok's face.

The pale morning sun

barely edged over the lip of the earth and flushed the sky of its blackness. Cimmera bolted up, clutching the blanket at her breast, breathing heavily. The dream had seemed so real. She was running, fear ripping through her as sharply as the point of a lance. Something or someone was in pursuit—coming after her. Then everything in her dream had slowed to an unnatural speed so that her movements were exaggerated. She could see the individual droplets spraying up as her feet splashed in the water. She looked behind her, her head turning so slowly. She felt her ankle turn, and then she saw herself fall face down in the water.

Cimmera held her forehead in her hand. If the dream had brought her a fragment of her lost memory she would have been thankful. But this was only a nightmare with nothing good coming from it.

She looked at Cherok and Talasee, who slept. Was it the Tegesta who had been coming for her, running her down, when she fell and lost her memory? She was sure that Cherok and Talasee believed she was Tegesta, but what would happen when they arrived in the village? What if someone recognized her—the same one who had pursued her that day? What would happen to her?

Suddenly she remembered the blood that had covered her. Had she used that knife, the star knife, on a Tegesta?

Cimmera held her hands out in front of her, staring at them, wondering if those hands had done such a deed. Her stomach churned. And where had that chant come from, the song she had sung over Kupah's body? Who was she to communicate with the spirits? An evil spirit herself? Perhaps it was better that she did not remember anything—better that she did not know.

She lay down on the bedding again and watched the sky ease into pastel swirls as the sun continued to rupture the darkness, extinguishing the fires of the spirits until only the morning star was left burning.

Cimmera sat up and used both hands to smooth back her hair. The white morning light would awaken Cherok and Talasee at any moment. She pressed the fur blanket to her nose and breathed into it. The warmth felt good.

She moved closer to the fire, seeing there were only a few small coals left burning. She added some of the tinder Talasee had piled nearby and gradually fed the fire larger pieces of wood, listening to it crackle and sizzle. Cimmera opened the fur robe so the heat could reach her body and warm the inside of the coverlet. She didn't notice that Cherok had also come to the fire and stood entranced across from her.

The sight of her naked dazed him. It was a moment before he could say anything, before he wanted her to know he was there. Talasee was wrong about this woman's body. Talasee had not seen her as he had, stripped bare, flesh adorned only by light gleaming and shining on crests and swells, and shadows shading and hiding sweet valleys. But he could not stand here forever relishing the sight.

"It seems colder this morning," Cherok said, moving to her side and sitting down.

Cimmera saw the warm moist vapor coming from Cherok's mouth as he spoke. She modestly closed the blanket around her, appreciating the secure and comfortable sensation it created. "Yes, it appears so," she answered, her eyes tearing from a cold breeze.

Not only was the air cold, but with the daylight came a fierce wind, chilling them all to the bone. Cimmera huddled in the canoe, but Cherok and Talasee were not as fortunate. Cherok poled the canoe for a while and then turned it over to Talasee.

"Our village is not so far," Cherok said to her.

Cimmera felt an extra shiver run down her back.

The shallow water rippled with the wind, and the swords of saw grass whipped and tangled. But the sky was clear and blazing, the sun a brilliant globe.

By midafternoon their stomachs rumbled with hunger, and they picked at the supplies in the baskets. Talasee cut a piece of smoked meat and carried it to his mouth on the blade of his knife.

"Take the pole, Talasee," Cherok said, sitting next to Cimmera, who kept herself hidden in the furs. He pulled his basket to his lap and fumbled through it until he found a piece of dried fruit, which he removed and held out to her.

"It is too cold," she said.

"Too cold to eat?"

"Too cold to take my arms out of this blanket."

"I can take care of that," he said, touching the fruit to her lips. "Open."

Cimmera opened her mouth just wide enough for him to slide the tidbit inside. She chewed and swallowed, wishing it were warm tea. "How much longer?"

"We will be at the village before the sun sets."

Cimmera felt colder and bundled herself up tighter.

"Others may have arrived since we left, found their way back on their own. And perhaps someone from your village has joined us."

"I do not think so."

"I know that your home is far away, but the storm has scattered us all. If some of your clan wandered this way— and certainly most would not wander to the north so close to the A-po-la-chee, as you did—they would see the smoke from the fires, and that would guide them to our village."

Cimmera nodded to convince Cherok that she believed him.

"You do not say much."

She stared into the distance.

"Do you refrain from talking to me because of the way

I touched my lips to yours?"

Cimmera spun around to look at him. "You have not apologized."

"No," Cherok said, "I am not regretful."

"But I did not want you to do that."

"Yes, you did. At least part of you did. You did not tear your mouth from mine at the very first instant. There was a struggle inside you, even if it was brief."

"You are vain," she said, looking away from the man who had such insight into her.

Cherok took a handful of her hair and lifted it free from inside the furs so that it trailed down her back. The tiny mark on her neck reminded him of how fragile she was. "It must have been terrible to be alone for so long."

"I do not want to talk about that," she said, the memory of the desolation coming at her with such force that she immediately felt her throat tighten and her eyes sting.

"You are not alone now."

Cimmera refused to look at him.

"I will not tell you that I will never try to touch you that way again. Think about this, Cimmera. Tomorrow another storm could come and be the end of us all. I have decided that I do not want to miss anything in this life, because I did not dare, because I lacked courage, because I waited till another day. The great storm has changed us all, I think."

"Cherok, you do not know anything about me. Why would—"

He cut her off. "What do I need to know? Tell me about yourself."

"Leave me alone," she snapped, twisting so that her back was to him.

Cherok shook his head, and a muddled expression

crossed his face. "I do not give up so easily," he said, standing and taking the pole from Talasee. "Woman, tonight when I rest my eyes just before sleep, I will say to myself, 'Cherok, you tarried not a moment of this day.' I will sleep quickly and peacefully."

Cimmera dismissed the idea of replying. If she knew who she was, if she knew she was Tegesta, knew she was not an evil spirit in the flesh, if there was nothing to hide, then maybe she would sleep as soundly and contentedly as he professed he would. Maybe she would allow herself to enjoy his attention, bold as it was. But she did not have such freedom, and she would have to keep her distance from him. It was imperative that she live every moment with prudence and regard.

Cherok looked at Cimmera. There was detachment in her gaze. He shook his head. Had she heard anything he said?

Talasee saw a discountenance in his friend's eyes. He slapped Cherok on the back and chuckled. "I must have a talk with you when we reach the village—about women."

Cherok pushed the pole down into the water and felt it sink into the peat. He pushed down, gliding the canoe through the trail. A disinclined smile sat on his mouth.

Cimmera lifted her face and sniffed. Smoke. Cook fires. Tender meat, succulent roots and tubers, fresh fish. "We are close?" she asked.

"There," Cherok said, lifting a hand and pointing.

The hammock loomed ahead.

"I do not feel well," Cimmera said. "Would you help me avoid the people of your clan so that I can rest? Tell them I am ill and will be happy to meet them with the next sun."

"Avoid?" Cherok said. "That is a strange choice of

words."

Cimmera bit her bottom lip. She had thought the word was good. "I mean that I fear I will not make a good impression—the way I feel."

"There are not many of us, Cimmera. Introductions will only take a moment. Then I will tell them that you feel sick. They will understand."

"No," Cimmera said a little too curtly. She took a breath and let it out slowly. "It is important to me that I am accepted. My stomach is sour, and my head aches. Please, can you help me, escort me away from the crowd quickly?"

He flashed his straight white teeth at her in a broad grin. "All right," Cherok said. The expression was similar to the one he had worn when he dropped her in the water, and it made her uneasy.

Cimmera saw a handful of people gathering at the edge of the tree island. The canoe had been spotted, and the people collected to greet their returning friends.

"Cherok," a thin man said in welcome as Cherok banked the canoe. Talasee hopped over the side and splashed through the shallow water, clapping his hands against the arms and backs of his friends as he met them.

"The cacique has brought back a woman," Talasee said as he watched Cherok help Cimmera out of the canoe.

Cimmera whisked her head to the side to look at Cherok. He had not told her he was their king. "Cacique?"

Cherok hiked a brow and tilted his head. "You did not ask," he said.

Cimmera heard the villagers murmuring. "Who?" she heard whispered. "Where is she from?"

"The woman is ill," Cherok began. "When she feels

better she wishes to meet all of you."

Cimmera shielded her face with the blanket as if she was terribly chilled. Her eyes were suddenly snared by the glare of an old woman in the crowd who held her arm about a young boy. Cimmera swallowed at the peculiar, sharply uncanny sensation that accompanied the woman's stare. Her feet became rooted and her eyes riveted, returning the gaze.

The boy broke free and ran to Talasee. "Father," he said, wrapping his arms around Talasee's waist.

Finally the old woman turned her back and walked away.

Cherok took Cimmera's elbow through the blanket and guided her, moving her through the small crowd. She glanced back to see if the woman was still in sight, but she had disappeared.

Over the rim of the furs Cimmera saw how Cherok's clan had started to rebuild the village. Piles of debris sat near the central hearth, ready to be burned. New shelters with green thatch stood nearby.

Cherok stopped at the base of a platform. He gripped the ladder and encouraged her to climb it.

From under the blind of the furs, Cimmera peered up. She was so startled that she gasped. She whipped around to face Cherok. Now she understood the big grin he had worn when he agreed to excuse her from introductions.

CHAPTER 8

AMID ALL THE AMBER and brown of the desolation, the dust and dirt, this platform sat on Sabal palm boles etched and painted with vibrant dyes. Shell ornaments dripped from the supports and chimed in the wind. The posts bore elaborate colorful designs, and four carved wooden animal heads, protective spirits, crested them, rising above the thatch.

"This is the cacique's shelter," Cimmera said. "Your platform."

Cherok handed her her basket, then swept his arm toward the ladder, a gesture suggesting she climb it.

"I cannot stay here," Cimmera vehemently objected.

"It is your request. You are feeling too ill to meet any of my people. Where did you think you would stay?"

"Well … not here. I did not think—"

"I have noted that about you." Again he indicated that she go up the ladder. "There is nowhere else now." Then his face broke into a teasing smile. "If I think you deserve it, I will see to it that a platform is built for you."

Cimmera shot him an angry glance, her eyes sparking with the seething fire she felt inside. She grasped a rung and began her ascent.

She could feel Cherok's eyes on her, watching her climb, the furs and basket becoming cumbersome and making her awkward. The blanket slipped from one shoulder. Cimmera stopped to adjust it, wedging the basket between her thigh and the ladder to hold it while she sharply grabbed the coverlet and repositioned it. She shook her head, whipping her hair to her back as she gripped the basket again.

Though the ladder had only a few steps, he saw her frustration. She made every effort to maintain her poise as she climbed, but the robe was bulky and got in her way, the basket occupying one of her hands.

At the top Cimmera huffed at how clumsy she felt. If he had not been watching, she was certain that she would have moved up the ladder with grace and agility. She looked back at him and saw that he still smiled crookedly.

"I hope that you feel better, woman," he said.

Cimmera tucked herself inside the platform and out of his view. "Arrogant beast," she said aloud to herself, setting the basket beside her, opening the aggravating blanket and rearranging it around herself. It was cold inside the shelter. Outside, the sun had helped keep her warm.

She fidgeted with the furs to nestle her feet snugly and watched out the opening of the platform, hoping that she could survey the village. At the same time she hoped no one would see her without coming close and deliberately trying to look deep inside.

Cherok chuckled to himself and walked away. "Fire Keeper," he called, seeing Talasee.

His friend turned around. "Where is the woman?" he asked. "Does she feel better?"

"I believe she will have a complete recovery in a very short time," Cherok said, casually looping his arm around Talasee's shoulders and sauntering with him toward the central hearth, telling him where he had taken Cimmera.

"You are a sly one," Talasee said with a lively snicker.

"We will build her a shelter, but I will enjoy watching her fret until then."

They stood by the fire. As the sun belted the horizon with purple and pink, they warmed themselves, feeling the chill set in with the approaching night.

"Where are Atok and Dacoma? I have not seen them," Cherok said.

"I was told that they have taken a canoe. They also look for more of our clan."

"Okemah!" Cherok said, rising to his feet as an old friend approached.

One of Okemah's eyelids was scarred and drawn tight at an angle over his eye, the result of a childhood sparring injury. The stick had narrowly missed damaging his eye and his sight. The man's body was sturdy, though his once taut, developed muscles had lost their youthful definition. Around his middle he now carried a paunch. Cherok remembered how as a youngster he and others had been encouraged by the older Okemah to hit his stomach with their fists. Okemah had laughed as they drew back their hands in awe after striking the rock-solid muscles of his abdomen. Okemah roused many glad memories.

"Cacique," the man said as they ruggedly embraced.

Talasee slapped Okemah on the upper arm. "There are more and more of us."

"My heart fills with happiness to see you again," Cherok said. "I hope that all who were on the Big Water journey the night of the storm will find their way home." The images of that night raced in Cherok's head: the frenzy, the rising river, the scattering of the men as they attempted to escape the flood and the wind. He blinked his eyes, which had been staring into the distance, then looked back at Okemah. "Ah, but you give me hope,"

Cherok said. "When did you get here?"

"I arrived just after the two of you left on your search," Okemah said as they sat. "I had stayed with the people of the turtle clan while I recovered."

"Recovered?"

"There were three of us. Pocola, Manche, and me. We managed to stay together that night, but a falling tree struck Manche. He could not feel his legs, nothing beneath his belly, and that was a good thing, because a bone stuck through the skin of his thigh. Pocola and I did our best to carry him and care for him. But ..."

Okemah's face twitched as he faltered. He paused, cleared his throat, then spoke again. "Pocola and I buried him, but I do not know where. The storm has changed everything. There are no landmarks. The trees that once stood green against the blue sky are now no more than barren sticks—if they stand at all. The world has changed since that night."

Again his voice choked, and he needed to pause. Okemah pressed his thumb and forefinger against his closed eyelids and pinched the moisture out of the corners of his eyes. He sniffed and looked up. "Pocola ..." Okemah took a deep breath. "He felt guilty over Manche's death, and he felt we would never find our way home. He had injuries also and tried to disguise the pain, but I could see it on his face. He seemed to have given up. One morning I awakened. I must have heard a noise, because I sat straight up and in my heart knew something was wrong. Pocola had sharpened a long stick to a point, hardened it in the fire, and planted it, point up, in the ground. He had flung himself upon it. I ran to him and pulled him off the stake. He was not dead. I wished he was," Okemah said, his voice trembling, the corners of his mouth quivering. "The spirits were slow in coming to claim him. Perhaps because death was his doing and not theirs."

The men nodded in agreement, too stricken by the horror of the story to say anything.

"I wandered for many days without eating, without any direction. I do not know how many days it was; one seemed to fade into the next. Finally I stumbled onto the village of the turtle clan and collapsed there. They tended me until I had recovered my strength and will."

"We will send them tribute when we can," Cherok said. "We are grateful to have you return."

"The villages far to the north of us did not appear to have suffered as much damage as we did here," Okemah said. "The storm was powerful but small. Some trees were blown down, but the people were spared."

"It is unfortunate it did not hit the A-po-la-chee." Talasee said, pitching a stick into the fire.

"We found one woman that far north," Cherok said. "Very close to A-po-la-chee territory. She rests in my platform. She is unsure about the location of her village, and when you pry, she becomes edgy. She had been alone on a hammock for a long time when we found her. She becomes disquieted at any reminder."

Okemah was rubbing his forehead. "I understand. I wish I could forget. Sometimes I wish that it had been me and not Manche and Pocola who died."

Talasee turned away from the fire to face Okemah. "But the spirits have spared you."

"I do not understand any of it—why the spirits allowed such a storm, why they took Manche, why Pocola took his life, what happened to my woman." Okemah looked up and around the village. "Nothing will ever be the same."

Cherok firmly laid his hand on Okemah's shoulder.

"We must get past the storm. We are doing that. Look around the village. We rebuild, and the village will be better than it was before, just different."

"Some of us will never get past the storm. The wind sucked the spirit out of many of us."

"Never," Cherok said. "I still see the fire inside you. That is why you did not do what Pocola did. You will be a part of the change."

"It has been several cycles of the moon, the season has changed, and still we have not recovered. I tell you that our lives are changed forever," Okemah said.

"I agree with you, old friend. Our lives are changed. But they have not ended."

"Where are our women?" Okemah said, his voice rising. "I can tell you where most of them are. They lie face down in the water, food for the alligators and fish. They putrefy out there." Okemah turned to Talasee. "Tashi is out there rotting in the stinking mud like my woman."

"He has not given up hope, Okemah," Cherok said.

"Then he is a fool."

"Okemah," Talasee said, "I cannot give in to those thoughts. Do you not see that thoughts like those are a trap? If you become tangled in them, you might never come free. Look about. There are other women here. They survived and have been found—brought back here."

Okemah looked across the village and saw Narchise tending to some basketry, the fullness of her breasts plumply rounding out her fur robe. "And what does a man do?" he asked. "Do I wait forever for my woman to return? What does a man do to satisfy his needs? How do you say I must get on with my life, past the storm, and in the same breath tell me to hold on, my woman may yet be alive? Hope is not a good thing."

Cherok sighed. "All the healing will take time. Be patient, Okemah."

"I know, Cherok," Okemah said. "I know. But my loneliness does not make living each day any easier."

Talasee shifted. "At night when I am alone I think those thoughts as you have. Every man who lived through the storm does. In the daylight I know I must stay busy doing things that occupy my mind. I have to concentrate to put bad thoughts aside—think about Jumak, my son. I have been with him today, and I see that Gaga-na takes good care of him. I must not weigh him down. He, too, has suffered a loss."

Okemah rocked back his head and looked at the stars, then at Talasee and Cherok. "It is good to have friends to share such terrible thoughts with."

"We are stronger together," Cherok said, rising to his feet. "Come, walk with me about the village. I wish to see how the rebuilding goes."

Cimmera strained to see the faces of the people as they passed in front of the fire, but she could not make out features. She searched for the old woman, the one who had stared at her when she arrived, but she did not see her. If there was someone here who knew her, wished her harm, would she recognize that person and remember?

While it was quiet and dark, Cimmera moved the pelts stored in her basket, exposing the star knife. Why had Kupah called it that? The name was fitting, she thought. The knife had saved her life, like a gift from the spirits. She recalled how she had learned to use it.

She had been so desperately alone on that hammock for so long.

One evening as she had sat by her fire stuffing berries

into her mouth, she stripped the knife from the stick, destroying the lance. In anger she had hurled the knife away. She heard the twang that it made as the blade stuck into the trunk of a tree. She sat for a moment, staring at what she had done, then retrieved the knife. She knew she had thrown it hard, but was surprised to find how difficult it was to pull the knife out of the tree. She wondered if she could do it again. A few steps back from the tree, in the light of the moon, she tried. How had she thrown it before?

Finally she had replicated the position and grip she'd had on the knife when she threw it into the tree. She lifted the knife and held it by her ear, then thrust it forward, whipping her wrist, releasing the weapon. It missed the tree, but traveled the distance.

The next morning she threw the knife repeatedly. Every day she practiced, throwing the knife again and again. And then one afternoon she picked it up, stared hard at the target and threw. The knife flew straight and stuck in the tree. She cried out with excitement. She had done it!

For days and days—many notches on the stick—she had continued to practice, and at last was consistently sending the knife into her target. After that she hunted with it, brought down the animals, gave thanks to the animals' spirits, skinned the creatures, cooked their flesh, and filled her belly with it.

The memory of her accomplishment made her smile. Cimmera stroked the star knife. She felt it grow warm in her hands and thought she saw a special luster—no, a glow—come from it. She put it back in the sheath, covered it with the pelts, and moved to the interior of the platform. She had to wonder if the first time she had used it had been on a man. The thought brought back the memory of her hair dripping with blood and rivulets of bloodstained rainwater coursing down her chest.

The sound of Cherok climbing the ladder made her jump. Quickly she fumbled with the furs on top of the basket, making sure the knife was hidden; then she pushed it aside.

"I have brought you some broth," he said, setting a bowl in front of her.

The soup smelled good, and her mouth watered as she raised the bowl to her lips.

"Is it so difficult to tell me that you appreciate my effort?" he asked.

Cimmera held the bowl at her lips. "I apologize. I have forgotten my manners. It must be the company I keep," she said, looking at him over the rim of the black clay pot.

"Perhaps it is just your disposition," he said, unrolling his sleeping mat. He tossed a hide over the mat, and on top of that a blanket of warm furs.

"You are going to sleep here?" she asked.

"This is my platform. It is where I sleep."

"But I thought you would stay somewhere else."

Cherok slid between the hide and the furs. "Why would I do that?

"Because I am here," she said, her voice sharp with disbelief.

"Be thankful for my hospitality," he said, turning onto his side and closing his eyes.

"But the people will think—" She stopped short. Maybe the Tegesta customs were completely different from those of the A-po-la-chee. Though she could not recall specific details, she knew the moral code of her people. Unless you were a man's woman, you did not sleep in his platform.

Cherok rolled back to look at her. "Things are not the same as before the storm. We have let go of many of our customs to survive. The people will think I am a generous man to offer you my shelter." He smiled broadly in the dark and settled into the bedding, turning his back to her. "Those good manners you say you have might have made these circumstances different. You could have stayed with a woman or a family…if you had met them. But you did feel so ill."

"You cannot stay here," she said, pushing on one of his shoulders. "You must leave."

Cherok sat up and breathed deeply with annoyance. "You are a very irksome woman. Let me explain this more simply," he said. "This is my platform, and I am allowing you to stay here out of the weather, off the cold ground. Now, that is not so difficult for you to understand, is it?"

Cimmera sat back, and beneath the blanket she folded her arms tightly across her chest. "You have no regard for me."

Cherok threw back his head and laughed. "I rescue you from near death, provide clothing and food, give you a place to sleep, and you say I have no regard for you. What is wrong with you, woman?" he said, leaning forward and touching his fingers to her temple. "I suggest you stop your tongue from saying such ridiculous things and get some sleep." Cherok reclined again and pulled the furs over him.

Cimmera sat speechless. She watched him lying there so peacefully, drifting into sleep. She looked out and saw Talasee, his son beside him, banking the central hearth for the night. She sat in silence as the sounds of the people moving about the village stopped, and the sounds of the wind in the trees, the call of the night creatures, echoed across the mound. Finally she said in a subdued voice, "But I have no place to sleep."

Cherok ignored her.

"I do not have a mat," she said. "Just these furs."

Cherok rolled onto his back and looked at her silhouette in the shadows. "You can share mine," he said.

Cimmera let out an exasperated sigh and curled up in the furs on the floor of the platform and closed her eyes. It was no wonder the A-po-la-chee and the Tegesta were enemies. The Tegesta were ill-mannered and most certainly ill-bred.

She licked her chapped lips and felt them sting. When the morning came, she would bathe herself and find medicine for her lips. She rolled over so she could look at the outline of the man who slept so close to her.

Much time passed with Cimmera too nettled to sleep. But as the night wore on, her indignation gave way to fear. She was afraid of what would happen when she went out to meet the people who lived in this village. Someone out there might know she was A-po-la-chee.

CHAPTER 9

A COMMOTION IN THE VILLAGE woke Cimmera. The sun streamed into the platform in a slash of jasmine light.

She sat up, clutching the blanket to her neck. Cherok was not on his mat. It was neatly rolled up and moved aside. She pulled the furs around her and edged closer to the opening of the shelter to see what the disturbance was.

"Talasee," a man in the distance called. "Come quickly!"

Cimmera bound herself in the robe of furs, descending the ladder, and moved behind the small band of villagers who stood at the canoe landing. A frail woman, her hair hanging in strings, her color as gray as ash, coughed violently. She moved forward in the canoe.

Talasee's son burst through the crowd. The woman reached out for him, but then her hand quickly returned to her chest for another bout of coughing. The boy cried softly when he saw the spot of blood in the corner of her mouth.

Talasee picked up the boy, held him close, then let him down, holding out his hand to his wife as she stepped out of the canoe. Tashi's eyes had dark circles beneath them; the skin of her cheeks was pulled tight across the bones in her gaunt face. She stepped onto the landing, and the spasmodic coughing began again. The child buried his face in his father's side, trying to hide his crying.

Talasee curved his arm about the woman and patted the boy's back. "Come," he said to the child. "Make your mother proud. Lift your head like a man."

The boy let go of his father, pulled his small shoulders back, tipped his chin up, and wiped away the tears that stained his face. The woman stumbled even with Talasee's support. "You are home, Tashi," he said, lifting her in his arms. He bent his head down to touch his mouth to hers.

"No!" Cimmera said loudly and sharply, startling Talasee and the others. She realized the attention her outburst had brought, and she stiffened.

Cherok followed as Cimmera walked close to Talasee so that she could speak softly.

"She must be isolated," Cimmera said. "The illness can jump into you also if you are too close."

"What are you talking about?" Talasee said.

Okemah came and stood beside Cherok. "Stop her, Cacique. She will have all of the people frightened of one another."

Cimmera barely let him finish before she continued. "The sickness—the bad spirit that has gotten inside her— it can get into you also, Talasee. You must put her down."

Talasee took a step, and Cimmera stood squarely in front of him.

The stranger's boldness shocked the onlookers.

"You will get the sickness, too, Talasee, if you stay with her," Cimmera said. "Then you will be of no use to her or to the rest of the people in this village." She glanced at the bewildered faces around them. "And you will carry the bad spirit to the rest of us." She looked at Okemah. "And to you," she said.

Talasee's eyes bored into her, and his nostrils flared.

"Let me pass, Cimmera."

"This child is your son, is he not?" Cimmera said. "Think of him. He, too, will become ill."

"Cherok," Talasee said through a clenched jaw, "quiet this woman and tell her to move aside."

"Cimmera," Cherok said, "move away. You are talking nonsense about a jumping illness—"

"It is not strange talk. Have you never seen this sickness before?"

"Of course," Okemah said. "We know it well in this village."

Cherok grabbed Cimmera's arm through the furs and pulled her out of Talasee's path.

"Many of you will die if you do not listen to me," she said to Cherok, watching Talasee move on. "If nothing else, you must persuade Talasee to send his son away."

"I will not listen to this," Okemah said, walking away. "Take care of your family, Talasee," he said.

Cherok squeezed her upper arm tightly and gave it a slight jerk to make her walk with him. "Woman, you have said enough. I do not understand you. Nothing about you makes any sense." He stopped abruptly and swung her around so she was facing him. "Why would you want to separate this family?" Cherok asked. "And where did you get such irrational ideas?"

Cimmera huffed in frustration, wrenching her arm from his grip. She turned away from him, took a deep breath, and then wheeled back around. "I want to save that family and what is left of this clan. Just because you do not know something does not make it not so. I cannot believe that anyone would be so arrogant as to risk the lives of his people just because—"

"I have never put my people at risk." Cherok took both her shoulders in his hands and glared at her.

Cimmera shook his hands off. She did know about the sickness. Though she could not remember her village, her people, she was convinced that what she was about to say was the truth. "My people understand that this sickness, the illness that makes Talasee's woman cough up blood, can get into others who stay too near her for too long. When someone in our village has this bad spirit inside him, we make him stay alone. Sometimes so many do not get sick."

"And sometimes they do?" Cherok said, arching one brow.

"Sometimes," she admitted. "But still, not so many become ill."

Cherok felt he had refuted her argument. He prodded her up the ladder and into his platform.

Cimmera promptly sat on the floor, twirling the fur wrap around her.

"I have never heard of the Tegesta doing such a cruel thing," Cherok said. "It is suggestive of the A-po-la-chee's cruel ways."

"And you tell me that you have seen this illness in your village. Then you know how horrible it can be. First one person is sick, then another and another. Listen to me, Cherok. Stop this sickness before it spreads to all of us. You are the cacique. The responsibility for this clan rests with you."

Cherok stared out the opening of the platform. The people of his clan were just beginning to rebuild, just beginning to recover emotionally from the devastation they had experienced. He was well aware of how fragile their well-being was. They would not survive an outbreak of this sickness.

"I do not really know you, woman," he said, his voice sounding distant. He looked back at her. "I question how you would have this kind of knowledge, if what you say is the truth. My father was a powerful shaman, and so is my sister. I have never heard this before."

"I speak with honesty," she said, looking up at him and feeling a jolt of sympathy. She was so sure about this, though she did not know how she knew it. She realized she was asking the leader of this clan to listen to a woman and a stranger. She had demanded a lot. He carried so much responsibility. She had convincingly told him lies from the beginning. Now when she spoke the truth he did not believe her.

"I have my doubts," Cherok said.

"There is no reason for me to lie. Surely you see that. At least ask that the boy be permitted to leave his mother's side."

"But Tashi is his mother. Talasee is his father. They will want to stay together."

"If you ignore me, they will die. Please believe what I say. The boy is so young."

Cherok looked back at the village. "I will think about it," he said.

"Go, now. Ask for the boy. That can do no harm."

In the distance he saw Talasee at his hearth, Tashi's head cradled in the fire keeper's lap, and the boy tucked under his father's arm.

"If she dies, I will wish they had never found her," Cherok said before walking away.

The village had grown quiet, he noticed. The initial excitement had dwindled. There was not enough time or energy for prolonged celebrations. So much work still remained to be done and so many were still missing.

Cherok stood a body's length behind Talasee, staring, feeling his friend's anguish, the misery that was at the heart of his people.

Talasee spoke but did not look up as Cherok sat next to him. "We have no shaman."

"I will send for my sister. I said that when our clan regathered I would bring her back to the village so that she could serve her people. She will heal Tashi."

"There is not enough time for you to send for Mi-sa," Talasee said. "Tashi could be dead before she arrives. The spirits will decide over the next few days if my woman is to get well or die. You know how this sickness is."

The boy tugged at Talasee's arm. "Will she die?" he asked, looking woefully at his father.

Talasee pulled him tight against his side but did not answer his question.

Cherok heaved out a heavy breath. "Talasee, if Cimmera is right …"

"Do not discuss her with me," Talasee said.

"But if she is right, if she knows something about this illness that we do not, we would be foolish not to listen to her and heed her advice."

"Tashi is my woman. I will not leave her," he said, stroking back the hair from her forehead.

"Then let me take Jumak back to Gaga-na," Cherok said.

The boy stood up behind his father and clutched Talasee's furs.

"He does not need to be here seeing his mother suffer."

Talasee studied Cherok's face, looked down at his wife, who had fallen asleep, then nodded approval. "But not because of what that woman has said. Jumak should not be burdened with this."

"Jumak," Cherok said, "come with me."

Before he left them, Cherok touched Talasee's back.

He took Jumak's hand and crossed the mound.

From the platform Cimmera saw Cherok and Jumak walking together. A great rush of relief flooded her. Even if she raised suspicions about herself, her conscience told her to tell them what she knew about this disease. There was little else she could do.

Now, she thought, she needed to review the faces she had seen. One more time she scanned the village. The appearance of the rescued people had provided a good opportunity for her to see everyone. The arrival of friends had so engaged them that she had been able to have a good look at each one without anyone taking notice. She recalled no face that kindled her memory. But what was it about the old woman that haunted her? They had stared at each other for so long when Cimmera first entered the village. But there was no memory of her, and the woman had finally turned from her and hobbled away without saying anything. Her stare had probably been no more than interest and curiosity about a stranger. Cimmera had to hope that no one in this village knew who she was.

She watched as Cherok led Jumak to the fire at the center of the village. How very tall he looked next to the boy. How gentle and strong. She closed her eyes a moment and wondered what it might be like if she were not A-po-la-chee.

Cherok stooped by the fire. "Your father is a very important man to this village. Do you know that?"

Jumak nodded.

"He is responsible for keeping the fire for all of us. Has he taught you some of his skills?" Cherok asked.

Jumak smiled and picked up the fire board and bow drill that lay on the ground. He put the end of the fire board under his foot and turned the bow drill so the sinew spiraled around it.

"The drill and the fire board should be of the same wood, or one will be consumed by the other," Cherok said. "Do not use oak because it is too hard. Do not use pine. It is too soft," he told Jumak, watching the boy demonstrate the sawing motion used to start a fire with the tools he held. "You will be a good fire keeper."

Jumak's face lit up, the dark sadness wiped away for a moment. But the gloom quickly resettled in his bright eyes. "I want to be with my mother," he said, putting down the fire-making tools and rubbing his eyes with his knuckles. "I do not want her to die."

"Yes, I know," Cherok said. "You have waited a long time for her return. I know that you have missed her. You are a fine son."

"I am afraid," Jumak blurted out, his nose wrinkling, his eyes squinting as he fought tears.

"It is all right to be afraid," Cherok said. He held the boy to his shoulder.

Jumak pulled up straight and wiped his runny nose. "But I will not cry. I will grow up to be a brave warrior."

"You are very courageous," Cherok said, standing up. "Come."

He led the boy through the village to Gaga-na's hearth. Cherok nodded at the old woman and Narchise, her younger friend who sat with her.

Gaga-na smiled at the boy as he came next to her. "We will have some tasty stew soon."

Narchise had ample breasts and plenteous hips set atop spindly legs. She dropped another hot stone into Gaga-na's pouch that hung over the fire, and then looked up. "Cacique," she said in a respectful greeting, subtly bowing her head.

"Has anyone in the village been ill?" Cherok asked.

Gaga-na shook her head as she spoke. "No. The spirits have spared us."

"She speaks the truth," Narchise said, revealing a pudgy hand, taking it from beneath her blanket to clear the windblown hair from her eyes. "No, no," she said, thrumming her fingers against her chest. "That would be awful if a sickness was visited upon us." Narchise's eyes filled with tears. She nervously pulled at her top lip. "You do not think we are going to become ill, do you? We are not all going to have the sickness, are we?"

"Narchise," Gaga-na said. "You frighten the boy."

"Oh, I did not mean to." She paused long enough to wrestle with the furs around her. "Who was that woman who talked to Talasee—the one who talked about jumping bad spirits?"

"Her name is Cimmera," Cherok said. "She is from another Tegesta village far from ours."

Narchise picked at a scratch on her forearm, then fingered the fur of her blanket as if she expected to find something hiding inside. "She is peculiar. Stood right in front of Talasee, bold and brazen." Her voice vacillated between shrill and squeaky.

"What did you think of what she said?" Cherok asked.

Narchise fidgeted incessantly. "I did not hear all she said, but I know that Okemah says she is no good."

Cherok attempted to still her. "Cimmera said—"

"No," Narchise objected, darting her eyes around her. "I do not want to know. No, do not tell me. It is not a good thing for me to know."

"Narchise," Cherok said, "calm yourself. There is no danger in knowing what the woman said."

Narchise shook her head vehemently. "No, no, no. Look," she said, "Gaga-na's stew is hot. Do you want some? What about the boy?"

The old woman stirred the stew. "Take a bowl," she said to Jumak, dipping a ladle in the stew. "Narchise, look there. Okemah is alone. Perhaps you can help him with his meal. He needs a woman."

Narchise gave her a big smile, exposing a row of white teeth and the crescent worn out of her first lower molar from the many seasons of working leather back and forth to soften it. She padded off in Okemah's direction, combing her hair with her fingers.

"Gaga-na, I know that you are old and your time for caring for children is over," Cherok said. "But Talasee has agreed to send Jumak away while his mother is ill. He is very brave and accepts the wise decisions of his father.".

Gaga-na sipped broth from the shell ladle.

"You are responsible for saving the boy when he was separated from his mother during the storm," Cherok said. "I feel he will be most comfortable with you."

Gaga-na nodded. "Jumak, what do you think of taking care of an old woman?" she asked, looking at the boy.

He gave her a smile.

"Tell me, Cacique, do you believe that the woman, Cimmera, speaks the truth?" Gaga-na asked.

"I do not know, but I am convinced that she believes what she says. I have given it thought and have decided that we could profit from her advice if she has knowledge about this sickness. Council must decide."

"Mmm," the old woman said in a monotone, reserving her judgment. She turned her head to the boy. "Perhaps this Cimmera can help me with Jumak," she said.

Cherok glanced at his platform. He could see Cimmera. At first he thought she was just daydreaming.

Cimmera sat in the opening of the platform. The thatch

kept the wind from her, and the sun felt delicious. Suddenly her vision became blurry, and she touched her temples with her fingers, gently massaging. She heard singing, softly at first. She looked toward the sound, toward the central hearth. The heat from the fire distorted the air, making everything appear wavy and unclear. The singing grew louder, but it sounded like an echo. Dizziness engulfed her, and she held on to the platform post.

She could see the back of the man who knelt before the fire. He was a large man, gray streaking his long hair, his voice creaking with age and wisdom as he chanted and shook a turtle-shell rattle. She heard the healing prayer he sang, a song for the spirits. She knew the words ... the voice ... the man.

"Tamar!" she shouted as she stood up.

The man whipped around. Cimmera heard herself gasp and quickly sat back down. The air no longer shimmered near the fire, and she could see clearly. The face belonged to a young man. No gray hair. No turtle-shell rattle. She had startled him, and he curiously stared at her. Cimmera looked away. Tamar, she repeated in her head. Kupah had mentioned that name.

CHAPTER 10

"I WILL BE BACK FOR JUMAK," Cherok said to Gaga-na, still staring in the direction of his platform opening where he had seen Cimmera.

The old woman did not look up. "Something is wrong?"

"I do not know," he answered, walking away.

Cimmera had not looked right, the way she held her head, the way she stood, then sat so abruptly. He had heard her call out, but had not understood her.

Once Cherok had his back to Gaga-na, she hoisted herself to her feet with a crooked walking stick and took a few hitching steps. She stopped and watched as Cherok trotted to his shelter.

Cimmera moved back into the shadows of the platform before he got there. When he reached the top of the ladder he saw her huddled in the corner.

"Cimmera, what is wrong?"

She shook her head, drew up her knees, folded her arms over the top of them, and hid her face there.

Cherok knelt next to her, running his hand over her hair as it tumbled down her back. "Tell me what has you so upset."

She kept her face concealed in the cross of her forearms. Cherok sat in silence, giving her time, patiently stroking her hair.

Finally she felt her voice was strong enough to speak, but still she could not look up. "You have persuaded Talasee to send Jumak away?"

"Yes. I have taken a risk, believing in you."

"No," she said, lifting her face, revealing tear streaks down her cheeks. "You would have taken the risk if you had not heeded my advice."

"But that is not what has you hiding in the shadows. I saw you in the opening of the platform before. What happened? What is wrong?"

"Nothing," she said, looking down at her arms covering her knees. "You have a strong imagination."

"You cannot look at me and say that. Your eyes would give away the falsehood." Cherok put his hand on her shoulder and gently turned her around. "Speak the truth," he said tenderly but firmly.

"Just memories," she answered. "Nothing you would want to be troubled with."

"Memories of the storm?"

Cimmera hesitated, knowing that with each lie she buried herself deeper. "Yes, the storm," she said, keeping her eyes from his.

Cherok lifted her face in his hand. "There is nothing you can do about what happened in the past. Your life must move forward."

Clearly the image of the man by the fire came to her again. Why could she remember only patches and fragmented visions? And what prompted those remembrances? Again she saw the blood running down her body as she crouched in the rain. That same feeling of horror and fear swept through her. Had she killed someone? Perhaps the man named Tamar?

"You must put the past behind you," Cherok said.

"We rebuild, not only our village, but also our minds. Let it go," he said, wrapping his arm around her shoulders and pulling her head close to his chest.

She could hear his heart thumping in slow, easy, comforting beats. She felt him gently press his lips to the top of her head. He made her feel safe, as if she really could dismiss her past, the past she did not understand, and start fresh again with no worries, no regrets, no fears.

"Cimmera," he whispered through her hair, "send those bad memories away on the wind. Set yourself free."

She had to pull away from him, but everything inside her fought that. What would he do if he found out he was comforting an A-po-la-chee?

"You still tremble," he said, cupping his hand about her head, his other arm binding her close. He could feel the rapid rise and fall of her small chest, the tremor in her hands.

Suddenly his mouth was on the column of her neck, wet and warm, his breath spiraling around her ear and into her hair, small streams of it working through the furs about her shoulders.

Cimmera closed her eyes and bent back her head as his mouth explored the hollow of her throat, the line of her jaw, her temple. "No," she finally protested, opening her eyes and pulling away. "Stop. I do not want you to do this."

Cherok sighed loudly. "Your words contradict your body. I saw the flush in your cheeks, heard your breath catch when my mouth touched you."

He stood up, lazily sliding his hand from the side of her face, down her throat until the furs guarded her bare skin.

Cimmera watched as he moved to the ladder, wishing he would come back—wishing he would leave her alone. Which was it?

"Was she all right?" Gaga-na asked Cherok.

"She says she is."

The old woman ground leaves in a bowl, thinking to the rhythm of her work. "Where did you find this Cimmera woman?"

Jumak practiced rolling a stone ring and then tried to throw a pointed stick inside the ring as it moved over the bumpy earth.

"Very far north," Cherok said. "A-po-la-chee territory actually. We dared to tread that far, but I am glad we did. Cimmera would be dead if we had not."

"I see a light in your eyes when you speak of her," the old woman said, but without even the hint of a smile.

Cherok threw back his head and stared at the sky as he assessed his feelings. "She interests me," he said, then lowered his head. "But I think perhaps her temperament discourages me."

Gaga-na pinched up a small amount of the herb in the bowl, rubbed it between her fingers, testing the texture and consistency. "Was she alone when you found her?"

"She had been alone for a long time—so alone that she wished for the spirits to come and take her."

Jumak hit his target, the stick stuck in the ground through the small ring. He jumped and squealed joyously at his success.

"With every practice your aim improves," Gaga-na said encouragingly.

"What else do you know about this woman?" she asked, returning her attention to Cherok.

"She does not talk much. She says remembering her

past is too painful."

Gaga-na tilted her head, more intrigued. "She tells you nothing about her past? Does that not seem strange?"

"I have asked her questions, tried to probe, but my curiosity upsets her. There is too much sorrow, and for now she wants to forget. Perhaps as time passes …"

"Maybe you should leave her be. Perhaps there is something she does not want you to know." Gaga-na looked toward Cherok's platform to see if she could catch a glimpse of the woman.

"Jumak," Cherok said, "do you like to fish?"

Jumak nodded.

"Good. We will fish together. Then Cimmera will help Gaga-na cook our catch."

He walked the boy to the edge of the hammock.

Jumak leaned out over the water, his sharp stick ready, when a sprinkle of rain fell, rippling the surface. "I cannot see the fish," he complained.

Cherok grinned. "Back into the trees. The rain will pass," he said, appraising the clouds in the sky.

Jumak followed Cherok into the cover of the hammock.

"Why does the cacique let a woman tell us what to do?" Jumak asked, testing the point of his spear with his finger.

"You are unhappy. Any boy would be reluctant to leave his mother. But a boy should not question his elders. Especially the cacique."

Jumak hung his head at the scolding.

"Tomorrow the Council will discuss this. For now you do as your father has instructed."

Drops of rain collected on the threads of a spider web so that it glistened and tempted the young one. Jumak poked his finger into it.

Cherok grabbed the boy's hand and made him slowly withdraw his finger. "No," Cherok told him. "A man does not disturb the flower on its stem or the spider in its web. Those things will come to an end on their own soon enough. It is not meant for man to end them."

Jumak's forehead furrowed, and his eyes filled with shame.

"There is no dishonor in what you did. The responsibility of teaching boys the ways rests with the men. Now you have learned. Be glad the spirits see you as worthy of a lesson this day."

There was no confidence in Jumak's smile. Cherok tousled his hair, and the boy's smile broadened.

"Look," Jumak cried, pointing to the rainbow.

"Ah," Cherok said. "The Great Spirit paints a circle around the earth."

"It is a good omen?" Jumak asked.

"Yes, he finds favor with us, so he shares beauty with the People."

"Then the Great Spirit sees my mother!" Jumak said excitedly.

"He sees us all."

The child ran out from under the trees. "The cloud did not have many tears to cry," he said, scampering to the water, ready to fish again.

Jumak's comment brought to Cherok's mind the disturbing concern over the recent lack of rainfall. This brief shower was not enough to make even a slight difference. He had seen droughts before and prayed this was not the beginning of another.

Cherok watched as the boy waded into the ankle-deep water searching for a fish. How wonderfully simple life was for children, he thought.

"We will catch so many that we will have to share with

the rest of the village," Cherok said, joining the boy.

Okemah watched Narchise approaching. Some men thought her figure too heavy, but he didn't. She was fleshy and full. Her kind of body felt soft beneath a man. A man could get lost there between her breasts, falling deep into the cushion of her, swallowed by the luxuriant depth of her body. He felt his thoughts arousing him, making his blood heat and flow into those parts of him that yearned for a woman.

"Okemah," Narchise said, coming next to him. She shuffled the furs around her shoulders, letting the front plummet low about the upper swell of her breasts. "A man should not have to do without the care of a woman."

Okemah wanted to speak, but his mouth became dry, and he could not stop the whirling of his thoughts. She was speaking words, and he was imagining low moans, feeling himself slide into the passion-swollen warmth of her, sensing her passage clench his manhood.

She sat across from him and stirred the ashes and embers of his fire with a stick, bringing small flames to it. "You are a good hunter, but do you know how to cook your kill?" she asked.

Okemah did not answer. His throat was too tight, his concentration too splintered.

"You have been without a woman since the storm," she said. "A good meal will feel gratifying in your belly. Why do you not go about your man's business and let me prepare your food?"

Every time she stirred the fire, the slow, heavy joggle of her breasts pushed at the furs, and he had a hard time taking his eyes off them. "True, I have not had a woman take care of my needs in a long time."

Narchise smiled up at him. "That is not good for a man. You know my husband crossed to the Other Side some time before the storm. It is a sad thing for someone to be alone. I have been without my man, and you without your woman."

Okemah was becoming acutely aware of how long he had been without his woman, and for the first time since the storm he put his mourning aside. "I do not think I will tend to anything now other than watching you cook," he said, captivated by the way she talked and moved, her body seeming so ripe and ready to burst with sweet juices, her bare flesh hiding just beneath those furs.

Narchise tugged at her earlobe and giggled softly, looking up at him without lifting her head. She allowed her robe to slip over her shoulder and then slowly pulled it back in place. The robe gapped, revealing one of her weighty breasts.

Okemah gasped at the taut dark nipple that reminded him of a spring bud, his lips spontaneously pursing. Then she shifted to close the gap, cupping her hand at the underswell of her bosom and letting a very soft, almost undetectable purr vibrate in her chest.

Okemah cleared his throat and pulled a basket into his lap to hide the sizable bulge that distended his breechclout, but not before Narchise had noticed. She stared where the basket sat askew and blindly tossed a few herbs into the pot by the fire.

"It is best when very hot," she said, suspending the sooty black bowl over the flames.

"Perhaps you will share it with me," Okemah said, speaking on the outflow of his breath, which he suddenly realized he had been holding.

Jumak split the fish down the middle and cut off the

heads. Gaga-na guided him, directing him in the use of the knife.

"I will get Cimmera," Cherok said! "She will help you with the cooking."

"Lay them on the grate, boy," Gaga-na said, pointing to the wooden framework over her fire.

The child spread the fish out evenly. "I could have caught more," he said. "But it would be a waste to take more than we could eat."

"You are learning the ways of the hunter," she said, watching Cherok walk away.

"Can I take some to my father and mother?" Jumak asked.

"No, boy. You must stay away until your mother is well. Cherok will arrange for food."

"Do you believe what Cimmera said?" he asked the old woman.

"Come close and sit by me," she said. After the boy sat, she draped a thin arm around him. "What do you think?"

Jumak swirled a stick in the dirt, then prodded a fish so that it would not fall through the grate. "Cherok says that tomorrow he will take the matter to Council, and the men will decide. But I do not believe what she said." He looked up at Gaga-na, wrinkling his nose at the sting of tears that wanted to come. "I want to be with my mother. I want to tell her that I love her."

"But what if Cimmera is right? You must protect yourself. It is you and the other young ones who will bring into the world another generation of our people. We have fallen off in number. The storm claimed many. We cannot risk sickness befalling our youth. Do you understand? The cacique is wise to deliberate and take precautions."

The boy nodded.

"The cacique is coming," she said, first spying Cherok, then returning to the task of keeping her fire alive.

Cimmera walked a step behind Cherok. "I am not hungry," she said when she saw the old woman.

"Then cook only," Cherok said.

"I am not going," Cimmera insisted, spinning in the other direction.

Cherok grabbed her by the arm, reaching harshly through the furs. "The old woman has agreed to take care of Jumak. You are responsible for her added work. At least you can help."

Cimmera turned back. The old woman was not looking, but she felt Gaga-na's eyes on her anyway. "I cannot," she said, feeling her heart flutter in her chest.

"You are most confounding," he said, yanking on her arm. "You come into this village, do not want to meet the people, hide in the shadows, cause a disturbance by telling a man not to stay with his woman, insisting a child be taken from his mother and father. And now you say you cannot help an old woman."

Cimmera opened her mouth to speak, but Cherok promptly clapped his hand over it. "I have been kind to you, patient and understanding. My people have accepted a stranger in their midst. You will come with me and you will help Gaga-na. You are obligated." He waited a moment before taking his hand away. "I will argue with you no more."

Cimmera knew she could not explain her reluctance to meet the old woman. Her reaction was just a feeling, not even a feeling she could identify. She looked sharply at Cherok. "Why did you not leave me where you found me?" Cimmera said, her voice low and troubled. "You could have let the spirits take me. That is what I wanted."

Cherok's eyes were fiery. "Perhaps I should have. But since I did not, you get this put in your head. You will behave respectfully to my people."

He tugged at her until she stumbled forward; then he planted his hand on her back and urged her on until they stood before Gaga-na's hearth.

"Gaga-na, this is Cimmera," Cherok said. "She will help you with your chores."

The old woman looked up, straight into Cimmera's eyes. At first Cimmera thought she heard the tinkling of shell bells, and the blankets did not keep back the chill of the air.

"Sit by me," Gaga-na said. "Keep warm by my fire."

But Cimmera did not hear her.

CHAPTER 11

THERE WAS SOMETHING about this woman, a familiarity, and Cimmera's senses deadened with fear. She knew the people around her were speaking, but their words were slurred and garbled to her ears. The only thing she distinctly heard was the pulsing of her blood.

"Cimmera!" Cherok said, annoyed at what he thought was rudeness.

Gaga-na reprimanded Cherok with her expression. "Here," she said to Cimmera, patting the ground next to her. "Get yourself warm. You are shivering."

Cimmera focused on the woman's mouth, watching her lips move. She made herself concentrate until her head stopped spinning. She followed Gaga-na's directions, the old woman's gestures helping her to coordinate her thoughts and movements.

"You will feel better now," Gaga-na said. "I despise this cold weather." With two sticks she tweezed a fish from the grate. Some white meat flaked away as she moved it. "Taste it," she told Cimmera, holding the fish in front of her.

Cimmera tore off a small portion of meat, felt for bones, then put it in her mouth, obeying the woman as if she were a child.

"Is it cooked enough?" Gaga-na asked.

Cimmera nodded, feeling her apprehension subside.

"Good. Take the fish off the grate, Jumak. Put it aside."

Cimmera was at last warm.

"I see all kinds of things in a fire," Gaga-na said, noticing how Cimmera stared into the flames. "Do you?"

"Yes," the young woman answered, her voice low and sounding far away.

Cimmera was seeing things that came forward from dark recesses within her mind, envisioning a brief reflection from her past. In the vision she was just a child, very young, perhaps four winters. She stood alone, surrounded by screaming people, sizzling and burning thatch, and men's war cries. Suddenly someone whisked her up and carried her on her hip as she ran.

She looked back to see her mother standing in the center of the village. She could not understand why the beautiful young woman was not running, escaping the attack. She reached over the shoulder of her grandmother, the woman who carried her, her small fingers grabbing at the air. Her eyes widened as she saw a brightly painted warrior come up behind her mother. Suddenly she was turned away as Grandmother spun to see what was happening behind her. But the child twisted around so that she could look back also.

The grandmother shrieked, the cry so near the child's ear that it made her blanch.

Her mother seemed oblivious to all that was happening, not seeing the threat of the approaching warrior, and not understanding or hearing the desperate pleas for her to flee.

The warrior raised his strombus shell club, and it gleamed in the daylight. It came down swiftly.

The child cried loudly and pressed her little hands over her ears to block out the horrible noise.

The warrior whirled his club in the air, his voice sounding a triumphant whoop. Cimmera, he child, screamed and pressed her face into the shoulder of the woman who carried her. Then suddenly they were going down, falling hard onto the black dirt.

She clung to her grandmother, but the woman's hands pushed her, shoved her away, wanting her to keep running.

She turned again and saw her mother sprawled on the ground. Her eyes darted back to the older woman, who was grimacing, holding on to her leg. An arrow shaft stuck out between her bloody fingers.

Grandmother's hands gripped the arrow and yanked. She heard Grandmother cry out and saw the blood spurt.

The child shook her arms, her body tense and rigid with fright. She was wailing and tramping her feet up and down, stirring up the dust.

There were more warriors—everywhere. Grandmother furiously waved her away.

She took a last look and then ran into the brush.

The flames of Gaga-na's fire tamed to small flickers. Cimmera's eyes fluttered, and the vivid flash of memory disappeared. But she kept seeing the arrow. What was it about the arrow that would not let her go? What had she remembered?

"They are in a basket beneath my platform," Gaga-na was saying.

"What?" Cimmera asked, trying to focus on the present, but still desperately holding on to the image of her grandmother's leg and the arrow. The arrow.

"The ant's-wood plums. Get them. There," she said, pointing to the dark space under her shelter.

"Oh," Cimmera said. "The plums." She moved slowly

at first, still reorienting herself. She pulled out a few of the baskets. At last she found the dark purple oblong fruit. Gaga-na had not done a good job of harvesting the fruit from its thorny branches, and Cimmera pricked her finger.

"Ya-ta!" she whispered, feeling the sting of the puncture. For an instant Cimmera went numb, realizing she had just spoken in A-po-la-chee. She felt her stomach turn in fear, and a tingling, burning fire shot down her arms all the way to her fingertips. How stupid of her! She spun around to see if she had been heard.

"And bring a few of the satinleaf fruits. Jumak will like to chew the skins," Gaga-na said, smiling at the boy. "Would you like that?" she asked the boy.

Jumak's eyes grew wide in delight as he nodded.

Cimmera quickly studied their faces. Apparently no one had heard her. She replaced the baskets she didn't need, swallowed and breathed deeply, trying to rid herself of the panic.

"Here," she said, holding up the satinleaf fruits to Jumak in one hand and the basket of plums in the other. Her voice was too high. It did not sound normal, she thought, hearing herself.

A bright red drop of blood rolled down her finger, over the top of her hand, and dripped off her wrist.

Gaga-na frowned. "I am getting too old to harvest those fruits. Always seem to leave some thorns," she said. "Come close; let me tend to that." She motioned for Cimmera. "Take the fruit," she told Jumak.

Cimmera wiped away the streak of blood. "I am all right. Just a small prick."

"Come here. Let me see your finger."

"Really, it is nothing," Cimmera said as she squatted next to the woman.

Gaga-na took Cimmera's finger and examined it. Then she put it in her mouth, sucked blood from the wound and spat it out. "Bad things happen to small punctures like that. Go and get some red maple bark."

"I do not need any medicine," Cimmera said, taking her hand from Gaga-na's.

"Go, as I told you. Bring it back, and I will prepare a decoction."

Cherok nodded at Cimmera, his expression also strongly suggesting that she do as the woman asked.

Cimmera turned and left, headed farther into the interior of the hammock where the maples grew. Nearly there, she realized she had nothing with which to strip the bark. She took a few steps back toward Gaga-na's hearth, but then decided differently. Cherok's platform was much closer. Quickly she slipped inside and looked through her basket, removing the star knife. She wrapped it in a pelt and continued on to the stand of maples.

There were few leaves on the maple tree because of winter. That helped her identify the tree. Many other trees growing on the hammock were evergreens.

Cimmera removed the sheath from the pelt, then withdrew the knife and sliced off a strip of bark. Suddenly her hand began to tremble, and the knife felt warm. A tingling started at the tips of her fingers and rose all the way up to her scalp. The knife, the bark, everything around her, grew blurry, and then she was on the wind, soaring like a bird. Below her was a village—not this village but another, from the time she could not remember.

"You can take the bark from this tree many times if you are careful," came a familiar voice.

She saw herself, this time older than she had appeared in the last vision. She stood listening to a woman who was carving bark from a maple tree.

"Never take the bark in a ring around the girth of the trunk or the tree will die. Take strips like these and then leave the tree to heal so that it will provide for you again."

The woman fell silent. A shadow came over them, and she looked up.

Tamar!

He took her small hand, covered it with his, and laid it against the wound on the tree.

"Close your eyes," he said.

She smiled at the big man and did as he said. She felt the heat radiate from his hand through hers, felt the vibrations beneath her hand.

She heard him sing, his deep voice chanting just a few words to the spirits. He repeated the chant, and she sang with him, feeling his power and then realizing hers.

"See what we do together," he said, opening his eyes and taking his hand off hers.

She pulled her hand away from the tree. New bark covered the space where the woman had stripped it. Her mouth opened in awe and she looked up at the man.

"It is remarkable," Tamar said. "Your power and mine. You were meant to be my daughter."

Cimmera heard the wind rushing by her, the flutter of a bird's wings, and the vision ended. The knife grew cold, and she lifted the bark to her nose, wanting the scent to keep the vision flowing. But it was over.

"Are you telling the truth?"

Cimmera spun around. "Jumak! What are you doing here?"

Quickly she wrapped the knife in the pelt, cramming the sheath inside the rabbit fur as well.

"What is that?" the boy asked.

Cimmera stammered. "Why—How long have you been standing there?"

"I just came. I came to ask you if you tell the truth."

"About what?" she asked.

"About my mother. About the bad spirits that can jump into a person."

Cimmera crouched so that she could look the boy in the face. "Yes, Jumak. I speak the truth. I am sorry that your mother is ill, and sorry that you cannot be with her. But I do not want the sickness to spread. Do you?"

The boy shook his head. "Will my father get sick also?"

"He could, Jumak. But he wishes to stay with your mother and take care of her. They are husband and wife. Their lives are as one."

"But I am their child. I think I should stay, too." His young voice cracked.

Cimmera laid down the knife, reached out for the child, then held him. He stood stiffly in her arms. "Oh, Jumak, I know how you miss them. You must feel terribly alone, even though you have Gaga-na."

Jumak sniffed, and then he put his arms around Cimmera.

"I feel that way sometimes, too," Cimmera said. "I am alone, even with all the people around me. I am not home."

Jumak pulled his head back and looked at her. "You are missing your people?" he asked, wiping his nose with the back of his hand.

"I miss them very much," she said.

The boy placed his head back against her furs.

"I cannot be your mother, but when you are feeling sad and alone, you can come to me and know that I will understand."

Jumak drew in a deep and cry-rattled breath. "You will not tell me that a man does not cry?"

"No, I will not tell you that ... ever."

They held each other a little longer, and then Jumak said, "We should get back. Gaga-na worries too much."

Cimmera grinned. "Yes, she does."

They returned to the village, her hand on the boy's shoulder.

"Wait here," she said at the base of the ladder to Cherok's platform. "Hold the bark for me."

Cimmera put the knife back in the basket and covered it. She thought about what she had said to the boy. She missed her people more than he could imagine. She did not even have any memories of them to cling to, only those tiny flashes that came and went so quickly. Yes, she knew what it was to be without loved ones, to feel so lost.

When Cimmera climbed down the ladder, she found Narchise keeping Jumak company.

"Hello," Cimmera said, looking at the woman who rocked back and forth.

"Good-bye, Jumak," Narchise said, ignoring Cimmera's greeting.

"Wait," he said. "Meet my friend." Jumak reached out and took Cimmera's hand.

Narchise shook her head in small, rapid shakes, backing away.

"I am Cimmera."

"Narchise," the nervous woman responded, still taking little steps backward, now nodding.

"I am glad to meet you, Narchise. If you are a friend of Jumak's, then you are a friend of mine."

Narchise's head still bobbed as she turned and walked two steps, then broke into a fast waddle.

Cimmera arched both brows and looked at Jumak,

who shrugged.

"She is always that way," the boy said.

"Always?"

"Well, I heard my father say she is like that except when she flirts with Okemah."

Cimmera laughed softly. "Narchise flirts?" She found it hard to believe that this nervous, skittish woman could actually be coy with a man.

"My father says she needs a strong man's affections to calm her down, that after one night in the furs with Okemah she would be back to singing tranquil songs."

Cimmera laughed again. "I think you have been listening to conversations you should not be listening to," she scolded.

Jumak's grin was a confession. Cimmera looked at him chidingly out the corner of her eye.

"She is nice, though," Jumak added.

"Maybe we can try another introduction sometime," Cimmera said.

Gaga-na had the pot of water hot and ready to receive the maple bark.

"Put it in there," she said, tapping the hot bowl with her stirring stick.

Cimmera dropped the bark into the water. "You really do not need to go to so much trouble." She looked at her finger. "I can barely see where the thorn stuck me."

Gaga-na pulled her walking stick close and stood it upright. She used the staff for support and balance as she struggled to stand up.

Cherok attempted to help, but she shooed him away. "I can do this myself," she argued. "I have managed for a long time."

Cherok shook his head at her determination to remain

independent though he knew her age was beginning to slow her down.

Gaga-na weaved as she stood, then took a staggering step, catching herself with the stick.

"It is time you let others help you," Cherok said.

"I will let you know when I need help," she answered. "I am not so old that I cannot care for myself."

"I did not mean that," he said. "But your leg does not make growing old any easier."

"I do not expect it will get any better or any worse. It's only an inconvenience."

"All right, Gaga-na," Cherok said, yielding to her.

"Now," she said to Cimmera, "let me see that finger." She glanced at Cherok. "Now that some people have stopped interfering."

Cimmera looked at Cherok and caught his smile. There was such sincerity in his dark eyes. Though he was strong and demanding, certainly insistent and confident, a vulnerability and tenderness shone through his eyes. She could not help but smile back at him.

Jumak turned his head from side to side, watching the unspoken messages pass between them. Finally he fixed on Cherok. "Is Cimmera your woman?"

Cherok did not answer, but stared long at Cimmera. Her smile had disappeared with her surprise at hearing Jumak's question.

"Well, I like her," Jumak said. "I think you should want to get her in the furs."

"Jumak!" Gaga-na said, stunned by the boy's comment. "What makes you talk that way?"

Jumak shrugged his shoulders. "It is the way men talk."

Cherok bent down and motioned for the boy to come close so he could speak to him privately.

"I have said something wrong?" Jumak said. "It has been a day of wrong things."

"Since the storm you have spent a lot of time with me and the other men. You have heard men's conversations. But they are men's conversations. Men do not talk like boys, and boys should not talk like men."

Jumak looked up. "But how am I to know what is good to say and what is bad?"

"Men and women together, those are the kinds of things that men sometimes speak about—not boys."

"Oh," Jumak said. Then he whispered, "Are Gaga-na and Cimmera angry with me?"

"I do not think they are angry," Cherok said, his voice low, "but perhaps you could apologize so they know you now understand the difference."

Jumak nodded and turned to face the women. "I am sorry," he said, his voice scratchy with embarrassment.

Cimmera gave him a polite and sympathetic smile.

"That is a good boy," Gaga-na said. She dipped a swatch of hide in the maple-bark medicine, then wrapped Cimmera's finger with it. "Cut this for me," the old woman said, picking up an end of a rawhide strip that had come loose from the handle binding of her walking stick. "I will tie the medicine cloth with it."

Cimmera felt a shock crash through her. "I do not have a knife," she said.

Cherok stepped toward them. "Then how did you cut the maple bark?"

CHAPTER 12

CIMMERA WAS AWARE of the long pause before she replied, and she was certain that Cherok and Gaga-na noticed. "I cut it with my woman's knife. I stopped and took it from my basket."

Cherok looked at her. Her hands were empty, and she wore no belt, nor did a sheath dangle at her hip. "Where is it now?"

"Jumak and I stopped at your platform when returning, and I put it back."

Cherok glanced at the boy, who gave no indication that she was speaking an untruth. "Did you not think you might need it to help Gaga-na?"

"No," Cimmera answered. "Gaga-na has a knife. I thought I could use hers."

The older woman placed fish and fruit inside a basket. Her gaze lit first on Cimmera and then held steady on Cherok. "Deliver this to Talasee and Tashi," she told him, strangely glancing back at Cimmera as if they shared a secret.

"How will you do that?" Jumak asked.

"I will leave it near your father and call to him. When I leave, he will retrieve it."

"That is the best way," Cimmera said, relieved that the conversation had turned.

"May I go with you?" Jumak asked.

The cacique did not answer right away. "You must

stay back and you cannot linger. Seeing your mother and father from a distance may be difficult for you."

"I will stay near you," Jumak said.

"Come, then," Cherok said. "Take the basket from Gaga-na."

When Cherok and Jumak walked away, Gaga-na passed a piece of fish to Cimmera. "What did you see in the fire?"

"What do you mean?" Cimmera asked.

"I was a shaman's woman. I know the look when someone has a vision."

Cimmera tensed and picked at the fish deliberately, trying to seem unruffled. "I do not know what you are talking about."

"Yes, you do," Gaga-na said. "You will tell me in good time, just as you will tell me how you cut the bark. As I said, I was a shaman's woman. Fire is a good place to see visions."

"I was just remembering things. That is all."

Gaga-na looked back at the hearth. "There are great mysteries about you," she said, poking at the embers.

"You talk in circles."

"Tell me about yourself. Where do you come from?"

Cimmera struggled to speak without choking. "I think your life sounds more interesting. The woman of a shaman! I would rather hear about you."

Gaga-na smacked her lips. "This plum is tart," she said.

"Was the shaman taken by the storm?" Cimmera asked.

"No," Gaga-na answered, rummaging through the basket for another plum. She picked one out and took a bite, speaking with her mouth full. "It was long ago. He is dead."

"Oh, I am sorry," Cimmera said.

"It is all right. Many, many seasons have passed since then."

"The loss of a loved one is painful no matter how much time passes."

"That is true," Gaga-na said, wiping plum juice from her lips. "The summer after he crossed over, a man from this village took me as his wife. I have lived here ever since. He was good to me, and I was thankful to have a man again. But I never loved another as I loved the shaman."

"You smile when you speak of him," Cimmera said, noticing the faint curl of the old woman's lips.

"I smile inside. I suppose it bleeds through to the outside." Gaga-na paused and spat out the plum pit. "Now tell me about yourself."

"My past was uneventful. There is nothing to tell."

"Give me your hands," Gaga-na said.

Cimmera held them out, and the old woman took them in her hands, turning them so that the palms were up. "Healing hands," she said.

The younger woman drew back and folded her hands in her lap. "They were not good enough to heal a man we found on our way here," she said.

"Sometimes the spirits call a person to the Other Side. When that happens, there is nothing even a spirit man or woman can do."

"Oh, Gaga-na, you are making me into something I am not. I am only a plain woman."

"You hide things about yourself."

"No, I do not. You know what there is to know. Nothing."

"Not so," Gaga-na said. "You do not allow yourself to be honest. If you did, you would not pretend that you do not enjoy our cacique's attentiveness."

"Gaga-na," Cimmera said, "now you talk like Jumak."

"Even the boy notices," the old woman said. "And see, you have not told me anything about yourself."

"What do you want to know?" Cimmera asked, hoping she could make up a story quickly enough to satisfy Gaga-na.

"I will make this easy. Begin with what I do know about you. How do you feel about Cherok?"

Cimmera felt relief at not having to invent a past, but still she did not know how to answer.

"Keep your thoughts and words simple. Speak from the heart, not the head."

"He is a good man, but he can be arrogant."

"No, no," Gaga-na said, stopping her. "Those are words from the head. Tell me what your heart says."

Cimmera stood up. "I told you what I think of your cacique. Now I believe |I should help you with the chores."

"Give me your hand and help me up," Gaga-na said.

Cimmera extended her hand, and the old woman grabbed it. She held on tight, squeezing as she stood. "You need a friend," Gaga-na said. "You have one in me, but you do not realize it." The old woman took the basket of plums and shoved it under her platform. "If you have a healing gift you should share it with us. Our clan is without a shaman." Thunder rumbled in the distance, and Gaga-na looked at the sky. "False hope," she said. "Pray that it rains soon."

"Do you think a drought has begun?"

Gaga-na stopped what she was doing. "I believe you are better suited to answer that question. Why ask an old woman?" She moved to the ladder of the platform. "Call up to me when Cherok and Jumak return. We will see that their bellies are full."

Cimmera still reeled at the woman's statement. Why did Gaga-na think she would know about the drought? It seemed the old woman was more certain of who she was than she was about herself.

"Arghh," Gaga-na mumbled, rubbing her thigh. "Perhaps Cherok is right. I am getting too old. It gets harder every day to climb this."

"Let me help," Cimmera said, boosting Gaga-na up the ladder.

"Is it difficult for you to sleep?" Cherok asked, seeing Cimmera sitting in the opening of the platform, the moonlight barely enough to give her form.

"Sometimes," she answered, surprised that he was awake. She had lain on the mat that Gaga-na had given her, but her eyes had remained wide open in the darkness. She had thought the woman would offer her space in her platform, but she hadn't. To Cimmera's bewilderment, she had felt relieved. She found a certain amount of comfort in sleeping so near Cherok.

She stared at the long silhouette of the cacique stretched out on his mat, comfortably resting beneath the furs. "Do you suppose everyone believes that we sleep together?"

She caught a glimpse of his white teeth as he grinned.

"There is nothing to suppose. We do sleep together."

Cimmera grunted her frustration with him. "You know what I mean."

"You wonder if everyone thinks that I join with you?"

"Yes," Cimmera answered.

"Probably," he said, turning over so that his back was to her.

"Cherok?" Cimmera scooted out of the entranceway

and nearer to him. She tugged at his shoulder. "Why?"

Cherok feigned sleepiness, tucking himself more snugly in the furs and yawning. "We will discuss it in the morning. Let me sleep."

Cimmera pulled at him more heartily. "But we are not doing that. I am not your woman."

Cherok finally turned so he could see her face as she leaned so close. "You sleep here. That is enough."

"How do you know they think such things?" she asked with an edge to her voice.

"The men give me that look. They clap my back at having such a beautiful woman sleeping in my platform."

"And you do not say anything? You just let them think—"

Cherok suddenly reached up behind her neck and pulled her head down to his. He planted his mouth soundly on hers, his hand tight at the nape of her neck. Then he let her go.

"Now there is some substance to what they say." He turned over, away from her.

Cimmera took a moment, sitting there, frozen in the awkward position in which he had left her. Finally she was able to sit back and lift her head.

Had he already stopped thinking about what he had just done?

Her face was hot, and she reached up to touch it with the backs of her fingers. She lay down on her mat, pushing the furs away, letting the chill of the air cool her. Now she was sure she would never sleep.

"Come down!" Jumak's young voice woke Cimmera. "I have brought her back."

Cimmera moved to the opening and looked out. There stood Jumak with his hand around Narchise's wrist.

"She says she would like to meet you again."

Cimmera rubbed the blurriness from her eyes, judging the lateness of the morning by the position and brightness of the sun. "Good morning. Will you wait a moment? I will come down," she said, looking at the woman who seemed to bounce, though she was standing still.

Narchise did not have an opportunity to speak.

"We will wait," Jumak answered.

In a moment Cimmera emerged from the shelter. "I am very happy that Jumak has brought you back."

Narchise took a quick step forward, Jumak still gripping her wrist. Briefly she looked at Cimmera's eyes, and then looked away. "Where is your village?" she asked, sounding hurried.

"To the north."

"Jumak says far north."

It puzzled Cimmera why the woman would ask her a question to which she already knew the answer.

"Yes," Cimmera said.

"Humph," Narchise grumbled. "You are close to the A-po-la-chee."

Jumak let go of Narchise's wrist and sat in the dirt, looking up at the two women.

"Have you seen them?" Narchise asked, her eyebrows wiggling up and down.

"I have," she answered.

"Yes, well, I suppose all the Tegesta know the A-po-la-chee," Narchise said. "They captured our cacique and Talasee right after the storm. The A-po-la-chee held them captive in one of their villages. I hear the men talk about the terrible torture they suffered. Cherok escaped, and Talasee was lucky to be rescued."

Cimmera looked toward the central hearth. Cherok

stood near it, talking with two men, his lean body golden brown in the morning sun.

"He must have great hostility toward the A-po-la-chee. Even more than most."

"We all hate them." Narchise's face squirmed as she spoke. "What they have done to the Tegesta! Their blood should cover the ground, fill the rivers, soak the soil!" Her voice rose at the end, and she formed a shaky fist.

"I am happy you have your cacique and the fire keeper back."

Narchise's eyes widened, and she leaned her head forward at an awkward angle to her shoulders. "Cherok's sister—our shaman, Mi-sa—she got the Kahoosa to take a war party to the A-po-la-chee village to save her brother and Talasee. Cherok had already escaped, but they did save Talasee. Now she is the woman of the Kahoosa cacique. But Cherok says she will serve the Tegesta when we need her. Soon, I suspect."

"There are not many of you—us," Cimmera said.

"When there are many, Mi-sa will come back and take care of us."

"But she is the Kahoosa leader's woman."

"She is also our shaman. Those responsibilities come first."

"I suppose they do," Cimmera said.

Jumak perked up and poked Cimmera's leg with his finger to get her attention.

"Gaga-na says she thinks you have special powers. I heard her talking."

"Oh, oh, oh," Narchise said nervously, rocking back and forth, her thick fingers playing at her lips.

"Who was Gaga-na talking to?" Cimmera asked.

"Herself. She does that when she is thinking hard."

"Well, Gaga-na is mistaken. There is nothing special

about me."

Narchise puckered her lips, and then tightened them into a thin line that twisted down to one side. "Gaga-na was a shaman's woman. She knows things."

Cimmera's head ached, and she rubbed her forehead.

"That is true," Jumak said, standing up. "Can you do magic?"

The pain in Cimmera's head grew stronger. "I am sorry," she said. "I do not feel well."

Narchise peered at Cimmera. "I hope you are not getting the illness—like Tashi."

Jumak's face paled.

Narchise took a step back and pulled the boy with her. "Maybe you should eat your morning meal," Narchise said, her feet barely moving, but taking her away.

"Yes, maybe that is it," Cimmera said, turning back to the platform, weakly grasping the ladder.

"Cimmera, do you want me to get you something from Gaga-na's hearth?" Jumak asked.

"No, I will be all right. I will join Gaga-na in a moment."

"That is good. Yes, a good idea," Narchise said, ready to leave. "We will talk again. Another time."

Cimmera nodded her head and climbed up the ladder.

"Do you want me to stay with you?" Jumak asked. "I will."

Cimmera looked back and smiled. "I know you would. You are a good friend. But I think I want to be alone for just a little while. Then I will join you and Gaga-na. Wait for me there."

Jumak skipped a few steps, turned to see her again and waved, then ran off. Narchise was already gone.

Cimmera sat in the platform, avoiding the bright rays of

the sun that sprayed through the opening. The sick feeling faded, replaced by frustration and anger. Who was she? Did Gaga-na see something in her? Was she a connection to the Darkside, a bad spirit, evil enough to kill someone? She had to know.

Cimmera held her hands in front of her face. Living in this village brought nearly as much isolation as living alone. Everyone was a stranger—even herself.

Suddenly Cimmera felt that someone was watching her. Slowly she took her hands away from her face and raised her eyes.

There in the shadows was a wavering image.

Tamar!

The image shimmered like summer heat rising off the water. Tamar was not real; he was an apparition.

The wind whistled through the thatch, and Cimmera had the sensation of being disconnected from the rest of the world. She felt her skin prickle, and a rush of cold fire ripped through her. The confines of the shelter vanished as if they didn't exist. White mist appeared, a thick blanket of fog swirling around her and the vision of Tamar.

What she saw entranced her. He was so large, his black and silver hair thick and long, his jaw heavy, his nose straight, his eyes deep. But then she blinked, and the big man disappeared; the thatch covering of the shelter reshaped itself. The wind settled.

Cimmera shuddered. Today the air was warmer than it had been for a long while, but she felt chilled. She was tired of the confusion that caused such fear to swell in her. She had to know if there was truth in Gaga-na's suspicions.

Cimmera moved aside the furs in her basket and took out the knife, wrapped it in a skin, and descended the ladder. Tamar must have given her the idea.

There was something she had to do before she did anything else.

CHAPTER 13

CIMMERA SLIPPED BEHIND the platforms so she wouldn't be noticed. She carried the fur-wrapped knife tucked inside her robe.

Quietly she moved through the brush until she reached the maple trees. Beneath the one from which she had stripped the bark, she sat on the cool earth and pulled out the knot of fur that hid the sheathed star knife.

Cimmera took a deep breath and sighed as she pulled the knife free. The polished bone handle caught a sliver of sunlight that highlighted the rich hues. It was so beautiful, she thought. She held it in both hands, stretched her arms out in front of her, and closed her eyes.

She didn't know where the song came from, only that it rested deep inside her and that it slid easily off her tongue. She sang louder, the song coming fully and naturally. Then it happened—what she had known would happen. The knife began to grow warm in her hands, and she felt that peculiar tingle she had experienced before.

She opened her eyes. An aura surrounded the star knife, a golden halo of light.

Cimmera stood up, held the knife in one hand, and placed her other hand over the oozing scar on the maple tree. She closed her eyes again, taking four deep breaths.

She waited, desperately hoping nothing would happen. Just as she was feeling relieved, certain that nothing extraordinary was going to take place, heat began to pool in her hand, then radiate outward. The trunk of the tree vibrated beneath her fingers. She wanted to pull her hand away, to stop it, but she didn't. She had to know.

Cimmera gathered her courage and kept her hand pressed against the tree, just as she had in the vision. She could almost feel the weight of Tamar's large hand on hers. Suddenly she knew the words to another song, a melody she felt she had known for a long time. The power in her hand became stronger, the heat more fiery, and the vibrations more vigorous.

At last the warmth ebbed and the vibrations stopped. The knife no longer felt warm, and the tingling vanished. One finger at a time, Cimmera rolled her hand away from the maple until she saw what was beneath.

She dropped to her knees, the air sucked from her, and her mouth fell open. The wound on the tree was gone, sealed up as it would have done in time. She sat shaking, her hands trembling, her heart racing. Now for the first time she wished she could return to knowing nothing about herself.

Cimmera held her forehead in her hand, covering her eyes as if not seeing would make everything go away. But she could still feel the knife in her lap. She could do nothing to change who she was—what she was.

She put the knife into the sheath and skin and tucked it inside her fur wrap. Gaga-na was right: There was some kind of power inside her. But Gaga-na did not know that it was a power that came from the Darkside. Someone in contact with good spirits could not have killed another.

The bushes rattled behind her, and Cimmera whipped around. She searched the brush. Her stomach lurched at the thought that someone could have witnessed what she had just done. If the Tegesta found out she was an evil A-po-la-chee sorceress, they would surely kill her.

She hurried back to the platform and buried the knife in her basket.

By midday the people of the village had shed their fur robes from their shoulders. The sun was warm and drenching. The dark soil was quick to take on the heat, and the villagers appreciated the warmth that it spread to their feet as they walked. They sought places in the sun in which to do their tasks, basking in the warmth as they worked.

The season was about to change, and even the animals celebrated the break in winter. The alligators and turtles climbed out of the water and reveled in the sun's rays. The snakes slithered through the grass in search of something to eat, their bodies roused by the warm air. The birds looked for butterflies, but it was still too early for the swallowtails to take flight.

The women kept their fires low, and the men perspired as they gathered at the central hearth to meet in Council.

"I believe the signs are all here," Atok said, addressing the group of men. "This is the beginning of a drought."

The small group listened attentively.

"Yes, Atok speaks the truth," said Dacoma. "The canoe trails grow more shallow, and the small ponds have begun to dry up. The fish huddle in the deeper water."

"Cacique," Okemah said, asking for recognition.

Cherok nodded, giving Okemah permission to speak.

"There is nothing we can do about the drought. We can pray, but the spirits control the rains. And of course we have no shaman," he said, his eyes narrowing as he looked at Cherok. "I think it is time for you to bring Misa back to us."

Cherok had anticipated this discussion, but he

preferred to wait before asking Mi-sa to return. It was too soon for her to come back. First the rebuilding had to be completed. If he could improve the morale of some men before the sourness contaminated others, he was convinced his clan would one day be strong again. Then it would be time for Mi-sa to return to her people. He chose to wait for another reason, also: Mi-sa had at last found some happiness.

"I will send for her when we are strong in number."

Okemah folded his bulky arms across his broad chest. "You have always protected her. Let her also work at the rebuilding. Let her perform her duties. She has the Gift. We are her people."

Cherok tapped a stick against his thigh, carefully choosing his words before he spoke. "Mi-sa stays with the Kahoosa. If a drought comes, they will suffer also. Our shaman cannot ask the spirits to end the drought for the Kahoosa and not for the Tegesta."

Okemah grunted. "You are weak when it comes to women—your sister and this Cimmera woman. That is another thing Council will discuss today." He looked around to see the eyes of his supporters. "You barely know this woman, and yet you permit her to make a decision for our people. I find this unacceptable."

Cherok kept his patience, his voice low and calm. "I will not be blinded by pride and take the risk of allowing harm to come to us."

"You do not even know if she tells the truth," Dacoma added.

"Think," Cherok said. "Do not be so stubborn. Open your eyes to other ways."

Okemah stood up, his face red with anger. "I believe you should think," he said, his voice loud and gruff. "One of our own has become outcast at a time when he needs us most."

"I will not allow my emotions to shut out good advice. If this woman, Cimmera, is correct in saying that the sickness could spread, would we not be foolish to disregard what she says? If she is incorrect, no harm has befallen us."

"No harm to you or to me, but it is a cruel thing for Talasee, Tashi, and especially Jumak."

"Our clan is weak. We have barely begun to rebuild. We cannot afford another tragedy. As cacique I must insist that Talasee and Tashi stay isolated."

Okemah spoke again. "Why Talasee? He is not sick. And I am not so certain that we should rebuild. Perhaps it would be better if we scattered and found homes in villages that survived the storm."

"Okemah, you argue now for the sake of disagreeing with me. You look for a quarrel." Cherok pulled himself up into a commanding posture. "I will not ask for everyone to decide now. Important decisions should not be made in haste. Tomorrow there will be no moon. We will have our ceremony, and then the next day we will come together again. Let the wisdom of the spirits seep into you."

Jumak scampered around the central hearth. He had moved from Gaga-na's side, wanting to be closer to the men, to hear the issues they discussed. As Cherok walked away, Jumak marched beside him.

"Is it difficult to be the cacique?" Jumak asked. "To make decisions when others disagree with you?"

Cherok stopped so that he could look at the boy. "You have much wisdom for your age. Being cacique is not easy, and sometimes my decisions make others angry."

"They should ask me," Jumak said.

"Ask you what?"

"How I feel—if I think Cimmera tells the truth. Talasee and Tashi are my parents. But I believe Cimmera. She is a good person."

Cherok put his hand on the boy's head. "So much inside such a small space," he said.

"Cimmera helps Gaga-na now. I think you should visit."

Cherok laughed. "Always plotting. You are a lot like your father, but I do not need you to persuade me to visit Gaga-na's hearth. I go on my own."

"I was right!" Jumak said, dancing in front of Cherok, kicking up the dirt. "Your man parts like Cimmera."

Cherok grabbed the boy, wrapping his big hand over the top of Jumak's head. "Do not talk like that in front of the women," he said, playfully tousling the boy's hair and then giving Jumak's head a final shove downward and away.

Jumak ran in front of Cherok, blazing the way.

Gaga-na looked up from her task. She drilled holes in the hard, glossy red and black crab's-eye seeds. Jumak squatted next to her and took a handful of the toxic seeds from the basket, then dumped them back in.

"Leave them be," Gaga-na said.

"I am not going to eat them," the boy said, stirring the seeds with his finger.

"Go on," she said, flipping her hand in front of him.

Gaga-na handed the finished seeds, now to be used as colorful beads, to Cimmera, who dropped them inside a small drawstring pouch. The old woman massaged her knobby fingers and looked at Cherok. "Council has ended?"

"For the day."

"What was discussed?" Gaga-na asked.

"Only opinions. About the drought. About Mi-sa."

"About me?" Cimmera asked.

"No, just your advice."

"The men are angry with you," she said.

"Some men are slow to adapt to change and new ideas. I have given them more time."

"Cherok," Cimmera said, "the disease does spread through contact. I do not understand why, but I am certain I speak the truth. I am just sorry that my interference is causing you grief."

"Come and walk with me, woman," he said.

Cimmera handed Gaga-na the pouch and walked away with Cherok. Jumak sprinted behind them.

"No," Gaga-na called to the boy. "You will wait here with me."

Jumak's shoulders slumped in disappointment. Cimmera looked back to see the boy returning to the old woman.

"He has a lot of spirit," she said to Cherok.

They walked through the hammock, and Cherok led her off the trails. "This is a special place to me," he said, stopping.

"I understand why." Cimmera looked around her, imagining what it had been like before the storm. Shield ferns covered the floor of the hammock, and the evergreen trees formed a verdant canopy. Wild orchids dripped from the trees with bracts of red, white, and orange. The delicate gray-green tendrils of the air plants the women used for skirts gracefully wept from the branches of the trees. "It will be beautiful again."

"It is a quiet place, good for meditation. My sister and I came here often. Even as a child she took spirit flights—and took me with her. This place reminds me of her."

Cimmera looked into his eyes, seeing the sensitive side of Cherok. She liked it.

He pointed to a green bud along the branch of a dormant tree. "I do not want you to think I sacrifice anything for you. I believe that you tell the truth, or think you tell the truth. I cannot put my people at risk. I will not, no matter how much anger is stirred."

Cimmera's gaze dropped, and Cherok was quick to lift her chin in his hand. "No matter what you hear, no matter how bitter this disunion should get, I do not want you to feel responsible. What you have done is good."

"You do not know me," she whispered.

Cherok took her head in his hands and ran his fingers back through her hair. He leaned closer to her and gently touched his mouth to her forehead, then to her temple, her eyelid, her cheek, the side of her neck. He slid his hands through her hair until he cradled the back of her head.

"I believe in you," he said as his mouth touched hers.

His breath was hot inside her mouth. The heat of his close body, the smell of his skin, cast out her thoughts of resistance. She felt her body relent, her tight shoulders relax, her legs become unsteady.

His hands wandered over her back, beneath the heavy fall of her hair, the strands slipping silkily through his fingers. She could barely stand, her arms dangling at her sides, splendidly helpless. His body gently pressed against hers, and then he stepped back.

Cimmera opened her eyes. He stared at her, his eyes searching the depth of hers. Then he turned and walked away. She stood there, trembling, confused, watching him leave. He had a power over her, a dominion that left her numb and defenseless. She ached for him to come back.

She wanted to feel him hard against her, but he had only teased her, let her imagine what it would be like if his strong arms held her tightly against him. And he trusted her.

Cimmera felt weak, and she sank to the ground, watching until he disappeared, afraid of what might happen the next time he was so close—startled by what she yearned to have happen.

The night covered the small village as Narchise looked for Okemah. She padded across the mound in the direction of his shelter. With the darkness the air had cooled down, and Narchise had wrapped a soft fur around her shoulders.

Okemah sat at his hearth, his lap full of sticks with which he was feeding the fire. He was not ready for sleep, as most of the others were. This period of the evening was a good time to think, to chew up the events of the day into small pieces.

Narchise could see him in the light of his fire before he saw her. "Okemah," she said softly, her voice deliberately low and husky.

Okemah looked up to see her standing on the opposite side of the fire. Immediately he stood up, the collection of sticks clattering on the ground. At the sight of her in the flickering light his imagination became untamed. The sensation of his breechclout rubbing against him as he moved sent a surge of warmth to his loins, and he staggered a step. He felt the urge to touch himself, to adjust himself, so the breechclout would not add to the arousal. It was too late, and he sat quickly, grateful for the shadows of the night.

"Narchise," he said, politely nodding his greeting.

"Okemah," she said again, fluttering her lashes. "May I

sit with you?"

"I would like that." He stared up at her, wondering if she would sit opposite him where it would be easy to stare, or next to him where his ogling would be more obvious.

Narchise eased up beside him and grandly lowered herself to the ground. "It is a beautiful night," she said. "I think the season changes."

As she sat, the moving air brought a woman scent to his nose, and Okemah could scarcely focus on what she was saying.

"I am happy to think the winter ends, but I do not find it pleasant to bundle up in these furs," she said, cuddling her bosom with her crossed arms.

Okemah imagined his face smothered there in the pillow of those overflowing breasts.

"Are you not cold?" she asked. "You do not wear a blanket."

"No," he said. "I am warm enough."

He felt a feathery touch on his skin. Okemah looked down to see Narchise's hand slither across his thigh and then quickly disappear inside her furs. The deed was so sudden and brief that he wondered if it had really happened. He looked at her, his eyes brimming with the most exquisite bewilderment. He swallowed and spoke. "What has brought you to my hearth? Do you want something?"

Narchise cocked her head and smiled. She arched her neck and shook her hair back. "I have thought about this all day. I can trust you?"

"Of course," Okemah said. "With anything."

"Good," she said. "Trust is important, do you not think so?"

"Very," Okemah said, watching the upsurge of her

142

furs each time she took a deep breath.

"Then this night will stay a secret, just between us?"

Okemah thought he was going to burst. His arousal had grown so large that he was certain it would rip a hole in the deerskin cloth that kept it hidden. His throat was too tight and his mouth too dry to speak. He nodded.

Narchise reached over, took his hand and slipped it inside her robe. Okemah groaned. If she did not get inside his platform quickly, he feared he would be on top of her right here on the ground.

"I saw something today," she said, holding his hand firmly against the flesh of her bare breast.

"What?" he asked, his hand so full of her that he could not resist the urge to reach for her with the other.

Narchise patted his groping hand and placed it on his thigh.

Okemah clasped her fingers and held her hand securely just above his knee, fearing that she might brush against him. He was pulsing and swollen and painfully hard. A slip of her hand, and it would be all over.

"Do you want to hear what I saw?"

"Yes," he said, his voice catching, his belly flopping with anticipation, though he was not the least bit interested in what she had seen.

"I saw Cimmera heal a tree, seal an oozing wound in its trunk, with nothing but her hand."

CHAPTER 14

"DID YOU HEAR ME?" Narchise asked. "Cimmera did magic on a tree. I saw her do it."

Okemah felt himself shrivel. "Magic?"

"Yes. She cut bark from a maple tree earlier. Later I saw her go back there. She sang a song—a spirit song, I am sure. She held a knife, and it glowed. Then she put her hand on the tree. When she took it off, the scar was gone. I was afraid."

Narchise loosened her grip that held his hand to her breast, and Okemah slipped his fingers out of her furs.

"Are you sure what you saw?" he asked.

Narchise took his hand again and squeezed it. "I had to tell someone. You do believe me, do you not?"

"Of course."

Narchise leaned her head on his shoulder. "Oh, Okemah, I knew you would. Such a wise and brave man you are. I am so frightened."

He looped his arm around her shoulders. "There is no need to be afraid. I will take care of this."

Narchise lifted her head to look at him. "But if she knows I saw her, she might do something terrible to me."

"Ah," he said. "I see what you mean." He wrapped his other arm around her waist, holding the full breadth of her.

Narchise snuggled against him, dropping her hand to his middle. Her fingers snaked over his naked belly. "You will not tell our secret, will you?"

"No," Okemah was quick to answer, shifting his weight from hip to hip, scooting even closer.

Her hand prowled lower, and this time he made no effort to hide his need from her.

Narchise laid her head on his chest, feeling his tight knob of a nipple against her cheek. She smiled at the ripening hardness nosing her hand through his breechclout. She used a single finger to teasingly draw small circles on his proudly rising manroot.

Okemah kicked dirt over the embers of his fire. "Oh, woman," he puffed, pressing her hand firmly on his swollen member.

Narchise was quick to weave her hand inside the bulging breechclout. "You are so large," she whispered in his ear.

Okemah moaned and pushed her onto the ground, nuzzling her through the wrap, getting a mouthful of rabbit fur. He sputtered, his tongue flicking out the unwanted hair. His hand clawed at the robe, pulling it away from those wondrous, waiting breasts. When the furs finally came away, he drew back his head so that he could see what awaited him, but it was too dark. He buried his face in the abundant flesh, pushing at her plentiful bosom from the sides with his palms so that he could feel more of them against his cheeks.

Narchise still had her hand uncomfortably wound in his breechclout. She tugged to free herself, but remained tangled. She encircled him and gave a gentle stroke.

Okemah bucked and then reared up, his hands fumbling between their fervent bodies, tearing at the knot of cloth.

She tried to help but was in the way. He rolled to his side, ripping away the troublesome deerskin.

"Hurry," Narchise whispered.

The sound of her needful plea was more than he could bear. He moved astride her, shredding her moss skirt, afraid that he could not even make the entry in time.

Narchise dug her fingers into his back and clamped her legs around him, driving him deep. Her head and shoulders rose off the ground at his penetrating thrust, and she cried out, sending Okemah into his final frenzy.

Narchise opened her eyes to watch. The sight of his passionate grimace and the feel of his huge stiffened body sent the same wild concussions through her. Their voices tolled out across the quiet village.

The night air swept across Okemah's sweaty body as he sprawled limply on her. He lay there thinking how he would never get his breath back, how fiercely frantic this woman had made him. Now he was satisfied and overwhelmingly weary. He did not want to move, content to lie there bedded in all that great softness.

Narchise tried to draw in a needed breath, but the weight of him squeezed her chest. Her husband had not been such a big person, and she realized she had never been so wonderfully crushed by a man. And the best was knowing how feverish he had been for her, how excited and desperate she made him.

When Okemah visited her hearth the next morning, Narchise returned to the story of watching Cimmera heal the tree. "I heard birds—their wings fluttering—large birds," she said. "And the strangest thing—a shadow descended, like a great wing blocking the light."

Okemah tore off a piece of coontie bread with his teeth. "And you did not see anything? A bird?"

"No. I looked. Then she started humming, like I told you." Narchise reached over and brushed the dirt and stains off his knees.

"You had me on my knees like some spirit!" Okemah said, laughing.

Narchise hid her grin behind her hand.

Suddenly the playfulness on Okemah's face disappeared. "That is it! A spirit. She is a bad spirit in the form of a woman. We have no shaman. The spirits of the Darkside know that."

Narchise shivered. "Why do you think she is bad? Maybe she is a good spirit."

Okemah dug his hand into Narchise's cooking pot and pulled out a piece of alligator meat. He kept it between his fingers, moving it about with his expressive hands as he emphasized what he said. "A good spirit would have identified itself. A healer or a shaman would have proudly claimed the gift." Okemah leaned forward and talked more softly, glancing about to see if anyone was nearby. "No, she came into our village and struck right at the heart, saying she offered good advice. She has pounded a stake between us. Then you see her doing magic in secret. She is after our cacique, to destroy our clan."

Narchise shook her head. "She does not seem evil. She has been nice to me."

"She is a trickster."

"Oh," Narchise muttered.

Okemah stood up and looked over the village. Some men were gathering and talking. Okemah strutted away.

At first Narchise thought he would turn back and say something to her—something like how he would like to see her later, or good-bye or something. In the night she had left him snoring on the ground, and this morning he had shown up at her hearth. Of course she had thought that he would speak about their joining last night. But he had not. Only the one comment when she attempted to wipe away the dirt he had ground into his knees while satisfying himself.

She tossed some herbs into her pot and mumbled to herself. "You just wait until tonight, Okemah."

Cherok had not gone inside the platform to sleep when Cimmera did. He had stared for a long while at the black sky, listened to the whispering breeze, thought about his sister, dwelled on Cimmera.

When he entered his shelter he quietly sat on his mat. Cherok had wanted to stare at the woman, but the night was too dark.

When the first rays of light came, he rolled onto his side so that he could see her. She was curled up on her mat, one hand beneath her cheek.

"Cimmera," he whispered, waking her gently, his hand barely reaching her cheek.

She opened her eyes.

Cherok stood and ran his fingers through his hair, then left the platform. By the edge of the water he sat with legs crossed and greeted the day. He said prayers of thankfulness and prayers for harmony among his people.

When he was finished, Atok came and stood beside him. "Dacoma and I are going to search for others again. There are not enough of us—not enough women to nourish our seed. There must be more of us out there."

"And if there are no more? What then, Atok?"

"I do not know. Perhaps we must do as Okemah suggests. Scatter."

Cherok stood. "Never. No matter how few, we will become one again. Even if we must wait for our sons and daughters to bear their children."

"Well, Okemah has wasted no time," Atok said. "He has made his effort."

"What do you mean?"

"I sat late at the central hearth. At first I thought there were animals lurking about Okemah's fire, so I walked close to frighten them away. When I got near I saw that the big man had Narchise spread on the ground, grunting and groaning. I think everyone must have heard them." Atok laughed. "Okemah's fire was hot!"

"Perhaps he will not be so disagreeable now."

"And maybe Narchise will be still and stop her chattering and fidgeting."

Cherok cuffed Atok's shoulder. "Let us hope that the two of them are good for each other."

Both men gave a hearty chuckle. Then Cherok said, "Come, we have many things to do to prepare for the night."

Dacoma's eyes reflected a bit of game and sport. "You are looking well this morning," he said to Okemah.

"I am feeling quite well," Okemah said.

Dacoma's mouth spread across his face in a wide grin. "How did you make her sing like that?"

"Sing? Who?"

"The woman. She was as loud as a screeching gull. Sounded like it came from there by your fire."

"You heard?" Okemah said and laughed.

Dacoma slapped his friend's belly with the back of his hand. "She is a noisy one."

"It's the scar," he said, pointing to his eye. "Makes the women act crazy."

"And I thought it was some special thing you do—or the size of your ...

"That, too," Okemah said.

"Who was this fortunate woman?"

"It does not matter. I make them all squeal." Okemah

pumped his hips, and Dacoma broke into laughter.

"I believe our cacique is also enjoying the pleasure of a woman in his bed," Okemah said.

"Do you think so? He has asked me to help build Cimmera a shelter."

"Dacoma, you are a man. If a woman slept in your platform, what would you be doing? Or do you grow too old?" He held up a finger and then let it wilt.

"Never," Dacoma said.

"And our cacique is a man also …younger than you."

"Maybe she does not let him."

"Impossible. She wants him."

Dacoma noted the scowl on Okemah's face. "Why do you say it that way?"

"I believe she is no good. She brings harm to our clan and uses our cacique. She probably pleases him beyond any way he has ever been pleased before. That is why he does everything she says. His man part cannot tear itself away from her. Watch and see. She has made him foolish," Okemah said.

Dacoma studied the big man's face. He was very serious about what he was saying. He knew Okemah had been a sour man ever since the storm. He had changed into someone who never saw good anymore. Dacoma wanted to lighten the conversation. Okemah was much too intense.

"I have not heard Cimmera sing in the night. He must not have the knack that you do." The effort to make Okemah's mood more pleasant failed.

"You will see," Okemah said and walked away.

The women cooked all day, preparing for the evening festivities. The moonless sky would mark the end of another cycle, another passage of time. The clan had not celebrated the new moon since the storm. Cherok insisted they carry on the traditional rituals and ceremonies.

Gaga-na sat with her long stringy gray hair trailing in front of her as she stirred the large pot of tea.

"I like the way this smells," Cimmera said, sniffing the tea.

"It is tangy. Some think it is a little bitter, but I find a strong tea appropriate for special occasions."

Jumak dipped a shell in the brew and ladled some out. He wrinkled his nose, then spat it out. "I like cassite."

"And when have you had that drink?" Gaga-na asked.

Jumak hung his head.

"I thought not. You try to be a man too soon. You must learn all the ways first. The time is coming."

Cimmera dipped the shell into Gaga-na's tea, and then sipped from it. "I like it. Yes, I think it is a special tea for a special occasion."

She glanced across the mound. Cherok stood with a group of men. She wondered why he had whispered her name in the morning and then left without saying any more. He was wonderful to look at, his shiny black hair reaching his shoulders, the single braid with feathers and beads framing one side of his angular face. She never wanted him to know her secret, that she was his enemy. Her eyes grew sad, and Jumak tugged at her hand.

"What is wrong?"

"Nothing," she answered.

Satisfied, Jumak went about playing with another boy who came by.

"I told you the boy notices," Gaga-na said. "You were watching Cherok. Why do you not give in to your heart?"

Cimmera tossed the shell down by the pot. "There is nothing to give in to."

"Stir this tea, but be careful. Do not stir too fast or

hard. Gently."

Gaga-na handed her the stirring stick and went to search her baskets for another herb.

Cimmera slowly swirled the drink. She needed to ask Cherok when a shelter would be built for her. She had to put some distance between them. She wasn't only fearful they would become lovers; a much deeper trepidation sprang from that empty hole inside her. If she was a bad spirit, would she hurt him?

Gaga-na tossed a handful of herbs into the tea, interrupting her thoughts.

"There," Gaga-na said. "The boy will like it better now." She nudged Cimmera. "Ara comes. She is Okemah's sister."

The woman stood in front of Gaga-na and Cimmera. She did not sit with them, waiting for an invitation first.

"Okemah says that I am to prepare the food for Talasee and Tashi. He says I should take it to them," Ara said.

Gaga-na did not ask the woman to sit. "Why? Is my cooking not good enough?"

Ara shook her head. "I do not think the problem is with you," she said.

"And has Okemah spoken with the cacique?"

"He told me that he intends to and that I should come to you."

"I will wait to hear from Cherok," Gaga-na said.

Ara shifted uncomfortably. "There is no need for you to take on added burdens. You already take care of Jumak."

"Cimmera helps me. Jumak is no burden, and I cook anyway. A little more or a little less does not make any difference." Gaga-na put her hand on Cimmera's. "This woman does not let me do much of anything. Now you go along, and you and your brother do not worry about me."

Ara shrugged and left.

"What is spinning in that man's head?" Gaga-na said. "I knew his vision was blurry, but I did not realize his head was, also."

"Perhaps he just wishes to relieve you of responsibilities."

Gaga-na did not answer. Neither she nor Cimmera had missed Ara's point when she said the problem was not with Gaga-na.

"Taste this," she told Cimmera, holding out a shell spoon. "Add more of this if it still seems too bitter," she said, giving her a small basket of herbs. "Try it out on Jumak if you can get him to taste it again."

Gaga-na hoisted herself with her walking stick, grumbling about her leg as she stood. "I will be back."

She moved slowly across the mound until she found Okemah. She tapped him with her stick. "I want to talk with you."

"In a moment," he said, turning back to the group of men he stood with.

Gaga-na smacked his shoulder with the stick. "No, now," she said. "Give an old woman respect."

Okemah sighed loudly and rolled his eyes. One man elbowed another, and they held back laughter.

"What is it, old woman?"

"What is wrong with you?" she said. "Ara came to me."

Okemah smiled patronizingly. "I was thinking of you," he said, putting his hand on her shoulder, but Gaga-na knocked it off.

"I am old, but I still have my wits. Speak the truth."

Okemah's face grew stern. "I do not believe the

woman Cimmera. I think she has caused harm to Talasee and Tashi and of course to their son."

"What else gnaws at your gut?"

"I told you. I do not think her advice is good."

Gaga-na jabbed his middle with her stick. "Bah! There is more. That is not enough reason to keep Cimmera from helping me prepare their food. Since when did you care who was doing a woman's work?"

"Go on, old woman," Okemah said.

"I will fix their food until I hear from Cherok. If you want to send Ara to deliver it, send her."

Okemah turned his back and threw both arms over the shoulders of his friends and walked away with them.

She was sure he said something hateful about her, for all the men laughed, one of them bending forward he laughed so hard.

Gaga-na ambled back to her hearth. She knew something else was brewing, something that Okemah would not talk about, and she didn't like his smugness.

She looked across at the woman who was at the center of all this discord. Gaga-na stopped. Who was Cimmera talking to? The young woman stood at the hearth, her hand outstretched, saying something. But no one was there.

Gaga-na approached quietly and slowly. She saw no one near the woman, and yet she was obviously speaking to someone. Who did she see?

Suddenly Cimmera spun around, her face draining of color.

"Jumak!" she screamed.

CHAPTER 15

MOST OF THE VILLAGERS turned their heads to see who had screamed and why.

Cimmera stood by Gaga-na's hearth, her face pale with fear.

"What is wrong? What? What?" Gaga-na said, hobbling up to her.

"It is Jumak!"

"I do not understand," Gaga-na said.

Cherok ran across the village to them.

"Cherok," Cimmera cried. "Hurry! Find Jumak!"

He stared at her, puzzled.

"Please!" she said.

Cherok raced through the brush, Cimmera running behind him. He called the boy's name and could hear others also calling for him.

Suddenly Cherok stopped, held his hand out to halt Cimmera. "Wait," he said. "Listen."

Coughing.

"It is Jumak," Cimmera said.

When they found him, Jumak's friend was pounding him on the back. Cherok knelt in front of the boys. "Are you all right?"

Jumak coughed so hard that his eyes and face turned red. His friend backed away, letting Cherok take over.

Jumak drew a ragged breath. "I think so," he said, followed by another short cough.

Cherok looked at the ground near the boy's feet. "What is this?" he asked, picking up a small hollow reed and a few crab's-eye seeds.

Jumak's friend Yoma turned to run away, but Cimmera planted her hands on his shoulders.

"Come here, Yoma," Cherok said. "Do not be so quick to leave."

"I told him not to," Yoma said.

"Tell me about this, Jumak," Cherok said.

Cimmera moved beside them.

"We were shooting the seeds at frogs and lizards."

Cherok nodded and held the seeds in front of Jumak. "You put these in your mouth and blew them out of the reed?"

Jumak looked away and nodded, giving another cough.

"You choked on one," Cherok said. "Did you swallow it?"

"Yes," Jumak answered. "I did not mean to. The seed just went down my throat. Gaga-na is going to be displeased with me. They are her seeds. I did not take many."

Cherok looked up at Cimmera, whose eyes reflected the gravity of the situation.

"Do you have any seeds?" Cherok asked Yoma.

"Jumak gave me these," he said, holding three of the poisonous seeds in his palm.

"Throw them away."

The cacique picked Jumak up and carried him back to the village. When he reached Gaga-na's hearth he laid the boy on the ground. "Be still," he told him. He looked back for Cimmera, but she wasn't there.

Gaga-na hunkered down next to the child. "What is wrong?" she asked Cherok, looking at the tears rolling out of the boy's eyes. She wiped them away.

Cherok's expression told Gaga-na how concerned he was. "He has swallowed a crab's-eye seed."

Gaga-na's eyes grew wide, as did those of the other villagers who gathered around.

"I only took a few," Jumak said to Gaga-na. "I am sorry."

"Shh," she whispered, stroking his cheek. "What should we do?" she asked Cherok.

When he was a young boy, Cherok's father had taught him the names and uses of plants that were effective as cures and medicines. He searched his mind, trying to remember an antidote for the crab's-eye poison, but he could not recall one.

"He must get rid of the seed," Cherok said.

Gaga-na scraped dirt away, forming a shallow basin, and Cherok held Jumak over it, giving him directions to make himself gag.

Jumak's first attempts were halfhearted.

"Do it!" Cherok ordered. "Or I will."

"Wait," Cimmera said, coming up behind them. She put a fresh pot of water over Gaga-na's fire and tore up some leaves she had gathered in the brush, then threw them in the pot.

"What is that for?" Gaga-na asked.

"Jumak. Medicine to aid in getting rid of the seed."

Cherok helped the boy to lean over the basin again.

Cimmera put her hand on Cherok's arm and shook her head.

"Are you sure you swallowed it?" Cimmera asked the child.

Jumak sniffed and nodded. "I am sorry," he cried, looking at Gaga-na.

Cimmera stirred the medicine, then left it and sat close to the boy. "Did you bite the seed?" she asked.

"No," he answered. "I had it in my mouth to shoot at a frog, but I swallowed it by accident."

"Was it cracked?"

"No."

Cimmera sat back on her heels, looking relieved. "Let him rest," she said. "I believe he will be all right. If the hard shell is not broken, the poison will not get out. This medicine will speed the seed through him."

Cimmera moved to the hearth and took the pot from the fire. She poured some of the medicine off into a conch shell ladle. She handed it to Cherok. "Make him drink this."

Most of the crowd broke up, but a few lingered.

"Go on," Gaga-na said when the boy squinted his eyes and wrinkled up his nose. "It does not taste as bad as it smells."

"Yes, it does," Cimmera said with a big smile. "But Jumak is nearly a man. He will drink the medicine bravely."

The boy opened his mouth and took a big gulp.

"What did you put in that drink?" It was Okemah.

Cimmera looked up. "I made a medicine."

"Yes, I know; that is what you said."

"Then what do you want to know?" Cherok asked, standing.

"I want to know what she put in it. Did you see? That could be a medicine to release the poison in the seed, to eat through the shell."

Cherok looked away and let out a heavy sigh that clearly expressed his irritation.

"Then you do not know what she gave the boy," Okemah said.

Cimmera stood to face the man. "I mixed leaves of the milk thistle and wax myrtle with blades of nut grass. A purgative."

Gaga-na cocked her head, thinking what a clever remedy Cimmera had prepared. She had never thought of that combination, but the woman was right. That mixture would make a powerful medicine, and the seed would come out of Jumak very soon.

Okemah still had lines of doubt and suspicion carved into his face. "And you know that your medicine will save him?"

"If the seed was cracked, it will improve his chances. If not, the seed will pass through more quickly, before the poison can get out of the shell."

Okemah shut his eyes and shook his head. "How would you know a medicine we do not? Who are you?"

"Enough," Cherok said. "She told you what the medicine is. You should be grateful, Okemah. The woman has tried to help. I advise you to go about your business."

"Watch the boy," Okemah said, leaving. "His father is your friend."

Atok squatted by Gaga-na's fire and pitched a small twig into it. "I thought perhaps he would be less disagreeable after last night with Narchise."

Cherok sat. "The storm has changed him. He does not seem to recover."

"What will we do, Cherok? We physically rebuild, but the spirit of our clan flounders."

"Move on. Continue. Put the past behind us. That is what we have to do."

"I hope so," Atok said, resting his hand on Cherok's shoulder after he stood.

Atok was the last of the crowd to wander away.

"Okemah is distrustful," Cimmera said.

"He lost his woman in the storm."

"Did Atok say that he was now with Narchise?"

Cherok laughed. "He saw them last night. Apparently Okemah and Narchise have found each other."

Jumak sat up. "Okemah and Narchise? Atok watched them?"

Cherok turned and looked at the boy behind him. "Your ears are far too big."

Jumak grinned.

"Drink some more," Cimmera said.

"You are nice, Cimmera, but your medicine is terrible."

"Drink it anyway," Gaga-na said, holding the ladle to the boy's lips.

Narchise sat by the water. She had cleaned her body and now she spread a paste of ground flowers over her, a sweet perfume. The sun was setting, and she anxiously waited for the ceremony of the moonless night to begin. She was ready. On her upper arms, she wore bracelets adorned with tinkling shells and colorful feathers. Around her neck she had tied a thong with a large pink shell that nestled between her breasts.

Narchise bent over and looked for her reflection in the water. But the evening was already too dark for her to see anything there.

She got up to leave, and when she turned to walk away she caught a glimpse of something moving farther down the bank of the hammock. She stopped so she would not attract anyone's attention. She had come here alone so that the other women would not witness her detailed preparations. That would have invited too many questions, and it was too soon to tell about Okemah. Maybe after tonight.

Narchise paused and stared through the brush, waiting

for whoever it was to move on. The wind came up and rustled the leaves on the trees, stirring the debris on the ground. She looked up. She wanted it to rain. Everyone wanted rain. But not tonight.

What she saw surprised her. The sky was clear. There was no thunderhead that could have brought the burst of wind.

Intrigued by a large white bird that flew overhead, she tracked it with her eyes. Its wings beat heavily, and for an instant she thought it might have been the bird's wings that caused the wind. But that was a crazy thought, and she quickly dismissed it, hurrying back to the village.

At first Cimmera thought it was only the breeze, the subtle fluttering of the leaves, but then the sound became more distinct. A voice—Tamar's voice.

"Come with me," he whispered in her ear. "Go away from the village."

Cimmera did what Tamar told her. She left the village and wandered through the brush, off the trails, until she came to the far side of the hammock.

"Close your eyes," he told her, his voice a part of the air, his breath blowing through the trees. "Do not be afraid. I have come for you."

Cimmera obeyed. She heard the beating of wings as a great bird settled nearby. Tamar. She felt the breeze it stirred on her face, felt her spirit gather in a place near the top of her head, and then she burst free.

"I will help you see," he said.

Cimmera opened her eyes. She hovered above a village.

"Is this my home?" she asked, but no answer came.

Below her a woman inspected a newly made pot, checking for cracks, running her finger over the finely incised designs.

"Sola," Cimmera whispered, the name coming out of the wind and into her head. Immediately she felt tears streaming down her face, and then she heard Tamar's voice again.

"Good. You are remembering."

She blinked. The village and the woman vanished. "Tamar?" she called.

The sun was going down, and the shadows of the trees darkened the wood. She rubbed her upper arms, feeling an eerie chill, then turned and went back to the village.

The drums, the heartbeat of the People, throbbed in the night. The villagers gathered at the central hearth as Atok fed the fire.

"I am glad that you take Talasee's responsibilities until he is back among us," Cherok said.

Atok threw an armload of pinecones into the flames. The fire sparkled and snapped, winking light showering the air.

Cimmera stood back, unfamiliar with the ritual. Blackness veiled the village, except for the area around the fire, the cinders floating near the earth like tiny stars.

Cherok's oiled body shone in the firelight. His face was lime white with three charcoal lines across each cheek. His black hair tumbled onto his wide shoulders.

A hush fell over the villagers as they watched their cacique raise his hands into the night, his voice echoing. The festivities began.

Around the hearth the men formed an inner circle, their arms and bodies moving in rhythm to the drums and the voices of the music makers. The music rushed through them, compelled them to give themselves up to the sound. Every beat ushered them closer to a state in which they would be oblivious to everything except the beating of the drums. They took large, exaggerated steps, swinging their arms through the air. Their bodies undulated in the firelight.

The women in the outer circle danced with smaller steps, moving in unison. Both circles moved around the blazing fire, traveling in the same direction, but at different speeds.

Cimmera watched, fascinated, catching glimpses of Cherok as he progressed around the fire, seeing a part of his face over someone's shoulder, through someone's windblown hair or fluttering feathers. Then he would disappear, hidden by other dancers.

Gaga-na traveled about the circle as she had so often, her bare feet stepping with experience, toe down first, then heel, the shell bells dripping from her, tinkling. She spotted Cimmera and gave her a curious glance. When the first song ended, she made her way to the woman.

"Why do you not participate?"

"I will next time," she answered.

"Ah," Gaga-na said, seeing Cimmera's eyes dart away. "You watch the cacique. He does move magnificently. If I were a young woman I would have a hard time keeping my eyes off him tonight."

Cimmera smiled.

"They pass the cassite," Gaga-na said, guiding Cimmera toward the crowd.

They sipped from the ladles and passed them on. Cimmera took a small taste first, then a bigger drink. Gaga-na thought that strange, as if she had tested the drink first.

"You appear unsure," Gaga-na said. "Do not all Tegesta enact the same ritual for the new moon?"

"Subtle differences, that is all,"

The women gathered in one group and the men in

another. "What do the men drink?" Cimmera asked, then added, "I just wondered if it was the same."

"A special brew. The women are not allowed to prepare it or drink it. Is that the custom in your village?"

"Yes," Cimmera said, taking the ladle of cassite again as it was offered to her. She swallowed, and this time a warmth flowed through her.

The drums and voices rang out again, and the men rapidly formed their dancing circle. Cimmera felt her body relaxing as she joined the outer circle to dance with the women. She tried to focus across the fire, to the other side of the men's inner circle, but her eyes were slow to adjust.

Narchise's high-pitched voice caught her attention. Cimmera leaned forward, looking down the circle until she found the heavy woman. Narchise was babbling to Ara, who stood next to her.

Cimmera looked across for Cherok. She scanned the circle and found him moving close. As he came by, she closed her eyes, sensing his passing.

The dancing continued, and then the feasting began. Okemah stood with Atok and Dacoma. They carried on, laughing and telling stories to entertain one another. Atok broke away from the group first and joined in conversation with some women.

A young woman paid much attention to Okemah. Narchise bumped her way into the group, coming between the young woman, Tichini, and Okemah. Tichini held out some dripping meat and put it to Okemah's lips. He sucked at the meat and then at her fingers.

"Are you hungry, Okemah?" Narchise asked. "I will be happy to bring you more to eat."

Okemah shook his head and kept looking at Tichini as the juice from the meat slicked his smiling lips. The young woman held up a small mushroom cap, and then rubbed it over his lips before popping it into his mouth.

Tichini's breasts were round, and Narchise was sure they were firm. They peeked through her thick hair, which tumbled over them. Her waist curved in above a flat belly. Her thighs were shapely and solid, and no sagging flesh hung over her knees.

Okemah groped at her as he stumbled. The young woman laughed as he made her stagger backward.

Narchise swept her arm beneath his, helping to steady him.

Okemah let go of Tichini, but then planted his hand on her round buttocks and flexed his fingers so that he held a handful of her.

Tichini laughed and pushed him away, scolding him. "You should take better charge of your hands," she said.

Okemah laughed loudly and smacked his lips, then wandered off.

"Okemah," Narchise called, following him.

He turned around and looked at her.

"Would you like me to come with you?"

Tichini came up behind Narchise. "Look what you have lost," she said to Okemah, dangling one of his fallen feathers.

"I am grateful," Okemah said, reaching out for it.

Just as Okemah grabbed at the feather, Tichini snatched it away.

Okemah's face expressed his amusement. "You like to play games," he said.

Narchise backed away a few steps, then turned and left, fading quickly into the darkness. She could still hear Okemah laughing and Tichini giggling.

She felt like crying, felt like screaming, but she didn't. She sat beneath her platform where the blackness held her tenderly, hiding her from all those faces that would stare at her and laugh. She had to do something to keep Okemah's attention. Something drastic.

CHAPTER 16

CIMMERA STOOD WITH HER BACK against a tree watching the celebration.

Cherok came and stood next to her. "There is something I have wanted to ask you, but we have not had a private time together until now."

Cimmera waited, one hand latching on to the other, pinching a finger with anxiety.

""How did you know about Jumak?" he asked.

The drums began again, and the singers' voices warbled.

"Should you not be with your people?" Cimmera said.

"I doubt I will be missed. I prefer to stand right here."

She looked down, sure he would see the flush in her cheeks even in the dark.

"You knew the boy was in trouble. How?"

A large hand came out of the night and landed solidly on Cherok's shoulder.

Okemah.

"Where is Narchise?" he asked. "Have you seen her?"

Cherok shook his head.

"What about you?" he asked Cimmera.

"No, I have not seen her," she answered.

"I need the woman," Okemah grumbled and walked away.

"I hope he finds her or he will be cross tomorrow," Cherok said and smiled.

Cimmera looked up at the starry sky, leaning back against the tree.. The sound of a few singing voices floated through the air. She felt heavy—not sleepy, but very relaxed.

"They are both lonely people. It is good they have found each other." Cherok paused, brushing his fingertips along the side of her face, then tracing the outline of her mouth.

He stepped forward and brushed up against her. She closed her eyes. She didn't care who she was, what she was. All she knew was that there was no more resistance left inside her. She was tired of refusing to admit what welled up in her heart. He had come so close to her so often, and he had done what she supposed he intended. Little by little he had worn away her will to deny her feelings. Tonight his touch, the blackness of the sky, the music, the ceremonial tea, all destroyed the last of her defenses.

Cherok drew her close, and Cimmera sank into him. "I will not stop this time," he whispered to her.

If he had not been holding her, she was certain she would have sunk to the ground.

He smoothed his hands down her body, her hair sliding beneath his palms. Cimmera did not pull away. Now she knew something else about herself, and the revelation had not come in a dream or a vision. The new knowledge came from this moment: She had never been with a man before, not this way.

"I do not know what to do," she murmured.

Cherok drew back his head, taking his mouth from her shoulder, her innocence sending a flood of heat through him. He gazed at her and smiled. He stepped back and held out his hand.

Cimmera hesitated a moment and then placed her

hand in his. Cherok led her to his platform, stopping only briefly to light a stick in the fire.

He followed her up the ladder, then took a clay bowl filled with tallow and lit the exposed fiber strand. The soft flickering light danced on the thatched sides of the shelter.

He kicked her sleeping skin aside. Easily he put his hands on her shoulders, gliding them down over the crests and into the recesses of her body. The last buried shred of reluctance inside her flowed out, leached free by his magical touch.

He knelt, tasting the thin flesh over her ribs. Then he held her hips, and his hands insisted that she come down to him.

Cherok pulled her close, his fingers smoothing her back, and then his palms cupping her buttocks. Gently he took her onto his sleeping skin.

Cimmera lay still, waiting, her eyes open in wonder. He untied the waistband of her skirt, held the small of her back, and pulled the skirt away.

He guided her hand to his breechclout. Cimmera slipped the knot undone, and the deerskin fell away.

His hands flowed over her waist, then moved upward to the underswell of her breasts. He opened his mouth and suckled her. Cherok heard the little whimper, and he lifted her from beneath, bringing her ripe breast more firmly to him. The rest of his body he kept away from her.

She arched up to him, aching for him to fall onto her. He took both her hands and stretched out her arms, pinioning her as his mouth continued to explore.

When he finally released her, she was desperate for something to hold on to, to keep her tethered to him. She threaded her fingers through his hair, holding him to her heart.

Cherok pulled up and knelt, straddling her, and gazed at her lying there, her eyes finally closed, her lips parted, her chest rising and falling with each quick, eager breath.

He slid his hands over her belly, then teasingly over her breasts, then up the column of her neck, out from her chin, spreading across her jaw, and through her hair, coming to rest beneath her head to cradle it. Still he kept his weight off her, supporting himself on his elbows and knees, letting her first adjust to the full length of him.

The contrast of his rough, hardened body against the softness of hers, the stretch of his muscle-corded legs fitting pleasingly astride hers, the intimate contact of their hot naked skin, stirred a need in her she could only compare to hunger.

Cherok lifted himself, and his hand wandered along the tops and outer parts of her thighs. Lightly then he moved to the soft, tender inside. Gently he urged her open and cupped the rise there before he sought the small, shrouded, more sensitive flesh. His slow and even caresses were as powerful as the jagged lightning that ripped through thunderheads, and as soft as the glimmering light of the small flame burning beside them.

He watched her face, watched the ecstasy steal over her, her hair all about, her head drifting to the side. He heard her tiny gasp and saw her teeth catch her bottom lip.

When she trembled and he could feel her tighten, her body strain, he carefully guided himself into her and finally lowered his weight. Cimmera's breath gushed from her. Patiently he taught her the rhythm, guarding himself until at last he heard the cry of repletion torn from deep in her throat.

Cherok groaned as the scalding thunderbolt of rapture

shook him to the bone.

Cimmera lay still beneath him a long time before stirring. His head was buried in the crook of her neck, the taste of his skin still salty in her mouth.

Cherok moved to his side and pulled her against him, holding her tightly. He put his lips to her forehead.

"Cherok! Look," Cimmera called from the opening of the platform.

A bright slice of sunlight coming in behind her made it hard for him to see her. He propped himself up on his elbow. "What is it?"

She moved to him and sat on her heels, her eyes filling with tears. "A ground dove sings below."

Cherok reached out and embraced her. "Come here. Why does that make you cry?"

Cimmera sat next to him. "Death. It brings a message of death."

"No," he said, kissing her eyelids.

She wanted to insist, tell him that everyone in her A-po-la-chee village knew the meaning of a ground dove's call at the door.

Cherok lay back and curled her against him.

Cimmera wanted to stay there forever. She turned over and pressed her forehead to his chest, then looked up. The morning sun bathed his face in waxen light.

A loud thudding sounded through the shelter.

"Cherok!" Gaga-na called, beating her stick against the ladder. "Come down and settle this!"

Cherok sighed, grabbed his breechclout, and secured it around him before moving to the opening.

"What do you want, Gaga-na?"

"Okemah has told Ara that she is to prepare and deliver Talasee and Tashi's food. I told her I have not heard that from you."

"Go back to your hearth and do your cooking. I will settle this in Council. Let Ara take whatever she has to Talasee this morning."

"I will go with Gaga-na," Cimmera said, combing her fingers through her hair. "It is because of me that this argument has arisen. I can at least stand with her."

Cherok bent to bundle up his bedding. He noticed a spot of blood on the skin that had been beneath them. Cimmera's face flushed.

"I will clean it," she said hurriedly, reaching out to take it.

"It means that you are my woman," he said, taking the blanket out of her reach. "Go and help Gaga-na."

Cimmera turned and took a step toward the ladder, but suddenly Cherok's hands were strong on her shoulders, turning her. He wrapped his arms around her and held her quietly for a moment.

"Now you can leave," he said.

She would have liked for him to pull her back.

"Give it to me," Cimmera said to Gaga-na. "Let me take the basket. If Ara comes back this morning, tell her the task is already done."

Jumak had shown no ill effects from swallowing the seed, but Gaga-na kept him close. He tried to wander off, but the old woman called to him.

"Can I go with Cimmera?" he asked.

Gaga-na thought for a moment. "No," she answered. "Not this time." She would have let him go but was afraid there might be an unpleasant confrontation with Ara or Okemah. Jumak's little head carried a heavy enough burden.

The boy plopped down by Gaga-na and watched

Cimmera stroll away.

The young woman turned around once and waved at him. Near Talasee's hearth, she called out and waited. When no one came out of the platform, she called again, louder.

Cimmera put the basket down. "I have brought you food," she called out, wandering a bit closer. "Fresh from Gaga-na." She stared at the platform, waiting for Talasee. "Are you there?" she called. "Talasee?"

Still there was no answer, and Cimmera took a few more steps toward the shelter. "Talasee?" she called again.

Finally the man appeared in the opening of the platform. His hair was disheveled, his expression twisted.

"She is gone," he said, his arms hanging loose at his sides, his shoulders slumping with sorrow. His voice sounded hoarse.

"Oh, Talasee, I am sorry," she said.

The man turned and disappeared into the shadows of his platform.

Cimmera left, but glanced back before returning to the hub of the village. She needed to tell Cherok.

The men were already gathering at the central hearth. She circled them, keeping a proper woman's distance, looking for him. He stood within the group of men. The Council had not begun yet.

"Cherok," she called softly, knowing that her summoning him away would cause some discussion.

Cherok looked over his shoulder.

Cimmera beckoned to him.

"What is wrong?" he asked.

"Tashi is dead."

Cherok took a deep breath, blowing it out his mouth. "And my friend?"

"Talasee looks distraught. He grieves, and I am certain he is exhausted. The end to that disease is not an easy one."

"I must go to him."

"No!" Cimmera said, too loud. "The disease lingers there and it may have jumped into Talasee. Please, Cherok, stay away."

"How can I do that? He has many friends. All of us will want to comfort him."

"You are the cacique, not just a man. Your people have already lost so much. What would they do if they also lost you? Tell them all to stay away, that Talasee must stay separated from the clan until enough time has passed so that we are sure he does not have the illness."

"Who will tell Talasee?" His handsome face sagged with the heaviness of his heart.

"Please," Cimmera said, avoiding Cherok's question. "Tell the men at Council. Protect yourself and your people."

Cherok walked back into the gathered men.

Okemah's distrustful eyes followed him as he left Cimmera. "That woman influences our cacique," he said softly to Dacoma.

The Council began with a prayer to the spirits for guidance. They prayed that their decisions would be made with wisdom.

Cherok began. "Atok and Dacoma will go on another journey in search of others. They will go soon." Cherok stood and walked over to Atok. "Take this with you." He handed Atok a small freshwater mussel shell that had a hole drilled in it and was threaded on a strand of fiber cord.

"And you, Dacoma," he said. "Take this." He held out a shark's tooth also threaded onto a loop of twisted fiber.

Atok and Dacoma nodded their appreciation.

"To keep you safe upon the waters," Cherok said.

The cacique looked over the men. Okemah wore a stubborn, challenging expression. Many things needed to be discussed, but first he had to tell them.

"Tashi has crossed over," he said.

Cherok heard their sighs and saw the defeat worming lines in their faces. He allowed them a moment.

He was ready to speak again when Okemah stood with his fists clenched.

"The spirits tell us to forget this idea of rebuilding. It is over for us here. Do you not see that? We will all perish if we stay!"

"No," Cherok said. "The times are hard, but we are a strong people. This earth is ours," he said, picking up a handful of the black dirt. "It is where our spirits linger. Do not be weak, Okemah."

"I am not weak. You are stubborn. Tashi has died. We will all die. Perhaps two or three of us will be spared, but the evil spirits that have killed Tashi are here in this village, and they will take us one by one."

"Not if we keep the evil spirits away. Did you not hear the woman, Cimmera?"

"Bah," Okemah spat out. "You listen to her because she relieves your man needs!"

"Hear what I say, Okemah, before you drown all our people in your discontent. If the woman's advice is good, then we will not die of the disease. Talasee will stay at his shelter, and we will continue to provide him with food. When enough time has passed, he will rejoin us."

"We cannot ask that of our friend," Dacoma said.

"We must."

"And what if the disease strikes us?" Okemah asked. "Then what will you do, Cacique? It will be too late to leave!"

"We wait and see, but for now I ask that you men of wisdom not forsake the pride and courage of our ancestors. Stand proud and do not be afraid to hear something new. If the time comes when another decision needs to be made, then we will make it. Talasee would not want to endanger us. He would give his life for his people. I know him."

"I know him, too," Okemah said, throwing a stick on the ground. He turned and walked out of Council.

"Do you have any pine boughs?" Cimmera asked. "Some that still have green needles?"

"She does," Jumak answered before Gaga-na had a chance.

"You get in too much of my business," the old woman said to the boy. "Go on."

Jumak gave Cimmera a big smile. "Well, she does. They are under her platform. I saw them there."

"Get!" Gaga-na said, shooing him away with her stick.

Jumak skipped away, taunting Gaga-na with his grin.

"The boy is …"

"I know," Cimmera said. "May I have a small portion of your pine?"

"What will you use it for?"

Cimmera fixed her eyes on the woman's. She knew that the Tegesta added green pine to their fires to create smoke and help keep the insects away. She also knew that, when cured, it made good kindling.

She was not going to use it for either of those reasons.

After a long pause Cimmera finally spoke. "May I have some?"

Gaga-na looked hard at the young woman in front of her. "There," she said, pointing under her shelter with her gnarled finger.

Cimmera nodded her thanks, more for not prying than for the pine. Gaga-na nodded back and watched her leave.

The men were still in Council, and none of them would see what she did and try to stop her. The women were busy with the children and daily chores, but they still might notice and question. So Cimmera left the village and walked behind the shelters, deeper in cover.

She reentered the village and stopped when she came to the basket she had left earlier for Talasee and Tashi. Bugs crawled over it.

This was a dangerous thing she did; she knew that. Perspiration beaded on her forehead. She hurried across the clearing, approaching Talasee's ladder. She paused at the base, said a quick silent prayer, and then climbed up.

CHAPTER 17

TALASEE SAT SLUMPED in the corner of his platform, his head lolling, his chin on his chest, and his shoulders sagging.

"Talasee," Cimmera said softly.

His dark-rimmed eyes found her standing in the light of the opening.

"I know that you are suffering," she said. "My heart feels your grief."

Talasee looked at the body of his wife. "No one knows my grief."

"I know that the pain is great. I know that you never want anyone else to suffer as Tashi has … as you have."

"I did what Cherok said I should."

"Yes, you did. You have spared so many." Cimmera stepped closer, then sat in front of him. "But it is not over."

"Tashi is dead," he said, wiping his hand down over his eyes.

"But the evil spirit that made her so sick, the horrid one that has taken her from you, never dies. Talasee, that terrible spirit may have found its way into you."

"No!" Talasee's jaw tensed.

"That is how it survives. The evil spirit jumps from person to person. You have been close enough to Tashi that it could have gotten into you."

"I am not sick."

Cimmera shook her head. "It hides for a while so that you do not suspect it is there."

Talasee clutched his face in his hands, clawing at his hairline.

"I have come to tell you what I know. You are a good man, and you love your people."

"Go away," he said. "Leave me."

Cimmera touched his hand, which had fallen to his side. "In my village we have seen how this bad spirit works. You and your people have suffered enough. You can keep even more anguish from them."

Talasee looked up at her. "What do you mean?"

"Cherok will sacrifice himself for you. You are his friend. He wants to come to you, be with you during your grief. I have told him how dangerous this can be for him and for all the clan. He must think of everyone, and you must, also. Hear what I have come to say."

Okemah's feet trod heavily, kicking up the dust from the dry earth as he strode toward Talasee's hearth. He would show them that this woman was a liar. Cherok was beguiled by her, trapped by the warm clasp of her woman's passage. Their cacique was no more than a rutting stag. He probably could sniff her scent even when she was so far away he could not see her. Yes, Cherok probably could not get his mind off how soft her flesh was in his hands, how sweet on his tongue. The cacique dwelled on the feel of that woman, wet, hot, clamping around his man part, squeezing him as he drove long and deep inside her.

Okemah shuddered and shook his head. He would look for Narchise as soon as he had talked with Talasee.

Talasee was his friend, and he would not leave him alone in his time of need. As he drew closer, he slowed down. There was the slightest chance that even if the woman was a bad spirit, she could be right about how the sickness spread. Her explanation did make some sense, but he did not believe any of her talk.

Okemah paused. No, he would not go to Talasee yet. Perhaps in a few days. No matter his feelings, he should not blatantly defy the cacique. That would do too much damage to the clan.

Out the corner of his eye he saw someone moving through the brush behind the shelters. His curiosity was piqued, so he crept closer, watching for more movement.

Then he saw Cimmera dash across the open space of the mound. What was she doing? Why did she go into Talasee's platform? This was indeed strange. Perhaps Cimmera was just what he had thought, an evil spirit. After all, if she was telling the truth about the sickness, she would surely avoid this place.

Okemah hid behind a stand of trees, waiting and watching. He regretted that he was too far away to hear what was said inside the platform. What were they doing in there? He grew impatient after a while and revived his thoughts of Narchise. Okemah decided to leave and find that woman who stirred his loins so, but just then he saw Talasee and Cimmera appear. They lowered Tashi's body down the ladder.

Okemah followed them, creeping in the cover of the trees and brush. He could hear their voices.

"There is no shaman to guide Tashi's spirit," Talasee said, his voice cracking. He held his woman's body in his arms as if she were only sleeping.

In one hand Cimmera carried a hoe. In the other she held a black pot and something wrapped in a small fur.

"I will help her find her way," she said.

Talasee continued on and carried his wife down the

path that led to the slough. Cimmera followed.

They sloshed through the shallow water, then up onto the hump of land where the clan buried their dead.

"Here," Talasee said.

Okemah stopped at the open slough and found cover in the brush.

Cimmera looked back, sensing someone was watching. "You must hurry," she said, "before Council ends."

Talasee laid Tashi's body on the ground and took the conch hoe from Cimmera.

"Our first child rests here. An infant boy," he said, breaking the ground, pulling away the top layer of dusty soil and leaves. Beneath that, the black muck, musty and dank, came away in clots.

He worked in silence until the shallow grave was complete. Cimmera gathered some stones. When Talasee stepped back, she withdrew a handful of petals and leaves from a pouch at her side. She sprinkled them in the grave, and after Talasee had laid Tashi in the depression, she spread the rest over the body.

"Talasee?" she said, taking a small lump of red ocher from the pouch and holding it out in her palm.

He stared at her a moment, then nodded and stepped back.

Cimmera knelt over the dead woman. She closed her eyes and hummed softly. She said the A-po-la-chee words in her head.

A warm breeze sifted through the trees, and Talasee's hair bristled on his arms and the back of his neck.

Cimmera finished the song and then drew spirit signs on Tashi's face and body with the red ocher.

Talasee recognized most of the markings. He had seen Mi-sa and the shaman before her, Mi-sa's father, make the same lines, but the last mark Cimmera painted on Tashi's forehead was a design with which he was not familiar. He opened his mouth to say something, but at the same time Cimmera lifted her arms toward the sky, and he thought he felt the earth vibrate beneath his feet. He looked at the few white clouds splattered on the brilliant blue. Where had the thunder come from?

Cimmera lifted the dead woman's pot she had brought with her. She placed it above Tashi's head, then smashed it with a stone.

"Her spirit is free," Cimmera said. "Cover her and put these stones at her feet and at her head. Two small piles. Stay here while I return to your platform. What I have to do will not take long. Watch the sky. You will know when to return."

"How have you come to know these things?" Talasee asked.

"I am from a different village," she answered, then walked away.

She stopped once, overcome by uneasiness. Someone was watching. She lit a pitch stick in Talasee's fire and carried it inside his shelter.

Narchise sidled up to Tichini. "Did you have an eventful evening?" she asked the younger woman.

"I thought the festivities were wonderful," Tichini answered. "Yes, I had a very good evening."

The youthful sparkle in her eyes told the story, Narchise thought. The older woman took up a pinch of herbs and held them over the brewing cabbage palm stew.

"No more," Tichini said. "I have added enough already."

Narchise ladled out some broth with a mussel shell and tasted it. "Not hearty enough," she said.

"Really?" Tichini spooned up a taste of the soup. She

let it sit in her mouth for a moment before swallowing it. "I think it is fine."

"Well, it is not fine. Cooking, like some other things, is best done by someone with experience. After many seasons your stew will be almost as good as mine."

Tichini blinked, thinking she had caught Narchise's double meaning. "Of course you have more experience. You are older. I am certain your stew tastes different from mine. Your pot has acquired all the old flavors. Almost anything you cook in that pot will taste the same ...good but no variety. My pot is not as old." Tichini sighed. "Some things you can change, and others you cannot."

Narchise tasted the broth again, then dropped in the herbs. She turned her back on Tichini and walked away.

The plump woman's eyes stung, and she feared she might cry. Okemah must have stayed with that skinny woman, joined with her last night. Anger took over, and her face turned red. She huffed as she walked, mumbling her discontent.

"Ugly old man," she said. If she ever had a chance to touch his man part again she would give it a quick hard jerk. Then the corners of her lips hiked up into a sassy grin. Perhaps even better, she would reach a little lower, grab those unsightly dangling skin pouches and surprise him with a less than tender squeeze. Why did men think their parts were so wonderful? Those things were strange-looking. If she had them she was sure she would not feel so much pride in such queer growths.

Narchise wrapped a lock of her hair around her finger, twirling it as she thought. Tichini did not know what she was up against. She might have those perky little breasts, but Narchise had experience.

She spotted Gaga-na at her hearth, repairing a basket.

"What do you think about this woman?" Narchise blurted out.

"What woman?"

"Cimmera. Is she strange? Does she do peculiar things?" Narchise swayed as she talked, and her finger danced on her lips.

"Sit, Narchise. Be still. You make me jittery."

Narchise sat. She chewed on the nail of her little finger.

"Why would I think Cimmera is strange?"

Narchise shrugged. "Do you?"

"No. I wish you would explain yourself. You did not just wake up this morning and wonder what I thought about Cimmera."

Narchise leaned forward and whispered. "Could she be an evil spirit?"

Gaga-na put the basket aside. "You have been listening to Okemah and his rotten tongue. He is so surly."

"I think she could have some kind of powers, but I do not know what they might be."

"You have no reason to say that." Gaga-na's voice was edged with anger.

"Yes, I do."

"What? Tell me something."

Narchise sat back, her fingers drumming on her thighs, her nose twitching like a rabbit's.

"And be still!" Gaga-na said.

"Just a suspicion," Narchise finally answered.

"Suspicion is not a good enough reason to insinuate such a thing. It is a lie."

Narchise vigorously shook her head. "No, no, no," she whispered, looking down at her lap and her hand as it cracked the knuckles on the other. "It is not a lie."

"Narchise, explain yourself. Get it out."

"I saw her do magic. No one else knows but Okemah."

"I do not believe that," Gaga-na said, picking up her basket again.

"I did. She healed a tree. I saw it happen, but she did not see me."

"What did you see?"

"She put her hand on the place where she had stripped bark, and a moment later the wound was healed. If she can do that, I think she can do other things. I want to ask her for some help."

Gaga-na's eyes were sharp and angry. "Leave her alone. You think you saw something. If she had magic, we would all know. Do not go around telling this to others."

Narchise rose to her feet. She remembered exactly what she had seen. Exactly. She ambled across the mound. The men were still in Council. When she passed in front of Cherok's platform she hesitated.

She edged closer to the ladder, humming nonchalantly while fretfully scanning the village. She glanced up at the opening, then back at the men. The woman curled her hand around a rung. She might be able to scramble up the ladder before anyone noticed, but she was bulky and clumsy. Narchise let go of the ladder and moved on.

Maybe Cimmera would agree to help her if she told her what she knew about her.

Cimmera moved away the sour cloths Talasee had used to sponge Tashi and made a circle of pine boughs in the center of the shelter, carefully overlapping the ends. The rancid smell of sickness and death was thick in the shadows.

When the circle was complete, Cimmera stepped inside and sat in the center of it, cross-legged, her hands resting on her knees, palms up with the star knife lying across them. The burning pitch stick rested inside a shell. She took several deep breaths, emptying her mind, preparing herself. She waited.

The warmth of the knife brought a smile to her lips.

"Sing with me," the deep voice said.

Cimmera left her eyes closed, relieved that Tamar was going to guide her. Talasee's shelter needed to be purified, and she was not confident she remembered everything that had to be done.

"Listen and you will remember," Tamar whispered.

Then his voice resonated within the confines of the shelter, and Cimmera soon knew the song. The words were simple, the song a gentle melody.

The chant ended, and then she heard the deep voice inside her head.

Cimmera lifted the pitch stick and stared at the glow.

"Yes, Tamar," she whispered. She held the small flame to the pine boughs.

CHAPTER 18

OKEMAH STILL HID IN THE BRUSH. What was Cimmera doing in there?

He rubbed his eyes. Were those wisps of ghostly spirits slipping through the thatch? His mouth fell open when the smoke billowed out of Talasee's platform.

He heard the thudding footsteps coming from behind him. Others had also seen the smoke. Okemah sank back into the forest.

"Stay back!" Cherok ordered those who followed him.

Talasee emerged from the trees. Cimmera had told him to watch the sky. When it cleared, the purification would be complete. But he heard the ruckus, and the smoke was thicker than he thought it should be, so he returned. Talasee glanced back and saw Cherok.

"Where is Cimmera?" Talasee asked, expecting to see her with the others. As soon as he asked, he realized where she was. He spun to see his platform, then back to Cherok. "She is inside."

A shiver of fear rippled down the cacique's back, and he ran to Talasee's ladder. He scrambled up, choking and coughing when he went inside the smoke-filled shelter. He put his hand over his nose and mouth and squinted as he fumbled through the platform, searching for her.

"Do you have her?" Talasee asked, following Cherok and dropping to his hands and knees to feel his way along the floor. The green pine needles had not caused a flame, only a thick, acrid smoke.

Cherok bumped into something. Frantically his hand explored.

"Cimmera," he said, feeling her shoulder and limp arm. He lifted her and carried her to the opening.

Talasee rushed down the ladder and helped lower her to the ground. Cherok knelt beside her. The villagers stared, their low mumblings to one another sounding like insects' droning. He put his hand beneath her nose, feeling for her breath. He bent over her, replacing his hand with his cheek. Everyone grew still.

Cherok picked her up, her arms dangling, her head tipped back, her hair falling free, swishing against his thighs.

"Is she alive?" Talasee asked.

"Yes," Cherok answered just as she sputtered and coughed.

"Hurry away," Talasee said. "The sickness may be inside me."

Cherok looked at his old friend, so thin and beaten-looking.

"Go," Talasee said.

Cherok carried Cimmera through the village. Jumak and Gaga-na cleared a space beneath Cherok's platform in the cool of the shade. The cacique laid her there, then propped her head in his lap.

The clan gathered around, curious about this woman who had asked their leader to forbid them to go near Talasee, and yet she had gone.

Narchise paced in the back of the crowd, peeking over shoulders and through bodies to catch a glimpse of the woman now and again.

Cherok wiped Cimmera's face with a damp cloth that Gaga-na provided. The coughing finally subsided.

"My mother is dead?" Jumak asked.

There had not been an opportunity to tell the boy.

Gaga-na pulled his head to her and held tightly. Cherok gave him the answer. "She has crossed over. The spirits have called her."

Jumak turned his face into the body of the old woman.

Cimmera opened her red-streaked eyes, reached out, and touched the boy's leg. "I am sorry," she whispered.

Jumak pulled away from Gaga-na and then bolted. Cimmera sat up and called hoarsely for him.

"I will go," Cherok said.

Cimmera fell back against him. "He needs to cry. Let him go. He does not want you to see him."

Cherok smoothed her hair back from her delicate face. "Come," he said, helping her to her feet, putting his arm around her waist and supporting her.

She took a step up the ladder and swayed. His hand against her back steadied her.

Inside the platform Cimmera lay down on the floor and coughed weakly. Cherok moved beside her.

"I am angry with you," he said.

Cimmera looked at him. "The smoke came too fast. I could not see—"

Cherok interrupted. "You talk such sense to me, and then you put yourself at risk. I cannot lose you, woman. I have just found you."

"I am not leaving you," she whispered, reaching up and touching her palm to his cheek. Cimmera's throat was raw and her words raspy.

"Do not talk now," he said, smoothing her long hair. He stared down at her. Her eyes closed, and Cherok tilted back his head. She had been purifying Talasee's platform. The smoke smelled strongly of pine. But only a shaman performed such rituals. The smoke carried the magical holy words. It seeped into every crevice and drove out the hiding evil spirits.

Cherok gazed at the woman as she drifted into sleep. He knew there was going to be more trouble. Okemah would never let this rest. He would use this to accuse her of being connected to bad spirits.

Cherok studied her face. He could not believe there was evil inside her. Still, she had known that Jumak was in danger, and there were other small things that gave him the sense she was someone special. Now this. If she was a shaman, why did she not tell them? Why would she want to hide her gift? Okemah would say that there was only one reason.

Cherok felt his gut tighten; He did not really know the woman who had his heart. She hid dark secrets.

Gaga-na tapped the ladder with her stick. "I am coming up," she said, already balancing on the lowest rung.

"Go and find the boy," she whispered when she was beside him. "I will stay with Cimmera." She waved her hand at him and sat.

Tichini hung back after the crowd left. She stood among the trees, watching. Talasee sat by his hearth.

When the smoke cleared, Talasee climbed the ladder, and Tichini turned to leave. Now that the air was clear; she could see what a beautiful day it was. She thought it refreshing to wander alone in the dense forest, amid the vines, trees, and wildflowers just coming into bloom.

Her bare feet made little noise as she wandered. She was good at moving silently. As a child she had watched the boys practice their stalking skills. She had mimicked them, and she had practiced, not because she wanted to hunt but because it was wonderful to get so close to so many creatures.

The noisy rattle of brush made her look toward the sound. Okemah lumbered through the woods.

She giggled with the notion to sneak up on him. She hid until he passed her, then hurried up behind him, her feet so lightly touching the ground that he did not hear her. Okemah was making enough noise of his own.

Tichini's eyes twinkled with mischief. She reached both hands toward him, then poked his sides with her fingers. He grunted, jumped, and wheeled around. She squealed, staggered back a few steps, then wrapped her arms tightly around her middle and bent over in laughter.

Okemah's face pulled into a snarl, but Tichini kept laughing.

"The look on your ..." She couldn't keep on, the laughter overwhelming her.

In a moment Okemah's mouth kinked into a muddled smile, and a low, unsure chuckle came forth. His laugh grew louder, spurred on by Tichini's inability to control herself.

Okemah's slanted smile warned her of retaliation.

"No," she said, backing up.

He bent forward from the waist, taking on a fighting posture. Okemah growled, his big threatening steps closing in.

"No, Okemah. No," Tichini begged through her laughter.

Okemah jumped at her, his fingers digging into her waist.

Tichini wailed and wrestled from his tickling. She twisted and broke away, running back to the village. The big man bounded right behind her.

"Stop, Okemah," she shrieked and spun around, running backward as she entered the village. "Stop! No!"

He stalked her, rumbling his threats. "I have you now.

There is no getting away."

Tichini stood still. Her sudden change stopped the hulk of man who pursued her.

"You are too much for me," she said.

"Arghh," Okemah growled as he lunged at her, his burly arms reaching out. They stumbled and went down onto the ground, Tichini's giggling and Okemah's grunting attracting a lot of attention.

He rolled to his back, giving up the game, too overcome. He bellowed his laughter, his eyes squeezed shut, his big belly shaking.

Tichini sprawled next to him, and she was suddenly silent.

Okemah opened his eyes.

"Narchise!" He scrambled to sit upright.

"Okemah," she said coldly, "perhaps I should send Jumak to join you." She walked away.

Okemah's shoulders dropped. Tichini tickled his waist, but instead of laughing, he sighed, then stood soberly and dusted himself off.

"Now you have done it," he mumbled to himself. "You will never have her now." He looked up, his dark eyes sad and disappointed, fixed on that luscious woman with the plush flesh as she walked away from him.

Narchise was glad he could not see her face, for she was sure that anyone who looked close enough would see through her expression of unconcern. Beneath that outward layer was hurt. Also shining deep in her eyes were perseverance and determination. She wanted this man and would have him!

She marched straight to Cherok's hearth and called up.

Gaga-na peered out. "Cherok is not here."

"Good," Narchise said. "It is Cimmera I want to see."

"Leave her be," Gaga-na said. "She is resting."

Cimmera sat up and coughed. Her head pounded, the pungent smell and taste of the pine smoke still in her nose, throat, and mouth. She couldn't rid herself of that sluggish and disoriented feeling. Her head was just beginning to clear. "Let her come," she said.

"I heard her," the plump woman said from below. She struggled up the ladder and then went inside the platform. She sat next to Gaga-na so that she faced Cimmera. "You can do magic."

"If you have come to be friendly, then stay. Otherwise curb your tongue and leave," Gaga-na said.

"What is wrong, Narchise?" Cimmera asked. "I see something in your eyes."

"It is Okemah. He is old and likes to feel young. Tichini makes a fool of him."

Gaga-na smirked. "I have heard that you make him feel young, also—rolling around in the dirt like opossums for all to see."

Narchise tugged at a strand of her hair, curling it around her finger. Her eye twitched. "He could not keep himself from me. He could not wait."

Cimmera smiled.

"This Tichini, she tempts him," Narchise said. "Have you seen her, Cimmera? Juicy red lips, breasts that bounce when she walks, her dark nipples peeping through her hair at just the right times, like two sniffing raccoon noses." Narchise made a jerky motion with her head, wrinkling her nose and mimicking the animals. "And round hips that sway with her step. Flat belly. Look at me."

"Okemah must like what he sees in you," Cimmera said.

"As I told you, he is old and wants to be young. I

cannot compete with Tichini."

"Why are you here?" Gaga-na asked.

"She does magic. I know she does. I saw her." Narchise faced Cimmera. "The tree. I saw what you did. I want your help."

Cimmera shook her head. "I cannot help you. I do not know how."

Narchise clucked her tongue, looking around inside. "That is yours?" she asked, pointing to Cimmera's basket.

"Yes," Cimmera answered.

Narchise reached for it. Cimmera's hand quickly gripped her wrist. Suddenly Cimmera felt panic pour through her. She had been so disoriented she had forgotten about the knife! Talasee must have found it by now. She had to go back to his platform and get it.

Narchise stared at the basket. "What do you have inside it? Magical talismans and amulets? A witch's knife? That is what Okemah says you are—a witch. Why will you not help me?"

"Enough," Gaga-na said. Narchise was upsetting Cimmera. "Leave," she said, prodding Narchise with her walking stick.

"I do not care if my help comes from the Darkside." Narchise descended the ladder.

"Never mind her," Gaga-na said. "You must know how she is."

"I would help her if I could." Cimmera sounded distracted. Her mind was whirling. She could not go and retrieve the knife now. She had to be patient. At least no one but Talasee would see it. But how would she explain to him?

Gaga-na rocked and started to hum, but Cimmera interrupted her.

"What do you think of me, Gaga-na? What do you

think I am?" Cimmera lay down again.

"I think you are the woman for our cacique. It is time for him to take a woman."

"Not that. You have many seasons of wisdom. Tell me what you think of me."

"All right," Gaga-na said. "When I first saw you getting out of the canoe, the day you arrived, I knew there was something special about you. I cannot explain it. But there have been little things. I think Narchise is right about the magic, but I do not think it is magic from the Darkside. I believe that even you do not know where it comes from. I also think you keep secrets."

Cimmera turned onto her side, away from the old woman, and curled her body into a ball.

"Everyone smelled the pine—the pine you got from me. People are asking questions."

Cimmera's voice was frail. "I did what was the custom in my village—to help your people."

"My people?"

"All of us," Cimmera corrected herself, feeling the clutch of her lies at her throat.

"Purification after death is only done by a shaman. That is the Tegesta way."

"My village was far away. Our customs are different."

"Yes, they appear to be," Gaga-na said with eyebrows arched.

They were silent for a while, each woman's mind winnowing and sorting through all the entanglements.

Gaga-na rubbed her aching leg and puffed a breath over her bottom lip, blowing a strand of hair from her face. She patted Cimmera's shoulder. "I have something to take care of," she said.

Okemah stepped inside Narchise's empty platform.

"Woman!"

Immediately he saw she was not there, but he could smell her. She had a certain scent, one that went straight through his nostrils to his groin. He picked up her sleeping skin and held it to his nose. She was going to have him crazy soon enough.

Okemah rubbed the soft hide against his chest, the bottom of it brushing against his thighs, reminding him of Narchise's hair touching him there. He threw the blanket on the floor. He could not stand any more of this arousal without relief. If he was to carry out the business of the day, he would have to do something about this.

At the base of the ladder he scanned the village. Narchise was nowhere in sight. Okemah shifted his stiff manroot, the touch of his hand deciding for him what he would do. He hurried across the mound to the privacy of his shelter.

Without removing his breechclout, Okemah slipped out his man part. He encircled himself, sucked in a deep breath, and felt his legs go fluid with anticipation.

"Okemah!" Gaga-na's gravelly voice called from below.

The big man froze for an instant. Then he ignored her, closed his eyes, pictured Narchise peeled raw of adornments and skirt, and went on with his crucial undertaking. He thought Gaga-na would leave.

"Come down. An old woman wants to speak with you."

He only needed a few more moments. Why would she not go away? She was destroying his concentration. His temper was rising, ruffling the image he held of Narchise, spoiling—

"Get your miserable self down here."

Okemah felt his need wither and wilt in his hand. He

tucked himself back in, feeling the low ache of denial cramp in his groin.

"What is it?" he said as he climbed down. "You have become a pest, Gaga-na. Were it not for your age, I would not give you enough respect to answer your call."

"I want your tongue to be still. Stop this cruel talk about Cimmera. You divide our clan at a time when we cannot be separated."

Okemah turned back to the ladder. She had called him out of his platform, interrupted him, for this chiding. He turned and climbed up the ladder.

"You hear me, old ugly man. Stop and think of what this talk will bring."

Okemah disappeared inside.

"You are going to have to be a strong spirit," Gaga-na whispered to Cimmera.

She brushed the young woman's hair away from her face, moving it back over her shoulder.

"What is this?" She leaned closer, her aged cloudy eyes taking time to focus.

CHAPTER 19

CIMMERA'S HAIR FELL over her neck as she rolled onto her back to look at the old woman. "What?" she asked.

Gaga-na's face was pale, her eyes reflecting the surge of shock that had just coursed through her.

Cimmera sat up, her head swimming. She steadied herself and worked to focus her eyes. The dizziness passed.

"Gaga-na? What is it?"

The old woman shivered. She reached out and stroked Cimmera's hair, tears pooling in her eyes. "Nothing, young one." Her voice was dreamy-sounding, as if her mind were drifting somewhere else. "These old eyes deceive me. I thought there was a bug crawling through your hair. But there was nothing. Only a clip of wind that blew through. Rest now."

Cimmera spoke softly, her throat still desiccated. "I feel much better now. I am growing restless. You fuss over me too much. The sunshine and fresh air are good things. This platform is too dark and gloomy."

Gaga-na's knobby old fingers gripped her walking stick, and she hoisted herself up. Her thready silver hair, sprinkled with a few strands of black, hung limp. Her cheeks were hollow, her sun-leathered skin creasing and folding, adding what many thought was a look of wisdom to her face. Her lips were thin and drawn with age, pulled in as if she had no teeth. Only once had she had trouble with her teeth. The crown of a molar had worn away, but that was not what had caused the pain. After many years of working leather, running strands of sinew between that tooth and the one in front of it, a deep crevice had formed, eating down past the gum line, exposing the sensitive root. She had removed the tooth herself. She positioned the strong columella of a conch shell against the molar, then struck it with a stone, knocking free the tooth that pained her. That tooth, along with her baby teeth and totems, was in the pouch she wore around her neck.

Gaga-na smacked her lips and ran her tongue into the hole where her molar used to be. She tossed her head, gesturing for Cimmera to leave with her.

Jumak stood beneath the platform.

"What has happened?" Cimmera asked, startled at the look of him. His hair hung in ragged lengths.

"You cut your hair," Cimmera said.

"I mourn," Jumak said.

Cimmera's eyes darted about the village as she looked for Cherok.

"It is the custom," Jumak said.

Gaga-na braced herself with the stick and walked closer. "You are a boy. This is the way a man mourns." She looked into the boy's face.

"I am a man in my heart," Jumak said.

"Lend me your knife," Cimmera said to Gaga-na. The old woman handed her the sharp cooking knife. Cimmera took the boy's hand and led him away. "Tell Cherok that Jumak is with me."

Cimmera lifted a handful of water and splashed it on Jumak's hair, then smoothed it. "We need to make it more even. You are in a rush to be a man," she said.

"My hair will take a long time to grow?" he asked.

"Yes."

Jumak wanted it to take long. "It will take a long time for my heart to heal."

"Sit down, now," she told him, backing him out of the ankle-deep water.

"The water used to come to here," the boy said, pointing to the old waterline. "What will happen if it does not rain?"

Cimmera took Gaga-na's knife and sawed at the longest strands of Jumak's hair. "The earth will turn brown and gray. That place where the water is will become dry and will crack and scorch. The fish will bake in the sun. The birds will find no minnows and no snails. They will abandon their nests. A drought is a terrible thing."

She watched the black hair fall to the ground.

"What else?"

Cimmera sat back on her heels. "The alligators will dig out holes that will fill with water. The animals will be so thirsty they will risk their lives to gather there to quench their thirst, predator and prey in the same space. The snail eggs that cluster on the saw grass will hatch, and the new lives will fall to dry ground, where they will perish. The snail hawk will find no food for itself or its offspring. The panther and the bear, the raccoon and the deer, will suffer for food and water. And the worst will be the fires, sweeping, blazing fires that will burn on and on off the dry tinder. The sky will be black with smoke, and ash will fall over us all. The People will have to be ever alert, ready to flee, even in the middle of the night."

"I want it to rain," Jumak said.

"Yes, we all do."

"Droughts have come before."

"After the fires leave and the rains return, new growth will sprout. The roots of the saw grass will live on, and the tender shoots will be fine food for the deer. The heavy branches that blocked the sunlight will be gone, and new young growth will flourish in the light. There is a plan to it all. It is a natural cycle."

Jumak drew one hank of hair toward his face to inspect it. "The Great Spirit does not make our lives simple."

The boy had more wisdom than most children, she thought. She gave him a smile. "You are growing up too fast, Jumak. Do not take on adult burdens too early."

He pitched a stone into the water. "Are you a witch?"

"Jumak!"

"You do magic. Everyone whispers about it."

"My ways may seem like magic," she said, "but that is just because they are different from yours."

"Only a shaman can drive out evil spirits." Suddenly he flung his arms around her. "I do not care if you are a witch."

Cimmera couldn't speak. Perhaps she was a witch—a terrible, evil one. What else could she be? she thought, recalling that day she forgot who she was, remembering the blood running over her body in the rain. Maybe all the A-po-la-chee were evil.

Cimmera embraced Jumak. "They whisper about what I did in your father's platform?"

Jumak drew back to look at her. "Yes. Okemah used to mumble, but now he talks aloud about it."

"Jumak, my village is different from yours. There are different customs. Where I come from, burning pine boughs in the house of the dead drives out the evil spirits."

"But here—" the child began.

"Shh. I know what you are going to say. Only a person of the spirits can do such things."

Jumak nodded.

"I wanted to help. It is not so strange for someone in my village to do such things."

"I am glad that you did," Jumak said, putting his arms around her again. "I miss my mother," he said, his voice cracking. "And I am so afraid for my father."

"When you are a man, if you are fortunate, you will know what it is to have a wife. Your father wished to stay with your mother, even if it meant endangering himself. He had great love for her. If he becomes ill and crosses over, he will be with her again. That is not a scary thing for him. And he sees you, so strong and courageous. He knows that you will carry on. Be proud, not afraid."

Jumak wiped his tears and nose. "I will come here each day. It is a good place to sing lamenting songs until my hair grows long again."

Cimmera touched the end of his nose with her fingertip.

"He has a courageous spirit." It was Cherok.

Jumak looked up and smiled at the cacique. "If I were a girl I would have scarified my legs …and I would not have cried when I did it. I would have cut deep enough to leave scars."

The evening star shone brightly as the men gathered, sitting on their haunches about the fire. Cherok took the reed stem of the pipe into his mouth and drew heavily on it as he lowered a small coal from the fire into the stone bowl atop the marlberry tobacco mixture. The soft wood of elder was sometimes used for the stem, but like the elder fruit, it was used only in times of scarcity.

Cherok blew a puff toward the sky and then passed

the pipe to his left, following the path of the sun. The men crouched in silence, listening to the lessons of the pipe. The stem was the connection to the supernatural world where the sagacity of all things was brought to a single point.

The pipe traveled around the circle, ending in Cherok's hand again. The cacique rose to his feet. "We know the story of the bear. Let us take heed. Bears were once men, but they were too lazy, and so they were changed into animals. We must not become so lazy, so afraid, so miserable, so doubtful, that we do not go on. We must not turn on one another."

There was a low rumble of agreement among the men. Okemah said nothing. He stared away from the cacique, across the village.

Cimmera took advantage of the shadows as she slipped across the mound toward Talasee, who sat outside his platform by his fire.

"Your son has also cut his hair," she said. Talasee's hair was shorter, and the lock he usually kept in a braid now hung loose.

"He becomes a man too soon." Talasee blew out a long breath. "You take your chances coming here. What keeps you from the sickness?"

"As you said, I take my chances. Someone must linger near the sick person for a long time or many times for the illness to get in."

Talasee shook his head. "We have all seen the illness pass more easily than that sometimes."

"Yes," she said, "we have. I put my health in the hands of the spirits."

"Why have you come?"

"I left something here."

"What would be so important that you risk your health

to retrieve it?"

Cimmera cleared her throat. "It is a personal item of sentimental value."

Talasee moved the food basket aside. "This?" He lifted the star knife that had been hidden by the basket.

Cimmera reached out, but Talasee pulled the knife back.

"Strange markings," he said, turning it in the firelight. "Some of them I have never seen before. What about this one?" he asked, pointing to the same design that Cimmera had drawn on Tashi with the ocher. He looked up sharply.

"They are all spirit symbols."

"And the blade ..." He thumped it with his fingernail. "Do you hear that? I know nothing that makes that sound." Again he turned the knife in his hands, scrutinizing it. "I do not know this substance. It is not wood or stone. Not shell. Tell me," he said, looking back at her. "What is this? Where does it come from?"

"The knife is from my village. I saved it during the storm."

"Fleeing from the great storm, you searched out this knife? Or was it yours already?"

"Talasee, I have done what I could for Tashi and for you. I have used the things I know to be helpful. I cannot tell you any more about the knife except that it helps me do these things. It was precious to my people, and so I saved it during the storm. The man who kept it was killed."

"This is not Tegesta," he said.

"I do not know what it is or where it comes from."

"There is more," he said, ending his statement with a slow, sure nod. "Who are you?"

"Talasee, please give me the knife."

He stared at her for a long time, and Cimmera held her breath.

"You were right when you said Cherok would sacrifice himself for a friend," Talasee said. "But why have you risked your life by coming to help me?"

"It is the right thing to do. I wish for your clan to survive. I want to help."

"He is vulnerable."

"Who?" Cimmera asked, confused by his jump in thought.

"Our cacique. I watched him even when we first found you. You have a place in his heart no woman has ever had before. He is responsible for those of us who are left, for how we will continue. Do not complicate his life. I do not understand who you are. Perhaps the spirits sent you to help us." He held the knife out to her.

"If others know about the knife, they will not understand," she said.

Talasee nodded. "I wish to show you something before you leave." He held out a large leaf.

"You have drawn figures in the leaf."

"Tashi," he said, pointing to the rounder figure. "And me," he said, indicating the other. "Do you know what we do with something like this?"

"No," Cimmera said.

"If you want a dream to come true, you draw it on a leaf and put it beneath your head when you sleep. I dream that I am with my wife."

"Your life need not be over. In time, when your hair is long again, you can take another woman."

"No," Talasee said. "I have had a dream. It has come to me four times. All dreams are sacred, but when it comes to a man four times, the dream is more than that. The dream forbids me to ever take another."

"Do not be hasty," she said. "Ask the spirits to speak."

Talasee looked at the leaf again, ignoring what she said. "Tell me about my son before I sleep," he said.

"He is strong and brave."

"Good." Talasee turned his face away from the fire so that it was hidden by the shadows.

Cimmera held her knife close to her chest and left. She hurried through the village, wanting to hide the knife before anyone saw it.

It was just past dusk, the early part of the evening. The men still sat with the pipe, and the women were preparing the shelters for sleep.

"Cimmera!"

She whipped around, holding the knife behind her back.

"It is Narchise. I am glad I found you."

"What is it, Narchise?"

"I know you can help me." She leaned to one side. "What is behind you? What do you have?"

Cimmera stepped back. "What do you think I can help you with?"

"I know what it is," Narchise said, moving toward her. "It is the knife. The one I saw you with when you healed the tree."

"Narchise," Cimmera said, "tell me what you want."

Narchise attempted to take a last peek around Cimmera, but she was unsuccessful.

"Help me get Okemah," the heavy woman said. "You have secrets, magical secrets. I will never tell. What can you do? Give me a potion? Say some magical chants?"

"I have told you before, there is nothing I can do."

"I did not tell others about the knife. Why do you not reward my discretion?"

Narchise edged closer and closer, her face twitching as

she talked, her hands rolling over each other.

"Go and tell Okemah how you feel. I believe that he would be glad to hear it."

Cimmera turned around, moving the knife in front of her. "Good-bye," she said, twisting her head over her shoulder and walking away.

Narchise mumbled her misgivings. She was so involved with her mutterings that she did not see Gaga-na.

"Why do you pester her?" the old woman asked.

"She could help me, but she will not. She should be grateful to me. I keep secrets about her."

"Your imagination works too hard. Leave the woman alone."

"Look there," Narchise said, pointing toward the central hearth. The gathering of men had broken up, and Tichini walked past them. "See how they watch her. I cannot compete with that for Okemah."

"Take care of your own business and leave Cimmera out of it," Gaga-na said. She tapped Narchise's leg with her stick.

Gaga-na hobbled off, moving as quickly as she could. The men were dispersing to prepare for the night. She watched Cimmera climb inside the platform. Gaga-na hid in the shadows, watching, guarding, even after Cherok also went into the platform. She would not let anyone hurt the young woman. No one.

Cherok slipped his hands down Cimmera's back as she stood looking out the platform. "Are you afraid?" he asked.

"Of what?"

"The talk. Okemah's wretchedness."

"Do you believe what he says?"

"I know that there is something special about you.

More than clan customs. You are a part of this clan now, and we will learn to accept different ways. Some people will just take longer to do so."

"I wish it was not like this."

"You should not have gone to Talasee's platform," he said, sliding his hands up and down her back beneath the sheet of her hair. "They do not understand. They grow suspicious when you perform the ceremonies of a shaman."

"Who would have purified his platform—driven away the evil that lurked there? Your sister, the shaman, is not here. I knew how and so I did it."

"Such mystery about you. You are strong and yet so soft. I do not want you to put yourself at risk again."

"I could not let you go to Talasee, and you would have. You would have sat with him and grieved, prepared Tashi's body. And it would have been too painful for you to explain that he must stay alone. I could not put that upon you."

"Those are my obligations. I am the cacique."

"But," she said, pressing her lips to his shoulder, "I could not bear it if you became ill. I owe you my life in many ways." She raised her face and kissed his jaw.

Cherok pulled her even closer, the heat of him flowing freely into her. She turned so that her back was flush against him, and he wrapped his arms around her. She leaned her head back against his shoulder.

"Gaga-na sits outside like a guard. Tell me about her," Cimmera said.

"I do not feel like talking now," he said, lowering her head so that his mouth fell in the crook of her neck.

Cimmera closed her eyes. She would hear about Gaga-na in the morning.

CHAPTER 20

CIMMERA LOOKED OUT from the platform. The burnished light of morning washed over the village. Gaga-na was gone.

Cherok sat below, his back to her, his legs crossed. He greeted the new day. Cimmera felt a tingle cross her body as she watched him. Her eyes filled with tears. Could she keep her secret forever? She did not feel like the enemy. She would go with this man anywhere, be whatever he was or whatever he wanted her to be. There was no past. Her life had begun with him.

She climbed down and passed the cacique as he sat with his eyes closed, his face serene as he spoke with the spirits. She found a lonely place where she, too, greeted the day. Her songs were different from his, the language A-po-la-chee, but she had the feeling that the spirits were the same. She whispered her songs and prayers. The wind will carry my words, she thought.

A sudden flicker of her past appeared in her head. She was hiding, crouched in the tall grass by the water's edge. She was a child, and her small shoulders shook as she cried. She was scared and confused. Her mother was dead. Her grandmother was dead. She could hear the whoosh and crackle of thatch going up in flames, the screams of the dying, and the whoops of the victors. She pressed her hands over her ears.

Through the web of blades she looked out at the

water. The canoes loaded with the warriors were moving away, all except one. A huge hulk of a man stood in that one dugout, his hand raised as if to still the others. The canoe halted, and the shouting warriors grew silent. Thick gray smoke cloaked his face, but his dark eyes pierced it. There was no place she could hide.

She shrank as small as she could, curled herself into a ball, peeking through the grass, her crying turning to wailing. The canoe was coming back, and he was looking straight at her. He saw her! He saw her!

A voice halted her remembering. "Have you finished?"

Cimmera turned with a start. "Gaga-na, you frightened me."

"I did not mean to. I waited quietly because I heard you pray."

"You heard?" Cimmera stood up.

"My old ears are not so good. Low sounds, like prayers, but I did not hear the words. I was not prying."

"No, I am sure you were not," Cimmera said, her heart still bumping in her chest, her breath still rushing in and out as if she had actually returned to that sliver of time in her past and relived it.

"Jumak is at my hearth," the old woman said, moving closer and stroking Cimmera's hair comfortingly.

Cimmera kept her face toward the ground. Gaga-na seemed to know that she was upset, and she was attempting to soothe her.

"He hopes you will join us for the morning meal," Gaga-na said. "Cherok fasts, but he will sit with us. He says the spirits spoke to him during his morning prayers. He waits at my hearth. For you."

Cimmera smiled and looked up.

"There, I like that smile," Gaga-na said. "The mention of Cherok does that to you. Finally! I thought you were going to be too stubborn to listen to your heart."

They went together, Cimmera walking slowly to stay at Gaga-na's pace.

"Look, the two of them have grown anxious," Gaga-na said. Jumak and Cherok stood at the hearth, looking in their direction.

Jumak trotted out to them. "Where were you?"

"Cimmera was greeting the day," Gaga-na answered. "Do not be a pest."

The boy danced in front of them. "The cacique was worried."

Cherok came up to meet them. Cimmera looked at him and smiled.

"He paced," Jumak said, bouncing about, his eyes twinkling.

Cherok put his arm around Cimmera. "I did not see you leave."

"Come get the bowls with me," Gaga-na said to the boy.

Jumak made a noise to express his disappointment. "I will be a man one day. I should listen to how the cacique talks to his woman. That is how I will learn."

Gaga-na took the boy by the ear and dragged him with her. "Well, you are not a man and you must obey your elders," she said, leading him away.

"Do not leave me like that again," Cherok said. He knew he could not bear to find her missing one day. He did not even feel comfortable when she was out of his sight. If he had had a choice, if he had been just a man without the responsibilities of the cacique, he would never even have left the platform this morning. He would have stayed with her.

"It will never be me," she said, her eyes meeting his, staring deep into him. "I will never leave you. It will have to be you."

"No," he said. "It will never be me."

Cimmera felt him lightly brush her cheek, then drop his hand to entwine his fingers with hers.

"Eat before Jumak has it all," Gaga-na called.

Cherok gave a tender squeeze to her hand. "Atok and Dacoma prepare to go on their journey."

"Go and be with them," she said. "I will be here."

"I do not like being away from you."

"Go," she said.

Cherok smiled and turned.

Cimmera took a bowl from Gaga-na. "Do you have children?" Cimmera asked.

The old woman slumped. "I did."

"Oh," Cimmera said. "I always ask the wrong questions."

"She had a daughter," Jumak said.

Gaga-na slurped from her bowl, then wiped her mouth. "Long ago. Long, long ago."

"What was her name?" Cimmera asked.

Two boys suddenly appeared. "Jumak!" they called. "Come with us. We are hunting birds."

Jumak's eyes brightened, and he took one last gulp of the coontie-thickened stew. He jumped to his feet; then his face fell. "My bow. My arrows."

Jumak's friend, Yoma, understood the problem. All of Jumak's things were in his father's platform, and he was not allowed to go there.

"You can share mine," Yoma said.

"No trouble from you boys," Gaga-na said, thinking about the seed incident.

"I will bring you a string of birds!" Jumak said.

They watched the boys leave. The old woman shifted. "Tell me about your village," she said.

"Nothing special about it," Cimmera answered.

"Surely you can tell me something," she said quickly, looking hard at the younger woman.

Cimmera's mind was blank.

After a meaningful pause, Gaga-na said, "You do not have to tell me anything." She stirred the stew, pursing her lips as she thought.

"Gaga-na, I—"

"Quiet," the old woman said. "You are safe with me."

Cimmera tilted her head. "Safe" was a peculiar choice of words, as if Gaga-na knew her secret. How could that be? Still, since the moment their eyes had met when she first arrived in this village, they had had some kind of connection.

"You have much insight into people," Cimmera said.

"Some. Do not forget, I was a shaman's woman. You learn things, being that close to a man of the spirits. My daughter was from his seed. I could never give him another."

"What was she like?" Cimmera asked.

"Beautiful. Looked more like her father, a ruggedly handsome man. His eyes, his face, but my nose. His nose was wonderful, very sharp. It would not have looked so nice on a woman's face."

Gaga-na's voice seemed to float when she spoke of him.

"Yes, he was the most splendid man to look at. When he wore his shaman's robes, white feather cape, shells dangling, and the magic in his eyes, every woman wanted him. I was the fortunate one. He had many women, but I was the one he loved."

Gaga-na paused and stared in the distance. Cimmera kept silent. Finally Gaga-na drew in a deep breath.

"As I said, it was long ago. Her name was Raina."

The old woman paused and watched Cimmera's face.

Cimmera wanted to ask Gaga-na what had happened to Raina, but thought it might be insensitive. "Raina," she repeated, wondering if she had heard the name before.

"You are prepared?" Cherok asked.

"A few more things and we will be ready," Atok answered. He sat with Dacoma near the central hearth. Collected in front of them were fishhooks made from birds' bones and from shells. There was also a petal-shaped piece of chert for fashioning those hooks. That piece, with a few chert and flint points, lay upon a small parfleche painted with diamond shapes. The points were separated into two groups. One pile contained the hunting points, with no barbs so the hunter could retrieve his point. The other group was made up of war points, those with barbs. When one of those stuck in a man, it could not be pulled out, only pushed through. Atok lifted a large spearpoint of smoky quartz.

"From my mother's mother's father. He traded for this when he was a young warrior." He held it out for the others to see before he put it down.

"People farther to the north have that stone," Cherok said. "Near the rivers."

The men nodded.

"Bah," Atok complained, holding a newly made arrow shaft across the tip of his finger, checking it for balance. "I need to shave this end a little more."

Jumak came up at a sprint, his eyes big, intrigued by the men's work. He eyed all the weapons Atok and Dacoma had. He bent over and touched the busycon club, the atlatl, and then the most frightening, the saber club with the teeth of the shark set in notches along the length of it, all turned toward the handle. These were the wonderful tools of men, the prizes and treasures that came with being a man.

"Will you help me make some arrows?" Jumak asked, dropping the white-billed gray bird he carried.

"You have killed a coot," Cherok said. "Now you must prepare it for food." He picked up the coot by its greenish legs and handed it to the boy.

"I will give it to Cimmera and Gaga-na," he said. "Yoma shared his arrows and bow with me. Will you help me make others?"

"Be patient, and I will. Save the wing and tail feathers. We will use them. Now, take your kill to the women."

Jumak hurried away.

Okemah pulled on his chin. "His father should be able to help the boy. His mother has no living brother."

"The clan has decided about Talasee," Cherok said. "This is not to be argued. Such talk might bring bad luck to the travelers."

Narchise ambled in their direction, puffing as she walked. She adjusted her wrap. The temperature was warmer than it had been earlier, and she let the skin fall down her shoulders.

"Everyone has said prayers for your journey," she said, not looking at Okemah. She folded her arms beneath her breasts and hoisted them up.

Okemah quivered just looking at her.

"Okemah," Atok said with a chuckle, seeing how the big man was so stricken by her presence. "Have you no greeting for this woman?"

Okemah smiled awkwardly.

"Is she not the songbird?" Dacoma said, his eyes sparkling with mischief.

Okemah's face grew red.

"What does he mean?" Narchise asked.

Dacoma rocked back, swallowing a burst of laughter.

"You have a beautiful voice," Okemah said. "Like a bird."

"A bird that sings in the night," Atok blurted through his laughing.

"Okemah?" Narchise said. "What are they talking about?"

"They act like children," Okemah said, finally standing. He put his arm around Narchise's back and guided her away from the men. He looked over his shoulder and scowled at them.

"We will be listening," Atok taunted.

"Pay no mind," Okemah said. They were out of earshot before Okemah spoke again. "Where have you been? I have looked for you."

"You have?" Narchise said. "I thought perhaps your eye had wandered elsewhere."

"Oh, no," Okemah said.

Narchise bumped against him. "You were wonderful that night by the fire," she whispered so softly that he wasn't sure that was what he heard. "I have thought about you every night since."

Okemah heard that and was about to respond by snaking his hand inside her wrap when he heard another voice.

"There you are."

Narchise knew the high voice, the cute little teasing lilt. Tichini.

Okemah quickly drew back his hand and turned around.

"You never did get your feather," the young woman said, holding it out. "I guess you were distracted and forgot all about it. We did have such a good time."

Okemah took the feather from her. "It was good of you to remember."

"How could I forget?" she said. "No one has made me laugh like you. Does he make you feel as good as he does me?" Tichini asked Narchise.

"Quite," Narchise answered, pulling the skin over her shoulders.

"He is a man I like to be with," Tichini said, slinging her hair out of her face with a toss of her head.

She wore no wrap and seemed to Narchise to ooze heat. Disgusting, she thought.

Tichini reached out and took Okemah's hand that held the feather. She guided it to his face and tickled his chin.

He grinned at the attention.

"I would like to make you feel as good," Tichini said.

Narchise had had enough. "That would be easy," she said, elbowing her way between them. "You just tickle him with that feather—right there." She gave Okemah a wrathful swat to the crotch.

Okemah grunted, bent over, and grabbed himself. Narchise offered them a gratified smile and walked away.

"Pull them all out," Gaga-na said.

"I did," Jumak answered, holding up the plucked coot.

"Even the small feathers," Gaga-na said, pointing to a few that were left.

"There," the boy said, his job completed.

"Now clean it out. Save the breast meat."

"Cherok said to save the feathers."

"Then save them, also," Gaga-na said.

Jumak looked at the small bird. There was not much meat. "I am feeling sad," he said as Cherok came up to him. "I think the spirits have sent me another lesson."

Cherok crouched next to the boy.

Jumak gazed at the bird. "Seems that this kill is wasteful. Such a little bit of meat."

Cherok held the coot and examined it. "The kill was clean. The animal died swiftly. Did you say the prayers?"

"Yes," Jumak answered.

"Then the bird has provided for you. Be grateful. The circle of man and animal goes on."

He handed the bird back to Jumak, who finished the cleaning and washing.

"It is ready," Jumak said.

Cimmera took the coot from Jumak and handed it to Gaga-na. Cherok looked at the young woman who preoccupied him. He had not done anything this day, had no conversation, without thoughts of her entering his head.

"Come with me. We will make some arrows," Cherok said.

Jumak jumped to his feet.

Cimmera gathered a basket of food. "I will take it to Talasee," she said.

"Leave that to Ara," Cherok said, his hand resting on the boy's shoulder. "If such a small thing helps settle Okemah, then we will humor him."

Cimmera nodded and watched Cherok and Jumak walk into the cover of the woods. He was a good man, she thought.

"First we need ironwood for a bow. A resilient sapling is the best," Cherok said.

When they had found the ironwood, they carefully selected a young tree about Jumak's height and as big around as his forearm.

"Now we need to find willows," Cherok said.

Jumak scanned the surroundings. "There." He pointed to a thicket of willows by the water.

As had happened all morning, the image of Cimmera drifted into Cherok's mind. She was as slender as a willow, pliable, tender, succulent. Since the night he had finally taken her, she had twined through his thoughts, never really leaving.

Jumak stood waiting for directions from the cacique. "You think about Cimmera," he said. "You forget that we are going to make arrows. But that is all right."

"I am sorry, Jumak. My mind drifts."

"Does she do magic on your ... in the furs?"

Cherok pushed on the boy's shoulder and turned him back toward the willows. "Now your mind is not with the task. Take the suckers growing from the base of the trees," the cacique told the boy. "They are the best for arrow shafts. No knots or branches. What are you going to hunt for?"

Jumak shrugged his shoulders.

"Cut some about the length of your arm, and then a few longer ones for frogs and birds."

Perhaps the boy was right, he thought. The woman did bewitch him, as Jumak had put it, in the furs. She made him need her in the most basic and nearly animal-like way.

Jumak used the knife his father had helped him make; the beveled edge of the macrocallista shell was ground sharp.

"That is more than enough," Cherok said.

They went back to Gaga-na's hearth and spread out the collection. Cherok found his eyes locked on Cimmera.

Jumak held each willow shaft to his eye and looked down it. "None of them are straight."

"Making them straight will be your job," Cherok said. "Shave the bark off first, and smooth the bumps. Then leave them here by the fire to cure until the sun is in the same place tomorrow." He had a difficult time concentrating on helping the young one.

Jumak looked at the sky, noting the sun. Then he quickly became engrossed in the task of stripping the bark and smoothing the shafts.

Dacoma and Atok walked past, carrying their supplies to the canoe. The rest of the villagers followed behind to see them off.

"Leave it for now," Cherok told the boy, and they joined the other villagers.

Atok and Dacoma loaded the canoe. "I see you take the totems I gave you?" Cherok said, meaning the mussel shell and the shark's tooth he had given them.

The sunlight glinted off the water into Cimmera's eyes. Suddenly she was off-balance, woozy, and the voices became echoes. New voices and images formed before her.

She was a child again and tightly hugged Sola's leg. Tamar was in front of them, and the entire village stood enthralled with him. Giant wings were strapped to his arms, though they appeared to be his, the way he danced with them, made them swoop so gracefully through the air, stirring a wind that kissed her face. Down the center of Tamar's face was a single white stripe. Around his throat he wore a thick necklace of shells.

He turned, bent his knees, swept close to the ground, closing the feathers about him, and then he surged upward, unfurling the wings, nearly leaving the ground. His voice warbled in song as he stretched the wings and slowly opened his hands. Appearing from nowhere, as if extracted from the very air, a white bird emerged from each palm and took flight. The villagers gasped in wonder.

Cimmera looked at the man's eyes and saw her reflection there. He returned her gaze, and then the huge wings enfolded her.

"The spirits know who you are, and now the people will be enlightened," Tamar whispered to her as she was swaddled in the feathers, the great wings.

She was sure her feet and his left the earth, and the air became a roaring in her ears. The wind was cold, but the wings, his arms, kept her warm.

Tamar's voice was deep and supernatural, reverberating across the village in a shaman's song. And then he touched the ground, settling softly, gently opening his wings, presenting her to his people.

"She is Walks in Stardust," he said.

She had a name.

CHAPTER 21

THE AFTERNOON SKY was a crisp, brilliant blue with only swatches of thin white clouds. No sign of rain, though a wind coming from the east, unusual for the season, held promise. The People looked toward the sky. The sunlight poured down onto the saw grass, where it was lost in all the gold and ripe brown bristling sedge. The shallow water flashed jewels of light. The air was cool.

Cherok raised his arms, and silence fell over the group.

"Oh, Great Spirit, creator of all things, be kind to us. We are your children, we with tired backs and woeful hearts. Hear us. See those who journey far. Until we meet again, make the sun rise in their hearts."

Atok raised the pole and pushed it down into the rotting peat, moving the canoe through the water. The small group watched them leave, the clan's hopes of finding others riding the wake behind them.

"Cimmera?" Cherok said softly. He saw that she stared into the distance, as if she could see something that was not there—like Mi-sa when she had a vision. He smiled at the thought of how Cimmera reminded him of his sister.

Cherok touched his hand to her cheek. "Cimmera," he said again.

She could still hear Tamar's voice in her mind, saying her name over and over. She tried to clear her head.

"Are you all right?" he asked.

"Yes," she answered, her voice sounding far away and unsure. As if in the distance, again she heard Tamar say her name: Walks in Stardust. She turned back toward the water. "I hope they find others," she said.

"So much time has passed since the storm, but we do not give up hope. When we let the storm take that away, then we are beaten."

"You are the one who keeps that hope alive," she said.

Cherok kept his eyes on her. He could not stop his mind from thinking of her. But there were tasks to be completed. The people depended on him. He could not just disappear into her flesh as he wanted to do now.

Behind Cimmera, Cherok saw Narchise kicking the dirt, watching Okemah out the corner of her eye.

"I thought Narchise would be more agreeable since she and Okemah have found each other," Cherok said.

"Narchise is not sure of herself. She believes Okemah would prefer Tichini's pleasures."

He still studied Cimmera's face, watching the lines gradually return to normal. "I worry about you. Something goes on inside your head, and still you do not share it with me.

"Is something wrong with Cimmera?" Gaga-na asked, her face kinked into worried creases. "Take her back to my hearth."

"You both fuss too much over me. Sometimes I daydream. Do you not do that?"

Gaga-na poked Cherok in his leg with her stick. "Take her back. Keep Okemah and Narchise away from her. Let her sit at my hearth. Jumak is anxious to make the arrows. Do that. I will be along."

Some villagers stayed by the water's edge, keeping a vigil until they could no longer see the canoe.

"Do you want to stay here with the others?" Cimmera

asked.

"No," Cherok said. "There is no reason."

Jumak did await them at Gaga-na's hearth. "Show me what to do," he said.

"Stand up," Cherok said.

The boy jumped to his feet. The cacique took one of the willow shafts. "Hold one end at the center of your chest and extend your arms out in front with your fingers outstretched."

The boy did as he was told.

Cherok cut off the part of the willow that ranged past Jumak's fingers. "Arrows must fit the man who uses them. Trim them all that way."

Cimmera sat with them, watching, catching small glimpses of a similar experience from her buried past. More and more fragments of recollection floated in and out of her memory, but never came together to give her a complete picture.

She saw Cherok and Jumak twirl filaments of sinew into a three-ply bowstring, wishing her memories could come together like that, forming something strong from all the threads.

"Put the bowstring aside now. When we fasten it to the bow, it will provide a lot of tension. Not too strong for you, is it?" Cherok said, grinning at the boy.

"No! I am strong," Jumak answered.

"Let these shafts smoke by the fire. Season them well." Cherok propped them over the hearth.

He took one of them after it had heated, smeared it with bear grease, and handed it to Jumak. "Take this one, since you are so eager," he said, giving the boy a piece of limestone with a hole drilled in the center. "Run the warm shaft back and forth through this hole," he said. "It will make the arrow straight."

"My father showed me this," Jumak said. "I wish I could show this to him. I think he would be proud."

"He would be pleased to see the fine job you have done."

Cimmera stirred Gaga-na's fire with a stick, keeping it ablaze. The way she moved so fluidly seduced Cherok as surely as if she spoke an invitation. Would the night ever come?

"What do you think, Cimmera? Will I make a good warrior?" the boy asked.

"You are brave of heart," she said.

"I am glad that you live at the cacique's hearth. He smiles more. A man has needs."

"And how would you know such things?" Cimmera asked, her face ablush.

"We men talk among ourselves. One day when I am a man, I will find a woman who keeps a smile on my face."

"Pay attention to what you are doing," Cherok said. The boy was right. This woman did keep a smile on his face, and right now just the thought of her made his body grow hot.

"Nock the shaft with this shape," Cherok said, drawing a U in the dirt. "If you used twisted fiber for a bowstring, you would nock it like this." Again Cherok drew in the dirt, but this time he made a V. "Do you see the difference?"

Jumak nodded and proceeded.

"What if this is all of us?" the boy asked. "What if Atok and Dacoma find no one else? What if they do not come back?"

"Your mind never stops," Cherok said, holding one of Jumak's shafts to his eye and looking down it.

"There are those who say we should give up and not rebuild. They say—"

"Do not listen to that kind of talk, Jumak. We are Tegesta! Proud and strong."

Cimmera moved against Cherok, her bare shoulder brushing his. "Hear your cacique. He speaks the truth."

"Will I have one arrow ready today?" the child asked.

"We can have this one, rickety though it might be."

"Good. I told Yoma that I would. He did not believe me. I told him that Cimmera would do magic on it!"

Cimmera drew in a sharp breath.

"That was not a wise thing to say," the cacique said, his expression scolding the boy.

Jumak's eyes drooped with humility. They sat in silence for a few moments. Cherok demonstrated how to shave the end of a shaft to a point. "We will temper it in the fire later."

"Can I paint it now?"

Cherok nodded.

Jumak held up a chewed willow stick brush. "What pattern?"

"You do not have a pattern to crest an arrow with yet. You will choose your design when you become a man. For now use the Tegesta pattern."

Jumak dipped the brush in a viscous yellow mixture.

"Make that band wide," Cherok said.

When the first band was complete, Jumak rotated the arrow to see how it looked all around. "It is good," he said.

"Now a narrow black band, then a wider red, and then black again," Cherok said.

"And another wide yellow band at the end," Jumak said, proud that he knew the Tegesta pattern.

When the painting was done, the boy held the shaft over the fire to dry. It dried quickly, much of the paint seeping into the grain of the wood.

Cimmera stared at the colorful shaft and the flames that lapped beneath it. Jumak's painted arrow brought back the vision she had before, of her mother and her grandmother, the attack, the arrow sticking out of Grandmother's leg. Why did that arrow keep flashing before her? What was it about that arrow and Jumak's arrow that kept catching her attention?

"Where are the feathers you saved?" Cherok asked.

Jumak twisted around and looked on the ground behind him. There, weighted with a stone so they would not blow away, were the coot's feathers.

"We will use the tail feathers."

After using pitch to glue the flight of feathers on the shaft, Jumak lifted the arrow and pretended to nock it to a bowstring and aim, one eye closed. "Through an A-po-la-chee heart!" he said.

Cimmera's stomach balled up into a sick knot. He might as well have shot the arrow. Her face drained of color. She dropped the stick she had been using to stir the fire.

"Shoot with both eyes open," Cherok said. He handed the boy a wad of sinew filament. "Put it in your mouth to keep it wet. Secure the fletching in a few places."

"When is Gaga-na going to cook my coot?" Jumak asked.

Cimmera's face was still pale. "Do you want me to cook it?" she asked, desperately trying to collect herself. Hearing the boy say how he would kill an A-po-la-chee had made her reel. His words were as sharp as any arrow, and they tore through her heart. No matter how she tried, she could never make this her home. At gut level, beneath everything else, she was A-po-la-chee. The enemy.

Something made Gaga-na uneasy, made her stomach

crawl: Narchise. Narchise was a threat. Gaga-na was not going to allow anything or anyone to hurt her Cimmera. The spirits had kept Gaga-na alive this long so that she would be around to protect Cimmera, and she promised them aloud that she would do just that.

Gaga-na rubbed her nagging leg. She had decided not to tell Cimmera what she knew. Not unless it became necessary. There were secrets and promises made long ago that she still honored. The young woman was confused enough, she supposed. The blood of Cimmera's father and grandfather collided inside her. The best protection Gaga-na could give her was to let her be whoever she believed she was.

She saw Ara approaching. She did not want to get into another argument with the woman. If Ara wanted to prepare and deliver food for Talasee, then that was how it would be. Gaga-na would not provide any more fuel for Okemah's fire.

"There is no need for you or that woman, Cimmera, to cook food for Talasee. Cherok has said that I may assume that task," Ara said.

"Then so be it," Gaga-na answered.

"Your attitude has changed. What has brought that about?"

"If such a small concession makes you and your brother content, then I relinquish my responsibility for Talasee's food."

Ara leaned her head to the side, one brow arched. "Somehow I find your new disposition puzzling."

"You are young, Ara. Do not try to understand the wisdom of your elders."

"Everyone knows you are a cantankerous old woman. I think you enjoy having that reputation. You think it excuses you when you are rude."

"Have I been rude?"

"That is my point. You are too good-tempered today."

Gaga-na smiled at the much younger woman.

That made Ara even more suspicious. "I enjoy my conversations with Talasee," she said. "I am sure he is happy that someone is not afraid of him."

Gaga-na straightened up. "What do you mean? When do you talk with him?"

"When I take him food. I take a little every day."

"Do you not call out to him and then leave the basket?"

"I do not believe that strange woman who lives at our cacique's hearth. Talasee has tried to discourage me, but I know he needs a friend. He needs something to take his mind off Tashi's passing."

"Does Okemah know you do this?"

"Okemah does not believe Cimmera."

"But does he know that you linger with Talasee?"

"I have not made a point of telling him," Ara said, "but if he knew, he would think I have a kind and wise heart."

"Ara, you are a fool. Stay away from Talasee. Fix his meals if you choose to, but keep your distance. If the sickness gets into Talasee and into you, you could bring it back to us all. You know what this disease can do."

"But I do not believe this nonsense about jumping illness."

"So far Tashi is the only one to become ill. Think about that. Is it because she was kept separate? Do not take such chances with yourself ...with us!"

Ara was dumbstruck.

"I will speak to your brother immediately," Gaga-na said. She walked away, mumbling loudly. "Okemah will have us all dead."

The shadows were getting long as the day drew on toward night. Gaga-na looked across the village. Where was the man? Then something caught her eye. There, near Cherok's platform. Was that someone peeping from behind the trees, or was it just the branches rustling in the breeze?

If someone was hiding there, she did not want him to know that she had spotted him. Casually she wound her way through the small village. The smell of fresh-cut palms was finally dwindling. Everyone's shelter was complete. Most of the rebuilding left to do was inside the People.

Gaga-na felt a chill and pulled up her wrap. Who would be lurking about Cherok's hearth? For what reason? She slunk into the brush, then stopped to watch. She cursed her old eyes. Things were not clear enough that far away, especially in the dim light of dusk, not like when she was young.

In a moment she did see some movement, but could not make out who was there. She had to get closer.

Gaga-na slyly crept beside the cover of the trees. She pressed her walking stick into the earth of the hammock. It should have felt soft, the rich black muck giving way beneath her stick. But the muck was dried out and hard. It crumbled in chunks. She moved slowly, concentrating on keeping her balance and being quiet. The weeds, wintry brown and brittle, made noise when she pushed past them, crackling, clattering noises instead of the soft swish of summer-moist green blades.

The old woman fumbled with her wrap as it shifted with her movements. She started to discard it but then thought better. If someone stopped her, how would she explain leaving the skin on the ground?

Gaga-na looked up again, peering around the trunk of

the sweet bay and through the cluster of wax myrtle. She stood still, hiding herself as best she could, waiting for the person to show himself. She was growing uncomfortable, her leg aching, her patience abating, when at last she saw the figure look out of the trees again.

The movement was fast but somewhat clumsy. Narchise scurried up the ladder of Cherok's platform! Gaga-na swung her stick in front of her, swiping at the weeds.

"What do you do in there?" she called out as she hurried ahead.

Narchise either ignored her or did not hear her. Gaga-na waited below the platform, staying hidden. Soon she heard heavy footsteps frantically descending the ladder.

Narchise tumbled onto the ground and anxiously whipped around, checking the foreground and the distance for anyone who might have noticed her. Convinced she had gone unobserved, she shook back her hair and started to move again.

"What have you done?" Gaga-na said, still obscured by the brush.

Narchise spun around. "Who is that?" she asked.

"Come here," Gaga-na said. "Explain yourself to me." The old woman moved out of the protection of the trees so that Narchise could see her.

"What do you want, Gaga-na?"

"Come this way so we can discuss this without an audience," Gaga-na said.

Narchise ambled toward her. "What do you want with me?"

When Narchise was close enough so that she could talk softly, Gaga-na said, "Tell me what you have done."

"Nothing. I have not done anything that would interest you."

"I saw you go into Cherok's platform. What were you doing there?"

"I was not in his platform. Why would I go there?"

"I do not know, but do not waste your time with denials. I saw you go inside."

"You could not have," Narchise argued. "I was not there. And what are you doing creeping about like an old snoop? Have you nothing better to do?"

"I stood over there," Gaga-na said, lifting her stick and pointing in the direction from where she had witnessed Narchise climbing the ladder. "I saw someone, you, peeping around the trees, looking suspicious, and I asked myself why someone would be doing that. So I came closer. I made sure that you did not see me."

Narchise turned around.

"Do not leave so fast. Tell me what you did."

"I am looking out for this clan," Narchise said.

"By doing what? Nosing about where you do not belong?"

"I am leaving," Narchise said.

Gaga-na lifted her stick and whacked Narchise on the shoulder. The plump woman whirled around.

"You are not leaving until I have an explanation, and if I do not get one soon I am going to start screaming for the cacique to come."

"Look," Narchise said, flipping open her wrap.

CHAPTER 22

GAGA-NA RUSHED her hand to her mouth to cover up her gasp. "What have you done? What is that?"

Narchise leaned forward, keeping the knife at her bosom. "It is Cimmera's. I saw this knife in her hands—glowing, it was. Then she did magic on the tree, healed it as if there had never been a wound."

"You—you do not know what you saw," Gaga-na said, stumbling over her words, scrambling for some explanation to give Narchise.

"I did see it, and this knife glowed in her hand. Look at it," Narchise said, holding it out. "Have you ever seen anything like it? I have not."

Gaga-na stared at the object. Indeed the knife was peculiar, and no, she had never seen anything just like it. She reached out for the knife, wanting to examine it more closely.

"Oh, no. You cannot have it," Narchise said, snatching it out of Gaga-na's hand.

"I just want to see it. Hold it out, woman. Let me see."

Cautiously Narchise held the knife out, but kept a tight grip on it. "Just look."

Gaga-na bent forward, squinting to see in the dusky light. In a moment she shot up straight. "I cannot see it. Come to my hearth."

Narchise followed the old woman, noticing how she limped, wishing she did not have to grow old like Gaga-na.

"Hold it up to the fire," Gaga-na said.

Narchise pulled the knife out from under her wrap and scooted closer to the hearth.

"I cannot see it clearly," Gaga-na protested. "Tilt it at an angle."

Narchise rotated her hand so the knife did not reflect so much light.

"Bah! If I lean close enough I burn up my face. Give it to me. "

"No," Narchise said. "It will not leave my hands."

"Then how do you expect me to see it properly? Perhaps all you say is foolishness."

"I have told you the truth. This is a magic knife, and if you were not so old and your eyes so poor, then you would clearly see how unique and strange this knife is."

"Maybe you do not want me to see it. Maybe you count on my failing eyesight. Perhaps you play a trick on an old woman. I have not seen anything strange. Just a knife."

Narchise huffed, twitching her mouth to one side. "I have told you what I saw. I have no reason to lie. If you cannot see, then you will just have to trust me."

"Give me the knife, Narchise, and stop all this nonsense. You act as though you think I will steal it from you. If you want to convince me that what you say is the truth and that you are not crazy, then hand me the knife so that I can see it. This has gone on long enough. You act ridiculous."

Narchise slowly extended her hand, and Gaga-na took the knife.

"You are enough to exhaust a person," the old woman

said. Gaga-na held the knife with both hands. It was heavy. That was the first thing she noticed. The blade was strange enough, but the handle designs were most curious. She turned it, the firelight showing off the luster of the handle.

"What do you intend to do with this? Why have you done something so horrible as to steal it? Cimmera has done nothing to hurt you."

"Okemah."

"What do you mean?"

"He will pay attention to me if I bring him this knife. He will see that there is something strange about it. He will be grateful that I have brought him proof that Cimmera does not belong here—perhaps proof that she is a witch."

Gaga-na shot an angry look at the woman. "You do this to win Okemah's affections? I cannot believe it."

"He will pay attention to me when I show him this. Tichini will not be on his mind then."

"This is a selfish thing you do. You do not know anything about Cimmera. She has only been kind to you, willing to be your friend, and you attempt to destroy her, all to get Okemah's attention. This is the most horrible, cruel, stupid scheme I have ever heard!"

"Give me the knife," Narchise said.

"I will not!"

"Give it back to me."

"You have stolen this from Cimmera. The People do not tolerate a thief. I will do you a favor and return this knife to its proper place. Then no one will know what a terrible deed you have done. Thank me. I will not tell."

Narchise scored her bottom lip with her teeth. How had Gaga-na turned this whole thing around on her?

"Where was it? Where did you find it?"

"Her woman's basket."

"Be gone, then. I will put it back where it belongs. We will forget this ever happened. Every woman has moments of being crazy, especially over a man." Gaga-na patted Narchise's shoulder. "Everyone would not understand as I do. Be off now."

Gaga-na watched the heavy woman traipse away. Narchise was not too smart, and Gaga-na was thankful for that. She was going to have to tell Cimmera about the incident.

The old woman stared down at the knife she held. A-po-la-chee markings, she thought. A shaman's designs. But the blade she did not understand. She had never seen anything like it. Part of the A-po-la-chee magic, she assumed.

Gaga-na got a small piece of deer hide and a rabbit skin, a strand of sewing sinew and a thin strip of rawhide. She wrapped the knife in the deerskin.

She had to speak to Cimmera alone, and now it was going to be too difficult. The evening was fully upon them. She would have to wait until the morning.

Gaga-na sat by her fire, sewing a rabbit skin pouch with her bone needle and the sinew. The fur would disguise the shape of the contents of the pouch.

She looked across the mound and saw Cherok's silhouette cross the fire as he went up the ladder into his platform.

Cimmera stood in the shadows of the platform.

All the while Cherok had helped Jumak, his eyes had wandered to Cimmera, taking in her slender shape, the curves and arches that he thought about his hands gliding over. If there had not been so many demands during the day, he would have taken her away and devoured her. Just the way she carried herself, the way she moved, like a song, kept his mind occupied, anticipating the way it would be with her after the night swallowed the daylight.

Cimmera heard him take a deep breath.

"You have tortured me all day, woman," he said.

"What have I done?" she asked, stepping closer.

Cherok embraced her. His hands slid down the length of her back as he held her against him. "You are so soft," he said.

Cimmera leaned back to look at his face.

"No, do not move," he said, not wanting her to take any measure of her flesh from his.

He held her there, still and quiet, in a slice of silver moonlight, the sheen of her hair spilling over his hands.

Cimmera leaned into him. His body was sleek like a panther's, the muscles taut as a bowstring. She breathed in, breaking the silence with the raggedness of her breath. The scent of him rushed through her. Cimmera opened her mouth and tasted his shoulder.

Cherok gathered a thick cord of her hair, then pushed his hand up through it until he cradled her head in his big palm, her hair tangled in his fingers.

She ran her hands down his sides, reaching for his thighs, then back again, hesitating at his groin.

"Do not touch me," Cherok whispered.

Cimmera bowed her head into his shoulder. She could feel his knees trembling against her, his naked chest intimately touching hers, the hardness of him pressed against her, and she was sure she felt his heart beating there.

"Move away," he said, his voice raspy.

"Why?" she asked, sounding hurt. She pulled back and sat on the mat, feeling ashamed or embarrassed, she wasn't sure which.

Cherok rubbed his face, then knelt in front of her. "I lose control. The touch of you, the nearness of you …"

Cimmera stretched up and touched her wet lips to his. He hungrily bit at her mouth, afraid to pause too long.

"I give you pleasure?" she asked, now understanding why he had asked her to move away. "Too quickly?"

"Much too quickly," he said.

Her hands clasped his face, and she sipped the sweetness from his lips. "I want to do that," she said.

He looked at her through heavy lids. Cimmera brought herself to her knees and slowly snaked her hands about his neck and drew him to her. "I never want to be without you," she said.

"Never," he whispered back, nipping at her ear.

She loosed the knot that kept his breechclout tied. The deerskin fell away, and she feathered her fingers across his belly, teasingly near that part of him that ached for her. She felt him quiver beneath her hands, his trembling muscles quaking.

Cherok heaved out a breath, filling her ear with his yearning.

"Tell me what you want me to do."

"Cimmera," he was barely able to say.

Her hands were suddenly between them, and one hand encircled him, then gave a long smooth stroke.

A moan gushed from him, and he folded his body over her, pressing her back to lie on the mat. His eyes were closed, his mouth open as he fell over her.

Driven by a hunger to see him, to see all this magnificent man as he needed her, she slid from beneath him. Cherok rolled onto his back.

"You are beautiful to see," she said, her eyes roving his lean, hard body and his sharp, handsome face.

Cherok smiled at the petite woman beside him. "You

are the one of beauty," he said, releasing the waistband of her skirt.

Cimmera bent forward and nibbled at his thigh. She placed one hand just above that part of him, pressing on the bone that lay beneath the skin. Slowly she tasted and teased. Lifting her head, she caught a glimpse of him through the curtain of her hair.

He reached for her and pulled her over him, a husky groan cast from deep in his chest as her weight settled on him. Cherok turned his head and bit into the soft flesh of her arm, then raised her so that her swollen nipple filled his mouth.

Cimmera arched her head backward, the gentle warm tug of his mouth bringing a whimper from her.

Cherok tore his mouth free and lowered her. He kissed her eyelids, her cheeks, and then her mouth, driving his tongue deep inside as he turned her to her side. Tenderly he bent her leg and pulled her knee over his hip.

A tiny moan ripped from her throat when his hand slipped between her legs and he stroked the heat of her.

He buried his head in her breast, so close to her that he could hear her shallow breath catch as he caressed her. Her heart beat loud and fast, and the fire inside her brought a glistening veil of perspiration to her skin.

She twisted, wanting him to fill her, to seal them together.

"Cherok," she whispered hoarsely, her fingers digging into the flesh of his back. A simple soft cry escaped her.

He murmured her name, suckling her, his fingertips feeling the dew her body prepared to make his entry smooth. She was ready for him, all damp heat and fire.

He turned her to her back and moved across her, parting her, lifting her knees.

Even before he penetrated her, just the touch of him waiting there, poised rigidly, made Cimmera press herself toward him.

He opened his eyes and watched her face as he entered her, slowly gliding into the sheath that coiled tightly around him.

"Please," he heard her plead as she tossed her head. He found exquisite pleasure in seeing the want he had brought to her. He drove all the way into her and then stopped, stealing a last look at the way her lips parted, the way her hair fell tangled across her cheek, the way the lines in her face gave her a look of desperation.

His head dropped as he began the ancient rhythm, and she was lost in the raw power of him. Cimmera clutched at Cherok, joining in the dance that evolved from some fire deep in their core. He stayed with her, leading her to the inevitable. And when their bodies could stand no more, they erupted into bone-rocking deep waves, especially powerful and delicious in knowing the other was feeling the same.

Cherok struggled to get his breath. "Our spirits have touched," he said.

A warm glow flooded her. Yes, she thought, their spirits had touched. For those wonderful few moments, his whole body had been inside hers, he had become a part of her, and she a part of him. What magic there was in loving someone.

The mantle of pale morning light came over the village. Cimmera opened her eyes and looked out at the windless day. Ground fog, thick and white, stood over the earth. The wet mist seeped through the thatch. The glossy leaves of the strangler fig dripped with dew, webbed patterns of moisture beading and shimmering in the first light. Tiny droplets fell to the ground and, in this time of no rain, gave the thirsty roots a small, secret drink.

Cimmera snuggled against Cherok, pressing her back to him, her body conforming to the contours of his. She loved this man. She held back tears when she thought of all the lies she had told him. She was embedded in them now; there was no turning back. Even if she could remember her past, she could never tell him about herself. There had been a time when she could have told him that her blood was A-po-la-chee, but no longer. Now if she told him everything she knew, or thought she knew, how would he ever forgive her ...ever believe her? Too much had happened. Too much deception to forget.

She felt him touch his mouth to her neck, breathing through her hair. She wished they never had to leave the platform ...wished she was only a Tegesta woman.

"Cherok," she said, turning to him, "tell me again that you will never leave me."

He reached his arm over her and drew her even closer. "Do you doubt me?" he said softly.

"No," she said, hiding her face against his chest.

"Then I will tell you again and again. Cimmera," he said, cupping her chin and lifting her face, "I will never leave you."

"It will never be me who leaves," she whispered, planting her head beneath his chin.

"I will make you my wife, the wife of the Tegesta cacique."

Cimmera felt her eyes sting as she fought back tears.

"Cacique!" It was Jumak below. "Look," he hollered, holding up the willow sticks. "They are all dried now. We can make some more arrows."

Cherok nuzzled his face in Cimmera's hair. "He is a pest."

"You are good to him," Cimmera said with a smile. "He needs you."

Cherok tied on his breechclout and stood in the opening. "Go back to Gaga-na's. I will come."

Jumak jumped up and down with excitement. "You will be pleased at how quickly I learn," he said before running away.

"He must have been awake even before the sun," Cimmera said.

"Gaga-na probably sent him just to get some relief from him," Cherok said with a chuckle.

"Will you still fast this day?"

He stared at her. He fasted to clear his head, to open a space for the spirits to come into him. He wanted to understand this woman who had riven his heart right out of his chest. "After the morning prayers I will break the fast."

She smiled at him and sat up, raking her hair back.

Cherok forced himself to leave her. He wandered through the hammock, finding a quiet place. He faced the morning sun in the east and sat, crossing his legs, straightening his back, and resting his hands on his knees, palms up. He took a deep breath through his nose and held it in his chest a moment, then slowly blew it out his mouth. He repeated that way of breathing several more times, feeling his body empty all the clutter, sending it out on his breath.

Cimmera watched him leave, hating the separation. She wished to see into the future; when the rains returned, when the days were hotter, longer, would he still hold her in the night?

She picked up her basket and held it in her lap. A shock spurted through her when she saw the jumbled contents of the basket. Someone had gone through it! The knife. The star knife! Frantically she rummaged through the basket. Where was it? Cimmera stripped everything out. No knife.

Her first thought was Talasee. He must have told Cherok, and now he had found her out, taken the proof from her basket to show the Council. What was he going to do to her? That was why he fasted, for advice from the spirits, advice on what to do about an A-po-la-chee in this camp. How he must hate her, she thought. She held her face in her hands, her throat painfully tight.

Fear gripped her so tensely that she did not see the shadow fall across the flooring.

CHAPTER 23

"WE ARE ALONE," Gaga-na said.

The voice startled Cimmera.

Gaga-na moved closer. "Cherok greets the day and then will be with Jumak. I have arranged that because I must speak to you alone."

Cimmera wiped her face and sniffed, hoping Gaga-na did not notice that she had been crying.

"What do you keep in that basket?" Gaga-na asked.

"Just things that belong to me, from when I was alone and from my home," Cimmera said.

"Would you be upset if you lost them?" The old woman reached out, and with her thumb she wiped away one last straggling tear from Cimmera's face. "Would you cry if you lost them?"

Cimmera picked up some things that she had emptied from the basket onto the floor and put them back. "I have nothing, really," she said.

Gaga-na held out the roll of hide. "This belongs to you."

Cimmera hesitated.

"Take it." Gaga-na laid the package in the young woman's palm. "Open the skin."

Cimmera peeled it away. Inside was the star knife. Her face dropped, and the tears started again. "Why did you take it?" she asked.

"I did not. Narchise saw you with this. She saw this

knife glow in your hands. When you did not help her with some magic to win Okemah, she thought she could get his attention with this."

"And Okemah has told Cherok?"

"No. Okemah never saw the knife. I intercepted Narchise and shamed her for being a thief. That was the end of it. I thought the knife must be important to you, and so I return it."

Cimmera clutched the star knife with both hands.

"I have made this pouch for you to carry the knife," Gaga-na said, laying the fur pouch in front of the young woman. "It is too dangerous for you to leave it about. Tie it on and keep it at your side. Put other things in it. The fur will disguise the shape."

Cimmera picked up the pouch. Gaga-na was correct; the fur would conceal the contents. It was better than the plain sheath she had made for the knife. She could never have worn that one. It gave away the shape of the knife.

"I made it in the night," Gaga-na said. "I thought there was no time to waste."

Cimmera slid the knife inside the pouch and ran her fingers through the soft rabbit fur.

"What do you know about that knife?" Gaga-na asked.

Cimmera shook her head.

They sat in silence for a few moments.

Gaga-na got up to leave. "It is all right. You need not tell me anything. But if you want a friend, someone to keep your secrets so you do not carry the burden alone, I will hear you. Whenever you are ready."

Cimmera bit down on the inside of her cheek. The old woman took a shaky grip on the ladder.

"Gaga-na," Cimmera called out.

The old woman looked up.

Cimmera paused before speaking. "Nothing. Just

thank you."

Gaga-na nodded and continued her descent.

At the base of the ladder she peered at the opening of the platform. "Gaga-na will keep you safe," she whispered. She left, her heart heavy.

"Now for Okemah," she muttered.

Gaga-na strolled by the water. She had not seen Okemah about the village. He could be cleaning himself, she thought. The fog still hovered. She could not see very well anyway, and this heavy mist made her search even more difficult.

She heard the ripple and splash of water ahead. She followed the sound.

On the limb of a willow she saw a length of buckskin. A breechclout. She spotted a blurry figure in the water.

"Is that you, Okemah?" she called out.

Gaga-na heard the water splash, and the figure came closer. He covered himself with his hands.

"You are crazy, old woman. What are you doing? I am a man taking a bath. Naked."

"Oh, I do not care about that, you old fool," she said, leaning on her stick. "I have seen other men."

"Why are you here? Sneaking a peek? Has it been too long since you have seen a man?"

"Your hands cover that little thing? My man's was too big to be hidden by his hands, so stop flattering yourself and listen to me."

Okemah had no choice but to stand still. "Then throw me my breechclout so I can dress."

"No, I think you will listen better this way."

"Get on with it," he said.

"Your sister, Ara, does not use good judgment."

"Gaga-na, you poke your nose into other people's

affairs. Ara prepares food for Talasee because she has a kind and decent heart. She does not trust Cimmera. That woman does not fool her. Cimmera brings strange notions to our village, ideas that separate us even further. Destructive notions. Ara and I know that she is a bad spirit. A witch."

"I am not going to argue with you now. I know the cool air must make you shrivel uncomfortably."

"Then be gone."

"You do not understand, you stubborn old bear. I thought only your eye was scarred, not your mind. I am concerned for Ara. I do not care that she prepares Talasee's food."

"Then what bothers you?"

"When she delivers the food, she stays. She goes inside his platform, and they talk."

Okemah bent forward, covering himself better, and bumbled onto the shore, snatching his breechclout from the branches. He stared at the woman, surprised that she did not turn away.

Gaga-na finally shifted her back to him. "Save the sight for Narchise," she said.

"How do you know this about my sister?" he asked, fumbling hurriedly with the strip of cloth.

"She told me," Gaga-na said, turning back to face Okemah.

"She has told you that she spends time at Talasee's hearth, inside his platform?"

"That is exactly what she has said. I know that you do not give credence to what Cimmera says, but to ignore her advice totally is to act irresponsibly."

"Ara does not believe what that woman has told us. Neither do I. If I could prove her to be evil, I would."

"You and Ara can have your opinions, but your

opinions should not endanger the rest of us. What if you are wrong? Think, fool. Tashi was isolated, and the disease did not spread as it did before. If Ara gets the illness, she will pass it on to us all."

"Bah! Talasee is not ill."

"Not yet. Cimmera tried to purify his platform, but she could not do the same for his body. If the sick spirit lives in him, then it has had a chance to jump into Ara also."

"Or maybe not. If Talasee is not sick, then …"

"Let us hope he does not become ill."

Okemah scratched his head, then pulled his long hair back and tied it in a knot.

"Talk to her," Gaga-na said. She took a few steps to leave. As she walked away, she said, "A bath is a good thing for a man. You smell better."

"A young man is judged by his skill in making weapons and his ability to bring down game," Cherok told Jumak.

"It is important to provide for the clan."

"Yes," Cherok answered.

"What about women? They do not hunt."

"Women are different. As young girls they are taught handicrafts and cooking. The woman serves the man, and the man provides for her."

"What about our women? Some do not have a man any longer."

"Then we all provide for one another. These are special circumstances. One day we will return to the customs with which the spirits have guided us. For now, we survive."

"Tell me more about women," Jumak said, cresting another arrow with the Tegesta signature.

"What do you want to know about them?"

Jumak grinned and blushed. "I know that they have their moon cycles. Will something like that happen to me when I become a man?"

Cherok tousled Jumak's hair. "Not really. The changes that will happen to you will be different. Your voice will get low, like a man's, your muscles bigger."

"But when a girl becomes a woman and has her moon cycle, then she can have babies."

"Yes," Cherok said. "That is right."

"What about me? When boys become men, they have the seed to plant inside a woman. How will I know when it is time?"

Cherok laughed. "You will know long before it is time. The spirits will give you very strong feelings. You will be sure. There will be no doubt."

"Will I feel it here?" Jumak asked, groping through his loincloth.

"Everywhere, especially there," Cherok said.

"What if I have those feelings and I do not have a woman?"

"That is the curse on men," Cherok said, laughing again. "We will talk about that more when you are a little older."

Jumak held the painted arrow over the fire.

"Take the ironwood," Cherok said. "Arrows are no good without bows. See which way it wants to bend."

Jumak stuck one end of the ironwood into the ground and braced it with his foot as he pushed on it to see which way it wanted to bend.

"Mark the way it bends. We will shape and string the bow so that it curves in the opposite direction," Cherok said. "Making a bow takes a lot of work if you want it to last."

Jumak wrinkled his nose in disappointment.

"Days of oiling so that it does not crack. If you make a fine bow, it will last a long time."

"But I am still growing. I will outgrow the bow. Maybe we will make just a good bow. One that I can hunt with today?"

"You are making a weapon. You must learn how to make the finest. You are not a patient spirit, are you?"

"My father helped me make a bow. No, he really made it, and I helped him just a little bit. I wish I had it."

Cherok looked at the boy. "You do without a lot and so little complaint."

Jumak shrugged. "I must show my courage," he said softly.

Cherok took out the piece of limestone with a hole in the center used for straightening arrow shafts. "Grease the rest of these shafts that are not already done, heat them, and run them through this hole."

"Where are you going?" Jumak asked when Cherok got up.

"Wait here. Do as I have said."

Jumak sat alone at Gaga-na's hearth and watched the cacique walk away.

"Will I wait long?" the boy called out.

Cherok turned around. "Not long," he said.

The child needed to hunt, needed to practice his skills, and needed something to occupy his time and mind. If his time was not full of things to do, he would dwell on the tragedy of losing his mother and the isolation from his father.

Cherok strolled across the mound, stopping to chat with a few people as he moved about. Okemah huddled with Ara, his brows dipped in seriousness.

Cherok moved into the trees, circling the village so he would not be noticed. Near Talasee's platform he picked up a stone and hurled it. The rock crashed into the thatch of the fire keeper's shelter. Cherok waited for Talasee to appear.

After a few moments he pitched a broken branch. The stick rattled the dry thatch and clattered to the ground.

"Talasee," he called out.

His friend emerged. He appeared doleful; his once proud and strong shoulders slouched, his head sagging.

"Friend," Cherok said, stepping closer.

"No! Do not risk yourself," Talasee called out, his voice sounding hoarse.

"What is wrong? You do not sound good."

"I do not use my voice much," he said. "It is surprised by the demand."

"I cannot stand this," Cherok said, walking toward his old friend.

"Do not let the evil spirits muddy your wisdom," Talasee said. "Stay back. Tell me why you have come."

Cherok thought about what his friend said. He supposed that Talasee was correct. The evil spirits would tamper with his good judgment, make him feel emotional and guilty so that he would discard good sense. They were indeed shrewd tricksters.

"I have come for some of Jumak's things. His bow. Some arrows."

"You teach him to hunt?"

"He will remember learning those skills from his father. I will take him to hunt to keep him occupied."

"You are my friend," Talasee said. "Teach my son so that he may become a man. Give him the experience he needs. Do not let him grow empty. I must know that you will do these things. Promise that you will do that for me."

Cherok raised his hand to confirm the pact, and

Talasee disappeared inside his platform. When he reappeared he came down the ladder with his son's weapons.

Talasee walked past his hearth and laid Jumak's things on the ground. He stood for moment. The distance he had closed between them gave him a clearer look at the cacique. "You look well," he said to Cherok.

Cherok could not say that about the fire keeper. He had dark circles beneath his eyes. His skin had a gray cast.

Talasee fingered the hank of hair that hung in his face. He pushed it back, sweeping his fingers like a comb across the top of his head. "Jumak probably did a better job cutting his hair than his father did."

Cherok tipped his head to the side. "Who have you talked to?"

Talasee stared blankly for a moment before answering. He decided not to reveal that Cimmera had returned for that knife. "Ara," he said. "When she brings my food she often tells me little things."

"Do you get enough to eat? What do you need?"

"The clan is good to me."

Cherok glanced back at the rest of the village. A few people had noticed that Cherok stood near Talasee's hearth. They watched the two men conversing with such an unfamiliar distance between them. "The clan straddles success and failure," Cherok said.

"Take my son's things before you linger too long." Talasee turned his back and headed toward his platform.

"Fire Keeper!" Cherok called. Talasee looked back from the opening in his platform.

The two men looked at each other. Cherok raised his hand; then Talasee disappeared inside his shelter.

Cherok retrieved Jumak's things. Perhaps it was time to send for Mi-sa. There were not many of his people, but they all needed healing, some in the flesh, some in the soul, some in both.

As he walked back to Jumak, the picture of his friend stayed in his head. There was more in Talasee's face than mourning, and Cherok's gut tightened. One other thing concerned him, something that just did not seem right. It rubbed at him like a rasp, like the skin of a shark. Never before had he had reason not to believe his friend. He knew Talasee so well.

"Push the pole," Cherok told Jumak. "Move the dugout into the trail."

Jumak plunged the pole down, felt it strike through the soft rot.

"Follow your heart," Cherok said. "Try not to think. Listen to Mother Earth. Hear, feel, where she leads you."

The two of them stayed silent, becoming more aware of the sounds and smells. Jumak moved the canoe through the water trails, which were sometimes so narrow that the saw grass swept against the sides of the dugout. Other times the saw grass parted, leaving great areas of shallow water with only small clumps of peat islands.

"That is the first step in the birth of a hammock," Cherok said, pointing to one of those small clumps. "And there," he said, pointing to another from which sprang a few willows, "that is the next step. If nothing goes wrong, the island will grow larger and larger."

"Cacique," Jumak said, "the water is too shallow to continue."

Cherok stood and looked over the tips of the saw grass that stretched to the western horizon. Then he pointed off to the left. Jumak looked where he pointed.

Baked into the marl were the tracks of an alligator, its trail made up of claw marks and the ruts made by its dragging belly and tail.

"Where we are now will soon be dry if the rains do not come. Take another direction," Cherok said.

Again the canoe moved silently through the dark water. "How do you feel now?" Cherok asked. "What do your senses tell you?"

"To stop," the boy said. He hopped out of the canoe and pulled it aground on a hump of tangled saw grass.

They crept through the sedge, Cherok demonstrating how to step, how to pause and listen. "Now gaze at the horizon and let your vision drift. Let your vision spread out. Do not focus."

Jumak's face was serious as he glared toward the horizon. "It becomes blurry."

"Yes," Cherok said, "but your eyes will pick up any movement. Then you sharpen your focus."

"Oh," Jumak said.

Cherok saw glimpses of Talasee in the boy's face, the expressions, especially the eyes.

"As we move along, you must slip in and out of that kind of vision."

Jumak flinched. "There," he whispered, sinking below the height of the saw grass.

Gaga-na rubbed ashes and water onto the hair side of a deer hide. She worked the mixture in, knowing that her efforts would be rewarded later with the easy removal of the hair.

"May I help?" Cimmera asked, appearing at the old woman's hearth.

Gaga-na looked up. "You wear the pouch. Good," she said. "And is the knife hidden there?"

"Yes," Cimmera answered, sitting across from Gaga-na. She watched the old woman work for a while, neither of them saying anything.

Finally Cimmera spoke. "I have not meant to keep secrets about myself. I have not meant to offend you."

"You have not," Gaga-na said, rolling up the hide, the hair on the inside.

"You have accepted me without many questions, trusted me, even risen to my defense against those you have known much longer."

"I do whatever I feel is right. It does not matter who is concerned."

"What you did with the knife … I owe you an explanation."

"You owe me nothing. Narchise was wrong to steal it from you. I do her a favor by not telling the others."

"Gaga-na, this is difficult for me, so please just let me talk and do not argue with me. Listen until I finish. I am so afraid that if you give me the opportunity, I will change my mind. You are right: I do need a friend."

Gaga-na put down the roll of hide and nodded. "I am ready."

"There is something I must tell you about me."

CHAPTER 24

"YOU ARE AN AGGRAVATION, old woman," Ara said, coming up behind Gaga-na.

"Go away, Ara." Gaga-na did not bother looking up.

"You talked to my brother. Okemah forbids me to visit with Talasee anymore. All because of you."

Gaga-na's face lit up. Now she looked at Ara. "Oh, he does? The man does have some sense about him. And I thought he was witless."

"Okemah is smart. He is certainly wise enough to know truth from untruth. He does not believe what she says, either," Ara said, tipping her head toward Cimmera. "He knows why she is here."

"I did not ask him to change his opinion, only that he be prudent and ask his sister to act with the same forethought."

"What I do is my business. Not my brother's or yours."

"That is true. There is a limit, however. When you do things that might affect me, then your business is of great interest to me."

"I do not do anything that affects you."

"Ah, that is where your brother understands and you do not. He does not believe Cimmera. He is stubborn, but he is not stupid. If there is a shred of truth in what this woman says, then you jeopardize the health of all of us when you come back into our midst after tarrying and dallying about Talasee."

"I will not defy my brother, but I do resent your interference."

"You should not have defied the decision of the Council."

"I will still prepare and deliver Talasee's food."

"I have no objection to that."

"We would all be better off if our cacique spilled his seed on the ground. He does not see his people for her." Ara turned on her heel.

"Do not pay attention to her," Gaga-na said to Cimmera. "She is venomous because she is angry. I think there is more to her indignation than she lets on. Perhaps she is interested in Talasee, the man. Everyone clambers for a mate. She would take advantage of this time. Men are vulnerable when they grieve."

"Do you really think Ara is that conniving?"

"She might not see it that way. May not even realize it. The need for a mate is natural, especially now so that we may grow in number again."

Cimmera considered what Gaga-na had just said as her eyes followed Ara. "If that is so, she wastes no time. Tashi has not been gone long."

"The storm has changed everything. There is no time to grieve properly. We have shrunk to such a small number. Now," Gaga-na said, "I am sorry she interrupted us. There was something very important that you were saying."

"Yes, but I think I have lost the courage to speak."

"You? I cannot believe that."

Cimmera's mouth curled into a faint smile. "All right," she said. "You asked me what I knew about the knife. I told you nothing because I do not know anything."

"Where did you get it?"

"I do not know that either."

"I am not understanding you."

"I am just as confused, Gaga-na. The truth is that I do not know where the knife came from or how I got it. I do not even know who I am."

Gaga-na cocked her head, addled by what she heard.

"You say you are Cimmera, from a distant Tegesta village that was also destroyed by the great storm."

Cimmera rubbed her forehead with her fingertips, staring down at her lap. "That is what I have said, but it is all a lie." She looked up. "Everything is a lie. When Cherok found me, he asked my name. I made one up. Cimmera was the first name that came to me. I have no memory."

Gaga-na shook her head in disbelief. "When? How?"

"It happened not long before Cherok found me. I remember running and falling. When I stood up, I found that my past had vanished, washed away as if there was nothing before. I hid on a small hammock and stayed there because I did not know where my home was. I had the knife with me." Cimmera buffed her upper arms for warmth and looked into the distance. "I am afraid of what I might have done with the knife. Maybe I did something so terrible that I do not want to remember. Perhaps that is why I was running." She looked back at Gaga-na to see her reaction. "Do you think that could be?"

"You are a good person. You would not have done anything to shame yourself."

"You only know me as I am today. Who was I? What was I like? Even I do not know that. I thought much about that when I was alone for so long. When Cherok found me, I had given up. I had tried to end my life. He saved me."

"Does he know you have no memory?"

Cimmera shifted, and she fought to keep her voice clear, although she wanted to cry. "No. He only knows the lies."

"You must tell him," Gaga-na said. "Tell him right away."

Cimmera looked down at her hands as she wrung them. "I cannot do that. I have told too many untruths. My life began with Cherok. There was nothing before him. If I lose him, I will have lost my life. That possibility terrifies me."

"It is dangerous to balance upon tiers of falsehoods. If one small prop collapses, then all of the others will fall."

Gaga-na felt a tinge of guilt. She had not lied to Cimmera; she just had not told her what she knew.

"I know that," Cimmera said. "Why cannot things just move forward from here? What does the rest matter?" she said, standing up. "I have created a past. It satisfies Cherok. There is no reason to tell him, is there, Gaga-na?" Cimmera paced, then spun around. "The truth would destroy his trust, destroy what he feels for me. He is everything to me. He fills up all the past I know. I have had no life without him. If I lose him I will have nothing—no past, no future. I will not exist."

"Do you ask my advice, or do you just confide in me?"

Cimmera sat again. "I do not know. Tell me what I want to hear."

Gaga-na thought about the knife, the designs she had seen on it, what she knew about this woman. "My head says you should tell the man. That is the best way."

Cimmera choked back a flood of tears.

"But," Gaga-na continued, "my heart says to tell you to keep your secret. Keep it until the clan is strong, when Cherok is less burdened, when the dissonance over the sickness has ended."

Gaga-na stopped and looked sympathetically at Cimmera. "The decision is yours to make. I am afraid I have not helped. What if you could remember? Would you tell him, then?"

Cimmera stirred the coals of the fire. "Maybe I do not want to remember. Maybe I would not like what I remembered. If my past was so bad that I have forgotten it, then I am better not knowing anything."

"Tell me who you think you are," Gaga-na said.

Cimmera shook her head.

"What will you do if your memory returns and you do not like what you recall? What if you are not who you hoped you might be?"

"If I am sure? If it all becomes clear, with no shadows, no fuzzy images? It would be better if that did not happen, better that I never remember."

Cimmera snapped the stick she had used to stir the fire, the jagged end cutting into the flesh of her palm.

"You have hurt yourself," Gaga-na said, taking the stick from her, opening the woman's hand and inspecting the broken skin. "Well, I know who you are," she said, closing Cimmera's hand. "You are Cimmera, Tegesta woman, woman of the cacique."

"I am glad that I have told you," Cimmera said. "I feel relieved."

Gaga-na looked away. Their conversation sealed her conviction. She would not tell Cimmera anything. The young woman was not ready to hear. Not yet. Even if Cimmera could remember, she would not recall everything that Gaga-na knew.

"Cherok!" Cimmera said as she stood.

The cacique approached, a stag over his shoulder, Jumak strutting by his side.

"It is my kill," Jumak said. "I have provided for the cacique, his woman, and Gaga-na!"

Cherok put the deer on the ground. "Jumak will have the antlers."

Cimmera's arms encircled the man's neck. "I am glad you return."

Jumak whispered in Gaga-na's ears. "They are so—"

Gaga-na shoved the boy away, scolding him with a glare.

Jumak looked up to see Cherok's arms go around Cimmera. The child leaned closer to see if he could hear any of their whisperings or spy on their touchings.

Gaga-na picked up her walking stick and tapped the boy on his back. "You are too absorbed in how men and women get on."

Jumak turned around and grinned. "I think I will like the touching when I am a man. The talk is silly, but I like the rest."

Cherok's hand slid down Cimmera's side. "What is this?" he asked, feeling the pouch.

Cimmera took his hand in hers and moved it away. "Gaga-na made it for me. Now I can carry things with me."

"She is good to you," he said, stepping back to look at it. Jumak had edged close to the cacique's feet and stared up.

"You have some work to do," Cherok said, looking down at the boy.

By evening the deer had been butchered, and the meat was drying on racks over the fire. Jumak gave the hide to Gaga-na, who began the process of cleaning it.

For days the sun continued to stream down, and the rains stayed away. The earth became scorched, and the canoe trails dried up. The winds returned, and the cool air turned warm. Everyone prayed for rain. They worried about Atok and Dacoma. The animals came close, seeking water and food, sometimes finding it in the clan's borrow pit, the hole the villagers had dug alongside the hammock during a past rainy season. They piled the spoil on top of the hammock to keep the village above water level.

Jumak and Yoma played by the man-made slough.

"Look, Yoma," he said, squatting by an old rotten log. "Bear!"

Yoma huddled next to his friend. "Ohh," he said after taking a closer look.

Jumak poked at the timber. "The bear has torn the log apart looking for grubs and beetles. He is hungry."

Yoma looked at Jumak. "The bear comes close."

The boys stared at each other. They did not often see bears, but knew how dangerous they were. They scanned their surroundings, neither wanting to admit his fear.

Stamped in the mud were the bear's tracks. Yoma put his foot inside the track. "He is a big one."

"Come on," Jumak said.

They ran back to the village. Yoma went straight to his father to tell him what they had discovered.

Jumak stopped and checked on his deerskin, which was stretched between stakes.

"That is a fine kill you made," Okemah said as he passed the boy.

"Yes, it is," Jumak said proudly. "Cherok helped me."

"Your father would have enjoyed the honor."

Jumak's face fell.

"That woman has caused you much pain."

Jumak looked up. "Cimmera has not caused the trouble. The sickness is to blame."

Okemah squatted so that he could look the boy in the eye. "Your father is my friend, also. If being so near Gaga-na all the time is difficult for you, then bide your time about my hearth. Ara will feed you well, and I will provide."

"I can provide for myself. I am a burden to no one," Jumak spoke up.

"I did not mean that you were a burden. I see by this kill that you contribute your share."

"My father asked that I stay with Gaga-na."

"She is old, and I know how restrictive that can be on a boy. That woman, Cimmera, stays about the old woman's hearth."

"She helps Gaga-na take care of me."

"Because she feels guilty, maybe, or because Cherok demands it of her."

"You are generous, but I am all right. My father will be with us soon."

"Has Cimmera told you that? Many days have passed already."

"She says it will not be much longer, when we are sure the sickness is gone and is not hiding in him."

"As I said, your father is my friend. If you wish to spend time with me, I would be proud."

Jumak nodded his head.

Okemah returned the gesture and walked away thinking about the situation. The conditions that Cimmera imposed were difficult for all of the clan to accept, but were most cruel to Jumak. The boy had his father's blood, the courage of the fire keeper. He did not show his sadness.

Okemah decided to sit by the water and talk with the spirits. Tichini was always about him, like a gnat. She was fun, but she put off Narchise. He had to think of a way not to hurt the young woman's feelings while winning Narchise. The way it was now, Tichini always buzzing about, Narchise would never receive his attempts to pursue her. Tichini made Narchise dreadfully hostile. Why, the last time she had rapped him solidly. He winced just thinking about the pain that had shot through him.

He sat in a quiet place in the shade of a tall tree. There was no wind, and the water was flat, without a ripple. Okemah filled his chest with air.

He drew back when hands touched both shoulders. He twisted and looked up. "Narchise."

Her hands gently massaged his big shoulders. "Do I interrupt your prayers?"

"No, no," he said.

"If I do, I will leave."

"No! Stay," he said.

"Does this feel good?" she asked, kneading the tight muscles.

Okemah's head lolled as she worked close to his neck. "Oh, yes," he said, his voice congested with the pleasure.

Narchise knelt behind him, lightly touching her bare skin to his naked back. She moved her hair out of the way so there was nothing between them.

Okemah could feel her great breasts rub against him.

"There," she said. "You should be more relaxed now." She withdrew, rocking away from him.

"No," he said. He touched one of his shoulders. "There is still stiffness here."

Narchise inched up to him again, her warm flesh smothering his back. One of her hands slipped around him and played with his nipple.

Okemah twisted and hooked his arm around her neck, dragging her forward, her head over his shoulder. His mouth was wild on hers, hard and bruising, his hand desperately trying to reach behind him to feel some part of her.

Narchise pulled up and moved around in front of him on her knees. He swept back her hair, which had fallen forward, and his lips opened, his mouth filling with saliva. He swallowed.

"Let me taste them," he pleaded, his hands cupping the outer swell of each breast, pushing them together, forming a deep valley between them.

Narchise bent her head back, offering them to him.

"Ohh," he groaned as he pressed his face into all that sumptuous flesh. His tongue lapped, and his mouth sampled and savored. The sheer volume of her overwhelmed him. He did not know where to focus, what to taste or nibble or lave next.

Narchise planted a hand beneath one of her breasts and pushed it up, the nipple centered at his mouth.

He nuzzled against her, then took in the dark nipple, drawing it to the back of his mouth with suction until he thought he would choke on the grand pleasure. Narchise held his head to her as she climbed onto his lap and wrapped her legs around him.

She could feel him hard beneath her, and it brought a triumphant smile to her lips. She reached down, lifting her weight, and pulled him free from his breechclout so that his man part stood proudly throbbing between them. Okemah grunted and tucked his buttocks more snugly beneath her so that their bellies hugged that part of him.

Narchise moaned at the intimate contact and began to rock gently, the motion and friction, the sound of her pleasure, drawing a groan out of his throat.

"Oh, no," he muttered, afraid that he might be finished too quickly. He lifted her up off him, stiffened as he fought back the release of his pleasure, then fell over her as he dared to touch her again. He probed for entry, his hips pumping.

Narchise slid out from under him. "You are in such a rush," she said.

"Yes," he mumbled, nipping at her belly, then back to those breathtaking breasts, making every effort to position her beneath him again.

"Be patient," she whispered. "Lie back."

Okemah trembled, his legs shaking with need. He rolled onto his back, gasping, his gut fluttering.

Narchise straddled his knees and bent forward. She held his manroot still. Lightly and teasingly she danced her tongue about, then slid him deep inside her mouth.

Okemah bucked, and Narchise slowly lifted her head. He reached for her, calling her name. His voice sounded like a cry as he begged for her.

"You like this, do you not?" she whispered.

"Yes, yes, yes," he said, his hands grabbing for her.

Suddenly Narchise stood up.

Okemah's eyes flew open, and he saw her looking down at him.

"I do not think Tichini can do it better. You let me know if she can," she said, pulling her long hair over her breasts and walking away.

Cimmera curled against Cherok, and a frail whimper came from her. She turned on the mat, slowly waking from the dream, keeping the finest details sharp and frightening. Tears rolled out of her eyes and one into the corner of her mouth. Carefully she turned away from Cherok, and then held still, her back to him, afraid that he would wake. She lay there, hushed, motionless, guarding her breathing until she was sure she had not disturbed his sleep.

She crawled to the opening of the platform, then

stood, glancing back at him, vaguely making out his silhouette in the dim light. She climbed down the ladder, then turned and pressed her back to it, hiding in the shadows.

The dream was still fresh in her mind, still wrenching tears from her. At least she hoped it was just a dream and not a vision. She would not sleep the rest of the night without knowing.

Cimmera darted across the crest of the mound, taking advantage of the dark, keeping her distance from the waxen light of the last glowing coals of the fires. The night was thick and black, forbidding. She slipped behind the trees, beneath the sooty night sky, on the perimeter of the village where there was no clear path. Fingers of grasses and vines curled about her ankles. An owl screeched, and she jumped. Her bare feet felt every lump and scratch of the forest floor. She was sure the earth crawled with scorpions and snakes.

She felt safer when she moved out of the brush and stood just below the platform. At the bottom of the ladder she paused, catching her breath.

CHAPTER 25

CHEROK REACHED OUT, expecting his arm to settle around Cimmera, and then he would tug her closer, but his arm fell onto the mat. He opened his eyes and peered into the dark, still reaching with his hand as if she had just drifted from him a bit.

He sat up and called her name. He hoped she was hidden in the deep black of the corners of the platform. She didn't answer him. He was impatient waiting for his eyes to adjust to the blackness, and so he stood and moved about. She was not there.

Cherok tied on his breechclout, wedged his knife between his breechclout and his waist, and grabbed a lance from the corner. If something was wrong, he would be prepared. He climbed down the ladder. All he could see was the reflection of things near the dying coals of the many small hearths. There was no movement, not even leaves blown by a breeze.

"Cimmera," he called softly.

There was no answer. Cherok moved about the village, near the central hearth, past the hoard of reeds, wire grass, and palms the women used for basketry, past the small mound of shells they had brought back from the Big Water. Meat smoked above the central hearth.

Cherok felt a pang of dread. Where was she, and why did he always fear that she would leave him? His anxiety stung like a premonition and kept him apprehensive most of the time.

Cimmera looked up to the opening of the platform. "Talasee," she called. "I must talk to you." Again she called to him, a little louder.

In a moment the man appeared.

"Please come down," she said.

"It is the middle of the night, Cimmera, and you should not be here. Go back."

"Come into the moonlight so that I can see you," she said.

"Leave," Talasee said, disappearing from sight.

"If you do not come down, then I must go up. This is important."

"No!" Talasee said. "Do not come up."

Cimmera backed away from the ladder and watched as Talasee descended.

"Back away," he said as he turned to face her.

Cimmera took a few steps back, but she could see him clearly enough. The moonlight fell on his ashen face. He was gaunt and haggard.

"You are sick," she said. "The illness."

"Go away, Cimmera. Do not be so close."

"Oh, Talasee," she said, her hand going to her mouth.

Talasee coughed.

"When? When did it start?"

"What does it matter?" Talasee said.

Cimmera felt queasy. She had experienced a vision, not a dream. The truth had crept into her while she slept: Talasee had the sickness and he, too, was going to die.

"Go," he said. Talasee climbed back up the ladder and went into his shelter.

Cimmera backed away, her hand still over her mouth.

She stumbled backward, tripping over a basket and falling. She rubbed her arm that had hit the ground first. It hurt from the elbow to the shoulder.

She saw the basket she had fallen over. It was still filled with food. Ara's basket. Talasee had not eaten. She thought of Jumak and Cherok especially, and how they were going to suffer again with another loss of someone they loved.

Behind her she heard the brush rattle. The noise had not come from a small animal scurrying through the dry grass. She heard twigs snap and leaves crunch. Something large moved nearby.

Cimmera scrambled to her feet. She moved quietly. Maybe the animal would not detect her if she kept her head and did not panic. She had to move back to the platform quickly and silently. A cloud passed over the moon, and the night was darker.

Again the brush rustled. Closer, she thought. It was following her, tracking her.

Cimmera swallowed. More quickly she moved, being less careful of the noise she made. She could barely make out the silhouetted outline of Cherok's platform in the distance. Safety.

Then behind her she heard it—the low growl, the heavy steps. In the brush it moved behind her. She took a quick look back, then turned and ran. She slammed into something and screamed.

"Cherok!"

"Cimmera," he said, his arms going around her. "What are you doing?"

"Shh," she said. "Something is there." Her voice quavered with fear. "Behind us."

Cherok pulled her down so that they crouched. "Do not move," he said. They hunkered quietly. Cimmera was trembling.

Then the creature suddenly crashed through the forest, breaking out into the clearing of the village.

"Run!" Cherok said, holding his lance in front of him, and whipping out his knife.

Cimmera froze in terror.

The bear stood on its hind legs and then lunged toward Cherok, its claws grazing Cherok's arm. At the same time, Cherok thrust the lance into the animal. He felt the point run through the fur and fat of its chest.

The bear reared up and bellowed, and Cherok yanked free his lance.

"Come again," Cherok said tauntingly. "Come for more. This time I will open your throat."

The bear leaned its head back and let out a horrible howl, shining spindles of saliva spiraling from its mouth.

Cherok rocked, shifting his weight from foot to foot, the knife firmly gripped in one hand, the lance in the other. "Do you want some more?" he said, jabbing at the bear.

The animal fell to all fours, the ground shaking from the impact. Cherok took aim and rammed the lance into the eye of the bear.

The bear roared and staggered, blood trickling out its eye and chest. It bounded forward, and Cherok grabbed its fur and swung himself onto the animal's back. He held on, gripping the bear with his knees, his arms around its neck. As the bear raised itself onto its hind legs, roaring and rumbling, Cherok drew the sharp blade of his knife through the neck of the bear, sawing it back and forth, cutting deeper until he felt the spurt of the animal's hot blood.

The men of the village awakened and rushed to the noise. They threw their spears into the big animal. The bear thrashed and tried to stay upright, but the blood flowed and the bear grew weak. Finally with a last gurgling roar, it crashed to the ground.

Cherok scrambled away, the bear's blood and Cherok's own blood covering him. The animal shuddered in a death throe.

Cimmera threw her arms around Cherok. "You are hurt," she cried.

Cherok embraced her, dropping the knife to the ground. She sobbed into his shoulder.

The men whooped and cheered, pulling free their spears. Bears were not easy to bring down, and they had great respect for the animal.

"It is the drought," Cherok said to Cimmera. "It makes the animals bold. They venture close, finding water in our borrow pit. We will become as desperate as they are if the rains do not come."

The men hauled the carcass into the center of the village where they would tend to it in the morning. Bear meat went rancid quickly. There would be no need to keep it, but the oil, the bones, and the fur were treasures.

Cimmera and Cherok sat on the ground, staring at the animal in the dim moonlight. She touched Cherok's arm. "You need medicine. I will take care of you."

The men gradually returned to their platforms.

Cherok looped his good arm around Cimmera and drew her face to his. "You could have been killed," he said, tasting her lips. "Why were you wandering around in the middle of the night?"

Cimmera lowered her face, then looked back into his eyes. "I dreamed that Talasee was sick, that he had the illness. I woke from the dream, but the image was so strong I could not sleep any longer. I had to see."

"And were you satisfied?" he asked.

"Cherok," Cimmera began. "My dream spoke the truth. Talasee has the sickness."

Cherok leaned his head back and glared at the moon. "We fight so hard," he said. "Why do the spirits torment us so relentlessly?"

Cimmera touched her hand to his cheek. "Perhaps they want to see your people's fiber."

Cherok stood up. "We have been stripped and broken, but we still say our prayers to the spirits, honor them with all we do." Cherok raised a fist to the sky. "It is time!"

Cimmera rose and put a hand along each side of his face. "They see you, Cherok. You have done all you can. Trust. Do not give up."

"Put this in your medicine bag, if you think there is bad luck," Cimmera said, handing Cherok a sprig of snakeroot. "This is a good-luck talisman."

"I saw the bear!" Jumak said. "It is a big one. I think Yoma and I saw its tracks. I believe it is the very same one."

"Yes, it may be," Cherok said, then gritted his teeth as Cimmera scrubbed his wounded arm.

"The bear could have torn out your heart. How can you think the spirits are not smiling on you?" Cimmera said.

"What is in that?" Gaga-na asked, watching Cimmera place medicine-soaked swatches of deer hide on Cherok's arm.

"You watched me make this, Gaga-na."

"But I cannot remember it all. Tell me again. This old mind does not hold things like it used to."

"Peeled stems of prickly pear, willow bark, a bit of brown from the cattail, juice of the pilosa."

Gaga-na studied how Cimmera bandaged the cacique's

arm. Strange how Cimmera could remember such concoctions but nothing about her past. She understood how it would be natural for her to instinctively know such things. After all, Gaga-na thought, look at the blood that flowed through her. What had happened to this child? What horrible things?

"Gaga-na, you look like you might cry. What is wrong?" Cimmera asked, tying the bandage around Cherok's arm.

"The wind is strong today. It stings my dry old eyes."

"I have seen other tracks by the pit," Jumak said.

Cherok put his hand over his bandaged arm and spoke to the boy. "If it were not for the drought, we would not have seen this bear, and there would only be small-animal tracks in the mud—raccoon and opossum. You must always be alert. Never let your mind drift or become distracted. Your senses must be extra keen. This is a dangerous time."

Jumak's eyes widened, and Cherok saw the sense of adventure that sparked in them.

"Take my words to heart, Jumak."

"He will," Cimmera said, smiling at the boy.

Jumak jumped to his feet and looked toward the central hearth. "They skin the bear," Jumak said. "I am going to watch."

The boy hurried away.

"I have given them the fur," Cherok said to Cimmera. "The men will gamble for it. They all watch and participate to make sure the skinning is done properly." Cherok laughed. "Jumak does so want to be a man. I hate to give him more bad news."

"What news?" Gaga-na asked.

"Talasee has the sickness," Cimmera said.

Gaga-na reached for her throat. "This is bad news."

"I will call the Council together later. We must discuss Talasee and of course the drought. The fires will come soon."

"We decided that I will tell Jumak about his father," Cimmera said. "While the Council meets, I will sit with the boy. Unless that is something you wish to do. I do not want—"

Gaga-na interrupted. "You do it. You are more like his mother. I am just an old woman. Take him somewhere quiet where no one will watch."

The boy and Cimmera sat in the shade of a large oak. A leaf fluttered down.

"If you catch it, your wish will come true," Cimmera said.

Jumak reached for the small leaf, but it eluded his grasp.

"There will be another," Cimmera said. "Jumak. I brought you here because I wish to speak with you. Sit closer."

"It is about my father, is it not?"

"Yes."

Jumak looked away from her. "I do not want to cry," he said, his voice rough and strained.

"I know that," she said. "If you want me to leave you alone, I will."

Jumak turned toward her abruptly. "No. Do not leave."

"The illness does not always—"

"It took my mother. It will take my father, also." Jumak drew up his legs. He crossed his arms over his knees and buried his face there.

Cimmera stroked his hair and then his back. She pulled him against her side, settling his head on her chest.

"I wish there was something I could do," she whispered, holding his head and rocking.

Jumak suddenly pulled away and looked at her. "You could if you wanted to."

"What can I do for you, Jumak? How can I help you through this?"

"You are magic. I know you are, Cimmera. I do not care where it comes from. I think it is a good magic."

"No, Jumak."

"You did heal the tree. You did know about me and the poison seed. You could heal my father with your magic. You could. I would never tell."

"I do small things that are not uncommon for people in my village to do."

Jumak's eyes filled with tears. "Please, Cimmera. Please."

Cimmera pulled his head back to her shoulder. "Shh. Shh," she whispered.

The men sat about the central hearth. The cool air of winter had gone.

"The heat of the sun is strong, but the rains have not come with the end of winter," Cherok said. "We all know what that means. The winds have also returned, and if the fires begin, the flames will be blown across the dry prairie," Cherok said.

"It is time to post a guard," Okemah said.

The men agreed that someone needed to be alert through the night, to spot the glow of fire in the sky, to listen and watch for animals, like the bear.

Yoma's father wiped a bead of sweat from his brow. "A few of us at a time should hunt for the entire clan. No one should venture out alone."

"Yes," Cherok agreed. He looked at the men's faces

and knew they worried about Atok and Dacoma.

Okemah spoke next. "All the women will prepare the food at the central hearth. No one will keep his own kill."

This was just another custom that was broken since the storm, and no one argued. Before the great storm, each man had been responsible for providing for himself and his family, or those for whom he agreed to provide. Now, no man would claim a kill for himself. If they were to survive they would have to accept change.

Cherok told the men not to be afraid of change, to ride the wind, and if the spirits wished them to return to the old ways when they were strong again, they would be told.

The men were nodding and agreeing, talking among themselves, ready to disperse.

"Another matter needs to be brought to your attention. Talasee has the sickness."

The men sighed and mumbled, some to themselves and some to one another.

Okemah stood up, his face twisted in anger. "That woman has brought all this misfortune upon us. The evil spirits sent her to destroy us. Can you not see that?"

Cherok struggled to keep his composure. He could not react with emotion; that would undermine his authority and the importance of what he had to say. "Surely you cannot believe that Cimmera brought us the disease."

"You are blind, Cacique!" Okemah said. "You cannot see how she has driven a stake between us. All her strange ideas, the tension between us."

"It is you who cannot see clearly," Cherok answered, deliberately keeping his voice low and even. "Cimmera has brought us good advice to keep the disease from spreading. As you see, Talasee alone is affected."

"Have you not heard the other accusations? I have

been told that there are those who have seen her do magic. Who else could do magic but someone connected to the spirits?"

"We have been through this before, Okemah. Cimmera is from a distant village with different customs. Let it go. See if what she says holds true."

Okemah kicked the dirt in frustration. "You will let your friend die alone," he said, scowling.

"Talasee will have it no other way. He knows what Cimmera says is the truth."

The men hung their heads. Such strong dissension within the clan was not good. This clan had once been very strong. Now it was unraveling, friends turning on friends, the men openly challenging the judgment of the cacique.

Okemah punched his fist into his other hand. "Ask your woman who she is. Ask her why she does magic, heals wounds in trees, burns pine boughs like a holy man."

There was much rumbling among the men.

Okemah was encouraged by the apparent support. "If I can find proof that she is not good for our clan, then you must listen to me. That will be the end of her. Will you agree?"

"There is nothing to find out about her," Cherok said.

"If I gather proof, do you agree that will be the end of this woman?"

The men were nodding.

"Yes, Cacique. If Cimmera is not what Okemah says, then nothing will be lost," Yoma's father added.

Cherok thought for a moment. If he refused, he would appear to have doubts. Why else would he avoid such a challenge? They needed to hear strong conviction from their cacique.

"Agreed," he said.

CHAPTER 26

"WE DO NOT HAVE TO TELL ANYONE," Jumak said.

Yoma shook his head. "I do not think we should go."

"Yoma, do you not have a sense of adventure? All we are going to do is look at the tracks, see what animals have come close."

"I think we should go with my father or the cacique."

"We are almost men."

"Almost," Yoma said. "Remember the bear?"

"Do you want the respect of men or do you want them always to think of you as a boy or even a woman? Show yourself for what you are. Or are you afraid?"

"No," Yoma said. "I am not afraid."

"Then come with me now."

Yoma followed Jumak to the edge of the mound where the borrow pit was.

"Maybe you should not tell your father we have been here," Jumak said. "Do not give him the chance to forbid it."

"No, I am not going to tell him. He might get angry."

"Look," Jumak said, squatting, studying a track in the mud.

Yoma leaned over. "What is it?"

"Bobcat. Too small for panther. It is a cat for sure. No claws showing. See how his back paw comes down almost right where his front paw was? It makes an overlapping print. That is how cats walk."

"Oh," Yoma said, looking even closer.

"You should know these things," Jumak said. "You cannot become a man if you do not know animal tracks. Be glad you came with me."

Yoma sat on his haunches next to his friend.

"Rabbit," Jumak said, pointing to more prints. "Do you know about rabbit tracks?"

Yoma shook his head.

"The back feet are longer and wider than the front. See how he jumps, the hind feet coming down ahead of the front ones."

Jumak stood up and walked around the edge of the pit. "Raccoon, deer." Suddenly he crouched again. "Look at this." His voice had a tinge of wonder in it. "Big cat. Panther. Big stride. Female."

"You are making that up. How can you tell?"

"Males are wider at the shoulder. Females' hind-feet tracks are more to the outside of the front. That is because they have the babies. Need more room there than the males. Know what else? Males walk more on the outside of their rear paws. Do you know why?"

"No," Yoma said, looking about, wondering if the panther was lurking just behind the bushes.

"They need to make room for their ...you know, their ..."

Yoma looked blank.

"This," Jumak said, cupping his crotch, rolling to the outside of his feet, and giggling.

Yoma laughed, then stood up, walking about bowlegged and on the outer edges of his feet, growling and snarling.

The boys laughed, finally dropping to the ground

holding their sides.

"You would know my tracks anywhere," Jumak said, barely able to speak through his giggling. "Mine are the ones that only show the little toe!"

Yoma was sprawled on his back, and Jumak had his knees bent. They lay there catching their breath, a loud chuckle now and again coming from one or the other.

Suddenly, Yoma sat up. "What was that?"

"What?"

"I heard a noise. Maybe we should go. That panther might be hiding nearby. He could be stalking us right now."

"She," Jumak corrected.

"Come on, Jumak."

Jumak took his bow, pretended to nock an arrow and take aim in the distance. "I could save you. I could bring her down."

Yoma and Jumak trekked back to the village.

Cimmera sat inside Cherok's platform. Jumak's words had gone straight to her heart. What if she could help Talasee? What if she did have that kind of magic, even if it was from the Darkside? Perhaps she could redeem some things she must have done in the past. Do something good.

She took the knife from the pouch and held it in her hands. Where had this instrument come from?

"What keeps you this morning?" Gaga-na called from below.

Cimmera put the knife inside the pouch and went to the opening. "I am lazy, I suppose."

"That is not a good quality," the old woman said. "Gives them something to talk about."

"I know," Cimmera answered. "I have been thinking."

"Well, that is always a good thing, but why do you not come down and do your thinking? Come to my hearth. Cherok is hunting."

"Yes, that is what he told me very early this morning."

"They will be back soon enough, and then our work will begin. We need to prepare."

"Cherok said they were not taking the canoes."

"There is no water except in the low spots. They walk. Come down and give an old woman some help this morning."

Cimmera climbed down the ladder.

Gaga-na stepped back and stumbled. She grabbed her leg, and Cimmera took her by the arm for support.

"How did you hurt your leg?"

Gaga-na looked up. "A long time ago. I will tell you about it sometime."

"I would like to hear."

"It is a dull story. I will tell you one day when we are both bored."

Cimmera saw Jumak and Yoma. "The boys amuse each other."

Jumak and Yoma were poking each other, laughing and making strange noises. They hunched their shoulders and tramped hard on the ground.

Gaga-na smiled. "It is fun to be a child. Jumak should enjoy this time and stop trying to be a man so fast."

"He does hurry. Do you think he would be that way if he had not lost his mother and was still living with his father?"

"Jumak was always precocious. Of course, now he is anxious to prove his courage. He hides his fear and sorrow behind a false face."

"I believe you know him well."

"And so do you," Gaga-na said. "Tell me, do you

spend less time in search of your memory?"

"A part of me wants to know, maybe needs to know. But another part of me does not want to know anything. That is the part I favor."

"Put it aside, Cimmera. Live this life and do not pursue the past. That is a quest that might better be abandoned. Your memory will return when the spirits deem it time and not one instant before."

"You sound convinced that I will not like my past, who I am."

"No, no," Gaga-na said. "How could I be certain of such a thing?"

Cimmera inspected Gaga-na's face, looking for telltale signs to judge if she was telling the truth.

"If someone has done bad things, and then later in life tried to do what was right, what do the spirits remember?" Cimmera asked.

"The good things, of course. It would be different if the person started out doing good and then was bad. Do you think you have done bad things? That is not a good way to think. After all, you do not remember anything."

Cimmera shook her head. "I guess I am afraid of losing what I have. My heart is filled with so much happiness I fear that it will be snatched from me."

"Stop that talk. I will hear no more of it. Now, take these," she said, handing Cimmera a bundle of long sticks to be used in making a grate.

Gaga-na helped Cimmera plant the supporting sticks in the ground. Jumak and Yoma, still laughing, came to Gaga-na's hearth.

"The smell of cooking meat will fill the air later," Jumak said.

"Does your stomach grumble already?" Gaga-na asked.

"I am growing. The more I eat, the faster I will grow."

"I do not think you can speed things along," Cimmera said. "What have you two boys been doing?"

Yoma glared at Jumak with wide eyes.

"We pretended to be hunting," Jumak said.

"Hunters do not make so much noise," Gaga-na said.

"You do not think I would be a good hunter?" Jumak asked.

"Not making all that noise. You would frighten away the animals."

"We were playing. Now we are really going to hunt. Is that not so, Yoma?"

Yoma shrugged.

"We are. You will see. We also will provide for the clan."

"Do not wander," Gaga-na said. "Killing a deer does not make you a man."

Cimmera smiled at the boy. "Be careful. Remember what Cherok told you about being alert."

"We will." Jumak patted his friend on the shoulder, and then they walked off.

"Gaga-na said not to wander," Yoma said, seeing where his friend was leading him.

"We will not go far," Jumak said, stepping onto the flat land that once had water covering it. "Come on. We cannot find anything here."

Yoma reluctantly followed Jumak through the tall, wilted brown rushes that surrounded them. "Why could we not hunt on the hammock?" Yoma asked, carefully watching every step.

Jumak, however, looked straight ahead, hiking through the brush with confidence. Suddenly he stuck his open palm in Yoma's face. "Listen and watch," he said.

"Can we not just catch a turtle?" Yoma whispered,

coming to a halt.

"Anyone can do that."

"Jumak," Yoma said, "I do not think this idea of yours is good. I want to go back."

"What is wrong with you, Yoma?" he said, turning around to face him.

"I just do not like it here. I feel that we are disobeying."

Jumak plopped down, crushing reeds and grass beneath him. "Do you think so?"

Yoma sat. "It does not feel right."

"Are you afraid?"

"I guess so."

Jumak looked around and then clapped his hand on his friend's shoulder. "We are supposed to be afraid. If we get all that out now, then we will have no fear when we are men."

Yoma grinned. "I wish I was like you."

"No, you do not," Jumak said, lowering his gaze, his voice low.

"This is a hard time for you. I am sorry. I would cry if my mother died and my father was also dying."

Jumak's head shot up. "But my father will not die."

"He is sick, is that not so?"

"Yes, but Talasee is not going to die."

"How do you know that?"

"I just do," Jumak said, standing up. "Come on," he said, giving in to Yoma's concerns. "We will catch a turtle or shoot a bird."

Yoma grabbed Jumak and turned him around. "How do you know your father will not die?"

Jumak stared at Yoma for a long time before he spoke. "Are you my friend, the best friend I have ever had?"

"Yes," Yoma answered. "We have always been friends.

Like brothers."

"Do you promise not to tell? Not even your father?"

Yoma nodded.

"Cimmera," Jumak said.

In the late afternoon the hunters returned. They brought back deer, alligator, small mammals—food for the whole clan. The women tended the fires and grates on which they smoked and cooked the meat. They soaked the hides in water and rolled them up to be taken care of later.

Jumak and Yoma took their catch to Cimmera.

"It is a fine turtle," Cimmera said.

Yoma hung his head, feeling responsible for the fact that they had not contributed more.

Jumak grasped the bear claw that hung on his thong necklace. "When we are men, we will fill the grates with our kills."

"I am sure you will," Cimmera said.

Yoma kept staring at Cimmera as she prepared the turtle, and she noticed.

Finally she looked at the boy, inviting him to say whatever was on his mind, but Yoma quickly looked away. He gazed across the village to where his father stood. Yoma had heard all the talk about this woman, the accusations. He liked her in spite of the things that were said, but now he was sure the suspicions were true, and that made him apprehensive. Jumak had said she was magic, but did not question where her magic came from. Yoma felt bad that he kept a secret like this from his father. But a promise was a promise, and he was a loyal friend.

Yoma stood.

"Where are you going?" Jumak asked.

"To be with my family," Yoma said, then trotted

toward the gathering.

Cimmera saw how Jumak's shoulders slouched, how his young face sagged with sadness.

"I have no family," he said.

"Of course you do," Cimmera said. "Cherok, Gaga-na, me, we are your family."

"Not really," Jumak said. The boy stood up and walked away, his head hanging low as he kicked a small stone.

Cimmera put down the turtle and rose to her feet. She touched the pouch at her side.

Cimmera leaned against the base of a tall Sabal palm. She propped her head against the trunk and stared up, seeing swatches of late afternoon light caught between the branches, palms, and leaves. No one had followed her; she had been careful. She was alone and hidden by the trees and brush.

Cimmera opened the rabbit-hide pouch and withdrew the star knife. She wandered around the area until she found the plant she wanted. She cut the stalk, touched the milky sap to her finger, and then her finger to her tongue. Four times she tasted the sap, facing a new direction each time. When she finished, the stalk slipped out of her fingers and fell to the ground.

Cimmera sat, legs crossed, and held the knife in both hands, laying it flat on her palms. She closed her eyes and hummed a slow, steady melody. While she focused her concentration, the words to the song came to her and flowed out. At first they were A-po-la-chee words, but then they changed. She understood them. They were ancient words in the magic tongue.

Cimmera felt the warmth seep into her hands first, then up her arms and through her body. Her skin tingled, the hair on the nape of her neck standing up. The warmth brought a flush to her face. She put the knife back in the pouch and felt the heat of it against her hip as she rose to her feet. These preparations came naturally, and she wondered if there was something else, something hidden in that dark hole in her mind.

This was the best she could do, Cimmera thought as she approached Talasee's platform. She had no idea if she was going to be successful, but she had to try, no matter the consequences. Jumak deserved her efforts.

The sun barely found its way inside Talasee's shelter. Dusty, dirty light hovered there. Talasee sat in the center with his medicine bag in his lap, the contents spread out in front of him.

Cimmera called his name.

Talasee dropped the bead he was holding. "Go out," he said. "You know the sickness is in me."

"That is why I am here," she said.

"There is nothing you can do."

Talasee's voice was weak and scratchy.

"What were you doing?" she asked, seeing the objects from his medicine bag.

"I assess my life. See what I am. It is time for me to do that. I thought I knew, but now that I am so close to the Other Side, I believe I have greater understanding."

Cimmera stepped closer. "Tell me about these objects. Tell me who this man, Talasee, is." She sat across from him.

"You should leave, Cimmera. This illness is a wicked one. Do not allow it in you."

Cimmera ignored him. "Tell me about this," she said, picking up a carved piece of antler.

"It is from my first kill. My uncle carved the designs. The shaman put it in my medicine bag."

"Cherok's sister, Mi-sa?"

"Their father, Atula."

"And this," she said, looking at the small fetish in her hand.

Talasee gathered all the articles, took the one she-held, and put them back in the bag and tied it around his neck.

"You must leave," he said.

Cimmera took the star knife out of the pouch and held it in front of her. The knife emitted a pale golden glow. "Close your eyes," she told him.

"Stop, Cimmera. Leave now, quickly, before the sickness finds you."

"Your son needs you," she said. "I am going to try to help."

"My son is young. He will grow and heal swiftly."

"I have promised Jumak," she said. "He trusts me. There is magic in the knife. Maybe just the right magic."

"There are greater things than my life. If you stay for any time, you will take too big a risk. Even if you knew the right medicine, the right prayers, this cure would probably take many days. You would have to visit me daily. Even then I might die."

Cimmera hung her head. If her life were at stake, she would have a better argument. Her life did not matter, what little there was of it. At least the spirits would remember the one good thing she had done—if indeed she could do such magic. She did not want to think of what would occur if she failed.

"There is too great a hazard, too much to lose," Talasee said. "The clan will not recover if this disease spreads among them. You could take it back to them. You understand," he said. "It was you who told us of the danger. Go!" Talasee stood up. "No more argument."

"I could attempt the healing. It might not take long. I

do not know the strength of the knife's magic." Cimmera looked up at the man with the pensive, stoic face.

"I will end this," he said.

"What do you mean?" she asked.

The fire keeper held the blade of his knife to his throat.

CHAPTER 27

"THERE WILL BE NO MORE of this disease! Go, or I will spill my blood!" Talasee said.

Cimmera got to her feet.

"If I must, I will," Talasee threatened.

Cimmera backed down the ladder. She put the star knife inside the pouch.

"What do I say to your son?"

"Tell him the truth."

"But I might have saved you."

"And you might have taken the disease back to Cherok, back to Jumak, and from there to all the others. You could not heal them all, maybe not even yourself. Some would die because I live. What kind of life would I have then?"

Cimmera felt the tears running down her face.

"Cimmera," he said before she left, "what if you had not been able to heal me? What then for you?"

Talasee vanished inside the platform, leaving her haunted by his last question. If she attempted to heal Talasee and failed, the villagers would be convinced she was a strange, evil woman with bizarre notions who thought she could do shaman's magic. At best she would be an outcast. At worst ... She hated to think.

Cimmera looked back at Talasee's shelter. She knew in her heart that if Talasee had not put the blade to his throat, she would have tried the healing. She had made a vow to Jumak. If the healing had taken long, she would have isolated herself, though she knew that the isolation would be difficult for her. She could never be alone like that again. But even that thought had not weakened her determination to honor the pledge she made to her small friend.

She wandered back to the village and found Jumak.

"Come with me," she said, leading him away from the village.

Jumak's face was bright and radiated with expectation. "You have done it!" he whispered.

Cimmera's heart tumbled. She led him to the edge of the hammock.

"It does not look like it is going to rain soon," Cimmera said.

Jumak plopped down on the ground, pulled a weed from the ground, and chewed on the stem. "Tell me about my father," he said. "When will he be well?"

"Jumak, there is something I must tell you." She sat beside him. "With our hearts we sometimes make promises to those we love. Those are oaths that are never taken lightly. They are the commitments that we would sacrifice anything to keep."

Jumak stared, eyes wide, taking in every word.

"My promise to you was one that I made from the heart. I love you, Jumak, and I would never break a promise to you."

"Then he is healed," Jumak said.

"No."

"Have you seen him yet? Do you want to break your promise?" Jumak's face crimped.

"I do not want to break my promise. Never would I do that."

"Then what is it, Cimmera? You bring bad news, or

good news would be told already."

"I have seen your father."

"Is he dead?"

"No. I have talked to him. I told him what I promised you, but he would not allow me to try the healing."

"Why did you not try anyway? You are magic; you could have done it, could have made him listen."

"I did what I could," Cimmera said. "I was willing to keep myself isolated if the healing took long."

Jumak stood up. "No! You were afraid. You are magic and can do anything you want to, but you fear the disease and protect yourself. You never meant to heal my father. Your promise was empty. A lie!"

Cimmera rose to her feet. "Jumak, that is not true. I wanted to keep my promise to you." She reached out to put her arms around the boy. "I wanted to—"

Streams of tears ran down the boy's brown cheeks. He tore himself from her hold and glowered at her. "They are right about you!" he screamed. Then he turned and ran.

Cimmera felt sick. Only a wicked person could cause so much disharmony and sadness. She stared out at the singed saw grass, the parched soil, the brittle brown grasses. There was nothing but great silence and loneliness out there. She shuddered.

Far from the Tegesta village Atok and Dacoma approached the small hammock on foot after abandoning their grounded canoe. They had followed the only water trail left, often portaging the dugout over shallow or dry spots. Now there was no trail, only the dry mosaic of cracked clay and soil where water had once stood.

This was the last hammock they would visit. It appeared to be inhabited. Smoke rose into the sky above the tree island.

Cook fires. Perhaps these people would be kind enough to share their food, they thought.

On foot they neared the bank of the hammock, calling out and waving, giving signals that they were Tegesta. A thin, aged man on the bank moved his hand in greeting.

Atok and Dacoma stepped onto the hammock.

"I am Wa-chee, cacique of the alligator clan. Welcome."

Atok and Dacoma introduced themselves as they walked with the old man. They surveyed the village as they entered. The alligator clan had been hit by the storm, too, but this far north they had not suffered so much. Yet there were fallen trees. They stepped over a dead cypress, some lacy leaves, now brown instead of bright green, still clinging tenaciously to the rough branches.

"We are from a clan to the south. Our leader is Cherok. Perhaps you have heard of us," Dacoma said.

Wa-chee stroked his chin. "Yes, I have."

"The storm of last summer did great damage to our village. Many of our people are lost. We are searching for those who may still wander," Atok said.

Wa-chee nodded reflectively. "And you stop here. You say you come from far south?"

"Yes, that is so. But after the storm some may have become disoriented. Our men were on a journey to the Big Water when it struck. They may have come this far north."

"In error, of course."

Atok and Dacoma looked at each other, and Wa-chee noticed.

"To the north are the A-po-la-chee. This direction would not be one of choice, I would think. In error," he repeated.

"We found another, a woman, this far north, but farther inland, to the west. She was not from our village, but she says the storm destroyed her village, also. There could be others, though not from our clan."

Wa-chee's old gray eyebrows arched. "I did not realize there was that much damage this far north. Tell me, from what clan did she come?"

They entered the center of the village, and Wa-chee invited them to sit beside the central hearth on a prominent earthen plaza they had built.

Dacoma answered. "We do not know. Our cacique says she does not speak about her past, that it causes too much pain in her."

"Hmm. Does she give you the name of her cacique or any man in her village? I should know them if they are my neighbors."

"No, she does not talk of anyone. Too many sad memories," Atok said.

"Well," Wa-chee said, "I am not aware of any neighboring village that was destroyed. We suffered some damage—fallen trees, scattered belongings, a few platforms lost their thatch—but no overwhelming destruction. This woman makes me curious."

Atok rubbed the back of his neck. "She is curious," he said. "Perhaps she is confused."

Wa-chee raised his hand and gestured for two elders to sit with them. "We have visitors from a clan to the south." He introduced Atok and Dacoma to Patok and Ocomee. "They search for survivors of the storm. They found a woman. She says she is from this area. Says her village was lost to the storm."

Patok and Ocomee listened intently. The strangers' tale was interesting.

"What was the woman's name?" Wa-chee asked.

"Cimmera," Atok said.

Wa-chee nodded his head and appeared to ponder it. Then he explained to the others. "She will not speak of her village or of clan members. The remembrance is too painful."

"She says she is from a village close to us?" Ocomee asked.

"That is what she has told others," Dacoma said. "But we have not asked her ourselves."

Ocomee turned to Patok. "Do you know of any village near us that was destroyed by the storm?"

Patok shook his head.

"Then we understand that you have not seen any survivors," Atok said. "No one has stumbled into your village?"

"No one," Wa-chee said. "We would have offered shelter and food. We know the terror of those great storms bred at sea. Many, many summers ago our village was hit hard. I was not so old and gray then. I was not afraid then. I would be afraid now. I am not as strong, but I am wiser."

They discussed the storm, those who had been lost to it and to storms before, the reason for storms in the first place, and why the spirits allowed such destructive forces. They talked about the drought.

"No rain for us, either," Wa-chee said.

"We took the only water trail that is left. It led here," Atok said.

Wa-chee peered up at the sky. "The rains will come. They always do. The drought will last long enough to do whatever the spirits have in mind, whatever they want accomplished by the lack of rain. We are not meant to understand. When the task is accomplished, the rains will come. All we can do is pray for that task to be hurried along so we do not suffer unnecessarily long."

"You think the drought has purpose?" Atok asked.

"Oh, yes. Nothing happens without the hand of the spirits guiding it. The wind that blows away the rain is the breath of the spirits. There is something to be learned or a message passed on. The spirits use the drought to deliver their message," Wa-chee explained.

"Is the message meant for a single man or a whole tribe?" Dacoma asked.

"The spirits may wish to speak to only one man."

"But a drought for one man?" Atok argued.

Wa-chee leaned closer. "If the message is important enough. If the goal achieved is meaningful enough."

"I suppose that could be," Atok said; "But I have never thought of a drought like that. I have cursed it."

Wa-chee smiled. "It does no good to shake your fist at the sky. The rains will not come until it is time."

Atok rocked back. "I see," he said. "That is interesting. Every man must listen to the spirits. The message may be for him."

"That is right," Wa-chee said.

All the men smiled.

"I will take back your wisdom with me and share it with my people," Atok said.

"Someone who sits beneath this same sky, feels the thirst of the earth, sleeps beneath this same moon, needs to listen carefully," Wa-chee said. "There comes something special, perhaps to his ear, his heart, his mind. This is how it has been explained to me," he said, nodding toward a lonesome man across the village.

"Your shaman?" Atok asked.

"Soltis understands the spirits."

As was the custom, Atok and Dacoma thanked Wa-chee and offered him one of their flint points.

"You travel far," the cacique said, pushing the offering away.

A sudden flurry in the village drew their attention. A woman screeched.

"Warriors! Warriors!"

Wa-chee got to his feet as many men scrambled to the edge of the hammock.

The word spread quickly that these were not Tegesta approaching, and it appeared they were not A-po-la-chee either. Panic swept through the village like wildfire.

Wa-chee and Soltis stood at the edge of the hammock. A long waving snake of strangely tall men trampled the saw grass, definitely headed for the village.

Wa-chee's leathery face rumpled, lines of age cut deep in his forehead.

Women hid, holding their infants to their breasts and toddlers to their legs.

"They are ugly," Soltis said.

Patok handed the cacique and the shaman their long spears, put quivers of arrows across their backs, and gave them their bows. The men of the village lined up behind Wa-chee and Soltis, gripping their weapons.

"I do not know this tribe," Wa-chee said.

Atok and Dacoma listened to the whisperings of the men.

"Who are they?" Atok asked a nearby man.

"We do not know them. Do you?"

Atok shook his head.

Soltis suddenly turned to Wa-chee. "The tribe that has been rumored. Thunderbolt. Enemy of the A-po-la-chee."

"It is said they are the fiercest tribe, that they feast on the flesh of their enemies. Such men are enemies of the Tegesta also," Wa-chee said, his stomach turning with revulsion.

Soltis closed his eyes and began a quiet chant. Wa-chee kept his eyes sharply focused on the approaching rope of gleaming brown bodies, glints of sunlight reflecting off ornaments around their necks.

Wa-chee's clan stood rigid, their black hair tied in knots on the top of their heads, polished bone pins securing the coils in place. They waited patiently, cautiously watching as a single warrior separated himself from the rest. Wa-chee suspected that he was their cacique. The unfamiliar warriors halted, and the one man moved ahead.

Wa-chee did not move, except to push back his shoulders, lift his chest and chin. Soltis took a step back.

About ten paces before he reached the hammock, the approaching warrior stopped. He lowered his bow, though the warriors behind him stood ready.

The two leaders stared at each other. The intruder was younger than Wa-chee. His chest and arms rippled with muscles; his legs were strung with taut tendons. He was lean and hard. But, Wa-chee thought, their cacique lacked the wisdom that came with a long life. Good that they would talk first.

Wa-chee estimated the number of warriors. There were many more of these strangers than warriors in his clan, even with Atok and Dacoma. Finally Wa-chee nodded a greeting.

The tension was as alive as lightning and nearly could be heard crackling in the air. The visitor waited for Wa-chee to speak first.

Atok and Dacoma stared. The warriors of this tribe wore bracelets around their arms and ankles, but dangling from them were not the usual feathers and shells. From these bracelets dangled teeth, and to Atok and Dacoma they appeared to be human teeth.

A ripple of disgust traveled through Atok. He studied this strange tribe even more closely. Their noses were perforated, and in them they had inserted fish bones and pieces of tortoiseshell.

"Welcome to my village," Wa-chee said.

"Kereb," the intruder said, revealing his name.

"Wa-chee."

Kereb bowed, then lifted his head. He looked behind Wa-chee, his eyes darting around the village.

Wa-chee stepped more squarely in front of him.

Kereb squatted and cleared a space in the dirt. With his knife he drew two shapely bodies ...women. He looked up to Wa-chee's face to see if he understood.

Wa-chee gestured that he did. But Wa-chee had no intention of bringing out his women, and for what reason did Kereb want to see them?

Kereb stood and made a wild flourishing sign to his warriors. They raised their bows, arrows already nocked.

"Why?" Wa-chee asked, though he knew the man would not understand the language. "Why do you want to see my women?"

Wa-chee knew the stories told about this tribe. He had heard what they did to women.

Kereb listened to the inflection in Wa-chee's voice. He crouched again, and in the dirt he erased one figure and circled the other. He held up one finger and said something in his language.

Atok and Dacoma watched, their hearts pounding in their chests. They wanted one particular woman. At any moment a battle could begin. Who were these strangely painted men? Never had they seen such designs in tattoos.

Wa-chee responded by raising his finger and shrugging

his shoulders.

Kereb drew something else in the dirt and waited for Wa-chee's reply. Then the intruder sketched another symbol. Atok and Dacoma strained to see what it was but could not.

Finally Wa-chee called for his women to come forward. The trembling women filed out from the brush, babies crying, small ones tearing at their mothers' skirts. The young maidens shook with fear, praying to the spirits that these men had not come in search of women to take back with them. They kept their eyes to the ground, their chins tilted down.

Wa-chee assured them that they were safe. He told them to cooperate and these strangers would leave soon.

Kereb strutted around the circle of women. He had them all pull their hair back as he marched around them, inspecting each one closely.

After several moments he went back to Wa-chee. With a combination of hand signals and drawings in the dirt, they communicated. Wa-chee did not ask who they were or where they had come from. He did not ask if it was true that they ate human flesh. It was wiser to stay focused on the moment. He would touch no raw spots and chance no miscommunication that could lead to battle.

Kereb stood up and signaled for his men to spread out around the hammock. Wa-chee told his people to sit.

"But, Cacique," a man said, "if we sit, we will not be in a posture to respond if there is an attack."

"Do as I say," Wa-chee said. "This will be over soon. Be alert."

Kereb's men made their way onto the tree island like a tightening band. Wa-chee's people watched, feeling the threat of being surrounded.

The warriors searched the brush and the trees. They entered every platform, looking to Atok like giant ants crawling over the entire village.

When the search was complete, Kereb spoke to his men, and they left the hammock, again forming that long line. Kereb said something in his language to Wa-chee, then turned his back.

Out of the corner of his eye, Wa-chee saw one of his clan fidget. The cacique raised his hand in a gesture to still the man and everyone else until Kereb had rejoined his warriors.

When the strangers became blurred by the saw grass, Wa-chee's people began to stir.

"Tell us," Soltis said.

"There was no danger to us. We do not have what they seek," Wa-chee said.

Atok and Dacoma worked their way over to where Kereb had been drawing in the dirt.

Atok walked around the drawings, then crouched to see them more closely.

Dacoma bent beside his friend.

In the dirt was the picture of the woman that Kereb had drawn and circled.

"What is that?" Dacoma asked, studying it even more closely.

"Looks like a knife in her hand. And look at this—a butterfly."

CHAPTER 28

AS THE DAYS WENT ON, the land gave up more of its moisture, and occasionally there was the scent of smoke. The People sniffed the air, and fear made the hackles on the back of their necks rise. They watched the horizon, waiting for a red glow to appear in the sky. Together they prayed for rain, and they prayed for the same when they were alone.

"Fetch some wire grass for me," Gaga-na told Jumak. "I need more for this basket."

"Do you ever wonder about things?" Jumak said, putting off answering her request.

"Of course. What is puzzling you?"

"Baskets."

Gaga-na looked up, surprised that such an ordinary thing would capture the boy's imagination.

"Well," he said, "how did the idea happen? How would someone have thought of making a basket?"

"Birds," Gaga-na answered. "A woman looked at a bird's nest and thought how useful something like that would be in which to store or carry things."

"Do girls just know how to make baskets?"

"Jumak," she said, startled by his ignorance on the matter, "you have seen women teach their daughters."

"Oh," he said. Absorbed for a moment, he paused.

"It is a craft that is passed down," Gaga-na went on.

"Who teaches the birds?"

The old woman put down her basketry. "The birds just know."

"How?"

"It is born in them. The spirits have given every animal certain gifts. For birds it is nest building."

"What about people? What is our gift?"

"We all have different gifts. Cherok's is the gift to lead. Your father's is the gift of keeping a fire."

Jumak shifted back on his heels. "And Cimmera's gift is magic." He sat quietly for a moment, then looked up and spoke hurriedly. "My mother said that if someone does not use his gift, it is taken away. It offends the spirits."

"Perhaps," Gaga-na said.

"Then the spirits will take magic away from Cimmera, and she will have no gift."

Gaga-na looked hard at the boy. "What makes you say such a thing?"

"She does not use her magic."

"That is not for us to judge, Jumak."

The boy saw Cimmera approaching them. "I will get the wire grass," he said.

"You have been this way for days. What has happened between you and Cimmera?"

"I hate her!" the boy said, his eyes tearing as he ran away.

"Are you going to tell me?" Gaga-na asked as Cimmera sat next to her with her own basketry. "Jumak cannot bring himself to tell me what has gone on between the two of you."

Cimmera put down her things. "I have failed him," she said.

"How can that be? You have been so good to him."

"I made him a promise I was unable to keep."

Gaga-na showed no reaction, her old experienced fingers continuing to weave.

"He begged me to heal his father. He thinks I can do anything. Because my heart ached so badly for him, I made the promise. Gaga-na, I did try, but Talasee would not allow it. He was afraid that I would get the illness and infect the others. He threatened to take his life. I could not tell Jumak that. All the boy understands is that he trusted me, believed in me, and I betrayed him, broke my promise."

"He has to be angry with someone or something. He has lost his mother, fears he will lose his father. He needs a focus, and you gave him one."

"I know. I agonize over his heartache. I wish I could do something."

"Let it lie for now. Deep down, he knows you tried. He just cannot see it now for all the pain and hurt. He does not cry or pound his fists. He does not have a way of showing his suffering. This gives him a way of expressing all that. In time. In time."

"Father!" Jumak called loudly, staying back the appropriate distance. He had been forbidden to come here. The others were all afraid that a boy could not control his emotions or that he might forget to stay back or that he might cry. No, he had not reached the age to be a man, but his heart was a man's. No one understood that.

Talasee appeared in the opening, and Jumak felt a stab of incredible pain. His father was sallow, his frame seeming to bend under the weight of his flesh.

"Jumak, are you there?" Talasee asked, squinting in the daylight.

"Tell me that you will be well. Tell me that you are

strong and will defy this evil sickness."

Talasee was quiet, his shoulders slouching.

"She could have done it," the boy said. "Cimmera could have healed you. She is all lies and is a coward. But I am not afraid!" Jumak ran to the bottom of the ladder and looked up at his father. "Tell me what to do," the boy said, his voice trembling as he cried.

"Jumak, what happens to me will be the spirits' choice."

"I will make Cimmera tell me what to do. I will hold my knife to her heart!" He was shouting, crying, tears rolling down his face, his throat pinching.

"She wanted to help," Talasee said. "She must stay away, and so must you. If you respect your father you will go and accept whatever the spirits decide."

"No!" Jumak yelled. "I am coming back. I will make her tell the magic secrets she has. If I have to, I will force her to come back here. Be strong, Father, and wait for me. I am coming back."

Jumak wiped away his tears with the back of his arm. "These are not crying tears. These are angry tears." He turned his back and ran. He did not head toward the village, but through the brush. His face was hot and red, his breath exploding out in sobs. In his secret quiet place he slumped to the ground and cried as he had not done since he was a very small boy.

"Where is that child?" Gaga-na asked. "He went to get me some wire grass and has not come back."

Cimmera looked across the village toward the place where basketry supplies were kept She did not see Jumak.

Gaga-na dusted off her legs. "Help me up," she said. "I cannot wait forever."

"Let me get it for you."

"I have grown stiff sitting like this. I need to move around if the old leg is willing."

Cimmera handed Gaga-na her walking stick and helped her to her feet.

"Come with me," Gaga-na said.

Cimmera suddenly felt a chill, and she turned around and stared into the deep woods behind her.

"Are you coming?" Gaga-na asked.

Cimmera shook her head. "No."

"Is something wrong?" Gaga-na asked.

Cimmera turned back to the old woman and stared a moment. "No."

When Gaga-na had gone, Cimmera walked into the cover of the trees. Something was nettling her. Something to do with Jumak. She did not feel he was in danger, but she felt him.

She wandered through the brush, following her instincts until a clear picture of him came to her. Then she knew the place. It was the spot he had chosen to sing his lamenting songs. Quietly she approached.

Jumak had his arms folded over his chest and his face toward the ground. Cimmera saw his little shoulders shaking. He was crying. She wanted to go to him, to comfort him, but knew he would not welcome her. Even if he felt differently toward her he would not want anyone to see him this way. She let him keep his dignity and turned away.

"They are coming!" Narchise screeched.

The villagers stopped what they were doing.

"Atok and Dacoma," she squealed, her flesh bouncing as she bustled about, breathless.

The villagers gathered and rushed to the landing.

Cherok stood with Cimmera. Atok and Dacoma

waved their hands in the air as they walked over what once had been covered with water. When they reached the hammock, Cherok greeted them with a strong forearm embrace.

"The spirits have blessed us," Cherok said. "Your return brings relief to us all. You have been in our minds every day."

The women stood back as the men met Atok and Dacoma, greeting the returnees, releasing that fear they had harbored and faced only in their dreams and private thoughts. Their smiles were broad, their laughter loud.

Gaga-na squeezed Cimmera's hand. "It has been a long while since good fortune has visited us. Though they have brought no one back with them, they have returned safely. No one else has been taken from us."

Cimmera glanced in the direction of Talasee's platform.

Bad news was not usually delivered too quickly when someone brought it home, and so Atok and Dacoma took part in all the festive talk. In the same custom, the villagers kept silent about Talasee. The time would come later to impart that information.

Ara and Narchise fluttered about, offering the returning men tangy teas and warm stew. Narchise found her way in front of Okemah as often as she could, sidling past him, giving him gentle bumps and cold but coy looks.

Gaga-na took Atok and Dacoma a bowl of food, hiding her grimace as she knelt to place it at their feet as they sat with the other men. Kneeling brought sharp pain to her joints and left her aching, but she declined to excuse herself. She did as was expected of every woman.

Jumak hovered around the circle of men, shushing his

friend Yoma so that he could better hear their conversation. He squatted beside a young cypress and pulled his friend down beside him. "Stop your babbling and listen to what they say. This is how we learn to talk man's talk."

"They banter and joke. There is no serious talk. Not until the sun goes down."

"How do you expect to talk like a man, to tell stories that make others laugh, if you do not pay attention?"

Yoma smirked and settled into a crouch next to Jumak.

The afternoon was hot and caused perspiration to dribble down the backs of the men.

"It is too hot," Yoma complained after sitting there for a long time.

"You have the shade of the cypress," Jumak said, not lifting his gaze from the men.

"But it is too late in the afternoon. The sun comes under the branches."

"You will be a boy forever," Jumak said as Yoma left.

Jumak sat, moving only to readjust his legs when they got tired or weak or uncomfortable. He was still there when the sun dipped under the edge of the earth. The men dispersed, ate their evening meal, then regathered around the central hearth. The time had come for more serious talk.

"Tell us about our friend Talasee," Atok began.

"Cherok tells us he has the sickness," Okemah said gruffly.

"Anyone else?" Dacoma asked, scanning the gathering to see if anyone was missing.

"No," Cherok said. "The rest of the clan is well, as Cimmera said we would be if we heeded her advice."

Okemah fluttered his lids, holding his tongue.

"We wait it out," Yoma's father said.

"There is nothing else we can do," another man said.

"Tell us more about your journey," Cherok said. "Tell us how the earth tolerates the lack of rain. What have you seen?"

"The drought is severe," Atok said. "Most of the trails have dried up. Fish bake in the sun."

"We abandoned the canoe several times. At the last, we gave it up," Dacoma said.

"Fires?" Okemah asked.

"We did not see any," Atok said. "But the prairie is tinder, and the black earth is ready to burst into flame."

The men sighed with the news. They had suspected that. The signs were all around them, but Atok and Dacoma confirmed their worst fears. The drought was bad. As bad as they had ever seen. The fires were going to come any day.

Atok settled more comfortably. It was time to speak of all they had seen and heard. "We visited a village to the far north, near where Cimmera said her village was. It is the village of Wa-chee."

"Yes, I know of it," Cherok said. "It is very far north in Tegesta territory. Close to the A-po-la-chee."

"Wa-chee wondered why we had gone so far in his direction looking for survivors of our clan."

"And did you explain?"

Dacoma nodded and spoke. "We did. We told him about you and Talasee and how you found Cimmera."

Cherok waited to hear more.

"Strange thing," Atok said. "Wa-chee's village did not suffer the destruction Cimmera said her village did. Yet they must be neighbors."

"I am certain there is an explanation," Cherok said. "Storms are unpredictable."

"There is more," Dacoma said. "Wa-chee was unaware of any nearby village that was destroyed by the storm. They all had some trees down, thatch blown away, those kinds of things."

Cherok pressed his fingers to his forehead and then spoke. "We do not know the cacique of Cimmera's village or exactly where it is."

"That is true," Atok said. "She must be confused."

"We have known that. She has so much pain recalling the storm that she does not wish to speak of it at all. I find no reason to probe her or doubt what she says."

Atok and Dacoma looked at each other.

"We have other news," Dacoma said.

"Tell us," Cherok said.

As darkness covered the village, Atok's voice grew more solemn, and the men strained to listen to him. "There is another tribe. Wa-chee says they are the fiercest people, even the enemy of the A-po-la-chee."

"Perhaps they will keep the A-po-la-chee engaged so that they will leave the Tegesta in peace," Okemah said.

"Wa-chee says they eat the flesh of their enemies."

The men reared back, appalled and shocked at what they heard.

Dacoma nodded at Atok before he spoke. "We have seen their leader. He is called Kereb."

"Where did you see this man, this inhuman?" Cherok asked.

"While we were in the midst of Wa-chee's village, Kereb and some of his warriors came upon the village. Wa-chee wished no battle, as his people were outnumbered and he had heard of the cruelties of these people," Atok said.

Dacoma continued the story. "Kereb was in search of someone. He drew a picture in the sand. A woman. He is in search of a woman."

"For himself?" Cherok asked.

"No. He looks for a special woman with some kind of knife. That is what he drew in the dirt, a woman holding a knife. He also drew a butterfly. There is some connection, but it was not explained to us. Wa-chee knew she was not among his people, and so he allowed Kereb and his men to search the village. They left without incident."

"Wa-chee's tribe is fortunate they avoided confrontation," Cherok said. "Where did these people, Kereb's tribe, come from?"

"I asked Wa-chee the same," Dacoma said. "He has heard they come from the Big Water in their canoes from a land far in the sea."

"I wonder why they search for this woman?" Cherok said.

Atok leaned forward. "Wa-chee said he wondered the same. He has heard the stories that these warriors battle just to take women away with them, that they have swept across the Big Water doing just that, killing the men and taking the women."

"Yet they took none of Wa-chee's women?" Cherok said.

"No, they were in search of just this one woman."

"That is peculiar."

"Wa-chee told us stories about these people. He does not know the name of the tribe, but those who know of them call them Thunderbolt," Atok said.

Dacoma clapped his hands loudly, startling the men. "Thunderbolt," he said, "because they strike at dawn, like a thunderstorm, slashing through villages like lightning. They ravage the women, and then take them as slaves. Their canoes are so large that you cannot count the men inside them."

"They must come from the far edge of the world," Cherok said.

Atok cringed as he spoke. "They come in their large dugouts, crossing the Big Water to eat the flesh of their enemies. They feast on the bravest man."

"What do they look like?" Cherok asked.

"Muscular, tall, savage. Their faces are ferocious, deep scars painted black," Atok said. "They have black and white circles painted around their eyes."

"They are frightful," Dacoma said. "They wear human teeth on arm and ankle bands and around their necks. They have put holes in their noses and wear fish bones or tortoiseshell in them."

The men sat listening in awe. What they were hearing was almost too incredible to imagine.

Jumak sat in the darkness beneath the same cypress where he had listened to the men during the day. His small mouth was agape as he pictured these horrific warriors in his head. What if they came to this village? There were so few of this clan.

The men listened to the crackle of the blazing fire on the central hearth, too stunned to say anything else. They let the new information trickle through their heads.

Jumak lifted his face in the evening breeze, suspicious of every rustling leaf behind him. The village was eerily quiet, as if even the trees and wind were aghast and dazed by the details Atok and Dacoma related. The boy sniffed the air. Smoke.

Jumak stood up. The men were close to the fire and could not smell what he could. He did not smell the gray breath of the fire burning in the central hearth. No, this scent wafted on the breeze. He scanned the moonlit sky, not blinded by the light of the flames from the central hearth as the men were.

There was a red glow and black smoke, but it was not a fire from the drought burning up the brush and coming toward them. This fire burned in the village.

CHAPTER 29

"FIRE!" JUMAK SCREAMED.

The men turned their heads, standing when they saw the radiance in the sky.

Jumak followed them as they ran toward the lit sky. Cimmera and the women hurried at their heels, Narchise huffing as she ran.

Jolted by what he saw, Jumak stopped, horror bleeding across his face. His father's platform was ablaze, flames leaping into the sky, the thatch popping and crashing down.

He watched as the men tried to get close. He heard Cherok and others calling his father's name, but Jumak already knew it was too late.

Cimmera came up behind the boy and rested her hands on his shoulders. "I am sorry, Jumak," she said.

The boy continued to stare at the blaze, unable to move, not even able to scream aloud as he screamed inside.

The men scrambled about but could not get close. Finally giving up their rescue attempt, they backed away from the heat and stood as still and helpless as the boy.

"I wish—" Cimmera did not finish. Jumak turned and yanked himself away from her hands.

"I hate you!" he shouted, flinging out his fists, pounding her.

Cimmera grabbed his wrists and held them still while

the boy cried and screamed. "It is your fault! All your fault!"

She dropped his wrists and pulled him to her by his shoulders, holding his head against her as they both wept, the child shaking with his tears.

Jumak sobbed and did not care who saw him now. Cimmera's chest muffled his cries. She stroked the back of his head, held him close, and leaned over him. She could think of no words to say.

She looked up at Cherok, who had come to them.

Jumak pulled back. His words were choked, and they stirred her deeply: "I believed in you, but your promises mean nothing. You have killed my father!" Jumak stepped back and glared at her.

Cherok quickly took the boy's arm and led him away. Cimmera stood alone, watching them go.

"The boy will be all right," Gaga-na said, coming up to her. "The child suffers."

"He is right," Cimmera said. "I am all lies, though the promise I made to him I meant to keep. Perhaps if I had never come here … if Cherok and Talasee had never found me …"

"Then we probably would all be dying of the sickness," Gaga-na said. "Walk with me. You are too hard on yourself. Jumak is only a boy and does not understand. Talasee has done what he felt he needed to do."

"What do you mean?" Cimmera asked.

"This fire was not an accident. He knew that what you said was true. He wanted to save his people."

"How do you know that, Gaga-na?"

"I am an old woman. I have seen many things. Now walk away from this with me."

From the distance Cimmera kept sight of the fire's flare in the black sky. Quickly it grew smaller and less bright. So swiftly it was gone, the charcoal sky closing in as if the fire had never happened.

The men dispersed. Yoma's father volunteered to stay to guard against a fire catching and spreading.

Cimmera sat at Gaga-na's hearth. Cherok approached with Jumak under his arm.

The boy climbed inside Gaga-na's platform without saying anything.

"These are difficult times for him," Cherok said.

Cimmera nodded and stood up. Cherok wrapped his arms around her and held her a moment. She hid her face in his shoulder.

"I told her that Jumak speaks with the voice of a boy," Gaga-na said. "He does not mean all that he says. He is just in so much pain,"

Cherok nodded at the old woman and then led Cimmera to his platform.

A slash of moonlight cut through the shelter. Cherok pressed his mouth to Cimmera's forehead.

"Gaga-na speaks the truth," he said. "Jumak does not mean what he says."

He combed her hair back with his fingers, and moonlight splashed over her face. His hand cupped her chin; then his thumb traced the outline of her lips. He studied her, the deep black pool of her eyes, the small delicate bones of her face, the long column of her neck. His eyes stopped there, the little birthmark reminding him of what Atok and Dacoma had said.

Kereb and his warriors had drawn a picture of a woman with a knife and a butterfly. Inside Cherok's head there was a distant, slight tingle of thought that Cimmera was that woman.

He let her hair drop back over her neck and shoulder

and held her tight. "I love nothing in this world as I love you," he whispered to her.

The rabbit-fur pouch bumped up against him. Cimmera untied it and tossed it aside.

Cimmera heard the voice, deep and compelling. She opened her eyes and felt the warmth of Cherok against her back.

Easily she slipped away from the man who held her even as he slept. She stood in the opening of the platform, the night breeze gentle on her skin.

Stars and moonlight filled the sky.

"Come." She heard the voice carried on the wind, pulling at her as if she had no will. She looked at the sky. Thin clouds drifted across the moon, blocking the moonlight for brief moments.

"Come, little Stardust."

"Tamar?"

"I have come for you."

She heard the voice, the breath of the wind, and she backed down the ladder and followed where the voice led her. She moved through the village, then into the brush.

"Come," the voice whispered.

Beside the tree that she had healed, she stopped.

She heard the wings of the great bird and saw the breeze that they stirred, felt the momentary chill in the air.

"Close your eyes. Come with me," he said inside her head. "I have something to show you."

Cimmera did as he said. Immediately she felt the comfort and security of Tamar close by. Strange as it was, this was a realm in which she felt content.

"I am ready, Tamar."

The leaves fluttered on the trees as the wind whirled,

and tiny spirals of dust spun on the ground, picking up fallen leaves and wisps of dry grass.

Had he spoken again or was it only the wind?

Cimmera stretched out her arms, palms up, her hair blowing behind her. She heard the song in her head and began to sing with it.

She opened her eyes, and there in the moonlight she watched the white bird come to rest in the tree. Her body tingled, and she drew in a deep breath before closing her eyes again.

"Take me with you, Tamar. Give me flight."

The sensation began in her feet, and then traveled up through her body. She raised her arms upward toward the sky, and in a moment she knew the transformation had taken place. On white wings, feathers floating on the wind, she soared with Tamar, seeing the earth from above, the moonlight splattered about in silver swatches.

"Do you see it all?" he asked.

"Yes," she answered, understanding why he had taken her on this flight. The earth was large, greater than she had ever thought, so large she could not see the edge, and she was only a small part. She was not to question her destiny. The hand of the Great Spirit had designed it all. A sense of reverence overwhelmed her. Below her was the vast Big Water, the moonlight glittering on the waves, their shadows falling on the surface. And there was the shore, land farther than she could see, stretching endlessly along the fringe of the sea.

"You are a part of this wonder," Tamar said softly.

The descent was slow and gentle, and in a moment she was back on the ground. She heard his voice as she caught a glimpse of his filmy shape, a sheer, translucent form that shimmered in moon shadow.

"It will all become clear to you," he said. "Do what

you must when the time comes. Have no fear for yourself. The magic is in you."

"When what time comes?" she asked.

"Follow your heart. The spirits rest there."

She watched as he faded into the night. He knew who she was, but she did not know about him. They were connected; their souls knew each other. If she was bad, then he was also. That thought gave her one glimmer of hope. She could not believe that this gentle spirit, Tamar, was evil. He was good and kind. He spoke of the heart, and she was sure he protected her.

She did not understand his message now, but was certain that what he told her would soon have great significance. A quick breeze, the beating of his wings, told her that he had gone.

"I will go with you," Cimmera said.

Cherok shook his head. "This job is for the cacique. I must do this alone."

"But if your sister were here, you would have a shaman to aid you."

Cherok pulled her to him and held her close. A few moments later he released her and strode away. Cimmera ladled another bowl of tea and sipped it, unable to keep her eyes away from him.

"Cherok," she called. She put down the bowl and ran to his side. "I will wait at Talasee's hearth."

He took her hand and rubbed her ann. "Are you sure?"

"I do not want you to feel so alone," she said.

Together they approached the fire keeper's shelter, the smell of recently burned palm and cypress still in the air.

Cimmera bent over Talasee's hearth. Ara's basket sat by the circle of stones that outlined Talasee's cook fire.

"He was not eating. The basket is full," Cimmera said and sat. "This is where I will wait for you."

Cherok stared at the burned-out platform.

Cimmera looked at all the things Talasee had placed about his hearth. There was a small bowl with some liquid in it. At least he had drunk some tea or broth, she thought. Then something next to the bowl caught her eye—torn stems of the white ghostflowers and a mushroom cap.

"Cherok," she said. "The fire was surely Talasee's doing, and he did not suffer."

Cherok looked down at what she showed him. "We will see," he answered.

The floor of the platform still stood, black and sooty. The thatch was all burned away. Cherok fumbled through the fallen ash and the burned roof timbers.

Something caught his eye, and Cherok stooped to see it better. He touched the trail of a burned cord. He understood what the presence of such a wick meant. Cimmera was right. Talasee had drunk a brew that would put him into a deep sleep. If Talasee had prepared a strong enough elixir, the sleep would have led to death. Just before falling asleep, he must have lit the wick, giving himself even more time to sink into his drugged sleep. If he was not already dead from the concoction, the raging fire would take his life and drive out any evil spirit from his platform and his body.

Cherok moved aside some timbers and debris, at last locating the remains of his friend. He hoisted the remains of Talasee's body over his shoulder and descended the ladder.

"I will go with you," Cimmera said, following Cherok to the burial area.

"He has no one to guide him to the Other Side,"

Cherok said.

"I have watched the ritual often," Cimmera said. "I will do what I can."

"But you are not a spirit man—woman."

"Leave him," Cimmera said. "Go and leave me alone with him. I will come for you when it is done."

Cherok stared at her. Anyone could attempt the ritual to lead a deceased man to the Other Side, but only a holy person could really do it. "I will stay," he said.

"No," Cimmera said. If Cherok stayed, he would hear her prayers, hear her speak the A-po-la-chee words.

"Do not ask questions," she said. "Do what you must do as the cacique and then leave."

Cherok laid down Talasee's charred body. Next to him he said the proper prayers.

"I will tell the others that we will bury our friend later, before the sun goes down."

"Trust me, Cherok," she said.

He gazed at her a long moment and then turned away. Whatever she could do for Talasee would be better than nothing. He walked back to the village.

"Talasee must have taken a firebrand into his platform. There is always danger in that," Okemah said, trying to explain Talasee's death.

"Yes," Cherok agreed, not telling him that Talasee had taken his life. "That is how it must have been."

If the others knew that Talasee had died by his own hand, they would bury him in disgrace, apart from the rest, with no grave goods. Cherok had decided that no one needed to know the truth. His people needed no more trouble on their minds, and Talasee should be remembered as the fine man he was. The storm had already destroyed too many lives, and in its own long, lingering way, the storm was still taking lives. Cherok felt his only defense was to break customs and fight back however he could.

"But why did he not awaken, if he had fallen asleep? Why did he not run?" Okemah asked,

"You forget how sick the man was. He had no strength," Cherok answered.

CHAPTER 30

THE VILLAGERS WATCHED as Cherok said prayers over Talasee in his shallow grave. Most of the cacique's formal accoutrements had been lost in the storm. Cherok painted his body and carried a newly made cacique's staff.

Cimmera watched him, admiring the elegance of his movements, enjoying the sound of his voice. The length of his arm as he reached toward the sky and the majesty of him standing before his people held her rapt. Even when singing death chants he was charismatic, the qualities of a great leader reaching out and touching every man and woman. He stood before them, a tower that stretched toward the spirits, and during these few moments all of the doubts and reservations that had haunted them disappeared. Their cacique led them along the sacred path.

When Cherok finished, he motioned to Okemah to come forward. Beside Talasee's body, the large man laid a fire drill he had found by the fire keeper's hearth. Other men also came forward on Cherok's cue, placing in the grave more of Talasee's personal articles that he had left by his hearth, out of harm's way. They brought a pottery bowl, Talasee's knife and atlatl, and the lined pouch in which he had carried burning coals on journeys. Talasee was a man, and a man of stature within the clan, the fire keeper. The burial ceremony was rich with respect for him.

None of the shaman's talismans were buried with him, though, and Cherok was sure everyone wondered if Talasee would find his way to the spirits without them.

Soon he would have to go for Mi-sa.

Talasee's body was so charred that Cimmera had not painted sacred designs upon it with ocher. It was better that way, she thought. The people would have asked questions if she had left her mark.

The women dropped flower petals into the grave, tufts of star grass, and some shiny gumbo-limbo bark. Most of them looked away rather than down at the fire keeper, afraid that the sight would sneak into their dreams.

Cherok pitched the soil over Talasee as the women wailed behind him. The grieving would go on through much of the night. The spirits would know what a good man this was.

Jumak stood near Gaga-na, his spine pulled straight, his shoulders stiffly wrested back, his chin bravely lifted. He watched the dirt spatter over his father's face. His throat tightened, and he dug his nails into the palms of his hands to fight back. The boy took a deep breath and locked his quivering chin. He would not shame his father by crying like a little boy. Talasee would be proud of him.

The villagers passed the boy as they left, the women whispering to one another how sorry they were for the courageous child. Yoma paused next to his friend, and their eyes met. Then Yoma, too, moved on.

Cherok escorted Jumak away.

After everyone left, Cimmera returned to the grave. She gathered stones and piled them on the ground above Talasee's head. Though she was certain that the spirit of the sickness had fled from the fire, she wanted to be extra careful. If the evil spirit had not yet left Talasee, it would be trapped in his body. She whispered A-po-la-chee prayers.

She hurried, knowing that Cherok would wonder where she was. Cimmera knew that people did not visit the graves after interment. Burials were the grounds of ghosts—mystical, unhappy, scary places. No one would notice the stones for a long time.

Dryness continued to creep over the land, and the winds grew more powerful. In many places the water shrank beneath the roots of the saw grass.

"It is the natural cycle of things," Gaga-na said to Jumak. "I have seen it before."

"But this is a dangerous time," Jumak said.

"Oh, yes. But when the time is right, the drought will end. Just when you think the earth will blister, the rains will come again. The black clouds of smoke will be replaced by the piling heaps of seething rain clouds. The wind will come ahead, and then rain will roar down, dousing the fires, ending the drought. The new season will begin."

The boy jumped up, having heard enough of Gaga-na's lessons for the day. "I go to find Yoma," he said.

Jumak's smooth brown skin glistened beneath the sun. He felt empty this morning and needed something to fill his spirit. He did not want to sit about. Too much time to think about things. He had to move on toward manhood.

He saw his friend with two other boys rolling the hollowed-out game stone along the ground, then throwing a stick, hoping it would go through the hole. The stick missed the target and skittered across the ground. The round stone tipped to one side, rocked, and then lay still.

"Give me a try," Jumak said.

Yoma collected the stone and stick and handed them to Jumak, who inspected the rock and then held the pointed stick to his eye and peered down the long shaft.

Jumak bent over and with a smooth swing of his arm rolled the stone down the path the boys had created for the game. He squinted and held the stick at shoulder height, gauging the speed and direction of the stone, his face hardened in concentration. Then he threw the stick.

The boys' eyes followed the stick as it glided smoothly through the air, and then they gasped as the tip penetrated the hole in the disk and stabbed the ground. The stone ring whirled around the stick in a rapid circle, then settled.

"Ay-ya-ya!" Jumak whooped and jumped in the air.

The boys slapped his arm and back in congratulations, yelping and whooping.

"Come on, Yoma," Jumak said, handing over the game parts to another boy. "Come with me."

Yoma and Jumak walked with their arms over each other's shoulders, still laughing and celebrating Jumak's skill at the game.

"You are amazing," Yoma said. "Did you see the looks on their faces?"

Jumak laughed loudly. "Practice and concentration. That is all it takes."

"I practice," Yoma said.

"But you must do it with determination and deep concentration. Over and over again."

"Where are we going?" Yoma asked.

"To the borrow pit."

Yoma dropped his arm. "I do not want to go there again," he said.

"Oh, come on, Yoma. You have been there before."

"And I saw all those tracks. The big cat."

Jumak took his arm from around Yoma and turned to face him. "It was adventurous, was it not? Did you not feel the excitement?"

"The drought has gotten even worse. We have been warned. I think it is too dangerous."

"Go back and play with the small boys, then," Jumak said.

"Come back with me. Do not go," Yoma said.

"You know where I will be if you find a little courage."

Yoma would grow up one day, Jumak thought as he hiked through the village and into the brush. He wished Yoma would change his mind, and turned around to see if perhaps his friend hesitated. An adventure was much more fun if there was someone to share it with.

Okemah sat by his hearth, sharpening his knife and thinking about his friend, Talasee. He thought about Pocola and how he had thrown himself on the pointed stick. He thought of Manche and his injuries, the storm, the many who were missing or dead.

Life did not go on forever. For everyone there came an end. Death could come swiftly and unexpectedly, or it could come slowly. What if it came for him tomorrow? What if it came before that? There was no way of knowing. He could be snuffed out like a tiny flame, with no warning. He had put off many things in his life, and he decided to change that.

Okemah blew on the edge of the knife, then gingerly ran his finger down it. Well, he thought, there were things he should take care of. There was no next time when it came to life.

Narchise was first on his list.

Okemah lumbered about until he spotted her. She was

standing with a small group of women.

"Narchise," he said strongly as he walked into the center of the group.

"What do you want?" she asked. "Can you not find Tichini?"

Okemah grabbed a handful of her hair. "I do not want Tichini. It is you I want."

The women giggled, but Narchise felt she was about to melt like a blob of bear grease in a hot pot.

He planted his hand firmly on the back of her head and pulled her face closer. Nose to nose, he whispered to her. "Come with me, woman."

Narchise neither looked at her friends nor closed her mouth, which hung open.

Okemah led her across the village, the group of women tittering and chattering behind their backs. When he had her far from everyone, and the deep brush hid them, he stopped.

"Do you know what you do to me?" he asked, taking her by the shoulders, kneading them. "You make me go out of my head."

"I do?"

"Look at you. When I am with you, the wonder of you swallows me. When you are out of my sight, you are all I think of."

His eyes could not stay put. They wandered over her, scouring every curve and dent.

"You really do not want the skinny one? The younger one?"

"Tichini? Never. What man wants to lie with a bunch of hard bones?"

"Some do," she said.

Okemah buried his face in the deep crevice between her breasts. Gently he shook his head, feeling her generous soft flesh flog his cheeks.

"Ooo," he murmured in a tremulous voice.

Jumak swatted at the tall blades of dying grass and sedge. He sat by the edge of the borrow pit, tearing a piece of grass into shreds. Yoma was not much fun anymore. Perhaps it was because he was becoming a man, and Yoma was still a boy. He wished he could hurry his friend along so they would enjoy the same things again.

He stretched out on the ground, watching the dazzling blue sky. He spied a couple of big puffs of white clouds that might build up during the hot day, fill with moisture until their gray bellies swelled, and finally burst. He felt the slightest hope that today it would rain. Then everything would start to return to normal ...except that his mother and father would never return like the rains.

Those thoughts made him sad, and so he sat up, determined to find other things to fill his mind. His father was watching him from his hearth in the sky, seeing how he grew into a man.

Jumak edged over to the mud and scrunched down, examining the tracks. He recognized them all. Raccoon, fox, opossum. He scooted around the perimeter on his haunches. Heart-shaped prints in a diagonal pattern. Deer. Jumak sat back a moment. Deer walked the way babies crawled, moving limbs on opposite sides of the body at the same time. It was a good observation. No one had taught him that. He did not follow the tracks any farther, pleased with his realization.

The boy stood up. "Do you see me, Father? See that 1 learn." He danced around, jumping, whistling, singing, moving along the side of the borrow pit, celebrating the pride he had in himself.

He caught sight of bigger tracks. He squatted. It was that big cat again. He noted the wide straddle and lengthy stride. She was big. Panthers were usually reclusive and did not come near the village, but this one had come twice. He was sure it was the same one.

Jumak followed the tracks. He saw that the cat had stood at the water a long time, her paws leaving deeper prints there. Her thirst must have been great. The prints moved toward the deer tracks, signs telling him the cat was stalking. Had the deer and the panther been at the pit at the same time?

Slowly Jumak slipped alongside the tracks, imagining the tension in the cat. Then the prints changed; the panther had charged. The deer prints and cat tracks overlapped, but then led away, out into the saw grass off the mound. Had the panther caught the deer? Jumak's curiosity was piqued. He had to know. Cautiously he followed the tracks, though they were less easily identifiable here.

The sedge swished in the wind, and Jumak looked up. He cocked his head, listening sharply, trying to decide if he had heard something other than the wind in the saw grass.

He looked back toward the village, surprised at how far he had wandered. The tall saw grass blocked part of the view, but he could see the tops of the cypress, palms, and oaks that grew on the hammock.

A trickle of fear ran through him, and Jumak balked at the feeling. That was the boy still in him, he thought.

Then there it was again, a whisper of a sound.

Cimmera made her way to a quiet spot on the edge of the hammock. There was a small puddle of water. She splashed the water on her face and rubbed it down her arms and legs. There was no good bathing water left. Every day the women filled pots of water from the borrow pit, always going in pairs, one to watch and one to dip.

She felt anxious, though she was not sure what was niggling at her. She scanned the surroundings, but saw nothing. A mist of rain dripped out of the clouds, and Cimmera turned her face to it. It was a tease of moisture, not enough to make any difference.

Maybe the sensation was just the rain on her skin, but she felt a tiny shiver. Cimmera searched for some plants for her tea and some to season the stews she cooked. The uncomfortable feeling was persistent. She was edgy and even jittery.

She decided to concentrate on the nuisance since attempts to ignore it did no good. She cleared a spot on the ground and sat, closed her eyes and forced her body to relax, fixing her mind on one small part of her body at a time, beginning with her feet, moving up her ankles, her calves, and the rest of her body. Tiny droplets of rain sprinkled her hair and skin as she waited, her senses clear and perceptive.

Suddenly her eyes flew open, and she bolted up. The rain stopped. Panic ripped through her. She ran through the brush, the ground cover tangling and ripping her ankles, the leaves of plants and trees slapping her. She kept looking ahead, frantic, pushing back obstructing branches with her hands. Her feet pounded hard on the ground. Her heart raced as she sucked her breath in and spewed it out.

Cimmera leaped over fallen logs, her arms pumping, her whole body working for greater speed.

Then clearly in front of her she saw the borrow pit

and then the ranging, endless saw-grass prairie. Her eyes skimmed the tips of the sedge as she sped through it, following her instincts as strongly as if a mighty rope yanked her.

Finally, she caught sight of him. Jumak squatted, inspecting the ground. Behind him, almost imperceptibly, a few blades of saw grass at a time disappeared, pulled down and crushed beneath large paws. The tawny coat of the panther blended with the dry sedge, and Cimmera strained to see ahead of her.

She was not going to make it! The panther was too close.

"Jumak! Look out!"

The boy looked up, a surprised expression on his face. Quickly he turned his head to see behind him.

Cimmera jerked to a stop and pulled the star knife from the pouch. With the accuracy she had learned when she was alone so long, she threw the knife.

The knife found its target with deadly precision, bringing the panther to the ground just as it leaped to pounce on the boy.

Jumak vaulted to his feet, shaken by what had happened. He turned back toward Cimmera and then looked at the panther again.

"What was that?" Narchise asked, pushing Okemah off her.

"Nothing," he said, breathing heavily, trying to climb back on her. "Just the rain."

"No," she said, sitting up. "Over there. Someone screamed—sounded like Jumak—and then I heard some words I did not understand. They might have been A-po-la-chee words. Did you not hear it?"

"My ears only hear your moans and whimpers."

Narchise cuffed his hand away as it grasped one of her breasts. "Stop. Something is wrong."

She stood up. "Put yourself together, Okemah."

He reluctantly obeyed and followed her through the brush.

"This way. The scream came from there," she said, pointing through the tall saw grass off the mound.

They trekked through the brush.

"It was your imagination," Okemah said as they wandered farther and farther from the mound.

"No, I am sure."

"Turn back," Okemah said. "I have no weapons. We should not be roaming out here."

"Jumak," Narchise called when she saw him. She shot Okemah a smug look. "You see, I told you."

Okemah and Narchise spotted the panther.

"Is that your kill?" Okemah said, moving closer.

Jumak did not answer. He looked at Cimmera.

Okemah and Narchise saw her, too.

CHAPTER 31

CIMMERA WAS BREATHLESS. The icy hot rush of fear spread through her like a lightning charge. She realized the words she had screamed were A-po-la-chee, and the knife sticking out of the panther was about to be discovered. She had saved Jumak's life and had given up her own.

Okemah bent forward and paced around the prone panther. He could not believe what he saw. He touched the handle of the star knife, then looked up at Cimmera.

"This is your knife?" he asked. Okemah pulled it out and wiped the blood on the ground. He had never known a woman who wielded a weapon, who could throw a knife as she had. His hands fondled the peculiar blade and handle, his fingers running over the incised designs. His expression displayed the puzzlement he felt.

Narchise stared at Okemah. "What does it mean?"

"It is the proof I needed," he said. "Cherok will listen to me now."

"I took this once from her basket, to show you. It is the knife she held when she healed the tree. But that old woman, Gaga-na, took it from me and gave it back. It is a magic knife. I know that."

"It is A-po-la-chee," Okemah said, glaring at Cimmera. "You are an evil A-po-la-chee trickster."

Cimmera swallowed hard, her throat pinched tight.

Okemah patted the blade. "What is this? What is it

made of?"

Cimmera did not answer.

Okemah held the knife up for a better look. He put the blade on his tongue and tasted it, then bit it. "Whatever it is, it means the end of you with my people." The taste was very different, he noted.

Jumak had seen and heard enough. When Cimmera had shouted the warning, she used words he did not understand. A-po-la-chee words, he assumed.

The boy glared at Cimmera, his insides wrenching with emotions so complex that he did not think he could sort through them, and knew he did not understand them. His bottom lip trembled, and the tiny muscles in his chin quivered. He turned his back to them all and ran into the village, throwing his arms about Gaga-na and burying his face against her.

"What is it, boy? What is wrong?"

"Cimmera," he sobbed.

"Has something happened to her?"

"She is A-po-la-chee!"

Gaga-na's head snapped up, and she looked in the direction from which Jumak had come. She saw Cimmera emerging from the brush, her head down, her shoulders drooping.

"Go into my platform," Gaga-na told Jumak. "Do not come out or speak to anyone until I return. Do you understand?" she asked, lifting his face so that she could look into his eyes.

Jumak nodded his head against her palm.

"Go, then."

The boy climbed up the ladder as Gaga-na gripped her walking stick and hobbled toward Cherok's platform.

The old woman climbed the ladder and stepped inside without announcing herself or requesting permission.

"What has happened?" Gaga-na asked.

Cimmera did not answer. She continued to gather her belongings and pack them in her basket, turning her back. Gaga-na watched, noticing that the pouch she had made for Cimmera did not bulge with contents. Gaga-na touched it.

"Where is the knife?"

"Okemah has it," Cimmera answered.

"How?"

She faced Gaga-na and explained the incident and then said, "I am A-po-la-chee. I am your enemy."

"You are no one's enemy," Gaga-na said.

Cimmera turned her back and put one of her plant-collecting pouches inside the basket.

"What are you doing?"

"Leaving," she said.

"No, do not leave yet. You must wait for Cherok."

"I will not be able to bear hearing Cherok tell me to leave. I do not want to hear the loathing in his voice or see the revulsion in his eyes."

Gaga-na glanced out from the platform. A commotion had already started in the village.

"Wait for him," Gaga-na said. "Explain to him."

"There is nothing to explain. I am A-po-la-chee. It is the only thing I know about myself. I am exactly what Jumak says I am. All lies. That is all I could tell Cherok, that I have lied to him every day, about everything."

"Give Cherok a chance," the old woman pleaded. "He loves you."

"Have you not heard anything?" Cimmera whipped around. "I am the enemy, someone every warrior and boy in this village dreams of destroying. I will not wait for their lances to be driven through my heart."

"Where will you go? It is not safe for a woman to

travel alone."

Cimmera shuddered, remembering her long isolation. "I have been alone before. I can take care of myself."

"Not yet," Gaga-na said. "Let me bring Cherok before they call for Council to meet." Gaga-na eased her bad leg over the edge of the platform floor and onto the first rung of the ladder. "Stay here. I want to talk to you both. There are things I should tell you."

Cimmera did not promise that she would stay. She did not want to face Cherok. She did not want to hear what he would say and see the way he would look at her. If she left now she could avoid all that pain for both of them.

She touched the skin on which they slept, her fingers lightly gliding over it. The image of standing before Council dipped in and out of her mind. The angry faces of the men, the women peeking at her out the corners of their eyes, and Jumak hovering near the men, listening and watching, despising her. And what would they recommend be done with her? That, too, frightened her.

Cimmera grabbed the basket, took one last look around the platform, and then climbed down. She was surprised to realize she did not feel like crying. Instead she was empty. Inside, she was hollow.

At the edge of the mound she looked up at the sun. There was time to get far away by the time the moon came up. On foot she left, moving toward the north, from whence she had come.

Jumak peeked out of Gaga-na's platform and saw her. He wanted to call out to her, to tell her not to go, but Gaga-na had said for him not to speak to anyone.

Gaga-na rushed through the village as fast as she could, the hitch in her leg worse than usual. Her eyes skimmed over the mound. If she could tell Cherok what she knew, it might make some difference. There was at least that hope.

She stopped when she got a clear view of the plaza around the central hearth. Already the men gathered. She moved closer so that she could hear.

"This is what the woman killed the panther with," Okemah said, holding up the star knife.

She heard the collective "Ooo."

"Touch the blade," he said, passing the knife among the men.

Atok thumped the strange material, then banged a small stone against it. The noise it made was peculiar. "What is it?" he asked, his expression of perplexity matched by the man next to him.

"Sit, Okemah," Cherok said. "Hand me the knife."

Okemah gave the knife to the cacique. Cherok studied it.

"It is the proof I told you I would find," Okemah said.

Cherok was also bewildered by the blade. He had never seen this material before. It was not rock. Not wood. At least not any kind he knew of.

"Perhaps it is a stone that comes from a distant place. That is why we do not know it," he said.

"Exactly," Okemah said. "It is A-po-la-chee. Either it comes from their lands, like flint, or they have traded for it. Maybe it even comes from the land of the tribe Atok and Dacoma have described. It is not Tegesta, and neither is Cimmera."

Cherok sat back, the palms of his hands beginning to sweat. "This is all your proof? Cimmera could have gotten this knife anywhere."

"There is more," Okemah said. "Narchise heard her scream words, and they were not Tegesta words. Ask Jumak. The boy heard it, also."

Cherok's gut kinked.

"And, Cacique, did you notice that the rain stopped? That was her evildoing, a punishment for us to suffer because we have found her out. She is wicked, and she has come here to finish off this clan. Do you not see how she entangled herself with you? Be thankful her plot is revealed."

"You make many grave accusations without questioning the woman."

"She will deny everything. There is no reason to ask her anything."

"I disagree," Cherok said, spying Gaga-na nearby. "Gaga-na," he called. "Step forward."

The old woman moved toward the plaza.

"Do you know where the woman Cimmera is now?"

Gaga-na nodded as she answered, "I will take you to her." She did not wish to tell everyone that Cimmera was waiting in Cherok's platform.

"We will all go," Okemah said. "We have a right to hear her explanation."

Cherok could not argue, or he would seem to be protecting her at the expense of his clan.

"Make them stay back," Gaga-na said.

"They must hear her explanations for themselves," Cherok said.

"Then let me speak with you first," Gaga-na said.

"If you have something to say, then tell us all," Okemah said. "This is no time for secrets."

"Okemah speaks the truth," Atok said. "Bring the woman here to us to face Council."

"I will bring her," Cherok said. "Gaga-na, where will I find her?"

"She waits in your platform."

Gaga-na started to follow the cacique, but Cherok

turned around and spoke to her. "No. I will go alone. Whatever you have to say, you will say before the Council."

Cimmera felt the long streamers of the sun. The tall saw grass blocked most of the breeze. The clouds that had teased them with rain had dissipated, and the sky was an empty, crisp, hot blue.

She walked, staying off what had been the canoe trails, the only paths that were clear, for fear she would be followed and found. The teeth of the sedge dragged against her skin, cutting thin, shallow, ragged slits. Perspiration made the cuts sting and itch, and tiny beads of blood collected along them.

As the day wore on, she became convinced she was not being tracked. She heard no calls, no voices. She stopped and put down the basket a moment to rest and check her bearings. The sun was about to set behind her left shoulder. Remembering her earlier exile, knowing the agony of loneliness that was to come, made icy blood flow through her. Somewhere inside, she supposed she had hoped that Cherok would come after her, scoop her up in his arms and tell her that everything was all right. She did not want to think about how he must really feel ...betrayed, angry, crushed by all her lies.

Cimmera picked up the basket and trudged on until she found a small hammock. She stood back, looking for evidence of habitation, cook-fire smoke, voices, canoes. Convinced the hammock did not support a village, she moved onto it and into the depth of the forest, which would keep her hidden. She cleared an area beneath a large oak and prepared a small hearth, then started a fire with her bow drill.

She had nothing to cook, and it was not cold, but the

fire brought to her a sense of security. Perhaps it would keep the animals away during the night. Man was the only animal drawn to flames.

Before sleeping, Cimmera made sure the space around the fire was clear. The earth was so dry that a spark could start a terrible fire. She kept the flames low and gave the fire no green wood, needles, or leaves that would spit.

Cimmera spread out a skin and then lay on it. The starlight sprinkled through the trees. When the sun came up, she would continue north, toward the A-po-la-chee. If she had done something, killed someone with that knife, then she deserved whatever they did to her. She was not going to run anymore. She would tell no more lies.

How could she have told him so many lies? Cherok wondered. If she had a trace of conscience she would have waited in his platform and explained. There was nothing good about her, and he was angry with himself for being so blind.

He sat by his dying fire and looked up at the sky. Somewhere she, too, sat beneath the same stars. Or perhaps, he thought, she was an evil spirit and had vanished into the air and laughed at him now, knowing how he ached inside.

Hard as he tried, he could not take his mind off her. She crept into his every thought. When he had entered his platform looking for her, he had smelled the fragrance she left behind. It still lingered there, and so he sat by his fire instead of going inside.

"Who is there?" he asked, hearing a noise and seeing a hazy silhouette through the bright glow of his fire.

"Jumak."

"What are you doing wandering about in the night?"

"I cannot rest," the boy said, coming into the light.

"Yes," Cherok said. "I understand."

The boy sat by the cacique, and into the fire he flicked small bits of things he found around him on the ground.

"She saved my life," Jumak said. "She killed the panther."

"Yes, she did," Cherok answered.

"She forgot to speak in Tegesta and her real language came out."

Cherok nodded, and they sat quietly for a while before Jumak spoke again.

"She did not mean to speak in her language. That was a mistake, but she must have known someone would see the knife. She threw the knife anyway."

Cherok continued to stare into the fire. That was the only good thing he could think about Cimmera. She had saved the boy, knowing that she would be found out. "She took that chance."

"She gave up her life for me," Jumak said. He rubbed a dirty line across his nose as he sniffed.

"This upsets you."

"I told her I hated her. I said bad things to her. Even so, she saved me and gave herself away."

"She loved you, Jumak. Perhaps you were the only one she really cared about."

"I want to be a man, but I know I am still just a boy, because I do not understand all this."

Cherok put his hand on Jumak's shoulder. "I wish I understood."

"Will she come back?" the boy asked, turning to look at the cacique.

"I do not think so."

"Should we go after her? I want to tell her that I am

sorry."

"No. We must let her go. If she had wanted to stay she would have explained to me."

"I do not think she is bad anymore. I was wrong. She must have had her reasons for not telling us who she was."

Cherok remembered the first time he had seen Cimmera. How fragile and innocent she had looked. Talasee had suspected that she was not Tegesta, and Cherok recalled his own response. And what if she is?

This situation was as much his fault as hers. He should have listened to Talasee, asked her more questions, not been so taken in by her. He supposed she had lied because she was afraid. She was an A-po-la-chee woman among Tegesta men. But why did she not tell him later, after they—

Jumak looked up at the stars. "You know what I think?" he said, interrupting Cherok's thoughts. "I think the stars are the campfires of the tribe that lives in the sky. It is a wonderful place there. It is always summer there, never cold weather that makes the old people sick. There, men and animals live together and do not hunt or kill one another. The bright one, there," he said, pointing to the brilliant star in the north, "is the cacique's hearth. And that one"—he pointed to a red star—"is his woman's. She is so beautiful that he cannot take his eyes off her. I think they all look down on us and watch us. Just as a boy has to grow to be a man, I think we have to grow to become members of the tribe that lives in the sky."

"Those are interesting thoughts," Cherok said.

"I think they watch to see who of us is pure enough, good enough, to be one of them. I do not think they will pick me."

"Why do you think that?"

"Because if I had listened and not gone to the borrow pit alone, this never would have happened. Cimmera would not have—" Jumak choked, and he could not finish.

"This is no one's fault, Jumak. You should not feel guilty. We would have found out about Cimmera someday. She told so many lies that she was bound to become tangled in them."

"Do you hate her?" Jumak asked.

"That is a good question," Cherok answered.

CHAPTER 32

IT WAS STILL NIGHT when Cimmera awoke. The crescent moon did not provide much light. At first she was confused, forgetting where she was. Her pupils dilated, straining to let in more light.

She sat up and stirred the dying coals of her fire, gingerly added twigs, then bigger pieces of wood. Huddled against the trunk of a nearby tree, a beady-eyed opossum stared at her. Opossums were spiteful, ill-tempered creatures.

She had a sudden flash of memory. She and another child spotted a baby opossum. She saw that one of its legs appeared to be broken. "Poor thing," she said to her friend.

She reached out to pick it up. The little animal hissed and bared its needle-sharp teeth.

"Leave it alone," her friend had said.

"No. It needs help. Wait here and keep watch."

Cimmera remembered running back to her shelter and asking Sola for a hide to wrap the opossum in so that it would not bite her. Then she had hurried back and gently captured the creature.

Cimmera smiled as the scene spilled through her mind. Tamar had helped her bandage the broken leg. Then she had kept the opossum in a contraption Tamar made like a fish trap. As long as she had the animal, it never became friendly. Every time she came near, even to give it food, it hissed and snapped. Finally they had let it go. She and Tamar watched as it scurried into the brush, leg healed.

How could the A-po-la-chee be such terrible people if they had hearts like Tamar and Sola? She lay back on the skin and curled up on her side. She would need more sleep if she was going to travel all the next day.

Sleep did not come easily. She missed the security and comfort of Cherok slumbering next to her. She missed being able to snuggle against him, to feel safe and content.

It was not easy sleeping on the ground. She felt crawling things move beneath the sleeping skin and sometimes on her. She swatted at them and brushed them off. The mosquitoes were merciless.

She was fortunate, she thought, to at least have gotten the sleep she had. She had no oils and no repellents. She chastised herself for not having covered herself in mud before settling in for the night. But it would have been much too dangerous to approach a watery area. All of the creatures ventured farther and farther, forgetting their fear of one another in their quest to satisfy their thirst.

Cimmera moved a hand beneath her head, her palm against her cheek. Thinking about the animals' thirst made her throat dry, also. She remembered how she had abhorred the nights when she was alone, and then how she had looked forward to the darkness with Cherok.

She closed her eyes again, wanting more sleep without ever seeing what was at her back. Behind her, on the northern horizon, the sky glowed orange and red.

Cherok greeted the day in his way, saying prayers, clearing his mind. Even as he prayed, visions of Cimmera distracted him. He prayed that the confusion he felt would end. At one moment he was filled with rage, angry with her for living those lies day after day, for never having loved him as he loved her, for never caring enough about him to be truthful. A moment later he was understanding, seeing how at first she must have been terribly frightened, but then had come the cycle of lies until it was too great to undo.

Always he felt melancholy.

This very morning he had decided to go after her, to find her, tell her nothing in her past mattered, but then he faced the reality that she did not want him. If he had meant anything to her, she would have given him some explanation. She owed him that.

Cherok prayed for rain, then stood up.

Jumak slit the belly of one of the frogs he had killed, then peeled the skin away.

"I miss her," he said as he worked. "Do you?" he asked Gaga-na.

"Yes, I do," she answered. "I try not to think about it." Gaga-na looked at the pot of frogs. "Is that the last one?"

"Yes," Jumak answered, tossing the frog on top of the pile.

"Skin this," Gaga-na said.

Jumak started to pluck the feathers from the bird.

"No," Gaga-na said. "Skin it. This duck dives for its food. If you leave the skin on, it will taste too fishy. Not good."

"Oh," Jumak said.

"Your mind wanders this morning. You do not concentrate."

Jumak shrugged.

"Are you going to tell me what is on your mind?"

The boy shrugged again.

Gaga-na put down her cooking utensils. "Enough of that," she said, "Speak up so whatever is bothering you does not eat through you."

Jumak looked up. "It is all my fault. Cimmera would never have had to leave if I had not gone to the borrow pit."

"I think it is time you stopped thinking about that. We must get on."

"Someone should have gone to search for her," Jumak blurted.

"The situation is very complicated, Jumak."

"I think I am bad luck. Maybe I should stay away from you."

"Come here, boy," Gaga-na said, holding out her arms.

Cherok saw the fleck on his forearm. He looked up. Ash was falling, carried on the wind, silently bringing the bad news. He scanned the sky but could not tell where the fire was. There was a dusty haze, but no great clouds of smoke.

He gathered the Council, and they sat sweating in the heat. "The fires come," he said.

"We have seen the ash," Dacoma said.

"Collect your things," Cherok said. "Tell your women. Be prepared to flee in the middle of the night."

Atok stood up. "The winds are strong. I cannot tell where the fire is, if the winds will drive it away or blow it to us."

"There may be many fires," Okemah said.

"That would be the worst," Dacoma said.

"Cacique," Yoma's father said, "perhaps we should leave now, move to the shore of the Big Water until the threat is ended."

"Not yet," Cherok said. "We need to know more about the fires. We could head straight into them, become trapped. Tonight we will see the glow in the sky. Then we will know."

Atok nodded. "We will keep our fires low so that we can see better."

"Go now," Cherok said. "Begin your preparations."

The men dispersed, and throughout the day they packed their most valuable things in pouches and baskets that could be easily carried.

Cherok wrapped the star knife in a skin and put it inside a hide pack. He hoped the fires would not come this way.

By dusk the people had completed their tasks. Nervous chatter spread through the village as night approached.

"Look," Jumak shouted from the top of a tree, pointing to the north.

The men moved to more open spaces and looked where the boy pointed.

They saw a deep orange flush tarnishing the northern sky.

"That is the way Cimmera went," the boy called to Gaga-na as he climbed down from the tree. "I saw her."

Cherok heard Jumak, also. The boy spoke the truth, he thought. She had headed back to her people. He stared at the reddened sky. The wind blew on his face. She did not have a chance.

"Okemah," he called.

The big man focused on the cacique.

"Come here," Cherok said.

Okemah left Narchise's side. "What do you want?"

"What do you think of the fires?" Cherok asked.

"You ask for my opinion?"

"It is a valuable one," Cherok said. "We may disagree about some things, but you know the land. You have seen the fires before."

"I think they will spread, eat up the dry tinder faster than we can imagine."

"The flames come this way," Cherok said.

Okemah turned his face in several directions, testing the wind. "Yes," he said.

"Cimmera is out there," Cherok said.

"That was her decision."

"I know we have disagreed about her, Okemah, and that is why I am telling you first. I am going after her."

"Arghh," Okemah grumbled. "Fire does not harm evil spirits."

"She is only a woman, Okemah."

"An A-po-la-chee woman!" Okemah shot his arms into the air in frustration.

"I must follow her, but I cannot leave our people without knowing there is someone here to make a decision if the fire comes too near. You are that man, I believe."

Okemah's mouth opened in disbelief. "You entrust that responsibility to me?"

"Should I not?"

"You should not go at all," Okemah argued. "This clan cannot lose another member, especially our cacique. We will dissolve into the black earth," he said.

"I am going."

"We should have given up on this village long ago, moved to other villages. Rebuilding has been too great a task. Now, at a crucial time, you jeopardize the well-being of our people once again."

"I leave them in your charge."

"Cacique," Okemah said, "you should not bring her back here. She is not welcome."

Cherok ignored Okemah's statement. "I will leave in the morning." The cacique wandered away to tell Gaga-na and Jumak of his decision.

Okemah went to Narchise.

"Cherok is going after the A-po-la-chee woman. He is afraid she will be caught in the fires."

Narchise shook her head.

"He leaves me in charge."

Narchise grinned. "You are so important," she said, fluttering her eyelids.

Okemah's chest puffed up. "He says I am the one to make a decision about the fires. I will know when they have come too close, when we should flee, if we should flee."

"Cherok is wise to have chosen you. The others will be glad to hear his choice. Tell Ara," Narchise said. "She will be so proud that her brother steps in for the cacique."

"Where is she? I have not seen her."

Narchise wrinkled her nose. "No, I have not either. That is strange."

They approached Ara's shelter. Her hearth was cold. No embers. Okemah called her name.

"Are you in there?" Narchise called.

In a moment Ara appeared in the doorway, the shadows hiding all but a vague silhouette.

"Come down," Narchise said, rocking from side to side. "Your brother has good news."

"Good news?"

"What is wrong with you?" Narchise asked. "Your

voice sounds odd."

"I was sleeping."

"Sleeping? It has just gotten dark. Are you sick?"

"No," Ara said. "I was very tired, that is all."

"Tell her," Narchise said to Okemah. "Tell her how important you are."

Narchise reached around behind Okemah and tickled his buttocks. Okemah slapped her hand away.

"Cherok is leaving in the morning, going after the A-po-la-chee woman, and he has told me that I am in charge."

The dry saw grass whipped in the wind, rattling its brittle swords against each other. In the remaining shallow water the armor-sealed garfish fed on the other fish. Finally the shallow water could not give even the ugly garfish life, and their carcasses lay rotting, stinking in the heat. The decomposing peat generated heat, and the ground smoldered, so much in some places that it burst into flame. The spreading fire hissed over the land, devouring the saw grass, jumping from crown to crown in the old pines, eating through the ground, traveling along the roots of the palmettos. Pillars of purple and cream smoke rose in the sky. Ash fluttered down, covering everything with a thin dirty veil.

Cherok stood at the edge of the hammock.

"It is a good thing you do," Gaga-na said. "When you return, I have something to tell you both."

"I want to go," Jumak said.

"It is too dangerous," Cherok said, looking at the clouds of smoke in the far distance.

"How will you find her? She did not follow the old canoe trails."

"She leaves tracks and signs like anything else. I am a

good tracker."

"I can help. My eyes are good."

"I will travel faster alone."

"I promise not to be in the way. I can help. I know what to look for; I read signs. You have taught me."

Cherok crouched in front of the boy so their eyes were level. "I count on you to stay with Gaga-na and help her," he whispered. "She is old, lame, and alone."

Jumak held out a fist, slowly opening his fingers. "I have the panther's canine teeth. I want to give them to Cimmera. She will know that I am sorry then."

"She knows you did not mean the things you said, but she will be pleased with your gift. Keep them in a safe place."

"I am afraid for her," the boy said.

"There is good reason to fear for her."

"Okemah says the fires may head this way."

"That is why I must find her quickly. When you speak with the spirits in your daily prayers, mention my mission. Ask them to go with me."

Gaga-na and Jumak watched Cherok disappear into the saw grass, his weapons in his waistband and across his back, the star knife in a packet tied around his middle.

The warm morning grew to a torturously hot afternoon. Cherok squatted in a spot where the water had once run deep. The mud stank and sucked at his feet. He threw his head back and looked straight overhead, thanking the spirits. There in the mud was the impression of a small foot. It had to be Cimmera's.

Throughout the day he had followed the faint signs of her passage—grass bent to one side, crushed patches of undergrowth. At last he had found a clear sign: this shallow print in the mud. The spirits were with him.

Cimmera stared at the discolored sky. She had no choice but to stay on this small, lonely hammock and wait out the fires. Heavy ash sifted through the trees. By afternoon the sky had taken on an eerie glow and rolling clouds of smoke covered the sun. The fires came closer. To the west was more saw grass that stretched on forever. To the east were more Tegesta. Ahead were the flames. She could go in only one direction …back toward Cherok's village, and she would not consider doing that. The fires were going to take her if the spirits willed it so.

CHAPTER 33

OKEMAH PACED and sniffed the air, smelling for smoke. He was pleased that Cherok had left him in charge, but now the responsibility strained him. Danger lurked nearby, and it was his duty to make the decisions that would keep the whole clan safe. For the first time he realized how much of a burden the cacique had to bear, how one in such a position must weigh all things, think them through, and then make a wise choice. His respect for Cherok was magnified.

Tichini flittered up to him. "You are not only big and strong, but now you also have great power. I like the way it makes you look. You move differently, seem even taller than you are."

"Go away, Tichini. I cannot think of anything other than the safety of our people. I must focus my mind on that."

The young woman shimmied closer. She touched his chest with her fingertip and lightly drew circles. "A little distraction would be good for you. Every man needs to relax sometime."

Okemah's eyes bulged as he saw Narchise approach, her eyes narrowed to furious slits, her breasts flouncing with the tempo of her angry pace. She bumped her way between them.

"This is my man, Tichini. He only wants me."

"Really," the younger woman said, running her hand

through the indentation of her waist and over the curve of her hip, ending at her thigh.

Narchise felt her temper bubble up, making her fidget, wiggle her toes, and pull her lips tautly to one side. "I might never have your long slender legs or your flat belly," she said. "But you will never have these." She lifted her breasts in Tichini's face. "These are what he likes, not those toadstool-size lumps you have. Why, if there were no nipples on them, they might be mistaken for mosquito bites."

Tichini opened her mouth to say something, but Narchise spoke again.

"Leave Okemah alone and find a man who likes to fondle bones. You are all sharp and hard. This man likes fullness, softness that he can bed in. He has no interest in you," she said. "Is that not right, Okemah? Tell her." Narchise slid her arm around his back and slipped her hand inside his breechclout, palming his buttock.

Okemah nodded.

"There," Narchise said, removing her hand and pressing her body into the big man's side. "Now go away."

Tichini's eyes darted from Narchise to Okemah. "You will never know the things a bony woman like me can do," she said, looking at Okemah, a coy smile wrapping itself over her lips. "There is merit in agility that you will never experience."

"Warriors!" Jumak screamed, running through the village and up to Okemah. "Warriors are coming. Great numbers."

Okemah whooped an alarm. The sound alerted those who had not already heard Jumak. The men dashed for their weapons and queued up along the edge of the mound. A painful spasm of fear gripped Okemah.

"Do not move," he ordered. Even at a distance Okemah immediately saw that these men were not the enemy he knew. These warriors were not A-po-la-chee. He arched one brow and anxiously called to Atok, "Are these men of the same tribe you and Dacoma saw? Are they Kereb's warriors?"

Okemah had faced warriors in battle before. His body was scarred with the proof. Nervously he eyed his meager rank of men.

"They are the same," Atok answered.

"Do not initiate a conflict," Okemah commanded. "Perhaps they will only ask questions, as they did in the northern village."

Jumak mounted the lowest branches in a tree, the rough bark chafing his feet as he climbed higher. "Come on, Yoma," he whispered to his friend, who stood numb at the base of the tree.

Yoma's mother had called her children into their platform, but Yoma's feet had become rooted where he stood. The boy looked up at his friend.

"Hurry, Yoma," Jumak said.

The boy obeyed, life suddenly entering his legs again, and he scurried up the tree.

"Look at them," Jumak whispered. "There are so many."

Yoma's eyes were wide and unblinking. The warriors spread across the prairie in a single line, the bright paint on their faces winking in the last of the sun, their oiled bodies catching the rays of the fading light.

"Like a long snake," Jumak said, watching them writhe in and out of the saw grass, slithering closer and closer.

Yoma's hand was at his throat, and he felt a choking

fear. "Did you hear what they do?"

Jumak nodded, his eyes taking in the full scale of the advancing warriors. "They eat the flesh of their enemies."

"What will our men do?" Yoma asked. "There are so many of them and so few of us."

"Okemah will know," Jumak said, turning his attention to the small group of Tegesta men.

Okemah watched them coming, like a giant wave, cresting above the saw grass and then disappearing into it again. Behind them, deep in the distance, the fires raged, producing a glaring florid horizon.

A Tegesta baby wailed in the background. Tension snapped inside the men, pulling every muscle and sinew as taut as the skin of a drum.

The wave of men swelled again, coming into clear view, surging through the sedge. The warrior in the center of the line raised his arm, and the wall of men stopped. The leader stepped forward.

Okemah did the same, then called out, "Kereb!"

Kereb cocked his head in interest. This Tegesta man knew his name?

"What do you want?" Okemah called out.

Kereb signaled his men, and they lowered their weapons.

Okemah gave no signal to his warriors, but he did lower his weapon and motioned for Kereb to come forward.

When they stood face to face, Okemah turned his back, a courageous gesture that told Kereb the Tegesta were brave, even though there were not many of them.

Kereb called two of his men to come forward and stand with him. He indicated that he wished for two Tegesta men to become temporary hostages to ensure his safety.

"Atok and Dacoma," Okemah said. "You have seen these men before. Take your place with them until this is over and Kereb goes back to them."

Atok and Dacoma walked forward until they stood with Kereb's ranks.

Okemah led Kereb and the other two men into the village. They sat at the plaza about the central hearth. The rest of the Tegesta stood guard, facing the enemy, who sucked fear from their very marrow.

Gaga-na peeped from the shadows of her platform. Jumak scampered down the tree, leaving Yoma clinging in fear to the branches.

Jumak slipped behind the platforms and made his way near the central hearth where he could see the men and hear their words.

Kereb brushed a space in the dirt, creating a smooth surface to draw on. He picked up a stick and drew a woman and then a butterfly.

"A woman and a butterfly?" Okemah said.

Gaga-na's hand flew to her mouth. He was describing Cimmera!

Okemah shook his head.

Kereb sketched a knife in the woman's hand, then thought for a moment before drawing lines to represent rays coming from the knife as if it glowed.

The sketch suddenly made sense to Okemah, and his expression changed. Kereb and his warriors were searching for Cimmera.

Kereb saw the change of expression on the Tegesta man's face. Okemah knew the woman. She was here. Abruptly he swung his arm up in the air and then in a circle, alerting his two escorts.

Kereb brushed clean the drawing space. With gestures

and pictures he persuaded Okemah to call forth all the women who were hiding in the platforms. Slowly they emerged, and the two men searched the shelters.

Kereb scrutinized every one of the women. Not finding the woman he sought, he grew angry.

He babbled something at Okemah, but the Tegesta man did not understand. Suddenly Kereb picked up a stick and held it at Okemah's heart. He gave a jerky push so that it hurt, clearly relaying the message that if Kereb did not get the woman he wanted, he would kill Okemah.

Kereb gave orders to his escorts, who quickly held their knives to the throats of two women. Okemah understood. They would kill not only him but everyone else as well, even the women.

"Wait," Okemah said with a trembling voice.

Kereb poked the stick harder.

Okemah very slowly leaned forward and cleared a spot of ground. He drew a picture of a moon. How many sleeps should he tell Kereb to wait? When would Cherok be back with the woman? He had to be safe. If he told this man to come back in too many moons, he might think it too long and become angry. If he told Kereb to come back too soon and Cherok had not yet returned with Cimmera, Kereb would kill them all.

The worst possibility was what Okemah imagined. He pictured their hearth broiling and boiling body parts and Kereb and his men feasting and laughing. The abomination made him shudder.

Okemah motioned toward the north. "She is there," he said. "Our cacique has gone for her. They will come back." He drew seven phases of the moon, then a woman with a knife. With his index finger he stabbed the ground. "She will be here in seven moon phases. She will have the knife." He felt a ripple of guilt, but quickly convinced himself he was doing the right thing. Cimmera was not Tegesta. She would have to be sacrificed to save the whole clan. After all, she was the enemy.

Kereb held up his hand and stretched out his five fingers, then two more on the other hand.

Okemah nodded.

Kereb said something Okemah was sure was a threat that if the woman and the knife were not here when he returned, he would butcher them all. What heinous things these people did. Okemah knew that if a man's heart and parts were not interred with him, if some monstrous enemy ate his flesh and organs, separated his body parts, the victim would never cross over to the spirit world. He would not be recognized. That was like a double death, robbing a man of his soul. Okemah took a deep breath and exhaled, warding off nausea. He had to protect this clan from such an atrocity. At all costs.

In the evening, after Kereb and his warriors left, the village was quiet. There was little activity.

Narchise came up behind her man and massaged his shoulders. "I must speak with you," she said.

"This is not the time," Okemah answered.

Narchise stepped in front of him. "I must speak to you about your sister."

"Ara? What is it?" he asked.

"She still does not come out of her platform. I called to her, and she said to go away."

"Why is she acting that way?"

"I do not know. I think you should check on her."

Okemah rose to his feet. "You come with me," he said.

At Ara's shelter Okemah called up to his sister.

"Go away, Okemah," she answered from the darkness

of her platform.

"What is wrong with you, Ara? Come down so we can talk."

"I am rest—" Her sentence was cut off by a furious cough.

"Ara?" Okemah said once her coughing stopped. "Are you sick?"

"I will be fine," she said. "I am just not feeling well, but I will be better in the morning."

Okemah shook his head. Then with the wide span of his hand over his forehead he massaged his temples. He looked up again.

"Do you have the sickness?" he was brave enough to ask.

Silence.

"Sister, it is true, is it not? You have the illness?"

There was no answer.

Narchise's face paled in the dim light of twilight. She looked at Okemah and whispered. "She spent time with Talasee. Remember?"

Okemah did remember. "But Cimmera could not have been right. She did not do anything good for this clan. She was A-po-la-chee."

Narchise's face squirmed. "Okemah," she whispered, "I have been with Ara every day."

The men sat about the central hearth, their voices low.

"My sister, Ara, has the sickness," Okemah said.

"She is the only one?" Atok asked.

"I have been about the village, and everyone else appears to be in good health."

"Is it true that she spent time with the fire keeper when he was ill? Did she take his food to him and stay and talk?" Dacoma asked.

"It is true," Okemah said.

"Then the A-po-la-chee woman was telling the truth," Atok said.

"We do not know that," Okemah said.

"But look how the disease has spread. Just as she said it would," Atok said.

"We must keep Ara isolated if it is not too late," said a small man with a missing little finger.

"My woman has frequently visited with her," said another man.

Yoma's father stood. "Ara should never have broken the rule of the Council. Cherok persuaded us to keep Tashi and Talasee away from the rest of us, just in case Cimmera spoke the truth. We came to an agreement."

"It is too late to place blame. That will not do us any good," Atok said. "Okemah, order your sister to stay in isolation."

"And anyone else who becomes ill. Every man and woman must judge his health every day. If there is suspicion, keep apart from the rest," Dacoma said.

The men waited for Okemah to say something. There was a silent pause.

"So be it," Okemah finally said.

"We are battered by too many things at the same time," Dacoma said. "We must discuss Kereb and his warriors."

"They might come back sooner than agreed," Atok said, "just to catch us off guard."

"That is right," Dacoma said.

Okemah's stomach crawled. "Look there," he said, pointing toward the firelit sky. "We have forgotten our other enemy—the fires. They come closer and closer, and this wind," he said. "The wind blows this way. The fires are spreading fast. If the fires drive us out, we will never be able to return. Kereb's men will come back and wait for us. We will have to scatter, and I fear they will make war on all the Tegesta. I wish Cherok were here."

Atok shifted. "What if Cherok does not come back with her in time?"

Cherok's progress was slow. Tracking was not something one did in a hurry. A small sprig of moss from Cimmera's skirt, bent grass—those were the kinds of things his eyes searched for.

He looked up, to the north. The sky was bright with the radiance of the fires. He was moving right into them. His head told him to turn around, but his heart kept him moving forward.

The evening was now upon him, and yet he pushed himself on. His goal was to reach the small hammock he could barely make out in the distance. Though he hated to admit it, he did realize that was as far as he was going to get. He would be lucky if the fires did not get there before he did.

Cimmera smelled the smoke. Her skin was coated with ash. She held a swatch of deer hide over her nose to filter out some of the ash as she breathed. The stars were veiled with sooty smoke, and there was no light except the fuming glare of the fires.

This would be her last night, she thought. She had experienced small burns before and knew the pain such an injury caused. She wondered if she would be dead from breathing the smoke before the flames got to her. She prayed that it would be that way.

She heard the fire roar in the distance. The wind blew her way, snatching free flames that rode the breeze over the small patches of standing water. There the flames caught, eating down the saw grass on the other side.

Cimmera saw sparks in the air and knew that it would not be long. She would not live out the night.

CHAPTER 34

CHEROK RAN through the saw grass toward the hammock. The sky churned with dun-and violet-shadowed smoke. Near the edge of the hammock he stumbled in mud and then in a shallow slough of water.

She had to be here. If not, she was lost to the blazing fires that took everything in their path.

He felt the gentle rise, the slope of the hammock, and he scrambled into the depth of the hardwoods.

"Cimmera!" he shouted, fumbling through the dense brush.

Cimmera winced as a hot cinder fell on her arm. The fire was going to arrive before the smoke. She was going to feel the flames, the intense, blistering heat, and finally the burning away of her flesh and hair.

Another spark landed, and she saw the fine dry ground grass ignite. She sprang up and stomped on the beginning fire. "No," she screamed, panic spreading through her body.

Cimmera picked up her basket. She thought she had come to terms with her fear of the fire, accepted that she was going to die in it, but she felt an overwhelming instinct to survive, at least not to be burned alive.

The ash fell heavily, and she saw bright flares in the hammock. She could feel the hot breath of the fire blowing on her. She turned her back to the fires and sprinted through the hammock, dodging trees and bushes.

Suddenly she stopped.

"Cimmera!"

"Cherok!" she cried, immediately recognizing his voice. "This way!"

In a moment he called to her again. Cimmera answered, moving toward his voice as he moved to hers.

She dropped the basket when she saw him, breaking into sobs as his arms went around her. He held her so tightly she couldn't breathe, and she didn't care if that was the way she died. She would happily perish in his arms.

He pulled her away and grasped her face between his hands. "I love you. I do not care who you are, only that you are mine."

Tears streamed down her face.

"Hurry," he said, picking up her basket, giving it to her, and then taking her other hand.

They ran through the smoke, feeling the heat grow stronger. The air was alive with sparks raining down on them.

Cimmera slid in the mud by the slough, landing hard. Cherok pulled her up.

"I am all right," she said, not waiting for him to ask.

They ran through the shallow water, it splashing up to mid-calf. When they cleared the slough they felt the hot dry earth under them again.

And then there was a brilliant light in the sky, cracking it open in a jagged line. The crash of thunder vibrated beneath their feet, and the rain poured down, huge splattering drops that stung on the skin and shot out halos of dust when they struck the dry ground.

Cimmera's whimpers turned to loud sobs of relief and happiness.

Cherok came to an impulsive stop, pulling her by the hand. They stood staring at each other in the shadows, the rain pounding down, craggy bolts of lightning illuminating the night enough for them to see into each other's eyes. He planted his mouth firmly on hers, nearly afraid to taste her again, afraid that she would slip away from him and disappear in the night, and that pit of anguish would open inside him again.

But her mouth welcomed him, and Cherok felt something inside him give way ...one of the barriers that he had always thought separated a man from a boy. But now he did not care about those things, and he felt the sting of tears in his eyes.

When he finally took his mouth from hers, they stood gazing at each other, their faces streaming with rain.

The rains had come, but it would take days to put out all the fires. They had to hurry, keep running. The fires were too close.

"What will they do with Cimmera?" Jumak asked Gaga-na. "Will they kill her and eat her flesh?"

"I do not know," Gaga-na answered. "Maybe all they will want is her knife."

"It is a magic knife, is it not?"

"Yes, I suppose it is."

Jumak stared into the distance. "Look," he said. "Lightning. Maybe it will rain."

Gaga-na did not look. "It is just the fires," she said.

"No, it was lightning."

Just then thunder rumbled, and Gaga-na looked up, a slow smile boosting up the corners of her mouth. "Maybe you are right."

Jumak stood up. He felt the wind. It was cooler. "A rainstorm is coming."

Gaga-na rose and put her arm around the boy. "Yes," she said. "A big one."

When the first drop splashed on her cheek, Gaga-na grabbed Jumak and hugged him.

Okemah fell to his knees and said a prayer of thanks to the spirits.

Atok lifted his arms in the air, feeling the cool rain streak down the length of him.

Tichini opened her mouth and tasted the fresh rain.

Jumak suddenly slumped. The end of the drought was not enough to sustain his happiness.

"Someone must warn them," Jumak said. "Cherok cannot bring Cimmera here. Kereb will kill her."

Jumak looked at Gaga-na, an idea brightening his face. He rushed inside Gaga-na's shelter and returned with the bow and arrows that Cherok had helped him make. They were larger, more fitting for his size than those he had made with his father.

"I have to find her. I will tell her not to come back," he told Gaga-na.

"No," she called, watching the boy run through the rain into the night.

But Jumak had already made up his mind. The old woman closed her eyes and said a prayer for him, for Cimmera and Cherok, for them all.

Jumak's small feet splashed in pools that were forming. The rain came too fast and heavy for the earth to absorb. The dried-out muck repelled the water. It would have to soak and soften first; then the earth would drink up the water.

The lightning kept the sky lit, as if especially for his journey. Jumak knew what to look for. Any man traveling alone would leave a deliberate trail; his father had taught him that, and Cherok had shown him, also.

He was happy when he spotted his first sign, a bundle of saw grass tied together. Jumak was reinvigorated. He felt skillful and confident, driven to find the woman who had saved his life so he could warn her.

The boy saw the glow still in the sky. The rains had not yet ended the fires, but this was the beginning. He felt a twinge of fear, knowing he was running straight for the fires.

"Be with me, Father," he said aloud as he kept moving.

Throughout the night the lightning continued to flash, sometimes as jagged bolts, and sometimes as flashes in the clouds. The rain kept coming, flushing the heat out of the black muck, satisfying the thirst of the grass. Curled gray blades unfurled and opened as they sucked up the water.

Jumak followed the trail Cherok had laid. When the sun came up, the rain dwindled to a drizzle. He felt the replenished earth under his feet. In some places he felt the return of the vast shallow river. The great lake to the north spilled over and flowed slowly through the saw grass, finally emptying at the end of the peninsula, adding fresh water to the salty sea, creating a perfect breeding ground for millions of thriving fish.

Cherok and Cimmera were happy to see the sunrise.

"Can we stop?" Cimmera said. "Just so that I can tell you about myself? I cannot go back with you unless you know it all." She looked at him, her eyes filled with love. "You have not even asked," she said.

"I do not need to know anything about you, except from the day I found you. That is all I need to know."

Cimmera laughed softly. "That is all I know," she said.

"When you found me, I wanted to end my life. Do you know why?"

"All that matters is that you did not," he said, taking her hands in his.

"No, Cherok. Please let me tell you."

"All right, Cimmera, but only because you feel you must. It does not matter to me."

Cimmera told him the story of her memory loss, of how she came to realize she was A-po-la-chee, of how she had fallen in love with him and was afraid of losing him.

When she finished, he held her in his arms. "Perhaps you were A-po-la-chee before, but the spirits took that from you, made it vanish when they took your memory. Now you are Tegesta."

After they had held each other quietly, Cherok stood back. "This is yours," he said, giving her the star knife.

She told him what she knew about the knife and what she didn't.

"Perhaps you are an A-po-la-chee shaman," Cherok said.

"A woman?"

"My sister has the Gift."

"No," she said. "Tamar, my father, was the shaman. I have remembered that."

"You will remember it all," Cherok said. "There is nothing to hide anymore."

"Your people do not love me as you do, Cherok. I think that my return will bring more trouble."

"Together we are strong enough to face the wind," he said. "Do not be afraid."

Cimmera twisted and tilted her head. "Listen," she said.

"A warrior's call," Cherok said. "When we separate

ourselves, we use that cry to keep track of one another."

They heard the call again.

"I know the voice," Cimmera said. "Jumak."

Cherok nodded. He put his hand to the side of his mouth to channel his call.

Jumak responded immediately.

They called to each other as they moved, until finally Cherok sighted the boy.

"Jumak!" Cimmera cried.

The boy sprang through the saw grass, his head bobbing above it. He threw his arms around her. "I am sorry, Cimmera. I am sorry. I did not mean what I said."

Cimmera stroked his hair. "I know that, Jumak. You do not need to tell me. You have not come all this way alone to tell me this, have you?"

Jumak pulled back. "No," he said, "but I would have."

"How did you find us, Jumak?" Cherok asked.

"You marked your trail well. Did you not teach me how to leave a trail and how to read one?"

Cherok roughed up the boy's hair. "What has made you do this dangerous thing? What brought you?"

"Those warriors came," he said, looking at Cherok. "Kereb and his men. They want Cimmera and the knife. Okemah has told them to return after seven phases of the moon. He said that Cimmera and the knife would be there then. The warriors are frightening. They have bones through their noses, and they wear human teeth!"

Cimmera remembered the strange men sneaking up on the hammock when she was alone. She recalled how she had hidden in the tree and watched them search the island. She now realized they had been looking for her.

"They have searched for me a long time," Cimmera said, and then explained.

"You cannot take her back," Jumak said. "They will

cut her up and boil her in a pot, skewer her and cook her over their fires."

Cherok pulled the boy to his side. "No, we will not let them."

"Do not take her back. Please!"

"We cannot escape from those warriors. We will keep Cimmera away from them, but we will not run. If we did that, it would be the end of us. All our work to recover from the storm would have been for nothing. The spirits would never forgive our cowardice. I will think of a plan as we return."

Gaga-na kept watch for Jumak's return. When the sun rose, she did her morning chores, then took some basketry to the edge of the mound. If anything happened to the boy, she would never forgive herself for not telling Okemah or someone else to go after him.

In her old bones she felt the boy needed to go, that if he did not, he would not like himself. He had to try to find Cimmera, and Gaga-na had to let him go.

Just before the sun was straight overhead, she saw them, figures so small in the distance that at first she wasn't sure if she had really seen anything. She struggled to her feet, pushing her walking stick into the rain-softened ground and hoisting herself up.

There again she caught sight of something, someone, moving in the saw grass. She found herself holding her breath as she continued to watch. A few moments later, there they were, all three of them.

Gaga-na walked beside them.

Okemah sighed with relief when he saw Cimmera enter the village.

"The rains have returned," he said to Cherok.

Cherok stared hard at the man. "Yes, I am aware of that," he said. "I want to speak with you about Kereb and your promises."

"Cherok—" Okemah started to explain.

"Stop, Okemah. I will not hear your explanation now. We are tired and hungry. Wait at the central hearth. When I am ready I will come for you."

"Will you be long?" Okemah asked.

Cherok turned and glared at him without answering.

"The warriors would have killed us all," Gaga-na said. "Okemah did the best he could …for Okemah. But now you are back."

"Yes, I am, and Okemah is going to break his promise to Kereb."

"Stop at my hearth," Gaga-na said. "I have food prepared. Fill your empty bellies, then rest."

Jumak grabbed a fistful of coontie and stretched out in the shade of a tree, wonderfully exhausted.

Gaga-na used a big conch shell dipper to fill their bowls with her stew. "Ara has the sickness," Gaga-na said. "The men have met in Council. They realize that Cimmera spoke the truth about the illness. Everyone is afraid now because Ara has wandered freely through the village. Narchise is especially frightened."

"Is Ara the only one?" Cherok asked.

"For now, but I think everyone knows the sickness is going to spread."

"I am going for Mi-sa. We can wait no longer," Cherok said.

"I know how you have tried to avoid this," Gaga-na said. "Mi-sa at last has found happiness, and now you must ask her to give it up and return to her clan."

Cherok looked at Cimmera. "The man Mi-sa loves is the cacique of the Kahoosa, and he cannot leave his people. He must serve his people, and she hers. She knew this day would arrive. Her people must come first."

"She means very much to you," Cimmera said.

"I would give my life for her," he answered.

A drizzle began again. Cimmera and Cherok got up to leave.

"No, wait," Gaga-na said. "Come into my platform. I cannot keep these old secrets any longer."

CHAPTER 35

"WHAT SECRETS?" Cherok asked as he sat in the shadows of the old woman's shelter.

The dim light revealed the darkness in Gaga-na's eyes. "I do not know how to begin this story, Cimmera. When I am done I will explain why I have kept this from you."

Jumak scooted closer. Cimmera leaned her shoulder against Cherok's.

Cherok looked at Cimmera, then back at Gaga-na. "We are ready," he said.

"When you first came to this village, Cimmera, I remember you stepping out of the canoe, and this old woman thought there was something familiar about you. I could not help but stare whenever I saw you. Then when I saw the butterfly mark on your neck, I knew for sure."

"Knew what?" Cimmera asked.

"Be patient. I must tell this story in my way." Gaga-na rubbed her aching leg. "Long ago I had a daughter. She was very beautiful. Like you. Her name was Raina. She had just taken a husband. They were very happy."

Gaga-na paused, cleared her throat, and blinked her eyes.

Cherok took Cimmera's hand.

"This is difficult for me. I tried to forget it all, and then you came here." Gaga-na drew her fingers through her long silver hair. "It was a day like any other day. We went about our chores as we always did. And then they came into our village, screaming, shooting fire into our thatch, killing anyone in their way." Gaga-na stopped a moment and then went on. "A-po-la-chee. They took us by surprise. One young A-po-la-chee warrior was a shaman's son; I could tell by his dress and colorful markings. He was too young to be the shaman, but he wished to flaunt his power and his bloodline. He had another man help him hold Raina down. Her husband tried to rescue her, but two men restrained him and made him watch as this warrior ravaged her. Then they killed Raina's husband. When the warrior got off her, he had his men drop the body of her husband on top of her. Our men fought hard and finally drove the A-po-la-chee out. There was so much damage. Raina did not talk for days. She grieved for her husband, scarifying her legs, keeping to herself, tying up her hair. Then the worst of her fears came true. She was pregnant. A child spawned by the A-po-la-chee's seed grew inside her."

"How did she know it was not the child of her husband?" Cimmera asked.

"He had been away on a journey and had just returned that morning. They had not been together since her last moon cycle. She knew right away that the child inside her had A-po-la-chee blood. When she told me, I said she would have to sacrifice the child when it was born. But Raina loved the child and said she could not do that. I promised her that I would keep her secret. She told everyone that the child was her husband's. If she had not, they would have killed the baby. I do not understand it all, but after the day of the A-po-la-chee raid something was wrong with Raina. Her mind was not right. I cared for her as if she were a child again. Some part of her mind was lost that day."

"Was the baby a boy or a girl?" Jumak asked.

"The baby was a beautiful little girl. She looked just like her mother." Gaga-na looked at Cimmera as she spoke. "The day she was born, I knew Raina was right to save her. My daughter wanted to be a good mother, but at times she did not make sense. Her mind was just not the same. She lived at my hearth with the baby. As time went on, Raina got worse."

Gaga-na rubbed her nose with the back of her hand.

"When the child had lived four summers, there was another A-po-la-chee attack, though it was not the same clan. The women ran to hide, but Raina just stood in the center of the village, staring blankly. I ran with the child. She looked behind me, watching over my shoulder. She saw her mother bludgeoned to death, and then I went down, an arrow in my leg."

Cimmera suddenly stood up. Images flashed through her head. "It was me! I was the child. Gaga-na, you—"

"Yes. I am your grandmother."

Now Cimmera knew why the arrows had troubled her. She could clearly recall the arrow sticking out of Grandmother's leg. The cresting, the signature, was A-po-la-chee. That meant she could not be.

"You told me to run, to hide. I hid by the edge of the village. I remember standing there, crying. Everyone was dead, I thought. I believed you were dead too. The village was on fire. Then a large A-po-la-chee man saw me standing there, crying. He turned his canoe around and came back for me. His name was Tamar."

Cimmera paced. "I was raised by Tamar, a powerful shaman. I know that Tamar was kind to me. I have bits of memory." She looked at Gaga-na, hoping she would understand. "He is with me even now."

The old woman nodded.

"His woman, Sola, cared for me. She was barren, and

Tamar gave me to her and said I was their child. He gave me a name before all his people."

"You are only part A-po-la-chee," Gaga-na said. "You also must think of the blood that runs through you. It is not only a mix of Tegesta and A-po-la-chee. There is more. Your mother was from the seed of the shaman of our village, the man I have loved all my life. Your father was the son of an A-po-la-chee shaman. And now you say the man who raised you was a powerful shaman. You must have learned the ways of a spirit man from him. You carry the Gift."

"But why is there still this blank? What happened that day that I lost my memory? What was I running from? Whose blood was on me?"

"I cannot tell you that," Gaga-na said. "Only you can answer those questions. I am just happy to have you back. I have not seen you since that day when you were but four summers old."

"Why did you not tell her this story before?" Cherok asked. "When you saw the butterfly?"

"I told you I would try to explain. I made a promise to Raina, my daughter whom I loved so. I promised that I would never tell anyone her baby was from the A-po-la-chee. Raina feared that she would die early; she had had a premonition. She never wanted her daughter to know that she was the result of ... Over and over she made me swear that I would never tell her precious baby girl that she had A-po-la-chee blood in her. I was not sure what had happened to the child. Cimmera, when you came here, I did not know what you knew and what you did not. When you told me you had no memory, I realized you had begun a new life, a Tegesta life. The spirits had brought you home where you belonged." Gaga-na looked at the cacique. "If I had told you, Cherok, you would have been obligated to take the matter to Council, and you know what the recommendation would have been. Though I was certain you loved Cimmera, you were still the cacique. If I had told, I would have complicated everyone's life. I hoped things would work out."

Cimmera felt dizzy as scraps and shreds of memory came together. She remembered that Tamar and Sola had raised her as their child, that at first the other A-po-la-chee had not accepted her because she was Tegesta, that Tamar had called her his own. She recalled how she had loved him.

"You are magic, Cimmera!" Jumak exclaimed. "Double magic!" The boy got up and skipped around the platform. "You can do anything," he sang.

Cimmera shook her head, attempting to clear it, to make sense out of everything she had just heard and recalled. Still, why could she not remember anything about the day she had lost her memory?

"Cacique," a voice called.

It was Narchise.

Cherok went to the opening. "What is it, Narchise?"

"Okemah waits for you by the hearth."

"I have told him to wait."

"He is patient."

"Good," Cherok said. He disappeared inside. "The rain has stopped. Tell him I am coming," Narchise heard him say.

"Let Cimmera stay with me," Gaga-na said. "You go tend to Okemah."

"Is that what you want?" he asked Cimmera.

"Yes. I will wait here," she said.

Cherok kissed her wrist. Cimmera followed him with her eyes as he left. He trotted to the central hearth.

Okemah jumped up. "Cacique," he said in greeting.

"I will get straight to it," Cherok said. "You have promised Kereb that what he wants will be in this village waiting for him when he returns. I do not think you can keep your promise."

"I could do nothing else," Okemah said. "And she is A-po-la-chee. Our first allegiance is to our own."

"Cimmera has as much Tegesta blood in her as she has A-po-la-chee. We must protect her. She is one of our own."

Okemah was stunned. "How can that be?"

"Her mother was Tegesta."

"I did not know that. What will we do? Kereb will kill us all if he does not get what he wants."

"We will deny that she is here. We will tell him that she died in the fires."

"And if he does not believe us?"

"Then we will defend her as we would any of our women. He will not strip away our manhood. We will not cower and betray ourselves."

"I did what I thought was best, Cherok."

"And you will continue to do your best, as we all will." Cherok sat. "Now tell me about Ara and how the sickness has spread."

Cherok lay with Cimmera wrapped in his arms, listening to the rain. He still breathed hard, and the warmth of joining still pulsed through him. He would have taken her again if he had not known how tired she was. Instead he settled for his hands on her naked flesh and her body pressed to his.

"We will leave in the morning," he said.

Cimmera turned over to face him. "Where are we going? I will not let you run from Kereb because of me."

"We are going to the Kahoosa village to get Mi-sa. She must come back and stop this illness."

"I would help if I knew how. All of that knowledge is lost, and I cannot remember."

"Mi-sa will heal her people."

"Will we return in time? I cannot run from Kereb forever. I wish this to end."

At dawn Cherok and Cimmera boarded the canoe. The rain returned with a booming thunderstorm just before the sun came up. "Do you think all the trails are filled with water again?" she asked.

"We must hope they are. Once we reach the river we will travel fast."

"But if we have to walk, our journey will take much longer."

"Then we must pray that the rain will continue."

"Take this," Jumak shrieked as he approached in an all-out run. "I was afraid you had gone," he said, out of breath.

Jumak extended his hand to Cimmera.

"What is it?" she asked.

Jumak unfolded his fingers. "The panther's canine teeth," he said. "They should be yours. Put them in your medicine bag."

Cimmera smiled, took the teeth, and hugged the boy. "I take with me the stealth of the panther," she said.

Jumak nodded once, suppressing a wide grin that he thought might be inappropriate at this sober time. "Gaga-na is coming. She wants to see you off."

The old woman limped toward them and joined Jumak. "Keep safe," she said.

Cherok poled the canoe into the shallow water trail. Cimmera sat in the dugout, her back to the hammock. She turned and waved to Gaga-na and Jumak.

Okemah stood in the distance. He prayed they would be back before Kereb returned.

The sun came out, and there was a break in the rain.

"The air is hot," Cimmera said, wiping the perspiration from her forehead.

"That is good. That means the clouds will cluster, and then there will be a thunderstorm late in the day."

Cimmera felt the bottom of the canoe scrape the ground.

"The water is too shallow. We have to portage the dugout," Cherok said.

On and off throughout the day they found parts of the trails too shallow until they finally reached the river.

"We go with the current," he said. "We will reach the Kahoosa village by nightfall."

In the afternoon, Cherok's prediction came true. The sky filled with forbidding clouds, swelling and darkening. The rumbles began in the distance, and as the wind whipped the water, the thunder and lightning came closer.

"This is the beginning of the season of rain," he said in the middle of the downpour as they huddled in the canoe beneath a deerskin.

"The fires are ended," she said.

Cherok's hand slipped behind her head, and he pulled her face to him. "You are the fire that burns inside me," he whispered.

Cota stood with Mi-sa on the bank. The young boy, Pa-hay-tee, had announced the arrival of the visitors, and the villagers had gathered to welcome them.

Cota put his arm around Mi-sa, knowing how happy she was to see her brother's face, but Cota's mouth and eyes did not express the same happiness. He knew that

Cherok had come for her.

Cota acknowledged Cherok and Cimmera and gave them permission to bring the canoe to the bank.

Cherok helped Cimmera from the canoe and introduced her. "I have much to tell you about this woman, but that will come later."

Mi-sa threw her arms around her brother. "I have missed you so," she said.

"And I you, Sister."

Cota's fire burned bright in the night. He fed it green wood and pinecones. They enjoyed the crackling and the showers of sparks.

"A disease has come to our village, Mi-sa," Cherok said as they sat together. "Cimmera tried to warn us about keeping those with the disease separate, but there were those who did not believe."

"Tell me about this belief, this method of keeping the illness from getting into others," Mi-sa said. "Where did you learn it?"

"I told you I had more to say about this woman," Cherok said. "Let me explain."

Cherok told the story of Cimmera's heritage while Cota and Mi-sa listened in awe.

Mi-sa fixed her gaze on Cimmera's eyes. "I see the magic in you," she said.

"But I have forgotten many things. My memory is gone."

"Some knowledge has returned and the rest will, also," Mi-sa said.

"Cimmera would help if she could," Cherok said. "I am afraid the time has come for you to return, Mi-sa. Your people need you."

Cota held Mi-sa's hand as he spoke. "We knew this

would happen, but that does not make it easier. I have looked forward to this moment with dread. I want Mi-sa to stay here with me forever."

Mi-sa looked at the fire, then at Cherok. "I was born to serve my people. That is why the Breath Giver breathed life into me. I have been blessed with a short time of wonderful happiness." She squeezed Cota's hand. "Now I am called home."

"I did not want to come for you, Mi-sa," Cherok said. "I waited as long as I could. I fear that the illness will finish us off. We are already so few."

"I understand," she said.

"Let us speak of other things now," Cota said. "Let us not end this evening so solemnly."

"Yes," Mi-sa said. "Tell me more about yourself, Cimmera. Tell me the things you can remember."

Cimmera laughed. "That will not take much time."

They talked until the moon was high in the sky. Mi-sa told wonderful, moving stories about the times when she and Cherok were small. She told how Cherok was the only one who had ever believed in her, how he stood by her when everyone in the village except her mother thought she was an evil spirit.

Cherok told the story of the night of Mi-sa's birth, about the shooting star that lit the sky the moment she was born, about the A-po-la-chee attack that same night, and how the clan thought Mi-sa was the source of their ill fortune. Then he smiled. "During her naming ceremony, when my father held her so that I could see her, I saw the magic in her eyes. She had touched the sky."

Mi-sa's eyes teared, and she leaned over to embrace her brother.

"We will be sleepy in the morning when everyone else is busy about," Cota said.

Just as they were leaving the fire to get some sleep, Mi-sa stopped. "Cimmera," she said.

Cimmera turned around.

Mi-sa stepped close and gazed into the woman's eyes.

"What is it?" Cherok asked.

Mi-sa finally broke her stare. "I think I can help her," she said.

CHAPTER 36

CIMMERA FELT THE COOL air brush against her cheek.

"There are things I must gather first. You can help me do that in the morning," Mi-sa said.

"Trust her," Cherok said.

"I cannot do anything until the sun comes up," Mi-sa said.

"What is it you want to do?" Cimmera asked.

"I think I can help you get your memory back. At least I will try."

"Rest well tonight," Cota said. "Share our platform."

The ground was still soggy from the storm that had come up in the night.

"Do you know this?" Mi-sa asked, pulling up a plant.

"Purslane," Cimmera said.

"Yes. Most know that if you lay it on your bed, nightmares will not creep in. It keeps evil away. But we will use it for something else."

Mi-sa took two fallen maple branches. "The wind has provided for us," she said.

When they had gathered all the plants Mi-sa wanted, they boiled them over a fire. When the pot cooled, Mi-sa took Cimmera's hands in hers.

"Are you ready?" Mi-sa asked.

"Yes," Cimmera said.

"If you are afraid of what you will see, let that fear go."

"The time for me to remember has come," Cimmera said.

Mi-sa's eyes went to her brother. "Assure her that you will stand by her no matter what," she said.

"She knows that I will," Cherok said, standing behind Cimmera and putting his hands on her shoulders.

"Then we will begin."

Mi-sa held the two maple branches. "Step through them," she said. Cimmera did as she was instructed. Mi-sa put down the branches and lifted the pot of special elixir to Cimmera's lips. "Sip," she said. "Four times."

Cimmera touched her lips to the bowl, closed her eyes, and tasted the tea. She swallowed, then sipped three more times.

"Keep your eyes closed and listen to me," Mi-sa said. "Hear only my voice."

Cimmera nodded.

"Clear your head. Empty it of all your thoughts."

Cimmera knew how to do this.

Mi-sa sang a soft song. At first the words were Tegesta, but then she sang in another tongue. Cimmera felt a vibration deep inside her.

The wind grew strong, and she heard wings, felt them flutter near her face. The haze that had clouded her spirit vision disappeared.

Tamar!

"I have come to lead you through," he said.

"But you are A-po-la-chee."

"We of the spirits are all of the same dominion. Give me your hand and do not be afraid."

Cimmera felt Mi-sa's hands on her temples and Tamar's big hand entwine with hers.

"Walks in Stardust," he said, "you are safe here. Let your eyes see what they must, what your mind has shut out all this time. Let in the truth. We are with you."

The mist about them thinned, and she saw her village, the A-po-la-chee village. Tamar was there. Sola was weaving. Then she saw herself rolling clay between her hands. She was not a child.

"This is the day," Tamar said quietly. "See what you must."

Crashing through Tamar's whispering came the loud shrieks and whoops of an attack.

She saw herself drop the snake of clay. Tamar stood, snatching up his lance and club.

"Who are they?" Sola screamed as she ducked inside her platform.

Fire soared through the air on the ends of arrows, setting the thatch of some shelters ablaze.

One warrior came behind Tamar, yanked his hair back, and held a knife to his throat.

Suddenly Cimmera realized this man was the same one who had come so close to her when she hid in the tree while she was alone on the hammock. She recognized his markings, the hideous adornments, even his smell. He had come so close. These were Kereb's men.

He spoke a few broken words of A-po-la-chee. "Want knife from stars," he said to Tamar, pulling the big man's hair hard.

Tamar said nothing.

Cimmera ran to Tamar's platform. "They want the knife, Sola. They have come for the knife."

"No," Sola said. "It belongs to the spirits. The knife is your gift and Tamar's. When you brought the piece of star out of the Stardust, it made you Tamar's daughter in the eyes of his people and the spirits. The warriors cannot have it."

"They will kill Tamar!"

"They will kill him anyway. Take the knife—quickly. Run. Get away." Sola was crying, and so was she.

"Here," Sola said, scrambling for the knife, then putting it in Cimmera's hands. "Go! I will help you get away."

They bounded down the ladder and across the mound.

"No!" Cimmera screamed. Tamar lay with a wound in his chest, bubbling up with bright red blood. She dropped beside him and pulled his head against her chest.

"No! No!" she cried, rocking him.

Tamar's eyes did not focus as he spoke. "Run, Walks in Stardust!"

"Tamar." She sobbed as she held him, her hair dragging in his blood. She bent her head over him, holding him to her as if she could keep his life from escaping.

"I will always be with you," he murmured, then went limp in her arms.

A man ran to them. "Take the knife," he yelled. "Run!" She looked up. It was Kupah, the injured A-po-la-chee she had later tried to save.

"Hurry!" he said to her.

A whistling sound in the air made her turn. Sola was down, blood dribbling from the corner of her mouth.

Cimmera looked at the knife, the devastation around her, the warrior who stared at her. Quickly she spun around, clutched the knife to her breast and ran, leaving the mound behind her. She ran from the burning village filled with death, just as she had before when she was small, when her mother and grandmother were killed, when she was Tegesta.

She sobbed, wanting to give up. She did not care

anymore. Let them come for her. Let them have her, the knife, anything they desired. All the people she had ever loved had been taken from her. Everyone left was her enemy.

"Take me, too," she screamed at the sky.

She did not look back, did not want to see the horror behind her. She knew it too well. Keep running, she told herself.

She stumbled and went down. Her lungs were on fire; she had run so far, so long. She lay there and did not want to get up, wished she would just disappear in the muck. The images were so horrible, flitting through her mind over and over. Her mother bludgeoned, her grandmother bleeding, fires, Tamar, Sola! Then she heard a loud noise, the beating of enormous wings. A great white bird enfolded her and made all those images disappear.

"You do not have to think about it now, Stardust. You do not have to remember. I will take the pain away until you can bear it. I am with you always."

Then she was standing in the middle of the saw grass, breathless, her muscles cramping in pain.

Who was she?

Cimmera's eyelids fluttered, then opened. Her hands flew to her face as she cried. "I know. I know."

Cherok held her, pressing his lips to her hair. "It is over now," he said. "You are whole, and we are together."

Mi-sa, Cherok, and Cimmera sat by the edge of the water.

"You have great power," Mi-sa said to Cimmera. "Do you know that? The magic that is in you comes from two tribes. And you say you remember that Tamar spent all his time with you, teaching you how to use the Gift."

"Yes," she answered. "He did."

Cimmera opened the pouch and took out the star knife. She told them about the star that had streaked through the sky. "When I brought this blade out of the Stardust, I became Tamar's daughter and an A-po-la-chee. The knife was a sign from the spirits. He gave me the name Walks in Stardust."

"That is a beautiful name," Cherok said. "As beautiful as Cimmera."

"I remember the days he spent carving this handle, how he made all the special markings," she said. "He used it at important ceremonies and rituals. It has never been used to cause harm." Cimmera looked up. "This knife carries great magic."

Cimmera held the knife out to Mi-sa, who took it and clasped her hands about the handle. She closed her eyes, and in an instant a pale light haloed the knife and her hands.

Mi-sa opened her eyes. "Good magic," she said.

Cherok suddenly glanced up at the sky with a huge smile across his face. "Mi-sa, when Cimmera was four summers old, you were born. The star that marked your birth also gave Cimmera her name and her place with Tamar. It was the same star."

"Yes," Mi-sa said, "we are connected by the spirits."

"Cimmera has the power," Cherok said. "The Gift is strong inside her. She was given to us, to our clan. Mi-sa, you need not give up your happiness. Cimmera will heal our people!"

"The river is deep," Cota said. "Have a safe journey." Mi-sa wrapped her arms around her brother. "When will I see you again, Cherok? I do not want us to be apart so long."

"When the clan is well and strong, I will come again."

"I will think of you every day," she said, her voice strangled.

"Are you not a part of me?" he asked. "And am I not a part of you? We are never really separated."

Mi-sa drew back and smiled. "You always say the right things. Just as you always did."

Okemah's big feet splashed as he ran through the shallow water. Jumak was right behind him.

Okemah grabbed hold of the bow of Cherok's canoe and pulled it up to the bank. Jumak jumped into the canoe and hugged Cimmera.

"The illness is bad. Very bad," Okemah said. "Narchise has the sickness. Ara is near death, I fear. Others have not come out of their shelters. I am afraid they are sick, too. This is the end of us. Even if a few of us live, our numbers will not be great enough for the clan to survive."

Suddenly Okemah realized Mi-sa was not with them. "Where is she? Where is Mi-sa?" he said, panicked.

"I bring good news," Cherok said, helping Cimmera from the dugout. "We have seen Mi-sa, and we have discovered things about Cimmera. She will tell her story in good time, but for now you must trust in what I say. Cimmera will heal our people."

Okemah sneered. "No, we need a shaman. We need Mi-sa."

Cimmera walked away with Jumak, leaving Okemah with Cherok.

"I want you to help me gather some plants. Will you?"

"Yes," the boy said. "I have keen eyes and I know all the plants. Tell me what to get."

Cimmera listed the plants and plant parts that she needed. "Bring them to me as quickly as you can."

Gaga-na hobbled across the village. When she was close to Cimmera, she stopped. "You are home," she said.

"Come with me," Cimmera said. "I have much to tell you."

"You remember?"

"I remember it all," she said.

They stopped and took a coal from the central hearth, and then Cimmera started her fire as she explained what Mi-sa had helped her see.

Jumak brought the plants, and the two women prepared a large skin of tea. Then Jumak ran to join the men as they gathered at the central hearth.

Cimmera dropped hot coals into the medicine, bringing it to a boil. "Last we add these," she said, peeling back the outer layer of some large stalks. She cut away small pieces, and in her wooden bowl with a pestle made from lignum vitae she ground the plant into a syrup.

"The words are most important," she said. "Without the spirits the potion is useless."

Gaga-na listened as her granddaughter sang in her beautiful voice. The words were foreign to her, and she did not know if they were A-po-la-chee words or the ancient tongue of holy men.

The young woman's hands danced over the brew, and the steam swirled through her fingers. "It is done," she said. They waited until the pouch was cool enough to handle, then poured the medicine into a bowl. Cimmera skimmed the plant residue from the top of the brew.

Cimmera carried the bowl and a shell spoon. She and Gaga-na approached the men, but stood back and waited to be seen.

Cherok stood and motioned for them to come closer.

"Begin with Narchise and Ara," he said.

Okemah filled with emotion. He wiped at his lower lids, sniffed, then straightened up, his face returning to normal.

"Do you wish to come?" Cimmera asked.

Okemah followed.

Inside Narchise's platform, Cimmera knelt next to the woman. "I am here to help you," she said. "Do you wish to accept my help?"

Narchise nodded and coughed.

"First you must pray to the spirits with me. You do not have to speak the words aloud; just say them in your head. Listen and believe," she said.

Narchise's dark-rimmed eyes looked up at the young woman.

Cimmera said her prayers, calling the spirits to come to the dedicated servant who suffered with the affliction and to be merciful. Narchise repeated the prayer in her head. Then Cimmera chanted, her voice growing louder until it filled the platform. Okemah, Gaga-na, and Cherok shivered, and the hair on their arms stood on end.

Cimmera's voice became even stronger until it seemed to be a part of the wind that blew through the platform, rattling the thatch and chilling them through. She dipped the shell into the medicine.

"Drink," she told Narchise. "Drink and believe."

Okemah lifted his woman's head as she sipped. Then Narchise shuddered.

"We are done here," Cimmera said. "Take me to Ara and the rest."

When the sun came up, Cimmera took more of her medicine to the ill ones. There were no new sick people today. Her medicine had worked.

Narchise sat up and sipped from the shell. Okemah

patted her hand.

"She will be well," he said. "Soon."

"It seems so," Cimmera said.

"We were wrong about you, Cimmera, and I am sorry," Okemah said.

"Do not feel bad. You suspected that I was not completely truthful, that I was A-po-la-chee. In some ways you were right."

The next day Narchise came down her ladder and sat by her fire. Ara was better but did not feel as well as Narchise. She had been much sicker. The others who were ill also came out of their platforms.

Cherok surveyed the small village. "We have come back," he said to Cimmera. "The spirits want us to survive."

"Tonight is the seventh moon," Cimmera said. "Kereb comes tomorrow."

CHAPTER 37

JUMAK AND ATOK sat in a tree keeping watch over the endless saw grass in the drizzle of rain.

"There," Jumak said. "Look over there. I think I saw something."

Atok stared intently. "I do not see anything."

Jumak kept staring in the same place. "Maybe Kereb will not come back," the boy said.

"He will come. He has heard of the star knife that came from the sky. He wants to have it and the magic it might possess."

Jumak sighed. "The others will not give Cimmera away, will they?" he asked.

"You mean give her over to Kereb? Never. She has saved this clan. The spirits sent her here. If we betrayed her, the spirits would never forgive us."

"Kereb has many warriors."

"Then we will die defending ourselves. We will die nobly, with honor." Atok turned to the boy. "Jumak, you must trust the spirits. Cast your fate in their hands. Be courageous."

"Yes," Jumak said. "I will."

Atok adjusted his position on the tree limb. "I think you are right," he said. "There is movement way in the distance. Go and alert Cherok."

Jumak scrambled down the tree and quickly found the cacique. "We have seen them. They are coming," he said.

Cherok's eyes locked on Cimmera's. He held her face in his hands a moment.

"Go inside the platform," he said. "The knife is hidden. They will never have it or you."

"I am not afraid for myself," she said, "only for you."

Cimmera rubbed the tender spot on her neck. Gaga-na had abraded the skin with a rough piece of limestone, rubbing it until it was raw. She did that in several spots, even on Cimmera's face, so the place on her neck would not stand out. The butterfly mark of birth was disguised.

The men of the village lined up along the edge of the hammock with their weapons. Kereb and his men rode the waters in their canoes.

When the two leaders could see each other's signals, Kereb gestured for his men to halt and get out of the canoes. They advanced the short remaining distance on foot. When they reached the hammock, Kereb ordered his men to stop. He moved four paces in front of them.

Cherok and Okemah stood in the middle of the Tegesta line. Even the recovering sick stood against Kereb.

"She is not here," Cherok said, shaking his head, hoping that Kereb understood.

Kereb's face distorted to a sneer. "Woman. Knife," he said in his newly learned Tegesta words.

Cherok shook his head again.

Kereb made a wild flourish with his arm, and two of his men came forward, their weapons ready. He addressed Atok, and Atok shrugged and shook his head, as did Dacoma, Okemah, and Yoma's father when Kereb stood before them. Every man denied that Cimmera was among them.

Cherok motioned to Kereb and his two men to follow him. He led them to the central hearth. There he threw fuel on the fire, and the flames blazed high.

"Woman," he said, pointing to the fire and then to the north where the fires had raged. "Whoosh," he said, imitating the sound of the fire.

Kereb's face displayed his disbelief. Okemah and Cherok moved apart, offering Kereb and his men passage through the rest of the village if they desired to make an inspection.

Kereb did not move. He growled something at Cherok, then suddenly shouted, and his men charged into the village.

Cimmera bolted from the platform and ran to the edge of the brush where the knife was buried. Frantically she dug through the dirt until her fingers finally felt the pelt in which the star knife was wrapped. She pulled it free.

Cherok faced Kereb. He bent at the knees in a fighting stance, and they danced in front of each other, dodging each other's blows and jabs.

The shafts of their lances clacked as they hit each other. Cherok's split. He threw it down and drew his knife from its sheath. Cherok rocked from foot to foot, tense, alert, waiting for Kereb to make a move. In a rapid maneuver, Cherok leaned back, thrust his foot up, and kicked Kereb in the chin, knocking him backward onto the ground. Cherok planted his foot on Kereb's chest, grabbed the warrior's lance, and held it at his enemy's throat.

The village echoed with war cries and sounds of combat. Cimmera ran into the middle of the battle. She stopped at Cherok's side. Her hands did not tremble as she held out the knife.

"No, Cimmera, take the knife," he said.

"I will not run anymore. I am home. Kereb does not want me. He wants the knife. Let him have it."

She glared at Kereb. "No more killing," she said. "No more."

Cherok kicked the man in his side and let up on the pressure at his throat.

Kereb dipped his head in agreement and warily sat up. He stretched out his hand, and with his index finger he poked the knife. More bravely he ran his fingers up and down the handle, then the incredible blade that had been cleaved from a star.

Cimmera nudged her hands forward. "Take it," she said. "End the fighting."

Kereb took the knife from her. He looked at it, then shouted to his men that the battle was over.

Cherok blew an eagle wing bone whistle, signaling the Tegesta men to stop.

The warriors pulled back, and Kereb guardedly rose to his feet. He backed away, a few steps at a time, still leery of Cherok. Then something peculiar happened, making him stop.

The knife moved in his hands. At first it vibrated gently and exuded a warmth that made him notice; then it grew hot, and the heat generated an unearthly light.

Kereb looked at Cimmera. The knife deepened in color, reaching a vermillion that equaled the heat that came from it, searing the skin of his hands. He smelled his flesh burning as he dropped the knife. Wildly brandishing his unharmed hand and emitting a piercing whistle, he ordered his warriors to retreat, but those of his men who were close enough to see what had happened were already running, fear etching deep lines in their faces.

The Tegesta cheered as the last of Kereb's men boarded their canoes.

"You should have let me kill him," Cherok said.

"They would have come back to seek vengeance. There are too many of them. Think of the things they do. I never want to run again. I want to stay here with you forever."

"Bring me all the pine in the village," Cimmera said to Jumak. "Pile it at the central hearth. Bring the branches, the wood, the cones. There will be no bad spirits left after tonight."

She wandered through the forest that surrounded the village, searching for the ingredients she would need. When she had them all, she returned to Cherok's hearth.

"You are fast." he said.

"Yes. I must make myself ready."

He watched as she removed the leaves, roots, lichens, and mushrooms from her gathering basket.

"What do you prepare?" Cherok asked.

"A special tea. You will see," she said.

Cimmera laid a leaf on a flat stone in front of her. With the tip of the star knife she incised a quatrefoil. She held it up toward the east, then toward each of the other directions.

On the other leaves she cut slashes and dots. Then she took them all in her fist and again presented them to each direction. She used the knife to cut up the other ingredients, then placed them all in a wooden bowl.

"I have seen Mi-sa and my father prepare such potions," Cherok said. He lifted her chin in his hands so that she looked at him. "It is a dangerous potion, I know. It is deadly if not prepared exactly right. Are you sure you know the exact mixture?"

"Tamar taught me well. I remember it all, Cherok. Everything. You have no reason to worry."

Cimmera took the star knife and drew it across her

fingertip. Blood oozed out the cut. She held her finger over the bowl, squeezed it, and let four drops of blood fall into the mixture.

Cherok watched in amazement as she put her cut finger in the palm of her other hand and uttered a soft chant. When she opened her hand, the slice in her finger had healed.

"Can you heal all wounds like that?" he asked.

"Only those made with the star knife," she said. "That is part of its magic."

Cimmera brewed her special tea as she waited for the sun to set.

At last, when the horizon was sprayed with color, Cimmera sipped her potion, felt the heat of it travel through her blood, bringing a transient flush to her face. Her head dropped to her chest, and her eyes closed. Her hands grew clammy, and beads of perspiration broke out on her forehead. Then in a moment the unpleasantness was gone.

"This is for you," Gaga-na said, lifting a beautiful feather cape.

"It is lovely," Cimmera said.

"You have no special garment and you should." Gaga-na draped the cape over Cimmera's shoulders.

The young woman smiled and touched her grandmother's hand.

At the central hearth, Cimmera fed the pine fire. The villagers gathered around. The sunset splashed colors across the sky turning the eastern horizon into a palette of violets and blues, and streaking the west with bands of gold, crimson, tangerine, and citron.

She waited until the sun slipped beneath the rim of the earth and twilight fell over the village. The indigo sky glittered with the early stars.

Then the young woman raised her arms to the sky and silence fell over the hammock. She summoned the spirits, singing words the people had never heard, but which they understood inside their minds.

A wisp of a cloud crossed the moon as a strong wind swept through the village. Cimmera's hair blew back from her face.

The spirits were truly upon them, the Tegesta believed.

Her voice echoed across the hammock. The firelight gleamed, and the silver luster of the moon cloaked her as she sang.

The people placed the backs of their hands on their foreheads and bowed their heads in respect. Not since Mi-sa had they witnessed such power.

Cimmera cupped her hands and held them out.

The people looked up when she grew silent.

Her eyes found Cherok's. Then she lifted her hands so that all could see. She sang another quiet song, then looked out over the crowd, her people. Whispering out of her palms, a white bird emerged, flew into the night sky, and soared over her village.

The air filled with sparks from the pine fire.

Or was it Stardust? Gaga-na wondered.

Excerpt from
SPIRIT OF THE TURTLE WOMAN

Prologue

SOUTHEAST COAST of the Florida peninsula, 2500 years ago.

Yurok planted the sacred stick in the sand. The clan sat, legs crossed, waiting for the spirits to speak through the stick and show them which way to go. The Jeaga, the People, depended on the spirits for such things. And now they waited for guidance to find the place where they would settle. The eyes of the Jeaga remained fixed on the stick. The staff swayed in the ocean wind, and then leaned, the turtle-head effigy at the top pointing south.

Kaya took advantage of the short delay and rested. If she lagged behind when the clan was moving, she would have to run to catch up, and she knew her legs would not carry her that quickly. She was much too weak. She kept her distance from the others because she was no longer allowed to dwell among them. To the clan, she was dead.

Yurok plucked the stick from the ground and held it overhead. Everyone gathered his belongings and took up the journey again. They traveled south, as the stick pointed, as the spirits directed.

The unusual chill of the wind bit at Kaya. There were only two seasons here, wet and dry. Both were usually warm, and sometimes stifling hot. The Jeagas' way of life was adapted to the heat. They were not prepared well for the cold.

Kaya held her new daughter to her breast. She was so very tired and wished they would stop for the day and set up camp. The brief rest while they had waited on the spirits' voices to enter the stick was not long enough. Only three nights ago she had pushed the new baby out of her belly. No one had helped.

The night when the child was born, Kaya had gotten no sleep, the birthing taking until dawn. When it was over, she wrapped the afterbirth and buried it. When the sun rose, the clan continued the trek. Kaya swaddled the infant in a blanket, put her to suckle, and trailed the group. For days now she had eaten only the clan's scraps. At night she huddled behind the dunes. She shivered in the cold air, keeping the child bundled close to her. In the dark Kaya felt the baby's cold skin, listened to her labored breathing. The child's suffering made her heart ache.

In late afternoon, at the mouth of a river, the clan watched the stick lean to the west. Yurok led them past the mangroves, upriver, where the foliage thickened with great oaks, lush vines, sabal palms, and strangler figs. There by the rushing water he planted the stick again. Kaya squinted in the distance, hoping the spirits had spoken. Relief spread through her like warm tea. This time the staff did not waver. It stood straight, claiming the spot as their new home.

Kaya's belly cramped as the baby suckled, and she was anxious to lie down on the patch of green ferns at her feet. She reached in the pouch at her side, withdrew a medicine leaf and put it in her mouth. It gave her a little relief, though it made the bleeding worse. She felt weak, her head dizzy.

"The stick speaks clearly," Yurok said. He scooped a handful of sandy dun earth and held it up, letting it slowly trickle out and catch in the wind.

Kaya sank to the ground. The infant whimpered. The child stirred fitfully. Kaya put her knuckle in her baby's mouth. She didn't have enough milk. They were both going to die.

The clan set up camp, and under the moon they celebrated.

Kaya chewed another medicine leaf and cleared a space beneath a red maple to sleep. Her head ached, and the dizziness grew stronger. She lay on the ground and pulled the baby against her. Her arms trembled with the effort.

In the moonlight she stared down at her beautiful child. Her throat tightened and her eyes teared. The child's skin had lost its wonderful deep reddish-brown tone—her Jeaga heritage. Instead, Kaya saw a gray pallor, dull eyes, and tiny chapped lips.

"No!" She scolded herself for not fighting back, for the child's sake. She could not let this happen. Perhaps she deserved to be dead. She was the one with the affliction. But the baby should not suffer.

She had to stop this before it was too late. Kaya got to her knees and put the baby in the deer-hide sling around her neck. She struggled to her feet. Yurok had to hear her.

Her head swam as she pulled herself upright. For an instant, she thought she would fall. She braced herself against the tree and focused on the small hearth fires. Her eyelids fluttered as she took the first step.

She heard the collective gasp as she stumbled into camp.

"Yurok," she called, seeing him by his fire. "It is Kaya, your wife. And this is your child."

A bulky shadow moved nearby. "He does not hear you," the shaman said, coming before her. "No one does.

Only I can hear you because I am a man of the spirits."

"No!" she said, taking another step toward Yurok. Her knees wobbled, and she hesitated before she continued. "I have been banished, but I am not dead."

"You have the affliction," the shaman said. "You must be cast out. It has been decided."

Kaya edged in front of Yurok. "I was your wife. Did you not love me before you discovered I carry a curse?"

Yurok's eyes watered and he bit down on the inside of his cheek.

"Do not speak," the shaman warned. "She is dead."

Kaya swayed with dizziness. Her mouth was dry. The bleeding was worse, and she felt it course down her legs.

"Let her speak," Yurok said. "I can hear her."

Kaya held out the baby. "She suffers, Yurok. She grows too weak to cry."

The shaman stepped in front of her. "Her line carries the affliction … passed through the daughters for generations until the debt is paid. It is the spirits' design. The punishment."

Kaya slumped to her knees, unable to stand any longer. A jagged stone sliced her knee, but she didn't flinch. She was numb to pain now.

"Move aside," Yurok told the shaman.

"Save your daughter," Kaya cried. "Your blood also runs through her. See, it is your eyes that she has, and the straight line of your nose. She is a beautiful reflection of her father. It is only I who brings you shame."

"This child might also bear the affliction," the shaman said.

"And she might not," Yurok answered. "Cheena, come here," he called loudly.

Yurok's sister came to his side, holding her own infant.

"Is your milk plentiful?"

Cheena nodded.

Yurok took the baby from Kaya's arms. He stared into the infant's face for a few moments, then handed her to Cheena.

Yurok gazed at the small group that gathered beside the shaman. "Be gone, all of you," he said. "Kaya," he said softly as he lifted her and carried her nearer his fire.

She felt the comforting warmth of him. He sat with her and rested her head in his lap.

"Keep her secret," she whispered. "Do not let your daughter be without a spirit."

Kaya's strength was quickly leaving, but it didn't matter, she thought. This was the way of the spirits, and the child was safe. She closed her eyes. She prayed the affliction ended with her and her death. She had suffered. Was the debt not paid?

Yurok stroked Kaya's hair and listened to her ragged breaths mingled with the sound of the breeze rustling through the tall grass. The moon was high above them when she crossed over. The strain in her face transformed to peace.

From somewhere in the darkness the shaman chanted prayers.

Yurok rocked her gently until daylight, and then, alone, he carried her body deep into the woods. He dug a shallow grave and lowered her into it. He knelt over her and brushed her hair from her face. His face tightened with grief. The spirits were difficult to understand.

Yurok said a prayer that the ground in which she rested be sacred. And before he covered her with the earth, he said another prayer and slipped a bird feather in her hand so her spirit could take flight.

CHAPTER 1

SOUTHEAST FLORIDA, one-half mile inland on the banks of the Loxahatchee River, 2380 years ago.

The Jeaga Turtle village was eerily still, though the women busied themselves with daily chores. The children ceased their romping and rested in the shade. The stillness seemed to have weight, and sagged over the village. The air was dense and stifling, and the mosquitoes were incessant pests.

Talli, the oldest of the three sisters, wiped beads of perspiration from her forehead with the back of her hand, and then returned to kneading clay. "Like this," she showed her youngest sister, Nocatee, using the heels of her hands for the task.

"Why do you add sand?" Nocatee asked.

"You ask too many questions," Sassa, the middle sister, said. Sassa was younger than Talli by only one full cycle of seasons.

Talli smiled at Nocatee. "How would you know things if you did not ask? Sassa, were you not the same when Nocatee's age?"

Sassa looked apologetic.

"Sand is the temper," Talli said. "The clay will not stay together without it."

Suddenly Talli felt a chill, like cold rain running down her arms. She looked up and her stomach knotted.

"What is it?" Sassa asked. She stared at Talli's face. "What is wrong?"

Talli stood up. "Stay here," she said, moving away.

Nocatee's face squirmed. Her nose wrinkled, and she squeezed her eyes tight as if she were about to cry. "Talli," she whimpered, but her sister didn't hear her.

Talli spotted Bunta as soon as he broke through the trees. She ran behind him to the center of the village, her heart drumming in her chest. She tried to see who the man was who hung over Bunta's shoulder. The injured man's arms dangled and flopped about, and a runnel of his blood trailed down Bunta's bare back.

"What has happened?" Talli cried, glancing back. More men burst out of the cover of the forest, carrying wounded warriors into the village.

Winded, Bunta laid the man on the ground, dust puffing up in a brown halo. Talli winced at the sight of the broken lance shaft protruding from the man's chest. "An Ais' attack on our hunt party," Bunta huffed.

Talli's hand flew to her throat. The Ais lived to the north and were a contemptible and murderous tribe. The Jeaga tried to stay clear of them, but this morning the men from the Turtle village and the Panther village had gone together on a hunt, and the Ais had attacked.

"Where is Akoma?" she asked, forcing the question out of her mouth.

Bunta shook his head. Sweat dribbled down his face as he lifted the injured man's eyelids. Bunta put his ear to the man's nose and listened for breathing, while his hand searched the man's chest for the feel of a heartbeat. "He is dead," he said and looked up. Talli was gone.

She ran through the village, squinting to fight the glare of the midday sun. Where was Akoma? Was he hurt … dead? Fear ripped through her like a jagged-edged chert knife.

Women wailed. Some stood rooted in their horror.

Other women darted about, searching for their husbands, their sons, their brothers. Some had found what they feared and knelt in the dirt, the sun hammering their backs as they hovered over their outstretched men. Bodies littered the earth like carcasses brought back from a hunt, but unlike the animals brought down by a hunter, these were not clean kills. Bewildered children shrieked and clutched at their mothers.

Talli wondered how many were hurt. The stream of bloodied men continued to come through the trees. There would be much for the Bone Cleaner to do.

The Bone Cleaner's job was to strip the soft flesh from the bones of the dead, and then bundle the bones and place them on the charnel platform in the mud along the bank of the river. The Bone Cleaner stayed isolated and was considered unclean, but was highly respected.

So many were injured or dead, Talli thought. She prayed Akoma was not one of them. "Please," Talli cried. "Please let Akoma be alive," she begged the spirits. Tears trickled into the corners of her mouth.

Akoma was sure his eyes were open, but something was wrong.

He was being joggled, bumped along in the darkness. He heard someone scream.

"Move out of the way!" a deep voice shouted. "I have Akoma."

"Is he alive?"

The jarring stopped with a thump, and Akoma became aware he was lying on the ground on his back. He could smell the dank odor of the soil. He felt heavy, as if he were sinking, being magically swallowed by mother earth.

Was that singing he heard or a woman's voice?

"His wound is bad," a woman said. "Where is his father?"

"He is coming."

Akoma felt pressure and a stinging on the side of his head.

"Hold this here while I bandage the medicine swatch," the woman said.

What has happened? He thought he asked it aloud. He was confused, and it was so dark. Maybe he had asked only in his head.

He strained to see, but still there was only blackness, not even a star in the sky. There came another voice and he thought it was Bunta's, the War Chief. If there was just some moonlight he would be able to see and know for sure. It was so dark.

A pain shot through his head. Akoma tried to sit up, but felt a hand on his chest restrain him.

"Can you hear me, Akoma?" Bunta asked.

Akoma struggled to get his dry lips and heavy tongue to move. He forced air through his throat and made a gurgling sound.

"I think he does hear," the woman said. "He is trying to speak."

The voices became distant echoes, growing softer and softer. He heard a faint buzzing, almost just a vibration, and then he was aware of nothing.

Yahga-ta knelt by his son. "Akoma?"

There was no response.

"He sleeps deep," the woman said.

Bunta turned Akoma's head so the wound could be viewed. "He has suffered a blow to the head."

Yahga-ta stiffened to speak without emotion. "Today my son became a man. He touched the enemy. It is not right that he dies and not know he has entered the world of men. Where is Putiwa? Get the shaman here for my son," Yahga-ta said to the woman. "Find him now!"

The woman obeyed and ran through the village, looking for the shaman. Near the central hearth, Talli caught her by the shoulder. "Have you seen Akoma?"

She nodded. "Over there," she said, pointing. "With his father and Bunta. I go for the shaman."

Talli scanned the distance and spotted Yahga-ta, Akoma's father, the cacique, the leader of the clan. He and Bunta stooped next to a body on the ground. Akoma? Did she dare go near?

Talli's chest tightened with dread as she hurried there. She hesitated before coming next to Yahga-ta. She wiped the tears from her face. When she saw the young warrior lying so still, she gasped and fell to her knees. "Akoma," she whispered, and then looked up at Yahga-ta.

"It is bad. He does not hear me," Yahga-ta said.

Talli swallowed and choked back a cry. She brushed Akoma's cheek with her fingertips, but quickly pulled her hand away. She should not have done that. "Will he be all right?" she asked. Yahga-ta did not answer.

She bent close to Akoma's ear making certain she did not touch him. She whispered his name. Blood matted his hair, and some of it was already caked on his face. "It is Talli. Wake up. Wake up."

"He is in the deep sleep," Bunta said. "He does not hear anything."

She straightened, afraid to be so close or it might happen.

"Talli!" It was Sassa. "Come. Mother needs you. Father is hurt."

Talli put her fear aside and lifted Akoma's hand in hers. It was limp and cool. She rubbed her thumb across his knuckles. Her shoulders shuddered subtly. Talli dropped his hand and stood up, but it was too late. The affliction. She grabbed her head, and shoved her fingers through her hair.

"Come now!" Sassa said, tugging on Talli's arm.

Talli blinked as she struggled to focus.

"Now!" Sassa said, pulling her away from Akoma.

On the way to the family shelter, Talli kept glancing back until the milling people hid Akoma from view.

Nocatee stood inside the shelter that was about man high and constructed of bent saplings covered with palmetto thatch. Her dark eyes were wide with confusion as she stared out the opening.

Talli knelt next to her mother. Kitchi stared at her daughter. Talli's eyes settled on her father's injured arm in her mother's lap. Ufala leaned his head back and grimaced as Kitchi's finger probed one of the wounds in his arm. Talli saw her father's heavy jaw clench, his eyes squeeze shut, and his large hands ball into fists, but he did not make a sound.

"The wounds are clean now," Kitchi said. "There is nothing in them, but I fear the bone is smashed."

Perspiration poured out of Ufala's skin, and his long, sweat-soaked, silver-and-black hair clung to him. He was a big man, full of muscle that seemed suddenly to lose definition.

"Be grateful the Ais warrior was not wielding a shark-tooth club," Kitchi said.

The thought of what her father's arm would have looked like if he had been attacked with such a club made Talli cringe. That kind of club was edged with shark's teeth set in notches along its length. It would have ripped the flesh off his bone and sawed through his arm. He probably would have bled to death.

"Get me some water," Ufala said to Sassa. The girl took a water pouch and hurried to the river.

"Sort through the baskets and find some pilosa and snakebark," Kitchi told Talli. "I need to prepare medicine. Stir the fire, and when Sassa returns with the water, boil the pilosa and snakebark."

Talli rummaged through the baskets her mother stored beside their shelter in the shade of a large oak. Her father would be all right, but what about Akoma? If she hurried, as soon as Ufala was settled, perhaps she could sneak away.

Sassa returned with the water. Talli splashed a bit into the pouch suspended over the fire, and then handed the remaining container of water to her father.

Ufala flinched. "Kitchi," Ufala said, nodding at his wife and gesturing with his head toward the pouch. He refused to take the water from Talli.

Kitchi grasped the otter-stomach from her daughter's hand and gave it to Ufala.

"Back away, Talli," he said after several swallows. "You should not be so close."

Talli stepped back, her head down in respect.

"Do you brew something for the pain?" Ufala asked Kitchi.

"I make a medicine to put on the wounds," she answered. "It will help."

"Something stronger," he said, palming his bruised ribs with his good hand.

"I will ask Putiwa," Kitchi said, wiping the sweat from her husband's face.

"The shaman is with Yahga-ta and Akoma," Talli said. "Akoma is injured and Yahga-ta has summoned Putiwa to help."

Kitchi's head shot up. "You have not been near

Akoma, have you? You did not touch him?"

Talli didn't have to answer because Ufala groaned, and Kitchi focused on her husband.

"Do something, woman," he said. "Forget Putiwa."

"Talli will gather the herbs as soon as she finishes preparing this medicine." Kitchi moved to peer in the pouch over the fire. She tweezed two rocks from the hearth and dropped them inside the pouch. There was an instant sizzling as the hot stones hit the water. A swirl of steam rose. "It is hot enough," she told Talli. "Put in the medicine plants."

Talli tore the leaves and stems and dropped them in. The solution bubbled. Kitchi scooted closer to Ufala.

Talli heard her parents talking behind her, but she did not follow their conversation. She stared across the village, straining to get a glimpse of something that would tell her how Akoma was. The center of the village, the plaza, was clear and the dirt steamed in the heat. The sunlight danced on the shelters as it splintered through the trees that shaded their homes. But there was nothing she could see that enlightened her about Akoma.

He had to be all right. How would she live if he was not?

"What is wrong with you, daughter?" Ufala asked sharply. "Your mother speaks to you, and you do not respond."

Talli whipped around. "I am sorry," she said. She looked back at the brewing medicine and saw the water had turned dark. "It is ready."

"Scoop off the residue from the top and bring it here," Kitchi said. "Pay attention to what you are doing. This is not a medicine to drink unless it is a time for cleansing. It is for dressing wounds. It keeps the bad spirits out of wounds and stops bleeding."

Talli prodded the pouch along the suspending stick until it no longer sat over the hot coals.

Her mother took a small busycon-shell ladle and dipped out some of the elixir. She let it cool for a moment, but the concoction was still hot. She tipped the shell and poured the medicine in Ufala's open wounds. The big man thrust back his head and his mouth opened as if to scream. His head came forward, and his chin pressed against his chest. Ufala let out a pent-up breath, grabbed Kitchi's arm, and squeezed until the pain abated.

The color drained from Talli's face.

"Move away, daughter," Kitchi said. "Go and gather the medicine plants that will ease your father's pain."

Talli stepped farther back. She saw her little sister hiding her eyes. "Can Nocatee go with me?"

Kitchi nodded at her eldest.

"Come, Nocatee," Talli called.

"Gather some sky-flower and pickerelweed," Kitchi said. Just as Talli turned to leave, her mother said, "Do not stray. Stay away from the others. You do understand?"

Talli picked up Nocatee. If she was careful, there would be no danger. Her mother did not need to worry. She would keep her distance.

Talli threaded through the thicket along the perimeter of the village. At at a range where she was sure Kitchi could not see her, she reentered the village and headed to the spot where she had last seen Akoma.

Nocatee's eyebrows dipped. "Mother said—"

"I know, little sister. We will only be a moment."

Near enough to see clearly, Talli realized Akoma was not where she had seen him earlier. Her heart jumped in her chest, and she felt weak. Had he died? Her arms tightened about Nocatee.

She spun around and looked toward the leader's hearth and his shelter, which stood at the head of the village in the east so the sun first shone on the place of the cacique. Yahga-ta's shelter was a lodge much larger than the shelters of the rest of the clan. The interior was also different. The inside was bordered with log benches on which clan members sat during council meetings. At the end of the lodge, slightly elevated, was the place where Yahga-ta himself sat during those times.

Talli saw a small group gathered in front of Yahga-ta's lodge. Did they stare down at Akoma's body?

"We will get the medicine plants in a moment," she told Nocatee, letting her slide down to stand on the ground. "Walk this way." She took her young sister's hand, moved a few steps, and then stopped. She felt a tingling along her spine. Talli looked at Nocatee and lifted her chin with her fingers. "It is all right," she said. She stooped to Nocatee's height. "Do not be frightened. Your little heart beats so fast."

Nocatee squeezed Talli's hand.

Between the men and women standing about, Talli saw someone did indeed lie on the ground. Her heart told her it was Akoma. Afraid of what she would see, she approached slowly.

She stopped outside the circle of people at Yahga-ta's hearth, behind Bunta's woman, Chinasi.

Putiwa chanted. His old weathered face was deeply wrinkled from sun, age, and responsibility. His eyes were filled with worry. Akoma was the spirits' chosen one and Yahga-ta's son. One day Akoma would take his father's place. If the shaman failed to save him, it would not be a good thing.

Chinasi looked back at Talli. "Putiwa does his magic. Only the men stand close."

Fear garroted Talli's voice, and her words came out cracked and strained. "Is he dead?"

"No, I do not think so. But I do not believe he will survive. He drifts in the deep sleep."

An unexpected wind whipped through the trees and a flurry of oak and bay leaves swirled about. Talli shivered.

Putiwa's chant grew louder as he strode around the unconscious Akoma. The shaman took his turtle-shell rattle, the hard seeds inside clattering against the shell to Putiwa's rhythm. The deer hooves, which were tied beneath the shell, clacked together. The peal of Putiwa's old uninhibited voice and the beat of the rattle made the shaman's music magical, and it saturated the village. The people watched and listened in awe, as they always did when the mystical man spoke to the spirits.

Chinasi rubbed the flesh that prickled on her arms. She spoke in a whisper. "If Akoma is to be saved, Putiwa will do it."

Talli nudged past Chinasi and stopped just outside the band of men.

Akoma's bandaged head inclined to the side. He was so still. Mora, Akoma's mother, wept on her sister's shoulder. Yahga-ta stood erect, donning a stern, determined expression. The colors the leader wore on his face for the hunt had already faded.

Talli took another step. Chinasi grasped her arm. "What are you doing?" she whispered. "Do not interrupt."

Talli shook her head as if confused. She was so close to Akoma, but could not tell if he was breathing. She should feel something, but didn't, and it frightened her.

Nocatee peeped through the mass of legs. She started to cry again and tugged at her sister's hand. "Talli? Is Akoma dead?"

"I do not know," Talli whispered. "Say a prayer, Nocatee. Say a prayer." She picked up the little one again and rocked from side to side, as she often did to comfort her sister.

Nocatee cried into Talli's shoulder. "Is Father going to die, too?"

"No. No, Nocatee. Father will be all right."

"But Akoma—"

"Shh," Talli said, stroking the back of her sister's head.

Suddenly, the shaman fell silent. The breeze ceased and there was a disturbing hush. Talli pressed Nocatee's cheek firmly against her shoulder.

Putiwa knelt at Akoma's head, drew smoke from his pipe and blew it in the young man's face. He uttered some magic words from the ancient tongue. The shaman stood and called out for two men to carry Akoma into Yahga-ta's lodge. Talli's heart thudded as she watched Putiwa present himself in front of Akoma's mother.

Putiwa put his hands on Mora's upper arms, and then drew a sign with his thumb on her forehead, smearing some yellow ochre above her brows. He said something Talli could not hear over Nocatee's whimpering.

Talli put Nocatee down and pushed through the crowd. She grabbed the arm of one of the men who lifted Akoma.

"Stop, let me see him!"

Shocked by Talli's boldness, the men paused, and Talli looked into Akoma's still face. Abandoning her fear, she let the tip of one finger touch his arm. She felt empty inside, all black, and barren, and hollow. Like death. "Akoma!" she sobbed. Her head jerked up so she could see the eyes of the man in her grip. "Is he dead?"

About the Author:

Lynn Armistead McKee has worked as a writing trainer for Broward County Schools and Citrus County Schools in Florida. Her interest in archaeology and her work with the Broward County Archaeological Society led her to write historical fiction about the indigenous peoples of South Florida.

Writing as Lynn Sholes she also co-writes thrillers with Joe Moore. Lynn is a member of International Thriller Writers, Mystery Writers of America, and The Authors Guild. She writes from her home in the Sunshine State.

Other Books by Lynn Armistead McKee
WOMAN OF THE MISTS
TOUCHES THE STARS
KEEPER OF DREAMS
SPIRIT OF THE TURTLE WOMAN
DAUGHTER OF THE FIFTH MOON

Other Books by this author, writing as Lynn Sholes with Joe Moore

THE GRAIL CONPSIRACY
THE LAST SECRET
THE HADES PROJECT
THE PHOENIX APOSTLES
THE 731 LEGACY
THE BLADE
THE SHIELD
THE TOMB
THOR BUNKER, A Short Story
BAM! JUST LIKE THAT (short story)

Connect With Lynn Sholes Online:

https://www.facebook.com/SholesandMoore
Website: www.sholesmoore.com

www.ingramcontent.com/pod-product-compliance
Lightning Source LLC
Chambersburg PA
CBHW070349260626
47161CB00001B/75